"YOU IDIOTIC LITTLE MANDRAQUE. I should kill you right now," said Graves.

"Don't," Gant immediately said. "Graves, don't do it."

"Yes, I don't think you should either," said Norda and without hesitation she turned the gun on Graves and opened fire.

It was difficult to determine whether Norda was genuinely aiming at him or was just firing off a random shot in his direction. Either way, it ripped across Graves' upper arm and he cried out, grabbing at it, as a thin line of blood rose up to the surface. He gasped, incredulous over what had just happened.

Norda, for her part, didn't seem to realize that she could have quite possibly ended his life if her aim had been just a bit more precise. Instead she cocked one brow ridge and looked at the weapon as if she was surprised that she was holding it. "Oh. Right. It does that," she said.

Crazy Eight Press is an imprint of Second Age, Inc.

Copyright © 2018 by Second Age, Inc.
Cover illustration and design by J.K. Woodward and Glenn Hauman
Interior design by Aaron Rosenberg
ISBN 978-0-9836877-9-5
www.crazy8press.com

First edition

THE HIDDEN EARTH

BOOK THREE
ORDER OF THE CHAOS

PETER DAVID

CRAZY 8 PRESS

TO ALL THE FANS WHO NEVER STOPPED ASKING WHEN THIS BOOK WAS COMING OUT.

THE ARGO

I.

JASON NEVER TIRED OF GAZING down upon the Earth.

It turned steadily below him, and he could never get enough of just staring at it, knowing that it was not for him and yet unable to erase from his imagination the visions of walking upon its surface.

He pictured what it would be like to have the sun beaming down upon him. He envisioned the sensation of the soft, gentle wind blowing across his face, messing up his long, unkempt brown hair or stirring up his equally disheveled beard. He saw himself standing in the middle of a vast plain of land…

No! At a beach. That was it. His mental image switched away from the emptiness of nothing and instead became filled with the picture of him standing at a shoreline. He had read that at such places, the land leading up to the lapping waters of the ocean was covered not with dirt or grass but instead something called "sand," which was composed of tiny granules that shifted when someone tread upon it.

Jason wondered, not for the first time or hundredth time but perhaps the millionth time, how he was supposed to call what he was doing "living." The entirety of his existence was in the abstract. His daily duties and maintenance consumed less than an hour of his time, and the rest he was left to do nothing but be curious about things to which he would likely never get the answer.

He turned away from his view and started walking. Even though he was not setting out for any destination in particular, that did not mean that he did not in fact have someplace to go in mind. He knew where he was going and whom he was going to see.

Medea Nussman. It was always Medea Nussman.

His dream girl.

It was the name that had first drawn him to her. Jason was well aware of the mythological origins of his name, and knew that he had acquired it because of the name of the vessel that they were aboard: the *Argo*. The Jason of the myths had been romantically involved with the sorceress Medea. Granted the relationship had ended disastrously, but nevertheless there was still that ancient sense of connection.

He walked past the weapons room and hesitated as he did so. There was enough armament in there for all one hundred and seventy five people to be able to open fire on just about anything that would come their way. Hell, in point of fact, there was enough armament to outfit five times that many people. It was Jason's understanding that that was typical thinking of humanity, or at least the humans who had resided in the United States of America

He wondered if he was an American. His parents had been, so he supposed that that made him American as well, but his entire relationship to the country was purely as a result of materials that he had studied. He had found its history endlessly fascinating. Going all the way back to when it had first been established, he had been fascinated by the country's ambitions and democracy. He believed that sometimes its ambitions had been far beyond what it had been actually capable of producing, but considering that America was pretty much ended as a concern, anything he might have in the way of an opinion was just after-the-fact criticism.

Perhaps he could talk to Medea about it. It was certainly something with which she was familiar. She had been born in someplace called "Brooklyn" in New York City. Her parents were Edgar and Helen, who had gotten divorced three years after she'd been born. She had been a lifelong New York resident until she had enlisted in the army and her particular skills had fast tracked her for Special Forces. She was a superb hand-to-hand combatant and Jason was convinced that if he ever met her, she would fall madly in love with him.

Which was likely never going to happen.

He was walking along the crystals corridor and now stopped outside Medea's tube. He had never had the opportunity to gaze into her eyes since they had been closed in slumber since he had first encountered her. Ever since he was a child, he had stood in front of her crystal and simply stared at her, imagining what she would be like. Initially he had imagined her as if she was a big sister to him, but as he had grown older and passed her in age, he had begun thinking about her in other terms.

Why the hell not? Why was it mandated that he spend the entirety of his life alone, anyway? His father had had his mother. Why should he be forced to go without?

Because that's what you were born into. That's the rules of your life.

Except it didn't have to be, did it. They were the rules that his father and mother had taught him, but who was to say that he couldn't violate the rules? What was to stop him from defrosting Medea Nussman, of bringing her back to wakefulness so that she could spend her life with him?

He had certainly seen enough pictures of her. He had thoroughly studied her files. He knew the sound of her voice, had heard her talk about her life, and had heard her laugh during interviews. She was a fascinating dichotomy, seemingly utterly focused on the army and the tasks that she had undertaken, and yet also had a firm sense of humor. He knew that she was not romantically attached to any guy because the army had been her first love, but perhaps he could shift her focus away from the military and onto something more productive.

After all, it wasn't as if the military was going to be of any use anymore.

Not since the creatures had arrived and destroyed humanity.

There had been twelve races that had emerged from the ships that had dropped through that massive hole in the sky. They had overrun humanity, and all of humankind's attempts to fight back had been thwarted when none of their weapons had been able to function.

Jason had, of course, seen none of it. It was ancient history. He hadn't been born yet and his father had been a newly married young man. And his father hadn't witnessed any of the chaos or destruction first hand. No, he and his wife and the one hundred seventy five people had fled the bounds of Earth.

Because the army planned for everything. Even the end of the world.

Except, of course, the world had not ended. It remained right where it had been left.

That was always the interesting thing, wasn't it? In the early part of the twenty-first century, mankind had been so obsessed with the concept of global warming and how it threatened the Earth. Except the planet had never actually been threatened. It was only the population that was facing imminent demise thanks to nature going berserk. As it had turned out, the entire matter had been rendered moot when humanity was basically hunted into extinction.

Were there any humans left on Earth? Jason very much doubted it. Creatures that had been spat out by mythology and fairy tales had overwhelmed humanity. Of all the manners in which the end of mankind had been predicted, that had certainly not been one of them.

Jason ran his hand gently against the exterior of Medea's crystal pod. It was referred to as a crystal because that was the code name of the project, but it wasn't genuinely any manner of crystal. It was some manner of high tech glass that could survive extreme temperatures, such as the ice cold that was currently pervading it and keeping Medea alive. Keeping all of them alive.

"Hey, Medea," he said softly, stroking the outside of her crystal. "How's it going?"

She said nothing, of course. There was nothing for her to say. His voice, however, reverberated within the crystal, because he had been sure to turn on the comm system. It had been installed in case there was some manner of emergency and it was necessary to communicate with someone while they were still awake or in the process of waking up. He liked to imagine that she was capable of hearing his words even in her slumber. That his voice was insinuating itself into her subconscious so that she was becoming familiar with him even as she slumbered.

Not that he would ever know for sure. He would probably be long dead by the time she was brought back to life, assuming that that ever happened.

Jason had seated himself on the floor and he ran his fingers idly through his tousled hair. As if she had responded, he said, "It's going fine with me. Same old, same old. Going to have to fire up the engines in a couple days to maintain orbit. Thirty seconds should do it. Wouldn't want to fall out of the sky, y'know. That would suck.

"Although I keep having this crazy dream. I imagine that every single one of the creatures that showed up and eliminated humanity are all standing in one place. And the ship crash lands on them, killing them all, so humanity is saved en masse and they cushion the fall so all the people survive. I know that's ridiculous, but, y'know, it's a dream. Do you have any dreams, Medea? Do you ever dream about…" He hesitated and then his voice drifted in a nebulous manner. "Do you ever dream about finding the right guy? Having children? Building a life? Any kind of life?"

She didn't reply. Yet her lack of response caused him to smile as if she had indeed responded to him. "Yeah, me too," he said.

He stared at the control dials upon her crystal that he could easily manipulate to bring her back to life. Could he dare follow that option? Ignore the rules? Find some happiness?

Except it was entirely likely that he was kidding himself. Who was to say that she genuinely would provide him with any manner of happiness? Yes, he had seen her when she was alive, but she had never had the opportunity to interact with him. Maybe he was kidding himself. Maybe she wouldn't have the slightest interest in him at all.

He wished he knew.

He had been sitting in front of her, but now he pulled himself to standing and continued to stare at her longingly. He brought his face close to the tube and breathed onto it, creating a patch of mist against it. Then he traced the outline of a heart against it.

You're an idiot, he thought, but when he turned away from her then, he did nothing to erase it.

And his father regarded him from on high.

II.

ISAAC TANNER WATCHED HIS SON mooning over that idiot soldier and rolled his eyes yet again.

Isaac did not have the faintest idea why someone had built in a complex video camera surveillance unit into the *Argo.* Why was there an intrinsic need for a metaphorical eye in the sky? They were a damned space ship. Was somebody expecting a burglar to show up? To somehow penetrate the vessel and creep about, stealing things before achieving his crafty getaway? The entire concept was patently ridiculous.

Yet here he was utilizing it. He was sitting in the security center, gazing at the several dozen screens that gave him a view of everything in the place, watching his son gazing in hopeless love at the unmoving figure of a frozen soldier. All because of her damned name.

"We should never have named him Jason," Isaac muttered. "Medea. Freaking Medea. Why did we call him Jason?"

A hand rested gently on his shoulder. "As I recall, it was your idea," a soft, female voice reminded him.

He sighed heavily. "Are you never going to get tired of reminding me of that?"

"Never," she said, but there was a deep chuckle in her voice.

He stroked her hand as he turned to gaze into her deep, blue eyes. He remembered when they had gone on their honeymoon to Hawaii and he had held her eye color up in comparison to the stretches of the Pacific Ocean that were rolling around them. He had opined then that the blueness of her eyes made the ocean pale in comparison, and even though all he had now of the Pacific were his memories—and a knowledge that he would never see it again—he was still of the same opinion.

She had aged, of course. Her blonde hair had started turning gray when she was in her thirties and entirely silvered by her fortieth birthday. She had thought about dyeing it; there were actually facilities on the space vessel that was their home that would have allowed her to do so. He urged her not to. "If this is what nature has in store for you, just accept it," he said emphatically, and so she had done nothing to try to stem the passage of time.

She was always there for Isaac whenever he needed her. She was the voice of reason when he would feel frustrated or upset or depressed or angry. She was the consistent sympathetic ear for whatever. He had no idea what he would do without her, and prayed that he would never have to find out.

He sat and watched as Jason continued to interact with the unmoving, unresponsive form of Medea. "Should we thaw her, do you think?"

"You know the rules," she said.

He turned and looked at her again. "Rules that were made up by people who don't have to live the way we live, Debbie. Day after day goes by, and we maintain the ship and the crew, waiting for some undetermined day when the creatures down there have killed each other off. Eventually we're both going to be gone and Jason will be on his own. He'll have to thaw someone or even someones out at that point because he would go insane from the solitude. To say nothing of the fact that his child or children will have to take over his maintenance duties when he's too old to do so."

"Yes, and every person who he winds up thawing out or reproducing will be a drain on the ship's supplies."

"We have enough supplies for a century, Debbie."

"Except that can be diminished very quickly. You know that. If we're up here for longer than a century…?"

She didn't bother to finish the question because it spoke for itself.

He lowered his head and sighed deeply. "I suppose you're right. But I just hate to see Jason leading an empty life."

"At least he has a life, which is more than the vast majority of humanity can say for itself. He should be grateful. So should you be."

"I guess so."

"You *guess* so?" She gently but firmly whapped him upside the head. He smiled. It felt good.

He flipped a switch and spoke into the overhead microphone. "Jason? I was going to grab some dinner. You hungry?"

Jason didn't bother to look up at the camera. "Sure. No problem. Meet you in the mess hall."

"Your mother and I look forward to it."

Jason moaned. Isaac had no idea why as he clicked off the microphone. What in the world was that boy's problem? He was consistently moaning, groaning, finding something to criticize about everything his father said. That would have made sense if Jason had been a teenager, but he was well into his twenties, far too old for teen angst. Sometimes he was convinced that he would never understand what was going through that boy's mind.

Perhaps it had been because they had had to wait so long to have a child. That had certainly not been anything that they had ever had any control over. They had never availed themselves of any sort of birth control, and yet it had not been until Debbie had hit her fortieth birthday that she had become pregnant. The whys and wherefores of that had always been a bit of a mystery to Isaac, but he had never chosen to question it. He'd been genuinely relieved because he had not been thrilled with the prospect of either him or Debbie—whichever one outlived the other—being alone on the ship.

"Don't worry about it," said Debbie as if she could read his mind. "You always said that people don't really become fully formed until they're twenty-five."

"He's twenty-seven. Almost twenty-eight."

"Yes, but look at the environment that he grew up in. He's never had anyone to interact with his own age. Isn't that likely to retard his progress somewhat?"

"Very much so," he said reluctantly.

"Then don't worry about it." She patted his hand. "It's all going to work out."

He believed her. Which was easy for him; he always believed her.

III.

THEIR KNIVES AND FORKS CLACKED together as they cut into the meatloaf. There were small portions of mashed potatoes and string beans on the plates in front of them, and Isaac was grateful for that. When he had signed on to the escape vessel, he'd been concerned that he would be subjected to eating dehydrated food for the rest of his life and was definitely glad that was not the case.

"You did a good job of preparing this, Jason," Isaac commended him. "You know, I would have been happy to do the cooking…"

"Yeah, I'm aware of that," replied Jason. "But let's face it, I'm better at it than you are."

"I'll give you that," said Isaac. It was a minor concession to him because no actual cooking was involved. Everything was frozen and the only thing the meals required was microwaving them back to life. So honestly, it was just a matter of setting a timer properly. A six year old could likely whip up a meal with equal facility, so why argue about it?

He studied the fork for a long moment, trying to summon his thoughts. The hell with the rules. Perhaps it was indeed time for Jason to try defrosting someone such as that Medea girl and attempt to build a life for himself. Certainly having a new voice around the *Argo* would not be detrimental to their lives. He knew that Jason would embrace the idea. Why not bring it up?

"Jason," he said slowly, "your mother and I were talking and—"

Jason angrily threw his fork down. It bounced off the plate and tumbled to the floor, clattering to a stop a few feet away. "Oh God, here we go again. Can we ever get through just *one* meal?"

Isaac blinked in confusion. "I…I don't understand. What are you so upset about? Why are you—?"

Jason slammed his hands on the table so forcefully that it caused the plate to rattle and almost tumble off to join the fork on the floor. He absently snagged it before it did so. "Do we have to have this discussion again, Dad? We've had it a hundred times! It's enough already!"

"What in the world are you blathering about—?"

Jason stood so quickly and angrily that he banged his knees on the underside of the table. He started to moan but then caught himself at the last moment. "She's dead, Dad. Mom is dead. She's been dead for years. I'm sorry she fell, I'm sorry she hit her head, I'm sorry she bled out before you found her, I'm sorry I wasn't there, I'm sorry, I'm sorry, *I'm sorry. Okay?!*"

Isaac stared at him uncomprehendingly, as if he had suddenly started speaking in a foreign tongue. Debbie was standing behind Jason, slowly shaking her head. It was clear she had no idea of what in the world Jason was talking about. All Isaac knew for sure was that Jason's attitude was frightening him.

"Jason…" He stopped, considered carefully what he was going to say. "I know we've talked about this in the past, and you've never been open to it, but we have any number of pills that you might want to consider."

"Pills?" Jason echoed.

"Yes. The computer med can certainly advise you as to something to take to calm you down…"

"You think that's what I need? Tranquilizers?"

"I'm not sure what you need, Jason. I don't have any sort of medical training. I'm just an engineer."

The rage seemed to have faded from Jason as quickly as it had possessed him. "Dad," he said, and he reached over and placed a hand on Isaac's. "You really don't understand. You're suffering from Alzheimer's. Or dementia. Or something. Some kind of mental disconnect. It might be some kind of PTSD as a result of the accident that killed Mom, or it might be aging, I don't know. But you've got to accept it, sooner or later. Okay? Will you promise me you'll try to focus and come to terms with it? You've promised me before and then every time we're right back where we started, so please—for me. Try. Okay?"

Isaac studied him with deep sadness. He had no idea why his son had such delusions, but it wasn't his place to try and correct him. So instead he just smiled, nodded slightly and said what he knew Jason needed him to say: "I'll do my best. I swear I will."

"Thanks, Dad." He nodded toward his plate. "I'm full. You want any of this?" When Isaac shook his head, Jason said, "Okay. See you later." He gathered his plate, picked up the fallen fork, and walked away.

Isaac leaned back and stared after his son long after he'd departed. He shook his head. "What in the world are we going to do with that boy?" he asked.

Debbie shrugged. "Kids," she said. Then she draped her arms around him and brought her lips to his ear. "Isaac...come with me."

"Come with you where?"

"Wherever I lead."

"All right."

She stepped back and he followed her through the corridors of the vessel. He smiled as he did so, confident that this was some manner of game.

But then he saw where she was standing and gesturing and he stopped walking and took a step back. Slowly he shook his head. "Debbie, I can't," he said softly. "I'll die."

"No, you won't," she said insistently. "You'll be fine. I'll keep you fine. I swear I will."

"I appreciate all your swearing, but..."

"It'll be fun! Come on!" she gestured eagerly.

He shook his head. "I don't like this game, Debbie."

"It's not a game! It's a show of faith!"

"I have faith in you, Debbie, I do, but…" He was backing up and didn't realize it until his back bumped up against a bulkhead.

Debbie crossed her arms and stuck out her lower lip. She was making no effort to hide her irritation. "Okay, fine. Be that way. I just wanted to play, but if that's too much of a problem for you…"

"Debbie, don't be that way."

"I'll be any way I want to be, thank you." She pivoted and strode off down the corridor. Isaac wanted to follow her at first, but came to the conclusion that it would be better to leave her be.

She would get over it. He was sure of that.

His gaze shifted to the large door that she had wanted him to open: the airlock. He shook his head. "Women," he sighed for what seemed the thousandth time.

THE SPIRES

I.

THE TRAVELERS CONVERGED AROUND THE Bottom Feeders, Eutok and Jepp. It was clear why that was so: in order to forestall any thought they might give to fleeing.

Slowly, ponderously, the powerful armored figure of the Overseer stepped out into the intersection. He simply stood there for a time, looking at them.

Then, finally, he spoke.

"What have we here?"

No one answered at first. And then Jepp walked forward, squaring her shoulders, and if she could not look him in the eye, she could at least take a guess as to where his eye might be and look there. "I am Jepp," she said. "I am a human."

"Yes. I know that."

"And I…"

"You what?"

She took a deep breath and let it out slowly, tremblingly. She realized that she was being seized with an almost primal urge to flee the scene. She had never heard the term "fight or flight," but if she had, she would have understood how it applied right then.

"I want there to be people again," she said. "People like me. Lots of people like me. I want the streets of this city to be filled with them. So many of them that, no matter which way you look, there are just…just people. Lots of them. And I just…I don't see why this world can't be big enough for the Twelve Races and human beings. I don't understand why the few humans who remain alive have to be slaves. I don't understand why everyone cannot be free to live their lives."

"You do not understand that? Would you like me to explain it to you?"

"I…I wasn't looking for an explanation actually. I just…"

"Human have always been slaves, child. Slaves to their desires. Slaves to their sex organs. Slaves to corporations. Slaves to their stupidity. To their greed and arrogance. To their endless, unrelenting pursuit of more and more pointless possessions, or drugs, or mindless entertainment. Corporations enslave employees. Religion enslaves minds and souls. Everywhere you looked, even when mankind was at its height, there was nothing…nothing but slavery. And the sick thing—the truly sick thing—is that everyone believed that they were free. They all thought they had free will. They all thought that they were masters of their own destiny, or at least could be if they had enough money or power or sex partners or whatever they needed in order to feel good about themselves. But it was all a joke. Just a big goddamn joke. Do you know what Voltaire said? No, of course you don't. He said that God was a comedian playing to an audience too afraid to laugh. Well, look where we are now, big guy. Look. You killed the audience. Absolutely killed them. Now who's laughing?"

Jepp just stared at him. "I have no idea what you're talking about," she said.

"No. No, of course you don't." He strode toward her, the ground shuddering beneath him.

Karsen's leg brushed up against hers and she could feel that he was trembling. She put a hand on his shoulder reassuringly. "Breathe," she said softly. "Breathe steadily."

"So you want to repopulate the Earth, then? Is that it?"

"The Earth? What's—?"

"My God, is there anyone with a brain left on this planet? How many times am I going to have to explain it! This! Here! This planet! Where you are standing! It's called 'Earth'. All right? Not 'the Damned World.' Earth! Urrrrrth. Earth! Are we all clear on this?"

Jepp nodded, not knowing what else to do.

"And I am supposed to just do what? Wave my hand and bring humanity back in full force? In case you haven't noticed, I am not humanity's biggest fan. The fewer humans there are, the better. And I would just as soon get rid of the ones we have. Which reminds me, Travelers, did you dispose of the ones who were scurrying around underneath the streets?"

One of the Travelers bowed slightly in a manner that indicated an affirmative.

"Good. There aren't all that many more. A handful out west, I believe, hiding out. Or at least they think they're hiding out. But they'll be found and dealt with. Just as you will be now, my dear…Jepp, was it? Yes. Jepp. And these are your…dare I say it…friends? You will all be dealt with."

"What do you mean?"

"You want to know? Really? All right, then. You have obviously gone to a great deal of effort to come here, and I feel it only right and proper to make it worth your while. And, most importantly, you deserve to have my personal attention. So here is what is going to happen:

"There is going to be a hunt. A huge, magnificent hunt. The lot of you are going to scatter, or stay in one group; it doesn't make any difference to me. I will give you a full day's head start. Go as far as you want. Run as fast as you can. Feel free to breathe a sigh of relief because you think I cannot possibly find you, and pat yourselves on the back for your own cleverness. And then I will hunt you down. I will use all the resources at my command, and I will track you and come after you, and I will kill you. You will all die, because that's just the way life goes in the big city. I will hunt you, Jepp with no last name, would-be savior of humanity. I will hunt you and I will kill you, and your friends, and your little dog, too."

"My little what?"

"Never mind. It's not important. What's important is that humanity never, ever get a toehold on this godforsaken world ever again. You will die, and those who have tried to befriend you will die, and the handful of humans will die, and then—if we're very, very lucky—everything else will follow. And even if it doesn't, well…at least this was a way to kill some time.

"Now run, little Jepp with no last name. You and all your friends. Run!"

"No!" said Jepp defiantly. "I'm not going to run. *We're* not going to run!"

"She doesn't speak for all of us," said Zerena.

"I'm not going to run because humans deserve more than you're willing to give them! They deserve more belief than you're willing to have in them! You all do!" and she turned and shouted to the Travelers. "You don't have to stand by and allow this! You can stand up to him! Together we can accomplish anything!"

"This is your last chance, child. Run now. You have until the count of three or you die right now. One—"

"I'm not afraid of you!"

"Two—"

"Humanity will live! I've seen it! And there's nothing you can do to stop it—!"

"Three!"

He advanced on Jepp, his hands outstretched toward her.

There was an explosion of thunder, but it was like no thunder any of them had heard. It was short and abrupt and repeated itself several times.

The Overseer staggered and looked down at his armored body. Three holes had appeared in the chest. Blood was seeping out of them. As if he was studying with great fascination something that had happened to somebody else, he touched one of the holes with his gloved finger. "Teflon bullets. Armor piercing. Has to be. I'll be damned."

A figure was slowly approaching. It was a female Mandraque. She was holding something made of gleaming blue metal in front of her with both hands. Jepp recognized her immediately; she had seen her in a dream.

The Travelers were frozen in place, looking as stunned as anyone else.

"She is right. We should all be free. Oh…and you killed New Daddy. You shouldn't have done that. So I gifted myself with this."

"I'll be damned," he said again.

"That's the plan," she said, and fired once more.

The fourth bullet slammed home and the Overseer fell backwards like a great tree and slammed to the pavement.

All was silent for what seemed an eternity. Finally:

"You stupid bitch," Graves said. "You've just destroyed the world."

"Have I?" said Norda Kinklash. "My. How very exciting."

"*Exciting?*" Graves said. "You idiotic little Mandraque. I should kill you right now."

"Don't," Gant immediately said. "Graves, don't do it."

"Yes, I don't think you should either," said Norda and without hesitation she turned the gun on Graves and opened fire.

It was difficult to determine whether Norda was genuinely aiming at him or was just firing off a random shot in his direction. Either way, it ripped across Graves' upper arm and he cried out, grabbing at it, as a thin line of blood rose up to the surface. He gasped, incredulous over what had just happened. Norda, for her part, didn't seem to realize that she could have quite possibly ended his life if her aim had been just a bit more precise. Instead she cocked one brow ridge and looked at the weapon as if she was surprised that she was holding it. "Oh. Right. It does that," she said.

"Put that down," Jepp said. She was approaching Norda very slowly. "What was your name?"

"Norda."

"Norda. I'm Jepp. I dreamt of you."

Norda blinked in surprise. "You did? I dreamt of you!" and to add emphasis to what she was saying, she pointed the gun in Jepp's direction.

Jepp immediately let out a startled shriek and automatically Karsen stepped between the two of them. "No!"

"No what?" asked Norda, momentarily confused.

"No…that thing," and he pointed at her hand.

Norda stared at the gun and was once again clearly surprised that she was holding it. "Oh. This is a gun. It was a weapon that Morts used. At least that's what the Morts told me."

"What Morts?" said Jepp. Karsen was helping her to her feet, but she was unaware of it because Norda's words filled her with hope. "There are others like me?"

"There were," and Norda's face darkened. "Now they're all dead. Thanks to them," and she pointed accusingly at the Travelers who were surrounding them.

Graves muttered to Trott, "How did she make that weapon fire? Our spells should still be in force. It shouldn't be possible."

"We'll figure it out later," Trott whispered back.

"If there is a later," said Graves and then he raised his voice, speaking angrily to Norda. "You have executed the Overseer. His life was protected by those who sent us here. Do you have any idea what manner of destruction you have visited upon us?"

"No," said Norda, and she appeared genuinely interested. "What manner? Will the sky begin to bleed? Will great bursts of wind come down and hurl us all away? Will our minds be reduced to the level of infancy? What exactly will happen?"

The Travelers glanced at each other but exchanged no words

until Trott said, with as much authority and anger as he could muster, "Come with us! Now!"

"And if we do not desire to?" said Karsen defiantly.

But the Piri that Gant was inhabiting put a hand on Karsen's arm. "No," he said in a soft voice. "Don't fight them. They're scared."

"Scared?" said Karsen, incredulous.

"Yes. They have no idea what is about to happen, and trust me, the Phey *always* know what is going to happen, so they are on very unusual ground right now. Let's just cooperate with them."

Karsen turned and glanced at his mother, but Zerena's face was impassive and the entirety of her response was a simple shrug. The leader of the Bottom Feeders clearly did not have it within her to fight against the Travelers, whether they were scared or not.

"All right, then," said Graves. "Come with us. Now." He started to assemble the people who were standing there, and then noticed that Norda was paying him no mind at all. Instead she was staring fixedly upwards. "What are you looking at?" he demanded in irritation and then looked in the direction that she gazing.

His jaw dropped.

Something huge was hanging in the sky overhead and drifting toward them. It bore a resemblance to a massive jellyfish except its hide was much tougher. It had dozens of tentacles hanging below it and, not only that, but apparently people riding atop it, although they were too far away to be able to discern them readily.

"It's a Zeffer," said Mingo. The massive Minosaur looked as surprised as anyone.

"I wonder if it's the one that brought me here," said Norda.

Graves' head snapped around and he gaped at Norda. "You came here on a Zeffer?"

"That's right!" She clapped her hands as if she were a delighted child. "It was ever so exciting! And if that's the same one that brought me, I wager we will have *so* much fun."

II.

ARREN KINKLASH BECAME AWARE THAT someone was shoving his shoulder. He had lost track of how many hours he had been asleep and now the jostling finally startled him back to wakefulness. The Mandraque shook his head and focused his vision and gasped as a single large eye stared down at him. It was Turkin, one of the two Ocular who had accompanied him on this potentially mad endeavor to catch up with his wayward sister. Arren shook off his slumber. "What's wrong?"

"Nothing is wrong. We're here."

Arren couldn't quite believe it. Pavan, the Serabim that was controlling the Zeffer upon which they were flying had told him that it would be reasonably quick as to when the Zeffer would get them to the Spires. But he had never dreamt that it would be quite this rapid. He sat up and called over to Pavan, "We are?" Pavan nodded. "How is that possible? This thing seems to travel so slowly, and I was under the impression that the Spires were days away."

"The Zeffer does not travel long distances in the way others do," Pavan told him. "It manages to do so through a process that I honestly don't quite understand. From what I've been told, it sort of just…" He seemed to be searching for the right word. "It just bends reality around itself."

"Bends it? How is that possible?"

"I have no idea, as I said. It just does it. My assumption is that it's some form of magic."

"Magic?" That was certainly news to Arren. "I had no idea that Zeffers were magic."

The other Serabim, the female, was walking toward him. Her fur was blowing gently as the wind passed them. "To the Morts," said Demali, "the very existence of a Zeffer would have seemed like magic. The creatures of the land we left behind are like nothing that has ever existed on the Damned World. In a way, magic is all around you if you're just willing to recognize it as such."

That was not something that Arren was particularly willing to do at that moment. Instead his focus was elsewhere.

He stared down upon the Spires below. The Zeffer was flying, or gliding, or drifting—whatever in the world it was that it did—toward the vast city that awaited them below. Arren had to admit that he was extremely impressed by it. It was definitely much larger than Perriz, of that he was quite sure. He was particularly impressed by the heights of the buildings, far taller than any that he had seen in his life. In Perriz only the Eyeful Tower was as tall, and that was not somewhere that Mandraques could easily reside. But many of these structures seemed much taller than the tower. He was having trouble understanding how the damned things were managing to remain upright.

"All right," he said, loudly enough for everyone to hear him. "If the other Zeffer brought Norda and Nicrominus to the Spires, then this is going to be the start of our search. It is possible that since the time they have arrived here, they might well have departed the area. So we are going to have to be extremely thorough in searching for them. It may require many turns to scour this city before we find the slightest clue of where they are. I know it's asking a lot of you to—"

"There she is," said Berola. She was pointing downward.

"What?" Arren didn't quite process what she had just told him. "What do you mean…?"

"We're looking for a female Mandraque, yes? There's one down there. Surrounded by Travelers. And some other people, including a…" She frowned. "What *is* that?"

"That's a Mort," Turkin said. He was apparently staring down at the same place she was. The sun glinted off the lens covering that was over his single great eye. "I've seen pictures of them." He frowned. "Ugly thing, isn't it."

"Wait, I don't understand," said Arren. He stared downward but everything was so small that he could not discern anything, much less determine the race and gender of people below. "You see her? Are you sure? How do you see her?"

Berola seemed amused by the question. "Look at our eyes, and look at yours. Who do you think has the superior vision?"

Arren was not about to doubt them. He was unaware that Ocular were able to see so well, but he was hardly in a mood to dispute it. All business, he turned to Pavan. "Can you bring us down where the Ocular are indicating?"

"Already on it," said Pavan. He was humming softly and then he began to sing. There were no words to his tune; just a seemingly aimless array of notes strung together at random.

Yet they were definitely having an effect. Arren could feel for himself the beginning of the creature's descent. He continued to be amazed by Pavan's ability to manipulate the great beast through song. Except it was obviously more than that. It was an entire language that Pavan had mastered that he knew as thoroughly as his own.

Evanna came to Arren's side, but her question was addressed to the Ocular: "Do you see any Firedraques down there as well?"

Berola squinted slightly and then shook her head. "No. I see a couple of Laocoon, another Mandraque, a Minosaur, a Trull…"

"A Trull? Are you sure? They never come above ground."

"It's definitely a Trull. I've never seen one, but I've heard about what they look like and that couldn't be anything else. And also there's a…" Her voice froze for a moment and then it dropped to a lower, angrier tone. "A Piri. There's a Piri down there. He's wearing a cloak for protection, but it's definitely a Piri."

"A Piri?" It was making no sense to Arren. "What in the world is a Piri doing in the Spires?"

"I don't know."

Arren glanced toward Berola, easily able to perceive the hatred in her voice. "I don't understand. You arrived in Perriz at the side of a Piri. I would think you, of all people, would be likely to allow them the benefit of the doubt."

"I've fought far more Piri than I've ever been enamored of," Berola said sharply. "I would just as soon crush one as trust it."

"She's right," said Turkin. "Clarinda had no love for them, and she *was* one. So you could say that that very much informs our opinion about them."

"All right," said Arren, putting up his hands in a gesture of surrender. "Piri are evil. I understand. Heaven knows I've seen what they are capable of close up."

"As have I," said Evanna.

"Fine, but the others don't seem repulsed by him or attempting to kill him. Which is, as I understand it, rather unusual behavior for our people, who tend to try and dispatch Piri wherever and whenever they are encountered. True enough?"

The two Ocular glanced at each other. As for the Serabim, they did not seem especially interested in the conversation at all. Obviously they had never encountered Piri and had no particular interest in them one way or the other. Berola finally nodded. "That would certainly be accurate. Gods know that's what our people did whenever confronted with them."

"Then let us get down there and find out what in the world is going on. Pavan, how fast can you get us down there?"

"Well, I could have the Zeffer grip us with tentacles and then have it turn over. That would get you down rather quickly."

It was not a bit of humor that Arren especially appreciated. "An alternate plan would be appreciated."

"Yes, I suspected it would." Pavan then pitched his head back and began to produce another series of musical sounds. Not exactly a song; it was more as if he were speaking in music. The Zeffer shuddered slightly in response and then drifted toward the ground.

Everyone down there was staring up at them, trying to make out the specifics of the individuals who were atop it. Arren did not care about any of them. His entire focus was upon the Mandraque that he was convinced was his sister. He balanced himself on the edge of the Zeffer so he could see her more clearly.

She was looking straight up at him and waving eagerly.

Well, that was certainly typical for Norda.

The fact of the matter—and it was not a fact that the Mandraques were especially enamored about advertising—was that a vast majority of their people were nearsighted. It was simply in the DNA of their race. That was the main reason that Mandraques preferred to get up close when battling enemies; their lousy vision precluded them from using weapons of distance such as bows and arrows or spears. So they were reduced to fighting tight in with swords and took pleasure in dispatching their foes so that the smell of their blood would waft to their nostrils.

But Norda was an exception to that. Her vision was uncannily sharp, so much so that Arren envied her visual acuity. He was seeing it on display now as well, for she had clearly spotted him. She was continuing to wave eagerly, or at least that's what Arren thought she was doing.

The Zeffer continued to drop toward the surface and with each passing moment, as his view of Norda became clearer, Arren felt relief sweeping through him. Part of him had actually doubted that it was she; that it was instead some sort of insidious trick. But no, it was definitely her, and though it was not the easiest thing in the world for Mandraques to smile, he was nevertheless sure that she was grinning widely. He waved back to her, shouted her name even though he knew that she could not hear him. He supposed that didn't matter. As long as calling a greeting to her pleased him, that was the most important aspect.

Evanna's hand was on Arren's shoulder. "What of my father? What of Nicrominus? Is he down there with her?"

Arren had, until that moment, completely forgotten about Nicrominus, so focused was he on the impending reunion with his sister. Evanna, for her part, likely did not give a damn about Norda. She was only interested in the fate of her father who had been absconded with by another Zeffer and taken away to this city of spires. The fact that Norda had come along for the ride was just happenstance. Arren surveyed the ground as best he could but was unable to discern any other Mandraques or Firedraques on the ground below. He shook his head. "Sorry. Can't see him. Just her and some others," and now he frowned, "including some Travelers."

"Travelers?" Clearly Evanna was not happy to hear that. "They're the bastards who were responsible for calling the Zeffer down upon my father in the first place. If they're down there with her, they certainly know where Nicrominus is. We'll make them tell."

"We'll make them?" Arren could not keep a bit of wry amusement out of his voice. "I don't think we can *make* the Travelers do anything at all."

Her face hardened. "You would be amazed what I can do when I put my mind to it. Plus we have them," and she nodded toward the Ocular.

"They're children," Arren immediately reminded her. "Not warriors, despite what they might have been able to do against the Piri back in Perriz. If it came to combat between them and the Travelers, they would…"

"They would what?" Evanna was challenging him. "They would what? What have you ever actually witnessed the Travelers doing? Their reputations certainly precede them, but whatever powers the Travelers might actually wield, they keep to themselves. Ever wonder why?"

"Because they are secretive."

"Or perhaps they have no powers at all! Only what the Overseer might grant…" Her voice trailed off and Arren saw that something else below them had attracted her attention.

"What is it?" he asked.

"That large figure in the armor. The one lying on the ground? Who in the world is that?"

"I haven't the slightest idea. Let's go down and ask them. In the meantime," and his gaze shifted to the Ocular who were likewise watching with rapt attention, "let me go talk to our 'warriors.'"

Long minutes later the Zeffer had drifted close enough to the ground so that it was able to reach up with its tentacles and it wrapped around the Mandraque, the Firedraque and the Ocular. The two Serabim remained aboard the Zeffer. Pavan stated it was easier for him to retain control of the vast beast, but Arren very much suspected that he simply had no desire to find himself face to face with Travelers.

He shivered slightly as the tentacle firmly insinuated itself around his body. It was surprisingly cold; surprising because he would have supposed that it would be warm since they were living membranes. But no, that was definitely not the case. It made the Mandraque feel as if he was being lifted by something unliving, and that alone was enough to send a chill down his spine. He had no idea if any of the others were feeling the same sensations he was, but if they were, he certainly felt badly for them.

Then the Zeffer eased them into the air and they descended towards those gathered on the ground. The closer he drew to them, the more confused he was by the diversity in the groups. There had to be half a dozen different races down there freely intermingling with each other, which was somewhat insane considering that typically the races remained solely with each other. Arren could not begin to imagine what they were doing together. And who the devil *was* that in the body armor?

He hoped he would learn the answers soon enough.

III.

NORDA CLAPPED HER HANDS GIDDILY as Arren alighted on the street, eased down by one of the Zeffer's vast tentacles. She wondered for a moment if it were the same one that had transported her here to this strange city, but then the thought flittered from her mind as all thoughts tended to do. She sprinted toward Arren and, when she got within five feet of him, leaped the remaining distance and landed in his arms. He embraced her tightly, whispering her name in her ear hole. "You had me so worried," he said over and over. "How could you have done that? How could you have taken off the way you did?"

"The flying thing took New Daddy," Norda said matter-of-factly, as if it was the only possible response to the question. "I thought he might be lonely. So I went with him."

"New Daddy?" Arren had no idea what she was talking about.

Evanna, however, did. "My father? You mean my father?"

Norda stared at her for a long moment, frowning, trying to remember from where she knew this Firedraque. Then it clicked for her: she had spoken any number of times with New Daddy. She oftentimes seemed quite impatient with him. He seemed to tolerate it with his customary grace, but Norda had found her very annoying. Her disgust with Evanna prompted her to push a startled Arren to one side and she took several steps toward the Firedraque. She cradled her gun in a manner that was clearly making Arren nervous; he didn't know what it was, but it was clear that he was finding her comfort with it somewhat disconcerting. As a courtesy to her brother's nerves, she endeavored to remember not to point the weapon in Evanna's direction, but it was difficult for her to focus on. "You were cruel to him," she said abruptly. "You always spoke disrespectfully to him. He hated you."

"What?" Evanna's jaw dropped in surprise. "He did not!"

"Well, I certainly didn't like you, and that's all that matters."

Evanna was seeming to have trouble figuring out precisely how to speak to her, and Arren stepped in before matters could devolve too quickly. "Norda, her father is Nicrominus, the Firedraque that the Zeffer took. The one that you hitched a ride with."

Her face cleared and then she understood. "Nicrominus. Yes. That's right. I remember. *He* called him that," and she pointed disdainfully at the armored figure that was lying unmoving some feet away. "He wasn't nice to him."

Trott stepped forward, looking extremely impatient. "We do not need to discuss this business here. We can retreat to our meeting hall—"

"We're not going *anywhere!*" Evanna whirled to face the Traveler, and he blinked in obvious surprise over her reaction and ferocity. Clearly he was unaccustomed to someone being so defiant to his face. "Not until you bring me to my father! Where is he?"

Then, to her surprise, Norda took her hand gently by the wrist, lifted it, and placed it against Norda's stomach. Evanna gazed at her, uncomprehending.

"I ate him," Norda said softly.

Evanna's hand fell from Norda's belly and she took several steps back, horrified, her eyes widening. It took her long seconds to process what Norda had told her, and then she let out a scream of shock and fury, opened her mouth wide, and blew out a huge gout of flame.

Had Norda remained where she was, Evanna would have set her on fire. As it was Norda barely avoided conflagration as Arren leaped through the air, slammed into her and knocked her flat. Evanna's head snapped around and she prepared to unleash another blast of flame. The fact that Arren was between her and her target did not even register on her.

That was when a sharp crack of a fist landed on the back of her skull. She went down, the half-generated flame discharging harmlessly from her mouth. Her head was ringing and for a moment she completely forgot where she was. Evanna endeavored to twist around and look behind her and saw only a large fist driving right toward her face. There was nothing she could do, no way to avoid it, and when it struck home it knocked her into unconsciousness.

Berola stood upright, shaking off the brief numbness in her fist. "That was exciting," she said and then switched her attention to Arren. "You all right?"

"I've had better days," he replied. He got to his feet and helped Norda to hers. "You okay?" he asked gently.

Norda nodded and then turned her attention to Evanna. "Are you all right?" she asked solicitously.

This garnered confused looks from the others, and then Trott stepped forward, his growing impatience with the situation undiminished. "Enough of this," he said. "To the hall. To what the Overseer called," and he hesitated, trying to pull the name up. "The Javisenter."

"Javisenter?" said a puzzled Karsen. "What in the hell sort of name is that?"

Trott shrugged. "Go argue with humans," he said.

IV.

THE WORLD SLOWLY RETURNED TO light for Evanna as her eyes opened and then squinted against the odd lighting from the ceiling above her. The bulbs within were most unusual; she could not recall ever having seen the like. She found it remarkably irritating.

She endeavored to sit up and was astounded to discover that she was chained down to some manner of cot. The only other furniture in the room was a single chair, and Norda Kinklash was seated in it. "Seated" might not exactly have been the right word. She was curled up on a simple gray chair, her legs crisscrossed and her arms draped around her shoulders in a manner that resembled a pretzel. Evanna saw an opportunity to unleash another blast of flame and Norda would unquestionably be roasted alive from it.

Evanna attempted to open her mouth and was astounded to discover that a muzzle was keeping it soundly shut.

"That's so you don't spit out fire or anything," said Norda cheerfully. She seemed oblivious to Evanna's mounting fury. "They were concerned about it, although I'm not sure if they were worried you'd burn me or this place." She gestured around, endeavoring to take in the entirety of their environment. "Apparently this place is called 'Javisenter.' Which is an odd name, if you ask me. Even the black caped men used to call it something else, but the man I shot said it was pronounced 'Javisenter' so that's what they're calling it now."

Evanna grunted. It was the only noise she was capable of producing.

Norda climbed down from the chair and approached her, cocking her head in curiosity. "If I remove that," she said cautiously, "will you promise not to blow flame at me? I don't think I would especially like being set aflame. I imagine it would hurt a great deal. Can I trust you?"

For a long moment Evanna simply continued to stare at her. Then, once more, she grunted, but this was accompanied by a brief nod of the head.

Norda clapped her hands together again. Evanna was already getting tired of that obvious means Norda employed of expressing satisfaction. It was like dealing with someone who was newly hatched. She was tempted to demand of Norda when she was going to grow up, but she stopped herself because she suspected that Norda would likely not understand the question.

It took a few moments for Norda to loosen the strapping around Evanna's mouth. Then she removed the muzzle from Evanna's jaw. Evanna considered the option of unleashing a flame blast, catching Norda flatfooted and blowing her out of existence. But her arms were still secured and she had no means of removing them. Which meant that she would be stuck there until someone came down to check on her. And when they did and discovered Norda's charred remains, it likely would not go well for Evanna, especially if Norda's brother had anything to say about it.

So instead she kept her word and took no offensive action against Norda. As if she were capable of reading Evanna's mind, Norda watched her warily for a bit before pulling the chair over to directly opposite her and then dropping into it.

"I've been thinking," said Norda, "which I have to admit is something that is kind of unusual for me. Usually I just feel things. It tends to make life simpler, you know?"

"Yes," said Evanna tonelessly.

"And what I was thinking was that when I told you I ate New Daddy, you immediately figured that I was the one who killed him."

"Why do you keep calling him that? 'New Daddy?'"

"Because my old daddy was not very nice," said Norda. "He shouted, he hit. He was very vicious." Her face darkened. "That's why Arren had to kill him, I expect."

That news caught Evanna by surprise. "He killed your father?"

Norda turned away from her as if her mind had taken her to

places that she had no desire to accompany it. "He was beating me. I had done something that upset him; I don't remember what. Maybe looked at him funny. In any event, he was striking me with such fury around the head and…" She reached up, her fingers tapping the side of her skull and she frowned. "I used to think differently. That may sound strange, but I think I used to ponder other things that don't occur to me anymore. It's hard to hold it all together. It's strange to remember your being another way, but there it is, I guess. You know?" She turned and looked at Evanna with curiosity, clearly waiting for her to respond.

"I suppose it would be," said Evanna.

"Anyway," Norda continued, shrugging slightly, "that's how I supposed all daddies were supposed to be. But then I saw yours. And he was not like that at all. Did he ever beat you?"

Evanna shook her head.

"That's nice." She sighed to herself. "That's very nice that he didn't. You were fortunate. But you never seemed to treat him like you realized how lucky you were. You seemed to argue with him a lot. I could never argue with my father. There would have been even more beatings. Like when my brother killed him. Did I mention that?"

"Yes, you did."

"My father never even saw him coming," said Norda wistfully. "Neither did I. I was lying on the floor, bleeding. There was blood all over, everywhere, even into my eyes, and my mouth was moving but no words were coming out. And my father was leaning down to keep beating me and suddenly a sword was sticking out the front of his chest. He was very startled, and he turned around and stared at Arren, who was just standing there looking as surprised as our father. Daddy tried to say something, but no words came out. He smiled. I think he smiled. Or perhaps he snarled; it is hard to say what expressions our father made at any given time. He turned around then and Arren let go of his hold on the sword. He just stood there, staring. My father tried to remove the sword from his chest and he managed to get a grip on it, but then his hands slumped to either side and his legs gave way and he just…just fell." She gestured toward the floor and made a sound akin to that of a body hitting it. "I was waiting for him to get back up and rage at Arren and start beating me again, but he did nothing. He just bled until he stopped bleeding and that was it. And I had no idea what we were supposed to do.

"And Arren explained. He said we were supposed to eat him. So we did. We just stripped the meat from his bones. It tasted rather chewy. Arren said that it was tradition. After that I saw your father and decided he was New Daddy."

"Why?"

"Well, I thought he would be a good father and you didn't seem to be making much use of him. So I decided I would. And then we came here, and that bad man in that strange suit…he killed New Daddy." Her face darkened for the first time and she looked ready to spit acid at the memory. "They were talking and then he threw New Daddy off the top of a very high building. He fell and fell and fell and fell and fell and—"

"I get it," Evanna said, having no desire to listen to a lengthy litany of her father's final moments. "And when you descended to the street level…"

"I ate him. Because that is the tradition."

No, it isn't, you little idiot, the words went through Evanna's head. *In ancient times, perhaps. Thousands of years ago. But not anymore, not for generations, not for ages. Your brother just told you that to cover up the death of your father. He saved you from the actions of a brute, and was concerned about the repercussions. So he used you to help him cover the evidence. Gods know what he said to the others to cover for his father's disappearance.*

Then her inner voice softened. *You believed what your brother told you. And gods only knew what sort of damage your damnable father did to your brain. Yes, you ate my father, but obviously you thought you were doing so in some manner of tribute. And it's not as if you were the one who killed him…*

"You slayed the man who killed my father," she said, understanding what had happened.

"Yes. I had to. I am not sure if your father would have wanted it, but I knew I had to. I wanted to. It was very strange. I have never wanted to kill anyone before, but I knew this person had to die."

"Except the person that you killed was the leader of the Damned World. His power stems from those who abandoned us here. They will be furious over what you've done. Even the Travelers are clearly afraid of the results of what you have done. They are expecting the sky to come crashing down upon us."

Norda tilted her head and stared curiously at Evanna. "And yet it hasn't. Nothing has happened so far. Why do you think that is?"

"I…" She had no answer and so she shrugged as best she could considering she was still tied to the chair. "I do not really know. I am beginning to realize that for someone who has spent the entirety of her life deep in studies, there is a sizable amount of things that I do not know." She pulled at the bonds but quickly gave up when she realized she was making no headway against them and then looked with some small measure of hope at Norda. "Listen: I am much calmer now. I understand that you did not hurt my father. And you believed that you were honoring him or some such when you…"

"Ate him."

"That's correct. So I would very much appreciate it if you could undo the restraints and release me from this chair."

Slowly Norda nodded. "Yes. Yes, I think New Daddy would want that. He would want the two of us to get on with each other."

It took Norda only a matter of moments to unbind Evanna from her imprisonment. Evanna stretched her arms and legs and groaned as her muscles played against themselves. Norda watched quietly as Evanna got her body back into shape. She noticed that Norda remained poised as if she were prepared to spring out of the way of a sudden attack. Slowly Evanna shook her head and said softly, "I am not going to attack you."

"If you were, would that not be the first thing you would say to convince me that you won't?"

Evanna considered that and nodded. "Yes. Yes, I suppose it is. Nevertheless, I assure you I am quite calm. I know that you did not hurt my father, and I suppose I must thank you for avenging his murder. Even though it is entirely possible that you may have led to the destruction of the world."

"Happy to do it," said Norda, and she really did sound quite pleased over her actions. In spite of the seriousness of the situation, Evanna shook her head slightly and laughed.

V.

JEPP KNEW THAT SHE SHOULD be impressed by seeing so many Travelers in one place. They were, after all, the most formidable beings in the whole of the Damned World.

Yet the several dozen individuals who had gathered in the large room—one of the largest she could ever recall being in—did not seem remotely formidable. They seemed concerned.

Pensive.

Frightened, even.

They looked remarkably similar to each other, extraordinarily beautiful with silver skin. Jepp was more familiar than any other non-Traveler in the world with what they actually looked like, since she had spent a length of time on a ship crossing with several of them. That familiarity was doubtless why she did not feel the least bit intimidated by being among them. In that regard, she was most definitely separated in attitude from the Bottom Feeders milling near her, who were clearly extremely uncomfortable in their surroundings.

They were seated along a row of chairs, glancing around suspiciously at the Travelers as they milled around. If they were speaking, it was in a low language that any who were not of their species was helpless to understand. It sounded more akin to a bird fluttering its wings than anything else, and yet it was clear that they were all engaged with each other.

Karsen Foux sat next to Jepp, squeezing her hand repeatedly as he surveyed the area, clearly alert for any attacks. Her eyes remained on him since she did not consider the Travelers to be worth her time, and eventually his gaze returned to her. "I cannot believe you're here," he said.

"I cannot believe *you* are here. To come all this way for me… it is absolutely remarkable. No one has ever done anything like that for me. No one has ever cared about me enough to undertake such a thing."

"I care for you. I care very much."

There was a sharp, annoyed gagging sound from nearby and Jepp knew immediately that it was Karsen's mother, Zerena. Mingo was seated next to her and seemed more amused than anything else, but Zerena was continuing to make loud retching noises. So loud, in fact, that it caught the attention of several nearby Travelers who glared at her but kept their silence.

"Must you?" Zerena finally said.

"Must *you*?" Karsen snapped back at her. "We are simply talking."

"You sound like two awful, clichéd lovers in some terrible romance work," Zerena said. "You care for her, she cares for you. I cannot understand why the two of you do not simply engage in sexual congress until you are bored with each other and then you can move on to something more constructive in your lives."

"You do not understand," Jepp informed her. "Perhaps it is because you have never truly loved someone in your life. I know nothing of your relationship with Karsen's father, of course."

"He's dead. Long dead."

Jepp lowered her head. "I am sorry for that."

"Don't be. I killed him."

That surprised Jepp, but wisely enough, she chose not to pursue it. Then Karsen rested a hand on her shoulder and said in a low voice, "Do not inquire further."

"Yes, I already decided on that course of action. Or inaction, as the case may be."

Jepp noticed that the conversation among the Travelers was becoming louder and more heated. Not only that, but the Travelers kept glancing angrily toward the Bottom Feeders and the individuals who had arrived in the air and were now hunkered down nearby.

Abruptly all conversation halted, and Jepp wondered why. She saw that all the Travelers were now looking past her shoulders and she turned to see what it was that had captured their attention. She was surprised to observe that the Mandraque, Norda, was walking into the room next to the Firedraque. There seemed to be no hostility toward them; obviously Norda had freed the Firedraque from the bonds that had held her in place.

Graves stepped forward and said warily, "Are there going to be further problems?"

"No," said Norda and, to the Firedraque's utter discomfort, she draped an arm around her shoulders. "Evanna and I are sisters now!"

"We aren't sisters," Evanna said in a low voice.

"We both have the same daddy!" Norda corrected her in a tone of voice that seemed to indicate that, as far as she was concerned, the debate was settled.

Evanna was clearly about to engage in a prolonged debate, but then she rolled her eyes and something in her face changed. Her body slumped a bit, losing the tension that had embraced it when Norda first put her arm on her shoulders and she said with a heavy sigh, "Yes. Yes, I suppose we do."

"See!" Norda said cheerfully. She turned to Arren who was approaching the two of them cautiously and continued, "Say hello to your new sister, Arren!"

Arren and Evanna exchanged looks and then Arren shrugged. "Hello, sister. You are looking well."

"Thank you…'brother,'" said Evanna.

Jepp actually found the entire exchange to be charmingly amusing. It was clear that the Mandraque and Firedraque were more concerned with sparing the feelings of Norda than hewing to accuracy or picking a fight. And it was Jepp's experience that when it came to picking fights, that was typically something in which Mandraques, in particular, were all too happy to engage. So it seemed to her that there was certainly something special about Norda, beyond the peculiarities that her actions thus far had displayed.

"Are we through with this?" said one of the Travelers. He had pulled back his hood as all the Travelers had done since they had entered their vast headquarters, and he was striding forward looking quite irritated. "Everyone getting along now? No one going to attempt to kill anyone?"

Jepp was struck by how musical his voice sounded, which was quite an accomplishment considering that he was obviously irritated. Nevertheless he sounded as if he were singing as he spoke. He gestured toward Norda, Arren and Evanna. "Sit. We are going to speak now and you are going to listen."

They did so. Evanna and Arren still seemed concerned over what the Travelers were going to say. Norda was too busy looking around the large room, her eyes wide with fascination. "This is the biggest room I have ever seen," she said in wonderment. "Did you make this?"

The Traveler hesitated for some reason and then said, "No. The Morts made it."

"It is amazing! Did they live here?"

"I do not know, nor do I care."

"Why do you not care?"

"Because they are dead. They're all dead," and the Traveler pointed in accusatory fashion right at Jepp. "Except for this one."

"If I am the last of the Morts," Jepp shot back at him, not the least intimidated by his status as a Traveler, "that is because you and your kind have slaughtered my brethren. Including, according to her," and she pointed at Norda, "a tribe of them that were living beneath the streets of this very city."

Another of the Travelers moved forward, and she immediately

recognized him as the Traveler who had been on the boat with her when she had almost drowned. "That," he said, "was not our desire or our wish. We were ordered to by the Overseer."

"You could have disobeyed him," said Jepp.

He shook his head and for a moment Jepp was captured by the displays of the overhead lighting that played off his face. "No. We could not have. His word was law."

"And yet he's dead." It was Zerena who had spoken up, and that impressed Jepp somewhat. Zerena had always been intimidated by the Travelers; even the very thought that they might be on the way would prompt her to gather up her things and flee in the opposite direction. Yet now she was standing and facing off against the Traveler and she did not seem the slightest bit concerned about incurring his wrath. "He's dead because she killed him," and she pointed at Norda.

Norda had picked up a random piece of string and was batting at it like a small animal trying to amuse herself. She wasn't paying the slightest bit of attention to the conversation.

"Yes, and we still do not know the outcome of her actions."

"Thus far there don't seem to be any," Zerena said. "Have any of you—*any* of you," and her rising voice took in the entirety of the meeting room, "considered the possibility that he was powerless? That you've all been bending knee to someone who had no puissance, no connection to our exilers at all?"

The Travelers exchanged blank eyed looks with each other.

Then one of them stepped forward and when he spoke to him, Jepp was surprised to realize she understood every word he said. Clearly he was making no effort to hide what he had to say. "Graves, we need help. We need to ask someone who actually knows about these things."

"Who would you suggest, Trott?" said Graves.

"Isn't it obvious?" said the one called Trott. "There is only one individual with the knowledge to explain why, so far, the death of the Overseer has not resulted in instant recrimination if not outright death. For that matter, he may well be able to explain why her weapon was able to function when we were able to halt the rest of the Morts' weapons from functioning."

At first Graves didn't seem to understand what Trott was suggesting, but then he did. His voice dropped to a near whisper. "You are suggesting...Obertan?"

"Yes," said Trott.

This immediately resulted in a repeat of the previous interaction as the Travelers spoke with each other, excluding everyone else from the conversation.

But Karsen knew that there was a way to understand what they were saying as he turned toward Gant. The green blob of a creature that had taken up residence inside the body of a Piri was sitting there, seemingly disconnected from the oddly quiet tumult all around him. Jepp, however, knew exactly what Karsen was going to ask before he did so. "What are they saying?" he whispered to Gant.

"How would I know?" replied Gant.

"Don't fool around with me," said Karsen, and there was clear annoyance in his voice. "I know you're a Phey and they obviously are too. I don't care that you're not in your body; your brain is working just fine and I know you can understand every word they're saying to each other. So tell us what they're talking about."

Gant shifted uncomfortably, and it was clear to Jepp immediately what the problem is. To his surprise, she reached over and laid a hand atop one of his. "You are not betraying them," she said softly. "They are no longer your people. You are a Bottom Feeder. They are your people, your tribe, and your family. And they need your help now."

Gant looked uncertain for a moment but then he set his face and nodded. He spoke in such a low voice that only those seated near him could hear him. "They are speaking about our leader. Obertan."

"I thought your leader was the dead man in the armor," said Jepp.

Gant shook his head. "The Overseer was our guardian. Our

warden. Our jailer. He did not lead us but instead oppressed us. We had to obey all of his instructions and we could not answer back. Our leader he most definitely was not."

"So who is this Obertan?"

"Some say," and Gant's voice dropped even more. It was the first time he had ever displayed something akin to reverence. "Some say he is the first of us. I am not sure how that would be possible, but I would not be surprised in the least."

"And where is he?" asked Jepp. "If he is your leader, where is he hiding?"

"He is not hiding. He simply is not here. He does not reside with the rest of the Phey. Instead he lives within the land of Dizz."

"Dizz?" Jepp and Karsen exchanged looks. The name meant nothing to them. "Where is that?"

"Many miles south of here. More Phey reside there. We Phey have never been much for living all together, you see. We are a somewhat…" He paused, trying to come up with a single word to summarize them. "Nomadic peoples, I suppose. Or perhaps we are simply overcautious. If we do not all live in the same place, then it would be impossible for an enemy to target us and wipe us from existence."

"I suppose that makes sense," said Karsen.

Jepp noticed that the rest of the Bottom Feeders were likewise nodding; apparently the caution of the Phey made sense to them. "So they believe that this Obertan would know why the death of the Overseer has not resulted in everyone and everything being obliterated?"

Gant was watching and listening to the Phey as they engaged in their discussion, keeping their tones hushed. Slowly he nodded. "I think that is exactly it, yes. In fact, I would guess that they are about to come to some manner of conclu—"

As if reacting on cue to his supposition, the Travelers separated from one another and then Graves turned and strode toward them. Instinctively Jepp drew nearer to Karsen. She was not remotely afraid of Graves. She had been through far too much to allow any residual fear of the Travelers to color her feelings toward them. Nevertheless, Karsen's proximity brought her a distant feeling of security and relaxation. She wrapped both of her hands around Karsen's arm, and he absently stroked her hair in an affectionate and reassuring manner.

He stopped a few feet shy of them and stared down at them imperiously. "It has been decided to consult our wisest to determine what we should do next. I cannot tell you who that is or where he is currently secreted, but—"

"You mean Obertan?" said Jepp. "Who lives in Dizz?"

Graves barely managed to conceal his shock at Jepp's innocent question, and then his eyes narrowed and he glared straight at Gant. Gant, for response, simply shrugged. "Is it not a bit late, brother, to be concerned over keeping secrets?"

"It is not your place to give those secrets away."

"Why not?" said Gant, who was now standing. "I'm not longer a Phey, after all. So what point is there in my being bound to our race's interests?"

Graves looked as if he very much wanted to discuss this at far greater length, but then he obviously thought better of it and instead shifted his attention back to the group in front of him. "I will be setting out on this mission shortly. As for the rest of you, you are free to go wherever you wish. We will not make prisoners of you."

"So you aren't going to attempt to punish Norda for what she did?" Arren was trying to sound casual, but Jepp noticed that his hand was drifting in an almost casual manner to the sword that was dangling from his hip.

Graves shrugged ever so slightly. "The fact is that we were never especially enamored of the Overseer. Had we not been concerned about the world being destroyed in retaliation for the action, we would have been happy to kill him ourselves. But one does what one must to survive, I suppose. So no, we are not going to try your sister. Not certain what the point would be. Within a day or so, judging by her discourse, she might well not even remember what she did."

"That's true, I might not," Norda said agreeably. "Some people think I'm insane. I don't believe I am, but then again, if I am insane, what do I know?"

Gant walked toward Graves and stood there with his arms folded. "Are you going by yourself?"

"Trott will accompany me."

"As will I," said Gant.

Immediately Graves shook his head, but before he could even speak, Gant continued, "It may be my only chance."

"Chance for what?" Then Graves understood. "Tania."

"She is down in Dizz, I assume?"

"I do not know. Tania goes where she will. She could be in Dizz, or she could be elsewhere. There is no way of predicting."

"She did this to me," said Gant. "She caused me to have to inhabit this…this shell. She is the only one who can change me back, make me what I was."

"And how do you know she would do that? How do you know she might not leave you worse off than when you started?"

"I'm a blob of green, Graves. How could I possibly be any worse off?"

"Given the opportunity, there is no saying she couldn't come up with something. She might even kill you."

"I doubt she would. I can't imagine her giving me that sort of release. But better that than the existence I have been living until now. Please, Graves. Do not make me beg."

Graves stared at him for a long moment, saying nothing. Then he sighed. It sounded like an autumn breeze. "Fine. Accompany us. But bring your cape and hood along to provide protection, because we are not going to change our travel plans in order to accommodate your…" He gestured vaguely at Gant's appropriated form. "…condition." Then he glanced around. "Does anyone else wish to come along?"

"It might be interesting," Karsen said. "To explore this side of the vastly waters. See what's here."

That immediately brought Eutok to his feet. "Oh no you don't!" he said angrily. "We had a bargain! An agreement! I've lived up to my part of it and now you have to live up to yours!"

Immediately Karsen's face fell but then he nodded, although it was clear it was regretful. "You're right. You are right."

"What agreement?" said Jepp.

"He promised me that he would aid me in finding...someone," said Eutok.

Karsen snorted disdainfully at Eutok's suddenly display of discretion. "Her name is Clarinda."

"Clarinda?" Both Evanna and Berola spoke at the same time. "The Piri?" Berola continued. Turkin and Arren were both also clearly interested in the conversation.

Eutok could not have looked more surprised if one of them had taken a two by four piece of wood and smacked him across the face with it. "Yes," he said. "Yes. You...you know her?"

"She was our leader," said Turkin. "She..."

"She's dead," said Berola softly.

Eutok slowly sank to the floor, missing a chair. His eyes were wide with shock. "Dead? How?"

"She sacrificed herself for me," said Evanna. "For us," she then amended, gesturing toward Arren. "When Perriz was under invasion by a combined force of Mandraques and Serabim. We were fleeing through the sewers and were under attack. She remained behind to face the attackers while we fled."

"You *left her behind?!*" With a thunderous roar that attracted the attention of numerous Phey in the hall, Eutok lunged at the stunned Evanna.

Arren immediately stepped between them, blocking the charge. He yanked out his sword and Eutok began to reach for his axe, but then Karsen came in behind him and grabbed his arms, halting the enraged Trull before he could mount a true attack. "Stop it, Eutok! This is accomplishing nothing!"

"They left her to die!"

"She made the sacrifice on her own," said Arren.

"We tried to talk her out of it but she wouldn't hear of it," Evanna assured him.

Suddenly, with no warning, Eutok stopped struggling. "Did you see her body? Did you see that she was actually dead?"

Evanna and the others exchanged puzzled looks. "No," said Evanna slowly. "Since we were under attack by someone in the sewers, it didn't seem to make sense to return and expose ourselves to further danger."

"So she could still be alive."

"I don't see how…"

"You don't know her as I do," Eutok said. There was no trace of desperation in his voice but instead firm determination. "She survived somehow. Someone like her is not going to meet her demise in the sewers of Perriz. If you did not see her dead body, then I have to assume that she still lives. And you, Karsen, are bound by your promise to me. These others," and he gestured toward the rest of the assemblage, "I do not care what they do. But you must come with me to Perriz and we have to find her."

"You won't be alone," said Berola. "She was our leader. Our teacher. If there is any hope that she lives, we will aid you in finding her."

"Absolutely," Turkin readily agreed.

The others were nodding as well and a strange, unaccustomed thing appeared on Eutok's face. It was a smile of genuine gratitude.

"All right then," said Pavan. "We can return to the Zeffer and get back to Perriz. It may take us a bit longer than it did for us to arrive here. The Zeffer is tired and needs to rest for a time before it can twist space again. But we will get there as quickly as is possible."

Zerena strode over to Gant and stared at him. "So this is it, then? You're going to leave us? Head off with this Traveler to try and be restored to what you were?"

"That is my plan," said Gant. "Zerena…I owe you so much. You took me in when—"

Zerena's fist flew before Gant was able to react at all. It struck him in the side of the head and Gant went down as if he had been hit with a bag of rocks. He lay there, stunned, his eyes rolling around in his skull for a few moments before he managed to repair his vision. When he did, he stared uncomprehendingly at Zerena.

She shrugged. "Tradition," she said. "It's what Bottom Feeders always do when one of them leaves. It's a way of wishing them luck."

"You couldn't just say, 'Good luck?' Shake my hand, perhaps?"

Once more her shoulders went up and down. "What can I say? One never argues with tradition." She walked past him and said loudly, "Let's go. We're going to catch a ride on the back of a Zeffer and get back to where we should never have left in the first place."

As she strode past Karsen, he said in a low voice, "I've never heard of that tradition."

"They have to start somewhere," she replied.

PERRIZ

JORMUND DESPISED THE OCULAR. HE always had, and he always would. He had despised them ever since he had first encountered them in an attempted raid on an Ocular outpost and the results had not gone remotely the way that he had hoped they would. The Ocular had slaughtered half his legions without it even being the slightest challenge for them, and when Jormund and his remaining allies had fled, the raucous laughter of the Ocular had followed him and haunted him for many sleepless nights thereafter. His nights had necessarily been sleepless because his followers had been so angry over his leading them into slaughter that actual slumber was a luxury he could not permit for quite some time.

But that had been a long time ago. The Ocular, as far as Jormund knew, were now nearly deceased. The last members of that damnable one-eyed race had taken up residence in the great Firedraque Hall and kept mostly to themselves. They were, every one of them, youngsters, and although their size and strength made them formidable warriors, they were still quite youthful. That made them pliable to Jormund's interests.

To Jormund, it seemed only yesterday when he had been attending that meeting of the Five Clans, gathered around the great table in the hall of Nicrominus. That was the meeting where that damnable trickster, Arren Kinklash, had somehow arranged for a gigantic bell to come plummeting from on high and crush Gorsh of Cheng. One minute he had been arguing with and threatening Arren and the next the bell had slammed down with unnatural accuracy and obliterated him. Gods knew what Gorsh's last thoughts had been, but whatever they were, they had most certainly been truncated.

Jormund, who was physically the largest of all the Mandraques on the council of the Five Clans—indeed, one of the largest of all the Mandraques in the entire city of Perriz—tended to keep his own council. When he spoke he was usually surprisingly soft of voice, and he chose his words carefully which tended to put him into stark contrast with many of the more bellicose members of the Mandraques. But as he entered the confines of Firedraque Hall and made his way up to the rooms that were occupied by the Ocular, he kept reminding himself that discretion was called for in this situation. "They are children, they are children," he repeatedly muttered to himself.

"Who is there?" came an uncertain tone from up ahead. Clearly their hearing was reasonably sharp as well.

"Jormund," he rumbled and then tried to pitch his voice slightly higher in order to make himself sound friendlier and more approachable. "I wish to speak with you."

"Go away," was the immediate response and several voices echoed the sentiment, but then another—a female voice, clearly— said with weary resignation, "Come up. Speak your piece."

Jormund required no further invitation beyond that. He strode the rest of the way up the steps and into a large room. It appeared to be some manner of chapel, for he had long ago discerned that Firedraque Hall had been a place of worship back when the Morts were running things on the Damned World. The Ocular were spread out through it. They looked beaten and weary, obviously still worn out from the mighty battle in which they had participated when the Serabim had assailed the city. They had lost at least one or even more of their own and the ravages of warfare were clearly a new experience for them. There were about half a dozen in the room at the moment. Jormund suspected there were more, but they were likely spread out through the Hall.

The one who was the female that had spoken was sitting upright, as opposed to the others who were in various states of recline. "What would you have of us, Jormund?" she said. She did not actually sound especially interested. She was simply asking out of a sense of politeness.

"To whom am I speaking?"

"Kerda," she replied. "I am the eldest of those of us remaining. So again: what would you have of us?"

"Why do you assume I want anything of you?"

"Because of course you do. Because you have no reason to come here unless you were seeking a boon or aid of some sort."

She was correct, naturally. Mandraques were not exactly renowned for caring about any race save for their own, and even then, not all that much. So rather than argue with her, Jormund nodded. He glanced around, looking for somewhere to sit and did not find anyplace immediately. So he shrugged and simply leaned back on his massive tail, using that to prop him up.

"You are familiar with Piri," he said. It was not a question. "You came here with one."

"Yes," said Kerda. "We came here with Clarinda. She was our leader. She…" Her single eye glanced downward and she sighed heavily. "She is dead."

There were a couple of choked sobs from the other Ocular and one or two head nods. They were clearly in mourning.

"It is…interesting that you would care so deeply about a Piri," said Jormund. "They are typically despised. As I recall, your people were at war with her kind."

"With her kind, yes. But not with her."

"She came to us," said another of the Ocular, a male, one of the younger ones. "She came to us in the forest and she offered to help us and protect us. And she did."

"I miss her so much," said a third.

Now several more of them started to sob, but Kerda immediately turned and said, with clear anger, "Stop. Stop that right now. She would have wanted us to be strong. Sobbing is not strong. So pull yourselves together."

The Ocular nodded in response, wiping their arms across their glistening eyes.

Jormund carefully assessed Kerda's obvious control over them. He found that to be quite intriguing and promptly lost all interest in the other Ocular. He sensed that Kerda was the only one whose opinion mattered at the moment. He took care not to lean forward because he was aware that his physicality could possibly be intimidating, although he then reminded himself that they were half again as tall as he was and thus were likely not especially afraid of him.

"How did she die?" he asked.

"I only know what we were told," said Kerda. "That there was someone beneath the streets."

"Probably some rogue Mandraques," growled one of the male Ocular, glaring rather fearfully at Jormund. "We know that some of them were in league with the Serabim that attacked us."

Slowly Jormund shook his head. "No. It was not any Mandraques. I believe," and now he glanced left and right as if concerned that someone was eavesdropping, "that it was Piri."

"Impossible," Kerda said immediately, but she did not sound as sure as the conviction with which she was trying to speak.

"Not impossible," said Jormund. "I was fighting in the streets and I am quite sure that I saw one. And it was definitely not yours. It was a male one, hiding in the shadows. I am unsure what his purpose was; perhaps he was some sort of scout. Maybe his job was to inform his leaders as to the whereabouts of certain others of his kind. Such as, say, your Clarinda."

The young Ocular were now obviously beginning to take quite seriously what Jormund was saying. Kerda had risen and was now walking toward him, studying him as if she were capable of seeing directly into his brain and extracting any untruths. Jormund's tongue reflexively lashed out and licked his lips, which were suddenly dry, but he kept his apparent position of leisure, leaning against his tail.

"You are serious about this?" she said.

"I am not sure how many times you are going to require me to say this, but yes, I am serious about it. And I am as concerned about the future security of Perriz as you are. Whatever disagreements we may have had in the past, we are at this point dependent upon each other for survival."

It was the longest series of sentences that Jormund could recall uttering in one sitting in some time. The Ocular did not know that, and likely would not have been impressed by it if they had. Instead they were clearly weighing his words and then Jormund watched as all their gazes shifted once more to Kerda. Yes, she was definitely their leader.

"Let us say," Kerda said slowly, "that we believe you. What would you have of us?"

"Your aid in finding the Piri and putting an end to them, once and for all."

"No."

The abrupt refusal caught Jormund completely by surprise. "But they may well have captured your Piri leader…"

"If there are Piri beneath the streets," said Kerda, "and they have indeed captured Clarinda, the last thing she would want us to do is risk our lives in a likely hopeless endeavor to save her."

"You do not know that…"

"Yes. I do." She was about to keep speaking and then her voice briefly caught. It was obvious that she was choking back tears, taking a few moments to steady herself. "We are tired of fighting. We have lost members of our ranks. We have buried them. And now you are asking us to…what? Throw ourselves into battle once more against a race that would love to drain the blood from our bodies?"

"Something that they may well do on their own initiative if they are left to do so," Jormund said.

"If you believe that they are a threat, then you are free to marshal your own forces to dispose of them," Kerda pointed out. "Mandraques, as I recall, do nothing in half measures. So if you think that they are lurking about and could harm us, you send your own forces down against them."

Jormund stared at her, unsure of how to respond.

As it turned out, he didn't have to. Kerda's single eye fixed on him and a grim smiled played across her lips. "You do not have forces, do you? Or at least not in any sufficient number to provide a genuine threat to the Piri that you believe are down there."

"I...do not," Jormund said slowly. He cleared his throat, looked down and then growled, "A significant portion of my clan chose to ally itself with Thulsa. I am afraid I had to slaughter a sizeable number of them." He glanced at the tips of his claws. "It will be some time before I am able to rid myself of their blood. The handful of remaining forces I have at my disposal are...ill equipped to be launched into battle right now."

"Well, so are we," said Kerda. She gestured around the room. "Look at us, Jormund. Do we look like warriors? Do we?"

"You look like Ocular, and the reputation of the Ocular precedes you."

"I am not interested in our reputation," said Kerda. "I am interested in surviving. We all are."

"If that is the case, then you may want to reconsider your position," said Jormund. "For if the Piri are truly lurking below, then it is only a matter of time before they turn their attentions to feeding. Considering the history of your people with them, it is very likely that you will be the first things to consume their interest."

The Ocular glanced nervously at each other and Jormund knew that he had struck a spot with them. The Piri had delighted in feeding upon the Ocular at any opportunity because their sheer size had provided a considerably large portion of food upon which they could feast.

"Kerda," one of the males said softly. "Maybe we should—"

"Quiet," she immediately silenced him and then turned to Jormund. "We have listened to you. You have had your say. Now I want you to leave."

"You say 'I.' Are you speaking on behalf of yourself or your peers."

"*Get out.*"

Jormund considered trying to hold his position there, but immediately dismissed the idea. He had definitely planted a thought, and now the wisest thing would be for him to depart and let it take root. So instead he simply stood to his full height and bowed to them slightly. "Thank you for considering my argument."

"We are considering nothing,"

"Of course you aren't," he said with an indifferent shrug. Then he turned and walked out of the room.

But he walked very slowly and so was able to hear the beginnings of intense discussions among the Ocular. Kerda was clearly determined to take no action, but the others were beginning to protest her intransigence.

That prompted Jormund to smile, which was a most unusual sensation for him. It made him most uncomfortable and he swore not to allow that to happen again at any time in the near future.

THE VASTLY WATERS

{GORKON MISSES JEPP. AND HE is most surprised to discover that this is the case.}

{He does not quite understand why that is. As beings went, she was certainly not the most useful of creatures. She would have drowned had he not rescued her from the ocean that she had tumbled into, helplessly, like an infant. Nor had she known how to swim, so she could not have helped herself for even a few moments. It had been nothing short of a miracle that he happened to be there at the right time to save her from her folly, thinking that she could stand upon the deck of a sailing vessel during a storm and not be swept overboard. If he had not seen the vessel passing by, if he had not spoken to Ruark about it, if Ruark's calm words had not convinced Gorkon to follow it, then she would be nothing except a dead lump of skin and bones at the bottom of the Vastly Waters.}

{And yet there had been something about her. Her determination to get to the city of Spires, to follow some path of destiny that was clear to her but no one else, spurred on by dreams that cascaded through her head…it had been somewhat sweet, really. She had struck him as a fascinating combination of naïveté and wisdom, and nothing that had occurred in the time that they had spent together had dissuaded him from that assessment.}

{And now she was gone, seeking her destiny in the Spires, driven to have some manner of confrontation with the Overseer that would doubtless lead to her death. But she had been determined to undertake that meeting, and Gorkon had been unable to convince her of the foolishness of that endeavor.}

{Why in the world did he miss her? He certainly has no romantic interest in her, for he had seen her completely unclothed and she was definitely the ugliest creature that he had ever been privy to. Not that he was ever attracted to any Markene, of either gender. He has come to think of himself as asexual and he is perfectly content with that. Was it possible that he had actually come to think of her as a friend? That was likewise a new experience since he did not have any friends, either, aside from Ruark. And Ruark was more of a teacher and mentor than a friend.}

{Well…of course there is the Liwyathan as well. Is he a friend? It is hard for Gorkon to be certain of that, since the creature is millions of turns around the sun old, and it is impossible for any mere mortal to know its mind.}

{He is, at the moment, lying in leisurely fashion atop the Liwyathan as it cruises the Vastly Waters. His breathing is slow and steady and relaxed, and he recalls the circumstances under which he originally met Ruark: lying atop a rock and preparing to cease breathing so that he could die. How far he had come since that moment.}

{Then Gorkon hears a noise passing high over his head. It is quite distant and yet the displacement of air makes it audible to him.}

{He slides off the massive back of the Liwyathan and into the water, immediately concerned that there might be some manner of attack coming from overhead. He has no idea what that attack could be, but he is not inclined to simply lounge there and permit it to happen. He is going to take refuge in the waters, counting on it to provide him shelter while he discerns the intentions of whoever or whatever is above him.}

{The moment he has secured himself, he gazes upward and gasps. He knows what he is looking at, from the stories and tales that he has heard, but it is staggering nonetheless to witness it first hand. It is a Zeffer, one of the magnificent creatures that reside in the far off land of Suislan. Supposedly they could be spotted in the skies from time to time, but none of them had ever passed near the City/ State of Venets, and that had been the only place where Gorkon had resided for the entirety of his existence. Or at least up until he had been moved to follow the Travelers and their vessel, a decision that had opened up the entire world for him.}

{Something stirs in the vast head of the Liwyathan. Gorkon is certain that its eyes reside beneath the level of the Vastly Waters, and yet he senses the creature inside his head, probing whatever is in his mind and apparently finding interest in it. The Liwyathan is truly capable of seeing the world through Gorkon's eyes, as well as projecting its thoughts into his mind. Since he first encountered and communed with the Liwyathan, their thoughts seem to be moving closer and closer together. He is truly uncertain how he feels about that. A remote part of him fears that he might lose his personality to the gargantuan beast entirely; become a simple tool of the ancient creature. Even as the thought occurs to him, he wonders if that would necessarily be such a bad thing. The truth is that he is not thrilled about many of the choices that he has made in his life, and perhaps the act of giving himself over to the Liwyathan would not be such a terrible idea.}

{"*It is a Zeffer,*" he thinks to the Liwyathan. "*A great floating beast that is controlled by the mind of its rider.*"}

{The Liwyathan does not reply immediately. It always appears to give thought to its words before it frames them. Gorkon waits patiently, because really, what other choice does he have?}

{"*No,*" returns the voice after a time.}

{"*No?*"}

{"*No. The Keepers control them via song. There are no thoughts of the mind involved. I would know.*"}

{The phrasing intrigues Gorkon. "*How would you know?*"}

{"*I am bound to all who inhabit the Damned World. None think any thoughts that are unknown to me.*"}

{Gorkon finds the sheer immensity of that claim to be unnerving. "*How is that possible?*"}

{"*I have been here for ages and have nothing but time on my hands. I scan all minds. None are closed to me. I simply find some more interesting than others, that is all.*"}

{"*Such as me.*"}

{"*Such as.*"}

{Gorkon considers what the Liwyathan has said, and suddenly a thought occurs to him. "*The Mort…Jepp…she spoke of dreams that she had. Dreams that suggested events of the future. Is there…did you have anything to do with—?*"}

{"*Yes.*"}

{The offhand confirmation from the Liwyathan startles Gorkon so thoroughly that he loses his grip momentarily on the creature before recovering his hold on it. "*What do you mean, Yes?*"}

{"*You asked. I answered.*"}

{The Liwyathan can sometimes be maddeningly vague in its responses. Gorkon forces himself to calm. "*Are you saying that you placed the dreams in Jepp's head?*"}

{"*She interests me. I did not place anything into her. I simply allowed her to share my perceptions of the world. Of time.*"}

{"*Perceptions of time? There is no perception of it. Time simply passes, one turn after the next.*"}

{"*For you, yes. For me, it is bendable. Mutable. Foreseeable. Because I am endless. A long time ago, I lived as you do: sequentially. No more. I am, and always will be, and have learned to live at all times simultaneously. It is more efficient. It helps to guide me. I allowed some of that to leak through to the human.*"}

{"*Why?*"}

{"*Because I felt connected to her. As I do to you. And the circler.*"}

{Gorkon is confused. This is a new name that has been introduced to him. He wonders momentarily if this "circler" is someone that he already knows and has simply forgotten. "*The circler?*" he asks.}

{"*Yes. The one who is coming.*"}

{"*Where is he coming?*"}

{"*I will show you,*" says the Liwyathan. "*And you will guide your people there. They are needed.*"}

THE SKIES ABOVE

I.

PAVAN WAS SINGING SOFTLY TO the Zeffer and was aware that its vast tentacles were trembling beneath it. It was taking pleasure as his voice caressed it, and he wondered if perhaps he should give the creature a name. It was not customary for Keepers to have such closeness with the beasts to which they tended, and yet somehow Pavan was developing a growing familiarity with the creature.

Slowly he became aware that someone was watching him, and it was not Demali. He had had his eyes closed, but now he opened them narrowly and glanced to his right.

One of the Bottom Feeders was watching them. It was the female Laocoon...what had her name been?

"Zeena," said Pavan, "right?"

"Close. Zerena." She swayed toward him, eyeing him with what appeared open curiosity. "And you're Pavan?" When he nodded, she continued, "Can I ask a question?"

"Of course."

She took in a deep breath and then let it out slowly. "What's it like?"

"What is what like?"

"This," and she gestured around her. "Being master of this creature. Being able to send it wherever you want. And the destructive power you have at your command!" She let out a low whistle. "It is truly remarkable."

Pavan stared at her uncomprehending. "Destructive power? What are you talking about?"

"Those tentacles hanging beneath. This creature could reach down and tear anything apart. It can kill anyone by just lifting them into the air and dropping them. Certainly it must have occurred to you that you are riding one of the greatest weapons in the Damned World. And it's not just the one; there are others of its kind. Frankly, I'm somewhat astounded that the Serabim have never attempted to use these creatures to take over the entirety of the planet."

"We would never do that. We…"

Then his voice trailed off.

Zerena cocked her head slightly. "What? What is it?"

"Actually," he said softly, "I have seen exactly the type of thing that you are talking about. The Zeffers were used to launch an attack on Perriz. An unholy alliance between our kind, led by Demali's father, and the Mandraques. What they did…what they were forced to do…it was horrible. I saw these grand creatures being abused, being turned into exactly what you referred to them as: destructive monsters. Killers. I felt as if I'd let them down."

"It is the way of the Damned World," Zerena said. "You should not feel remotely ashamed or embarrassed. Did you in any way encourage the Zeffers to take the action?"

"No. They had riders who controlled them."

"So it was not your responsibility. You did not make them kill anyone."

Pavan was silent.

She raised an eyebrow. "Did you?"

He spoke without looking her in the eye, as if he suddenly could not tolerate her gaze. "I commanded them to turn upside down. Everyone who was riding them fell to their deaths."

"Oh," she said quietly. Then she shrugged her shoulders. "Well, it could be argued that they had it coming."

Pavan turned and stared right at her, and then—as much to his surprise as to hers—he actually laughed. It was not a laugh that was familiar to Zerena. It sounded more like an angry bark than an expression of amusement. "I suppose you are right," he said once he had recovered his calm. "It is kind of you to point that out."

She moved closer to him and said in a low voice, "Out of

curiosity…can you command this one to fight again?"

"I suppose…" He realized that this was a rather odd question and he studied her in a different way than he had up to that point. "Why would you ask?"

She glanced right and left and was satisfied that no one else atop the Zeffer was paying them any attention. "That damnable Trull," she said, speaking barely above a whisper, "is bringing us into a battle zone. He is expecting us to go in and fight on his behalf to rescue his beloved Piri. Why in the world should we risk our lives when alternatives present themselves?"

"Alternatives?"

"We use the Zeffer to attack Perriz. To demand that the residents there act on our behalf. Tell them that they have to find the Piri and present her to us, and if they fail to do so, the Zeffer will destroy their entire precious city."

Pavan could scarcely believe what he was hearing. "Is this some sort of joke? I am unfamiliar with what Laocoon would consider to be amusement, so I am unsure if—"

"What? No! This is no joke. You can control this beast and have it inflict untold damage on Perriz. You said so yourself. Others did it. Why can't you?"

"Because I am their Keeper. It is my job to care for them. To prevent them from doing harm to others and themselves. These are not creatures of war and it would be a perversion of their essence to use them in that manner."

"Pavan, listen to m—"

"Why should I listen? You are not saying anything that I wish to hear."

It was clear that she was beginning to get irritated with him. She gripped him firmly by the arm. He stared down at it as if he were a scientist studying some new form of bacteria. "Then hear this: my idiot son has promised that damnable Trull that he was going to fight by his side to rescue some stupid Piri bitch, and I'm not going to stand by and allow that to happen. As long as we are riding atop this monster of yours, we are actually in a position to demand that someone else take care of this insanity. It would be nothing short of madness for Karsen or, even more specifically, me, to risk our lives just to keep his idiotic promise."

Pavan didn't seem to be paying attention to what she was saying. "I would strongly recommend that you release your grip on my arm."

"Not until you admit that what I'm saying makes sense."

In what seemed a very odd response, Pavan—rather than speak in words—replied with a steady stream of soft musical notes, as if he were singing to her. Zerena stared at him, not understanding what manner of reply that was supposed to be. "Why are you singing? What is that supposed to mean?" Impatience laced her tone and she began to drum impatiently on the surface of the Zeffer. "Listen, I'm trying to have a conversation with you, and you aren't making it easy to—"

That was when a tentacle wrapped itself around Zerena.

The Laocoon let out an alarmed shriek as the tentacle lifted her into the air.

Her outcry immediately drew the attention of the other Bottom Feeders, as well as the others who were strewn around on the surface of the Zeffer. Karsen let out a cry of alarm, Jepp gasped, and the others hurried toward Pavan to find out exactly what was going on.

A second tentacle had snaked up from beneath the creature's vast bottom area and had wrapped itself around Zerena's feet while the first one remained secured around her upper body. Pavan ceased whistling but kept his attention focused on the tentacles, even as he addressed his comments to the people who were approaching him. "Your mother is most aggressive, Karsen," he said calmly. "She wanted me to use this Zeffer as a weapon of war. I felt it appropriate to provide her with a first-hand view of what these creatures are capable of accomplishing with just a small bit of urging."

Karsen raised his hands carefully, as if he was giving a very gentle back rub to a touchy gorilla. "Pavan…whatever she said, I assure you…"

"I am not interested in your assurances, Karsen," said Pavan, his voice continuing not to be raised in the slightest. "Just as I am not interested in cooperating with your mother's desires. Whatever her ideas and recommendations are, I think it behooves her to keep them to herself. Otherwise I will quickly dispose of her. I would not hesitate to do so in the slightest. I find…" His voice trailed off for a moment and then he shook his head to remind himself that he had something more to say. "I find that, thanks to recent events, I hold the concept of life to be far less sacred than I used to. Once upon a time, I would never have even considered doing damage to Zerena. Now I could have the Zeffer rip her in half and not feel the slightest bit of concern over it. So, Karsen, I would strongly recommend that you keep your mother in hand if you wish her to be alive at the other end of this journey. Have I made myself clear?"

"Abundantly," Karsen assured him.

Pavan nodded once and then whistled what sounded like another aimless tune. Yet the tentacles immediately responded, lowering Zerena to the Zeffer's surface and unwinding from her, leaving her unmolested. Jepp got to her before Karsen, extending a hand to help Zerena to her feet. Zerena's first impulse was obvious as she started to shove Jepp away. But then she seemed to think better of it and instead accepted the outstretched hand, allowing Jepp to help haul her to her feet. Then Zerena turned and scowled fiercely at Pavan. "You could simply have said no."

"I did say no, and you were clearly not inclined to accept my word for it," he reminded her. "So I thought I would say it with more emphasis. I trust it was emphatic enough for you?"

Zerena was about to make an annoyed and even snarky response, but then to her obvious shock, Jepp squeezed her hand warningly. She glanced at the Mort's face and, somewhat to Pavan's surprise, he saw an air of command in Jepp's face. It was as if she was silencing the Laocoon without saying a word and, even more surprisingly, Zerena was deferring to her. All she did in reply to Pavan was to nod, indicating she understood and accepted the law that he had just laid out.

For just a moment, just a heartbeat of an instant, Pavan was able to discern just how it was that the Morts had ruled the planet.

"Good," said Pavan. He had been standing, but now he dropped back down into a sitting position, drawing his legs up so that they were folded. "I now desire to return to my meditations."

Zerena nodded once more.

As the Laocoon slunk off, Demali moved over to Pavan and sat down next to him. "What was that about?" she asked in a low voice.

"A simple difference of opinion. That is all."

"I thought you were going to kill her."

"I would have," said Pavan, still not looking at her. "Without hesitation. She wanted to have the Zeffer used as a war machine."

"And you would have had the Zeffer kill her in response?"

"Yes," he said without hesitation.

Demali stared at him for a long moment and then admitted, "I have no idea how to feel about that."

"Neither do I," said Pavan.

II.

EVANNA SCARCELY PAID ANY ATTENTION to the odd scuffle that was transpiring on the far side of the Zeffer. She noticed two tentacles of the creature come rising up from beneath and lift Zerena high in the air, but she wasn't especially concerned about what was causing it.

Instead she was staring down aimlessly into the great abyss of water that sprawled beneath her. She had spent the entirety of her life without ever seeing any water beyond the river that wound through Perriz, and yet now she was making her second voyage in as many days across the vast expanses of ocean that lay between her continent and the Spires. She found it endlessly fascinating, staring down at it. At one point they had drifted past what appeared to be a large island of some sort that seemed to be drifting, which puzzled her severely. She was unaware that landmasses were capable of any sort of movement, but then she decided that it was one of the things that she just hadn't learned about and wasn't actually all that interesting. The fact was that her thoughts were very far away from anything having to do with islands, whether moving or not.

"Are you all right?"

A soft voice was speaking to her from behind. She did not even have to turn to know immediately that it was Norda. She honestly did not feel like speaking with the erratic Mandraque, but she obviously didn't have a choice. "I am all right, yes," she said. "You do not have to worry."

"Oh. All right, then." She paused and then dropped down next to the seated Firedraque, who rolled her eyes and prayed that Norda would lose interest in her or even forget that she had initiated the conversation. Apparently, however, her wishes were not to be granted, because Norda's stare was fixed on Evanna and didn't seem to be easily distracted. Then she said something that was quite surprising: "Did you see the beast down there?"

"Beast? What beast?"

"It was very big. And floating. I've no idea what it was, but it was very big. Did I mention how big it was?"

"Yes, you did."

"Very," said Norda for added emphasis.

"I think you saw an island."

"No," said Norda firmly. "It was definitely a very big creature. Although not from up here. From here I could hold it in my hand. But if I were down there, I would need a much larger hand."

"I suppose you're right," said Evanna, having no other clue of what to say.

Norda nodded and seemed content with having had her point validated, despite the fact that her point made little to no sense. Then, as if she had not asked the question a mere thirty seconds ago, she said, "Are you all right?"

"Why do you keep asking that?" Evanna was having trouble restraining her annoyance.

"Because you aren't answering me."

"I did answer you!"

"Yes, but it wasn't a true answer."

"How in—?" She was about to ask *How did you know* but then realized that if she said that, she would be admitting that Norda was right. And the fact of the matter was that she knew Norda *was* right. She just had no clue how in the world Norda could know so easily what was going through her head at any given moment.

That was when she realized that she was at a significant disadvantage in the conversation. Somehow the young Mandraque was aware of what she was thinking and Evanna realized that she was just going to remain there and continue to hector her until she received an answer that she was satisfied with. The harsh truth was that there was only answer that would suffice, and Evanna sighed deeply when she realized that she was going to have to talk about what she had genuinely been pondering.

"I was just thinking about how you were right."

"Hurrah!" said Norda, clapping her hands together with great excitement. Then she tilted her head. "About what?"

"I didn't deserve my father." Evanna took a deep sigh and then let it out slowly. "All I ever did was criticize him and pick fights with him. I cared about him, yes, but I was often impatient with him and argued incessantly. I don't see how any reasonable analysis of our relationship could possibly—"

Norda's hand flew so quickly that Evanna never had the slightest chance of dodging it. She struck Evanna across the right side of her face with such force that the sound of the slap reverberated through the air. Several of the passengers looked around in confusion and Arren stared in bewilderment at his sister. Evanna's hand moved up to her cheek and she simply gaped as she rubbed the point of impact.

"Don't talk like that," said Norda. "Do not ever talk like that."

"Why?" Evanna said with a puzzled gasp.

"Because he would not like it. Because New Daddy loved you very much, and cared about everything you had to say, and considered your constantly challenging him to be proof of how intelligent you were. He had nothing but respect for you and your determination to stand up to him whenever possible. It made him stronger. *You* made him stronger."

She put a hand to her chest. "He told you all that?"

Norda shrugged. The intensity with which she had spoken seemed to dissolve and now she appeared indifferent. "No. But he didn't have to. I saw it in the way he talked to you. The way he smiled at you, but always when your back was turned. How he would repeat things that you said to him and chuckle over them. I was watching him. Always watching him. Most of the time he didn't know that. But I always knew. I always know. That's the funny thing about me, that I know so many things."

"Really?"

Once more she shrugged. "I don't know. Maybe I'm just making things up. It's hard for me to keep track. Do you ever have that problem?"

Evanna actually laughed. "All the time."

"See!" Norda clapped her hands briskly in obvious joy. "We are almost sisters already."

Evanna reached out and wrapped her fingers around Norda's hand. "I suppose we are."

THE UNKNOWN FOREST

IT WAS EVERYTHING GANT COULD do not to cry out in joy or even sob as he held tightly to the back of the draquon that pounded along the road. Graves and Trott were doing likewise, Graves riding in front of him while Trott came up behind him. To them there was nothing special about riding on draquon-back, but for Gant it was a glorious return to the creature that he had once been and, he hoped, would once again be someday.

The draquon had been most uncertain of him at first when he had initially attempted to climb on. It had backed up, lowering its head as it glared at him with suspicious eyes, its short wings down on either side and a low, warning hiss being emitted from between its lips. Gant couldn't blame it. Draquons were accustomed to being ridden purely by members of the Phey, and Gant was clothed in the body of a Piri. He very much doubted that the draquons would be any more enamored of his own green body of slime, though, so he took his time gaining the beast's confidence. He spoke to it softly, whispering gentle affirmations that he had every business riding the creature's back. It took him an hour to coax it into allowing him astride it, but once he did so, the calm and confidence with which he manipulated the draquon caused it to become far more relaxed with his presence. Now he had spent a full day on it, steering it down the remains of the great road that stretched between the city of Spires and the far off land of Dizz.

It was not the first time that the Morts' ingenuity and creativity had impressed Gant. The road they were hurtling down was quite vast. There were many broken spots along the way, places where the pavement had been chewed up or heavily cratered due to anything from vicious fights to simple lack of maintenance. Yet certainly they had managed to build it in the first place, and that alone had been a remarkable achievement. The draquons alternately glided and ran along it, and Gant was especially impressed by the lengthy bridges they crossed in order to get from one land mass to another. The water bubbled and roiled beneath them, and Gant couldn't help but wonder what sort of beasts lay beneath the surface, perhaps even creating civilizations of their own.

Every so often they would guide the draquons off into some heavily wooded areas, allowing them to drink or hunt small game in order to satisfy their hunger. Graves and Trott scarcely exchanged any words with Gant, tending to keep a wary eye on him from a distance. Even though they both knew him from old, and Graves was his brother—in spirit if not in blood—they continued to seem uncertain about him, as if they were not sure that they could trust him. That didn't bother Gant in the least. He knew what he looked like, and he knew that they definitely had no love for the Piri as a race. It was difficult even for the Phey to set aside what someone looked like and instead embrace that that was inside him. They would come around. He was positive of it.

After a full day of traveling, the draquons were clearly getting tired. Both the beasts and riders needed somewhere to rest and perhaps even slumber. It was a lovely night, and Graves decided that they would seek somewhere outdoors to take up residence. In that respect, Gant was able to provide some assistance because he was able to discern an assortment of Mort words, including one that was particularly useful in this instance: "Campgrounds." He took the lead, guiding his draquon and serving to lead the two Phey with him to somewhere where they could rest. The vast pavement they were following gave way to more forested areas, and the change in environment made Gant breathe more easily. He had always preferred the outside to dwelling within a building. Let the other Phey reside in their vast hall in the Spires; give Gant the great outdoors of the Damned World and he would always be happy with that.

A simple spell created a small burning fire for them to gather around . They roasted some of the partly cooked meat that they had transported with them and ate in relative silence until Gant finally turned to Graves and said, "Do you ever think we made a mistake?"

"Mistake?" Graves stared at him in confusion and then looked to Trott for possible clarification, but Trott simply shrugged. "Mistake about what?"

"About conquering the Morts."

Graves snickered slightly at that. "What else were we supposed to do with them?"

"This was their world," Gant pointed out. "They greeted us in peace."

"No, they did not. They attacked us from the very first."

"The very first was many of their centuries ago. They might well have grown up and developed as a race since then. But when we were exiled here in the third wave, we acted as if no time had passed. As if they were just as fierce and savage as their ancestors."

"Better to be safe than sorry."

"But it is really better?"

Trott abruptly spoke up, which was somewhat surprising since Trott was hardly the chattiest of individuals. "What shaped your thinking on this?"

Gant shrugged. "I've been studying the world. When you are thrown out of your own body and become a protoplasmic blob, it forces you to see things differently. For one thing, a Mort girl named Jepp—you met her—fell in with us, and I've become impressed by her. She is determined and loyal and loving and strong, and there is hardly anything special about her in terms of her ranking in hooman society. She is just an ordinary girl. And the more extraordinary of the creatures created things like the roads upon which we traveled, and the…" He paused, saying the word slowly. "…the 'Javits' center in which so many of you reside. Plus the underground tunnels for travel, and tall buildings, and so many other things. I am simply saying that if we had just sought to treat them like allies instead of enemies, things might be very different for us."

"Or perhaps they might have killed us."

"Why? Why would they have done that?"

"Because we were invaders," Graves pointed out.

"We were invaders simply because we arrived? I don't know that I accept that. It is entirely possible that they would have welcomed us. Unfortunately we will never know."

"No, we won't. So it is ridiculous to even keep discussing it." He studied him carefully. "Are you bringing this up because there are things you wish to avoid talking about?"

"Like what?"

"Like what you could possibly say to Tania to convince her to take the spell off you?"

"Oh, I have no idea what I'm going to say to her. Then again, she never was much for listening to what I had to say…"

"*Quiet.*"

The abrupt and wholly unexpected interruption from Trott instantly grabbed both of their attentions. Trott was among one of the more sensitive of the Phey, far more aware of his surroundings than others of his race. So when he abruptly called for quiet and focused on the world around him, that was more than enough to capture the attention of the others.

Trott sniffed the air, his nostrils flaring. Then he said, "Mount up. We have to go."

Gant was tempted to ask why, but decided there was no need. If Trott said they had to leave, it was best to take his word for it and get moving, saving the queries for some point when they were safe.

The draquons had been peacefully slumbering and were not pleased over being rousted from their sleep. Gant's in particular was slow to respond, but then its nostrils flared in a manner similar to the way Trott's had and immediately it stopped moving so that Gant could climb aboard.

"Which way?" said Graves.

"Back to the road, obviously," Gant said.

But Trott shook his head. "No. The path out is blocked."

Gant glanced in that direction. He didn't see anyone or anything impeding their way out, but he wasn't about to argue with Trott on the matter. "All right. So…?"

Trott didn't hesitate. "This way," he said, swinging his draquon around, and the beast galloped obediently deeper into the forest. Without hesitation, Gant and Graves followed.

Despite the fact that he had to remain covered with a cloak and hood to shield his sensitive skin during daylight hours, Gant was wishing that the sun had not set. He had no idea what threat had tripped Trott's inner warning system, but he would much rather have faced it in the daytime. At night it was far too easy for their attackers to spring out at them.

The three Phey rode their mounts through the forest. The trees were too close together so the beasts were unable to fly, but even when they ran their speed was impressive. For a few moments, Gant thought that they were going to be able to escape whatever it was that was supposedly pursuing them.

Then abruptly Trott swung his draquon around, so suddenly that Gant and Graves nearly collided with him. "We have a problem," said Trott.

Shadows moved through the forest in front of them, and Gant's eyes narrowed. The one advantage he had was that his eyes were sharper in the dark than the Phey's. That made sense, after all, since his Piri host spent his time living in the dark the entirety of his life. Gant scanned the forest and was instantly able to make out what the shadow was.

It was a Whoresman.

Somehow it made sense that it would be. The Whoresmen as a race absolutely despised the cities of the Morts. They typically resided in forests or woods, making it extremely difficult for them to be kept track of. The trees hid them quite well from any attempted inspection by the Phey or any other races.

The Whoresman's back half was far more suited for the forest since it was the lower body of a whores. Its hooves stamped defiantly on the ground as if it were creating a line in the ground that it was challenging the draquons to cross. His upper body could easily have been mistaken for a Mort except naturally the bestial lower part of it precluded any confusion. There was a bristling grayish brown beard decorating the lower half of his face, and his long brown hair hung down to his lower back. His lips were twisted back in a sneer as he studied the three of them. "Travelers," he said. "In our territory."

"As Travelers, we go where we wish," Graves said, prodding his draquon forward. The draquon growled low in its throat and Gant's own draquon matched the warning noise. Graves drew to within a few steps of the Whoresman. "What is your name?"

"Chyron," he informed them.

"A very old and respected name," said Graves. "Now stand aside and let us pass."

"Why would we do that?"

The use of the pronoun "we" did not sit well with Gant. It implied that there were more of them hiding in the shadows, and Gant intensely disliked that idea.

"Because we are Travelers. None may impede us in our business."

"Or what? We will face the wrath of the Overseer?"

"Do you dare take that risk?" said Graves.

"A very judicious response, and one that avoids the truth we both know: the Overseer is no more. The basis of your power is deceased. So what else do you have to threaten us with?"

Chyron's pronouncement stunned Gant. The Overseer and the Spires were many leagues away. How in the world could this Whoresman have learned the truth? The answer occurred to him immediately and he muttered, just loudly enough for Graves to hear, "They have a Visionary."

To his surprise, though, Chyron heard him as well. "Yes, we do." Then Chyron tilted his head forward, studying Gant more closely. "You are not a Phey. You are a Piri. Why are you riding with the Phey?"

"That is none of your concern," Graves said immediately before Gant could respond, which was fine with Gant because he really couldn't think of what to say in reply. "Out of our way."

"We would have words with you. Our Visionary would as well."

The situation was rapidly spiraling into a direction that Gant did not like. There was historically no love lost between the Phey and the Whoresmen. The only race that the Phey got on even more poorly with were the Serpenteens. No one knew or understood why the Serpenteens had such inbred hostility for the Phey; the two races had been hostile to each other for as far back as anyone could remember. Sometimes the Phey would speculate over what had caused the rift, but no one could recall, nor did they especially care enough to wonder all that much.

"No one has words with us," said Graves. He turned to his companions and nodded that the three of them should precede.

Abruptly two more Whoresmen were there, blocking their path. One was male, with hair so red and wild that he seemed like a shooting star streaking through the sky. The other was a female. Her head was shaved, and her thick breasts hung down unencumbered and not particularly attractive. Gravity or motherhood or both had had its way with her.

"No one leaves," said Chyron.

Very softly, very intently, Graves said in a low voice, "Take them."

The draquon that he was riding roared and opened its mouth, and a huge blast of flame lunged from deep within its throat. The brush and trunk of the nearest trees instantly erupted, and black smoke filled the night air. The aroma was incredibly intense to Gant, who discovered that his host body had a much stronger sense of smell, and it was all he could do not to choke on the acrid smoke.

Gant's and Trott's draquons were blasting fire as well. Neither of them had as powerful jets of flame as Graves' did, though. It sprayed the blast in a full 180-degree semicircle, and then Graves ordered his draquon to cut hard to the right. Gant's and Trott's followed suit, and seconds later they were tearing through the forest. They heard the infuriated roars of the Whoresmen behind them, and the abrupt galloping of hooves. They were in pursuit.

It was all Gant could do to hold on to his draquon's back. He kept his knees clamped and gripped the reins as tightly as he could. His night vision was formidable enough, but he didn't have to steer the draquon at all. It knew where it was supposed to go: away from the Whoresmen. The exact whys and wherefores didn't matter. The other two draquons were matching its pace, and even though they were heading more deeply into darkness, Gant prayed that they would be able to get away. He knew that they were eventually going to get to the end of the camping area, and they would encounter one of two things: either water, in which case they were in trouble. Or they would discover a new paved road, and if that were the case, they would easily be able to get away.

Gant's draquon abruptly skidded to a stop, and the others did so as well. It happened so suddenly and violently that Gant and the others were almost thrown off their mounts. As it was, Gant slid halfway off before he was able to right himself, and he squinted ahead using his formidable night vision to see what it was that the draquon had reacted to.

He gulped deep in his throat.

It was a Serpenteen.

Where he had come from, Gant could not even begin to guess. But he had seemingly materialized out of nowhere, and there were several more with him. The Serpenteen looked quite young, as most of their race tended to. His skin was pale green, and his red eyes seemed to glow in the darkness. The most noticeable feature that he sported, of course, was his hair. Well, not hair, exactly. Instead it was a thatch of snakes, somewhere between five and seven, perched atop his head. They were writhing and hissing, clearly reflecting the agitated state of the Serpentine who was before them. Shadows indicated that he was not alone, and the hisses of the others with him almost made it deafening.

"Run them down!" shouted Graves, and Gant did not hesitate to

do as ordered. He snapped the reins and the draquon immediately barreled forward. If the Serpenteen didn't move, the draquon would easily run him over. The Serpenteen wasn't especially tall and Gant was certain that when it came to strength, he had the edge.

And the snakes atop the Serpenteen's head began to spit. It was unclear to Gant what it was, but the first wad of it struck his draquon and the second hit him directly.

The draquon pitched forward, completely immobilized. It was as if the creature had frozen solid. Even more problematic was Gant's situation, for the instant the liquid struck him, he was feeling exactly what it was that his draquon had felt. But it was even more severe as the Piri's mind completely shut down. He pitched forward and toppled off the unmoving draquon.

Gant did the only thing he could think of: he evacuated his host. Within seconds he had managed to force open the Piri's mouth and Gant seeped out of the Piri, free of the paralyzed body. The Piri remained unable to move, the Serpenteen's venom pervading his form and keeping him immobile.

Graves and Trott were right behind him, and they instantly saw what had happened. Gant supposed that they would turn around and gallop away, leaving him in the hands of the Serpenteens. Somewhat to his surprise, they did no such thing. Instead they reined up their beasts and Graves called, "Gant? You all right?"

"*I have been…better,*" he said. He hated the fact that speech was once again a labored endeavor for him, but he had no choice. In his green mass of existence, it was just hard for him to talk. Unless he could take over the Piri again, that was not going to change.

The Serpenteen stared at Gant in confusion. He drew back his lips, exposing a pair of extended fangs. "What have we here?"

"We owe you no explanations," said Graves imperiously. "Allow us to pass."

"I don't think that's going to be happening," the Serpenteen informed him. "As you must know by now, you are completely surrounded. Outmanned and outgunned."

Gant was quickly able to survey the area and he could see that the Serpenteen was quite correct. There had to be a dozen individuals around them, a combination of Whoresmen and Serpenteens. Even more problematic, they were armed, each of them holding bows with nocked arrows. Furthermore, he could see that the glittering arrowheads were fashioned from silver, and that was indeed very bad news. There were many materials against which the Phey had natural invulnerability, but silver was not one of them. A silver arrowhead buried in a Phey's heart spelled instant death, and Gant suspected that their aim was quite precise. He wasn't honestly sure if he still shared that vulnerability to silver as his brothers did. Who knew the resistance that his green blob of a body might provide. But Graves and Trott were definitely vulnerable. Gant was certain that if they made the slightest wrong move, the arrows would be unleashed and they would be dead within seconds.

Graves glanced at the unmoving Piri. "How long will the paralysis last?"

"A while. It depends on the individual," said the Serpenteen.

"Then I suggest you bind the Piri since he will very likely attempt to escape the moment he can move," Graves suggested. "He is not exactly a willing accomplice in this undertaking."

One of the Whoresmen strode forward and he had rope coiled around his midsection. Quickly he removed it and lashed the frozen Piri's arms tightly to its sides. The Piri was staring up at nothing, but clearly there was consciousness in his mind because here was fear and confusion in his eyes.

"Come with us," said Chyron, "and do not attempt to depart the area again, because if you do it will not go well for you."

"Nor will it go well for you," Graves warned him. "It never ends well for someone who trifles with the Travelers."

"You can sound as important as you wish. But the Overseer is dead and all your authority stemmed from him. Here, out in the midst of the woods, all you are are Phey who are far from home. Now you are ours."

Gant definitely did not like his attitude. It had been quite some time since he had served as a Traveler, and he had very much preferred the days when the Travelers were feared rather than spoken to with vague contempt. But he kept his silence, which was not hard for him to do considering that the act of speaking was quite the challenge for him.

Graves stared down at the thick green goo that was his brother. "Hardly an improvement," he said dourly. Gant did not bother to respond and then Graves said, "Can you move?"

"Yes."

"Get up here."

Gant immediately did so. It was an action that Graves' draquon clearly was unenthused about. It started to back up and it lowered its head, snarling a warning that caused Gant to halt in his tracks. This in turn made Graves extremely impatient, and he cuffed the reluctant draquon on the side of its head, gaining its attention. "Don't be difficult," he ordered the beast.

For an instant Gant thought that it was going to buck and throw Graves over its head, but instead the well-trained animal accepted the rebuke from its owner and waited patiently as Gant slithered up the side and draped himself over the creature's back as best he could. *"What about…mine?"* he asked.

"When it comes to, it will follow us," said Graves. "That's what they're bred to do. I would not be concerned."

Gant tried to nod but naturally was unable to do much more than burble.

Graves and Trott guided their draquons to follow the Whoresmen and Serpenteen. This apparent teaming up of the two races was truly puzzling to Gant. Each of the Twelve races tended to keep to themselves, so the concept of two races having formed some sort of coalition was just odd.

Apparently it caught Graves' attention as well. "Since when are Serpenteen and Whoresmen allies?"

"We have mutual benefits," Chyron said. "Our tribes have

coexisted for many turns. Hunting is particularly effective. The Serpenteen are miserable as hunters whereas we Whoresmen are quite exceptional at it. But once we bring the Serpenteen within range of the prey, their venom is able to paralyze it with no problem. Mutually beneficial to all."

"I'm very happy for you," said Graves drily.

Chyron was staring intently at Graves. "What has transpired with your skin? Since when are the Phey silver? I thought your lot despised silver."

"We are what we are," said Graves with an indifferent shrug. "It is probably best not to question it."

Chyron simply nodded.

They continued through the woods in silence. Gant was wondering the entire time if perhaps Graves had some deeper plan in mind. If he was conjuring up some sort of magiks or spell that he would unleash on the Serpenteens and Whoresmen and use that opportunity to get away. But Graves seemed not to be the slightest bit interested in doing anything like that. Instead he simply kept his interest focused on the world around them and appeared content to allow the Whoresmen to exert their will on them.

Such passivity seemed curious to Gant, and once again he spoke, this time in a voice so low that he was positive even the sharp-eared Whoresman would not detect it. What he said was a single word: "*Why?*"

Graves immediately understood the question. "I want to see their Visionary. Someone who knew that the Overseer was dead that quickly is someone I want to meet."

Gant grunted. He hated to admit it, but it made sense.

The long remaining minutes passed in silence, and then bright, flickering lights ahead of them alerted the Phey that they were almost at the encampment. Gant heard murmurings from behind them: the Piri was starting to come out of his locked-in state. The venom of the Serpenteens was legendary. The Morts had morphed them in their retellings of earlier encounters with them to the notion that just the act of looking into the eyes of a Serpenteen would cause you to be transformed into stone permanently. Morts had a tendency to exaggerate everything that they encountered, which Gant considered to be both curious and amusing. Why did Morts have only a passing familiarity with the truth?

There was a burble of discussion that was audible to Gant coming from the encampment, but as they drew nearer the conversation stopped. Obviously their coming was expected. Perhaps that was also the work of the Visionary. Gant had to admit that even he was curious over the identity of this individual. Was it an insightful Whoresman or Serpenteen? Or was it someone else? Only the Phey were true magic users, and even their abilities had become diminished the longer they resided on this throwback of a world.

The Phey rode into the midst of the encampment. The fire was the centerpiece, but there were a variety of old Mort vehicles surrounding it that clearly served as homes of some sort. They were reasonably large and some had printing on the sides that said "Winnebago," but Gant couldn't read it and had no idea of what their significance was. He shrugged mentally since shrugging physically remained something of a challenge. Morts also seemed to enjoy labeling things, perhaps as some sort of boast of creation. They were certainly a peculiar race. Or might be again. Once more Gant's thoughts turned to Jepp. There was definitely something extraordinary about her, and he could not help but wonder if she might somehow be responsible for bringing her race back from the brink of extinction. Then again, Gant wasn't entirely sure how much more time he himself might have in this sphere.

The Serpenteens and Whoresman slowly approached, and then Chyron called out in his booming voice, *"Visionary! Your presence is required!"*

Gant heard slow movement coming from within one of the vehicles that read "Winnebago" on the side. There was a rustling at the small door and then it banged open, and a figure stood in the dim light provided by the fire.

"*Oh no,*" said Gant.

It was a tall, stately looking Phey. Rather than tinted silver, her skin was instead a pale but lovely gold, which matched perfectly the color of her long hair as well. Her eyes were pale green and she stared straight at Gant and laughed.

"You look well, Gant," she said.

"*Really?*" replied Gant. "*You look...like shit...Tania.*"

THE ARGO

I.

JASON UNWRAPPED THE SANDWICH THAT he extracted from the picnic basket and sighed heavily. "He's losing it, Medea," he said sadly. "He is really losing it."

Medea did not respond, of course. Instead she remained securely in her tube, unresponsive and unaware of the world around her. That was fine with Jason, really. The more he thought about his environment, the less enamored of it he was. There were times that he even considered leaving it. Just blowing himself out the airlock and putting an end to this…this non-life that he lived.

He was a babysitter. A full time babysitter for a spaceship full of comatose individuals who were likely never going to wake up in his lifetime. And what would he do when he was approaching the end of his own existence? He would have to designate someone to be the inheritor of this floating, empty realm. It would be his job to select his successor and condemn some other poor bastard to the empty existence he currently inhabited.

He wondered if he should choose Medea and realized that he couldn't do that to her. He had grown far too fond of her during their lengthy if one-way relationship.

"Maybe I should start studying everyone's bios," he said, as much to himself as to Medea. "Start figuring out who would be the best person to give this lousy job to. Crap. It's more involved than that," he began to realize. "What if I died unexpectedly? Just keeled over from a heart attack or aneurysm or something." He stroked his chin thoughtfully. "I could probably rig the computer to monitor my life signs and build a program where, if my life signs abruptly cease, the computer would just automatically wake up my successor. Yeah.

Yeah, that makes sense. But it just brings me back to who the hell I should choose. Do you have any thoughts on this, Medea?"

Unsurprisingly, no response came.

As he chewed his sandwich, his obsession with Medea began to pull at him. In his own way, he was mirroring his father's attitude toward his mother. Isaac was constantly engaging in conversations with thin air. Of course, the difference was that Jason was perfectly aware that Medea really couldn't hear him. That he was just engaging in a harmless fantasy as a means of keeping himself sane, whereas his father genuinely believed that his mother was standing nearby, listening to everything he said. She was effectively haunting him.

But, when it came down to it, was it really so bad, what he was doing? Jason was having his own problems over dealing with the constant loneliness, and his father had been doing it for longer. It was entirely possible that by the time Jason was Isaac's age, he might come to believe that Medea was really standing there speaking with him rather than just rooting around in his imagination. Maybe he didn't have the right to be bitching to himself about the deterioration of his father's mental facilities considering he had no idea what lay in store for he himself. What was the old saying about walking a mile in another man's shoes? Certainly those shoes were waiting patiently for him at the end of his own journey.

He tried to imagine an array of endless days before him, living in utter loneliness once his father passed. Just him and the incessant sounds of the ship thrumming along, its machinery constantly in operation, keeping him in…

Wait.

Jason slowly put down the remnants of his sandwich and turned his attention to the empty air. Something was wrong. Something was missing. He wasn't sure what it was at first, but the longer he listened, the more aware he became of just exactly what it was.

The engines.

The steady, dependable, life affirming "thrum" of the engines as they continued to propel the ship around the Earth in its endless orbit.

He had started them up fifteen minutes ago. It was necessary for them to fire for exactly fifty-seven minutes in order to maintain their orbit, and yet now he wasn't hearing them. Which was a situation that, if not corrected immediately, could result in catastrophic consequences.

He sprang up off the floor, his sandwich and Medea completely forgotten as he sprinted toward the engine control room. His mind was already racing through everything that could possibly have gone wrong, and everything he in turn could do to effect repairs. Say what anyone would about his father, but Isaac had been scrupulous about teaching his son everything there was to know about the vessel. Information on how to fix everything from the engines to the plumbing was rattling around inside Jason's head. So he was convinced that, whatever had gone wrong—and clearly something had—he would easily be able to repair it.

Except something was warning him that it was wrong. He was sure there was a cause for it, stemming from the fact that things on the ship did not tend simply to stop working for no reason. The fact that he had no idea what that reason could possibly be similarly alarmed him.

He descended to the depths of the engine room and the moment he strode in he saw what the problem was. In fact, he saw both the problem and the reason why it was going to be impossible to fix it.

The engines had indeed shut down. The massive conduits that powered the entire thing were sitting as silently as if they were dead, or perhaps even still born. The engines were idle, the thrusters likewise immobile. The engine room was about the size of a football field and experiencing that much silence was breathtaking, and also alarming. It wasn't just that the engines themselves were dead. Everything there that drew any power and caused anything to function on the ship was out. It was only now that Jason noticed the overhead lights were flickering and dimming. There was only one possible reason for it: the emergency breakers had switched on because the engine supply had already gone dead.

Nor was it difficult for Jason to determine why exactly that was. The control panels had been destroyed.

He could only assume that someone had shut down the engines first, and then—as near as he could determine—had taken an axe to the controls. They had been completely smashed to pieces. And whoever had done it had been damned systematic about it, because it wasn't just the main controls. The back-ups as well had been…

"Whoever had done it?" Jason was questioning aloud the thoughts that were going through his mind. He knew exactly who had done it because there was only one other damned person on the whole ship. His father, Isaac, had clearly undertaken the destruction of the control panels in the engine room, and the only thing left for Jason to do was demand why in God's name he had done so, and then perhaps blow him out the nearest convenient hatch.

But he's your father. You can't just execute him! His angry conscience was trying to scold him, but Jason did not care. His father, in his lunacy, may well have destroyed the entire vessel. If the man who had done this had been just another crewmember, death would be the immediate and indeed only reasonable response for such a destructive madman. The fact that this particular madman had been responsible for his birth was utterly beside the point.

"Dad!" he bellowed. He had no idea why he shouted in that manner. He was either nearby or he wasn't. If he wasn't, then he wouldn't hear him. If he was, then Jason didn't have to shout. The yell came more from his inner frustration than anything else. He was not sure what he would do if his father just magically appeared in front of him in response to his name. It could be even more problematic if he was still carrying the axe with which he had done all the damage. Would his father really attack him? Try to chop him to bits? He knew that his dad was deluded over the existence of his late mother, but it was a huge step from partial dementia to becoming a demented murderer.

For the moment, the entire question was moot, because there was no response.

He tore through the ship then, shouting Isaac's name, hoping the entire time that he would not find him. That perhaps this was some insane murder/suicide stunt and his father had already taken care of his own end of the bargain. But that, as it turned out, was not the case. Jason's voice echoed all around him, but Isaac continued to provide no response.

His search ended when he strode into the eating room.

Isaac was sitting there, munching on a cookie. He was wearing a headset and his head was bobbing slightly as Jason heard musical notes flittering from the earpieces. It was some sort of classic composition. Mozart if Jason wasn't mistaken. Yet Isaac was bobbing along with it as if he was experiencing the music of some rock and roll group.

"Dad!" he shouted once more, and this time Isaac noticed his presence. He reached up, removed the headset and stared at him quizzically. Clearly he had no idea what it was that had gotten Jason so worked up, and so just regarded him with a look of quiet confusion and a single cocked eyebrow. "How could you?!"

Isaac frowned. "How could I what?"

Jason could scarcely believe what he was hearing. All at once the strength went out of his legs; his knees were trembling terribly. He grabbed the back of the nearest chair and sank into it, staring at his father as if Isaac had just sprouted an additional eye in the middle of his forehead. "We're playing games about this?" he asked incredulously. "You're going to pretend you don't know?"

"I'm not pretending," Isaac assured him. "I have absolutely no idea what you're going on about."

Jason realized that there was no point in just telling his dad what had transpired. He would likely deny it. It was clear that he was utterly losing attachment to reality. His only choice was to show his father what he had discovered.

He grabbed him by the wrist, pulling him out of his chair, causing him to lose the grip on his doughnut. The pastry fell away and Isaac let out a protest, but Jason wasn't paying the slightest attention. His father apparently realized that he had no choice save to try and keep up with his son as best he could.

It took several minutes for him to haul Isaac through the length of the ship to the engine room. Isaac at first kept asking what the problem was but then eventually realized he was not going to get a response from his son, and so lapsed into silence. But when Jason finally got him to the engine room, he gasped in shock at what he beheld. Jason hated to admit it to himself, but he was almost relieved to see the disaster that had sent him into a barely controlled panic. Part of him was afraid that he was going to arrive there and discover everything in perfect shape, and he was going to be forced to the conclusion that it wasn't his father who was going insane, but he himself. So that was one less thing to worry about.

What was more astonishing was what his father said to him upon discovering the wreckage: "What have you done?"

"Me?" His voice was tinged with incredulity and actually went up an octave when he spoke. "What have I done? What have *you* done?"

"You think I did this?" Isaac came across as astounded as Jason was. "This may well have destroyed the ship. If we can't get the engines fired up, then this vessel will plummet to its destruction. Why would I do such a thing?"

"Because you're insane! Because you think Mom is still alive! You're crazy, that's why!"

Isaac's face paled. "I can't believe you would say that. I can believe that you would think it, but that you would say it to my face…"

"Dad, I didn't do this!" He gestured widely to the damage. "By process of elimination, unless we have a stowaway somewhere, it was you!"

And then Isaac gasped. "Oh my God. You're right. It was Debbie. It had to be. She—"

Jason didn't know he was going to do it until he did it. His right fist flew and cracked Isaac in the jaw. Isaac, not remotely prepared for the blow or expecting it, went down in a heap. He slammed down onto the deck sounding like a bag of wet cement as he hit the ground. Then he lay there for a few moments, shaking his head and trying to get the world to stop spinning.

Immediately Jason wanted to apologize. He felt mortified, ashamed for hitting his father. But then, just as quickly, he reminded himself that this madman had just doomed the ship. A punch in the mouth? He deserved to be thrown out of the ship.

So Jason fought his instinct to reach out and help his father up and do whatever else a normal, rational, contrite son would do. Instead he turned around and stormed off, determined to try and study the problem and see if there was any way to repair it. He was certain that it could, in fact, be repaired, but it would take weeks. Weeks he did not have. The only alternative that he could discern was to study the central computer core and see if there was any way to bypass the controls that had been destroyed.

But he very much doubted it.

II.

ISAAC LAY THERE FOR A long while. At first he rubbed his jaw but eventually that got old, and then his mind wandered back to Debbie. Was it really possible? Had she destroyed the controls of the ship?

"Debbie," he called out softly. "Debbie, where are you?"

"What happened to you?" her reply came back immediately. She was standing a short distance away, looking very concerned over the fact that he was lying on the floor. She reached out to help him up but he waved her off as he slowly got to his feet on his own. The ache from his jaw wasn't disappearing; if anything, it was becoming more pronounced.

"Did you do it?" he asked.

"Do what?" She tried to sound confused, but he was easily able to pierce her shroud of bewilderment. She was covering up. He knew her far too well for her to fool him with appearing unclear as to what he was asking about.

"You know what," he said more forcefully. "Did you destroy the controls in the engine room?"

"Why in the world would I do that?"

"That's what I want to know. Why did you do it?"

"But I…" She started to protest once more, but then her voice trailed off. She sighed deeply and stared at the floor, and seemed to be considering what she should say, if anything. Then she looked up at him again and there was a seriousness in her tone and demeanor that wasn't there before. "That's not really the question you want to ask me, is it. Go ahead. Ask me what's really on your mind."

He hesitated for what seemed ages and finally brought himself to ask what he really didn't want to know the answer to: "Are you dead?"

She nodded.

"Am…am I out of my mind?"

"Not at all, honey," she said quickly. She crossed to him, put her hands on his shoulders. He didn't understand how she could possibly be dead, because she was touching him. She felt real. He could sense the warmth coming off her skin. She smelled real as well; the scent of her perfume wafted from her. How could this not be genuine? "You're not out of your mind. It's just that you…well, you have the ability to see me because you haven't let go of me. And I'm fine with that. I haven't let go of you either."

"And…and heaven is okay with that? I mean, I'm assuming there's a heaven. It's okay with the hereafter if you just hang around?" He was asking questions he couldn't believe were coming out of his mouth.

"Well," she admitted, "not really. You feel a kind of pressure. Not of people talking to you, but just…in here." She tapped her heart. "They really want me to move on. But I can't. I'm weak. The truth is," and she dabbed at her eyes as they started to tear up. "The truth is that I don't want to move on without you. I want you to come with me."

That was when it was all clear to him. He understood completely. "So you destroyed the engineering controls—shut down the engines— because you wanted me to die so that I could go on with you. So that we could go together."

She nodded and now she was unable to restrain her tears. "I feel so selfish. It's going to kill Jason and everybody else on this ship. But really, why are we circling the Earth, anyway? Those creatures are never going to go away. They're just going to rattle around on our world and if we ever land they'll either enslave us or kill us outright. So honestly, we're just saving them from a long, lingering death. It's really the right thing."

"The right thing," he echoed. "Condemning all those people to death is the right thing."

"It absolutely is. You know it and I know it. We're talking about quality of life, Isaac. Something that none of them, including our son, will ever have. We are doing them a favor by sparing them that."

The entire notion was difficult for him to wrap his head around, but the more he thought about it, the more he began to come to the slow but unavoidable conclusion that maybe, just maybe...

She was right.

"We could be together," he whispered.

"Yes." Her head was eagerly bobbing. "Together. Forever. Wouldn't that be wonderful?"

"It would," he said. "Of course, Jason could wind up fixing it."

"Don't worry about that," she assured him. "I have another plan."

PERRIZ

I.

JEPP LOOKED AROUND IN WONDERMENT. She had never seen anything quite like Perriz in her life.

Perriz was well known to be a hub of industry and interest for the Mandraques, and that alone had appealed to the fundamental perversity of her previous master so that he had never had the slightest interest in going there. Indeed, as she recalled, the Greatness had relatives there that he absolutely could not get along with. Which was not atypical for him: the Greatness had excelled in not getting along with most of his kind.

From her vantage point atop the Zeffer, she was able to see the majesty of the city spread out beneath her. In its own way, it seemed even more magnificent than the city of Spires. Granted, those buildings had been taller and more impressive, but the city of Perriz below her seemed far more artistic. It was, she also sensed, much older than anything in the Spires. The older buildings stood beside the newer ones and blended together into one great tapestry of art. She found it fascinating and felt as if she could stay up there and stare down at it forever.

She also saw that the residents below her had noticed them. Their reaction was quite amusing. They pointed and immediately ran in all directions, obviously fearing that the Zeffer was the harbinger of yet another attack. None of them wanted to deal with it. She smiled; yes, definitely amusing.

No. More than that. For the entirety of her life, she had spent it being beaten or threatened or compelled to do whatever it was that others wanted of her. Never had anyone fled from her presence, believing her to be a threat. In point of fact, they weren't really doing that now, either. They were running from the Zeffer and the danger they believed it presented. Nevertheless, she was atop the thing and therefore they were kind of, sort of, running from her. She decided she would take her triumphs where she could.

Pavan, the Zeffer's guide, called out, "We're going to be descending. Everyone who is going down, now is the time."

"Where do we go exactly?" asked Zerena. Jepp noticed that Zerena was not sounding as combative or challenging as she normally did. Clearly the fact that Pavan had threatened her had diminished her typical bellicosity somewhat.

It was Eutok who responded. "We go where we said we would go. We go below to track down the Piri and rescue Clarinda."

"We could use some help," said Karsen. "The lot of us against the Piri, who can hide in the shadows, leap out at us wherever they want. We could be dead before we head a mile under ground, plus we have no idea where we're going."

"I can find her," Norda said in her typical off-hand manner.

Everyone looked at her with a mixture of surprise and skepticism. "You can?" said Eutok doubtfully.

Arren had walked over to his sister and rested his hand on her shoulder. "She can. Norda is an excellent tracker. If you can provide her something with Clarinda's scent on it, she can definitely find her once she picks up the track."

Karsen turned to Eutok. "Do you have anything of hers?"

"No," said Eutok grimly.

"But I imagine we do," Berola spoke up. "We can go to the chambers where the Firedraques placed us. I'm sure there's something there of hers."

"Plus we can ask the others of our kind if they are willing to go down and rescue Clarinda," Turkin suggested.

"That's an excellent idea," said Berola. "I'm quite sure that, now that they've had the time to get rested, they would be up for endeavoring to find her."

II.

"DID JORMUND SEND YOU?"

That was certainly not the question that Berola had been expecting.

Hers and Turkin's initial entrance into the room did indeed go exactly the way that she had expected, with joyous whoops as the Ocular greeted the return of their mates with genuine enthusiasm. The floor of the room shook from the impact of their gigantic feet storming across it as Kerda and the others fairly leaped into their arms. It was obvious from their reactions that they had not expected ever to see them again, and they were thrilled that the older Ocular had returned to them safe and sound.

"What kind of dangers did you encounter?" "Were you almost killed?" "What were the Travelers like?" These and other questions were thrown at them with the speed of rocks being hurled as part of an attack. Berola and Turkin fielded the questions as best they could, Berola laughing somewhat at the enthusiasm from her fellows.

"And now," Berola said once she had managed to calm them down so that they could have a conversation, "we have a new mission. Clarinda is still alive. We're going to go rescue her."

That was when Kerda asked her about Jormund.

Berola cast a confused glance at Turkin, who simply shrugged. He was crouched over in a corner and was clearly as puzzled as Berola was by the question.

"Jormund? The Mandraque? No. Why?"

Kerda let out a low breath. "He was here just the other day. He tried to convince us to go with him on an exploration to find the Piri that are lurking below and, ideally, save Clarinda."

"And you didn't go?" asked Berola and then closed her eye in annoyance at her own question. "Of course you didn't go. I mean, obviously, since you are all seated right here."

"But why didn't you?" said Turkin. "If you have reason to believe Clarinda is alive…"

"We didn't trust him," said Kerda, as other Ocular nodded in agreement. "And also, we are tired of fighting."

"Tired?" Berola couldn't believe what she was hearing. "Stalking the Piri, eliminating them…that was what we were trained for."

"Yes, and all that happened was that we lost our parents because of it," one of the Ocular pointed out.

"But our lives were saved," Turkin said. He now rose from where he had been crouched. "If we had not been out in the woods, training, we would have died with our parents."

"Then maybe we'd be better off!"

There were more nods from all around the room, and sniffles, and that was when Berola picked a bowl up off a table. It was filled with fresh fruit. She overturned it, spilling out the contents, and in one swift movement flung it across the room. It shattered against the far wall and the pieces flew in all directions. The Ocular flinched back, placing their arms defensively in front of their eyes to shield them. A silence fell in the room.

"You disgust me," Berola said tightly, her voice quivering with fury. "All of you. The Ocular are supposed to be warriors, not whining babies. Upon reflection, the lot of you should just stay here. You will contribute nothing to the battle."

She strode across the room to a freestanding closet and flung it open. She immediately found within what she was looking for: the tattered cloak that Clarinda had been wearing when they had first arrived in Perriz. She had changed it out for a different cloak that the Firedraques had provided her to take the place of the worn one she had been sporting. This one would serve nicely for providing Norda the scent that she required.

"And when we do find Clarinda," Berola continued, "you can rest assured we will not tell her of your cowardice in this regard. I feel we owe you that much." She nodded toward Turkin. "Come."

"Right behind you," said Turkin and he followed her out of the room.

They trotted down the flight of stairs, and the entire time, Berola was muttering in frustration and anger. "You need to calm down," Turkin told her at one point.

"No, I don't," Berola replied. "They were training to be warriors and as it turns out, they're just cowards."

"They had friends die just a few days ago. They're in mourning. They're in shock."

"Stop making excuses for them," Berola said testily.

"I'm not making excuses. I'm just trying to explain to you why they're reacting the way they are."

"I don't need explanations. I needed their fists backing me up. But if they want to stay up there, that's fine with me."

Evanna and Arren were waiting for them in the main foyer. "Well?" said Evanna, but then she immediately answered her own question. "They're not interested in coming."

"The less said of it, the better," said Berola. "Come; let's get out of here."

They headed out the large exit doors of Firedraque hall, Evanna in the lead. And then she jumped back, startled, as Kerda landed directly in front of her.

Berola stared in shock. "Where did *you* come from?

"I climbed out the window," said Kerda, sounding almost indifferent to her feat. "I wanted to catch up with you."

"You could have just come down the stairs behind us," Turkin pointed out.

"No. I didn't want to come running after you. I wanted to stand here and face you and tell you I'm no coward."

"You—"

"Do I sound like I'm finished?"

Her anger was palpable. Berola was clearly taken aback. Turkin, standing behind her, managed to stifle his smile, but just barely.

When Berola made no attempt to resume speaking, Kerda continued. "None of us are cowards. But we do not have any desire to fight. If others want to go and save Clarinda and bring her back to us, we will be happy to have her. But we have no disposition to creep around underground, seek out the Piri, and risk our lives, especially because we know fully well that that's the last thing Clarinda would desire us to do. Are we clear?"

"Yes, we're clear," said Berola, who had suddenly lost her taste for arguing the matter extensively.

"Good. So let's go," and Kerda turned away from her and started walking.

"We?" Berola asked. "I thought you weren't interested in fighting."

"I'm not."

"But—?"

"There's no 'but,'" said Kerda. "I've simply decided I'm going with you. If you don't like it, that's too bad. Have I made myself clear?"

Before Berola could respond, Evanna spoke up. "Abundantly clear. Welcome to the battle. We're happy to have you on board."

"Yes, I can see just how enthused you are," said Kerda, making no attempt to hide her sarcasm.

Passing Mandraques were casting them suspicious glances. There continued to be no love lost between the Ocular and the scaled warriors. That suited Berola just fine, although then a thought crossed her mind. "Should we summon Jormund to aid us?" she asked. "He could be most formidable in battle."

"Ideally the fight will not come down to the presence of one individual," said Kerda. "And I would rather he not be with us if it can be avoided."

"It can be," said Turkin.

"I prefer to proceed without him as well," said Evanna. "I do not fully trust him. In point of fact—no offense to you, Arren—I don't trust any Mandraque."

"Can't say that I blame you," said Arren. "I have to say, I don't especially trust us either." He turned to Berola. "You acquired what we needed?"

She held up the cloak. "Right here."

"Then let's go find her," said Arren, "and hope we don't die in the process."

"I'm all for not dying," Evanna said.

III.

"YOU'RE SURE YOU'RE NOT GOING to join us?" said Karsen.

The entire group was standing near the door that Arren had indicated would allow them to descend directly into the underground sewers that ran the length of Perriz. Karsen was addressing Pavan, and the large Serabim was standing next to Demali, one arm draped around her shoulder.

"I am not a fighter," said Pavan. "When forced into it, I can defend myself well enough. But I do not seek out battle, nor does Demali."

It looked to Karsen as if Demali was about to disagree with that assessment, but then she caught herself and stifled whatever response she was going to make. He understood her reaction fully. She was determined to remain in line with what her male said. She probably loved him; Karsen could see it in her eyes. That was fine with Karsen, because he knew the feelings he himself had developed for Jepp.

"So if it is all the same to you," Pavan continued, "we are simply going to return to our mountains and try and reassemble the Serabim into a single, unified race once more."

"I understand," said Karsen. "The best of luck to both of you."

Pavan saluted to him in the manner of his people, thudding a fist to his chest and then tapping Karsen's to complete the gesture. Karsen automatically did likewise, and then the two of them bowed to each other once more. Pavan then sounded a loud, distinct whistle, and seconds later a tentacle stretched down from on high and wrapped itself around both Pavan's and Demali's waists. It lifted them skyward toward the Zeffer that was hovering above them.

"I don't think I'll ever get used to that," said Jepp.

"Fine, they're gone," Eutok said with his customary lack of

patience. "Now who is going to come down with me to rescue Clarinda? Karsen, you, of course."

"And we are with you," said Turkin. Berola and Kerda nodded as well.

"I'm coming, too," said Jepp.

Immediately Karsen turned to face her. "No. Absolutely not. I won't have you subjected to danger."

"You're insane."

To Karsen's surprise, it was his mother who had addressed him. Zerena swayed forward and pointed at Jepp. "Don't you remember what this Mort is capable of in a fight? Especially if you are threatened? Of everyone here, she is quite possibly the most devastating weapon we've got, because she looks like nothing but can kill you where you stand. You'd be crazy not to bring her along. In fact, I'm going to save you some time. We're all going."

"Absolutely correct," said Mingo with a low growl in his throat. "I owe the damnable Piri some payback for the last time we encountered them. I very much like the idea of goring a few of them."

"Indeed!" bellowed Rafe Kestor. He had yanked his sword defiantly from his scabbard and now he was waving it around his head with such vehemence that anyone standing near him was flinching away for fear that he might lose his grip on it. "We must save the young damsel, else we do not deserve the titles of heroes!"

"I don't especially think we *do* deserve the titles of heroes," Zerena said with her typical sourness. "But if that's the situation that Karsen has gotten us into, then we've no choice but to undertake the endeavor."

"Are you sure you are okay with this, Evanna?" Arren asked her. "You were never much for combat. You were always the most studious of individuals I had ever encountered."

"One reaches a point in one's life where simple study isn't sufficient," said Evanna. "Sometimes one encounters things that are worth fighting for. These creatures lurk beneath our very feet and present an ongoing threat to all of us. I say we go down and exterminate every last one of them."

"As long as you're sure you're up for it," said Arren.

For answer, Evanna swung her head around, opened her mouth, and a huge gust of flame ripped out, scorching the nearby wall and blackening it. The eruption lasted for several seconds and then she closed her jaws and swung her attention back to Arren. "I think I can handle it," she said drily.

"I would have to agree." Arren then turned to Norda. "Are you ready?"

Norda inhaled deeply from the cloak once more and then tossed it aside, her nostrils flaring. "I'm ready. Let's go."

Eutok strode forward, grabbed the door firmly, and yanked it open. "Let's find Clarinda," he said.

One by one, they descended into the darkness.

THE UNKNOWN FOREST

I.

"WHAT IS HAPPENING?!" SCREAMED THE Piri, struggling in the grasp of his captors. They were shoving him toward a large tree with ropes dangling from their hands. Gant thought that if the idiot hadn't started fighting and had instead just gone along with the situation, that they would have had no trouble with treating him in a polite manner. Then again, no one ever accused Piri of being especially bright.

"I don't understand," the Piri continued as they tied him to the tree. "How did I get here?! Where *is* here?!? None of this makes any sense!"

"Oh my gods, shut up," Chyron said, making no attempt to hide his irritation. "If we want you to say anything, we can beat it out of you. Actually, on second thought," and he turned to Gant, "can you attend to him?"

"*Yes,*" said Gant and he slithered and slimed his way toward the Piri.

The Piri saw him coming and, in his bound state, nevertheless tried to pull himself away from the advancing Gant. "You! I remember you! Get away from me! Get away! *Don't touch me! Stay ba—!*" That was as far as he got before Gant's gelatinous mass enveloped him. Reflexively he screamed, which was the one thing he should not have done because Gant insinuated himself into the Piri's open mouth and down into his body. The Piri's scream transformed into a helpless gargle and then, seconds later, he was blinking his eyes repeatedly. He stared quite calmly at Chyron and the other Whoresmen and Serpenteens. "I think you can remove these," he said, glancing left and right at the ropes that bound him.

Moments later he was standing up, freed of bonds, shaking

out his arms as if he were trying on a new suit. "That was more excitement than I needed."

"Believe me, Gant, whatever mishaps you encounter, you brought them on yourself," said Tania. She was standing a short distance away, her arms folded.

He took several steps toward her and two Whoresmen placed themselves between him and her in a guarded manner. He stared at them and smirked. "You require protection, do you? From your own kind?"

"My own kind? You are a blob residing inside a Piri. That is hardly my own kind."

"You did this to me!" He chucked a thumb at himself. "You transformed me into that blob!"

"You did it to yourself when you betrayed me."

"I did not betray you! You said you were no longer interested in being my lover!"

He had stopped moving but now she strode toward him, pushing the Whoresmen aside as if they were not even there. They were evidently surprised by the strength in her arms as she shoved them out of her path. "And you made no effort to change my mind, did you. Never sought to make up with me. Never tried to win me back."

"You said I shouldn't waste my time!"

"And you *believed* me? Fool!"

Gant was able to feel the Piri banging around inside his mind. The creature had had enough time to pull itself together—as opposed to the first time when Gant had leaped into it and caught it off guard—that Gant could sense it trying to fight back against him. It was a useless effort; Gant was firmly in control. But some of the creature's bloodthirstiness was leaking through into Gant's consciousness and for just a moment, he felt a deep desire to leap forward, tear out Tania's throat with his teeth, and drink deeply. He envisioned the startled look in her eyes and the fast dwindling of her life, sheer surprise being the emotion that swept over her in her final moments. Would she regret it at that point? What she had done to him and how she had completely screwed up his life?

Then, very slowly, he managed to push back the animalistic impulse to attack. His mind regained control of his personality and he sensed the Piri howling in fury as it was shoved into the recesses of his brain. He took in a deep breath and let it out very slowly, and then managed to refocus on Tania.

She was frowning at him, looking confused. "What's wrong?" she said.

"How kind of you," he managed to get out, "that you care enough to ask."

Graves had taken a place next to a roaring fire that was blazing from a nearby cooking pit. He crouched in front of it, extending his hands and basking in the warmth. "So you are the Visionary of the Whoresmen and Serpenteens. How did you come into that situation, may I ask."

"You may ask, Graves," said Tania imperiously, "but I can't say that it's any of your business."

"I somewhat think that it is. You are one of us."

"No," said Chyron firmly. "She is one of us now. She is our Visionary and she provides us sight into the rest of the world."

"She always did have the touch for the grand picture," said Gant. "Although that being said, you'd think she would have seen my becoming involved with her sister and not overreacted the way she did."

"You know perfectly well I can never perceive my own future or those close to me. And I did not overreact. I reacted exactly in the way that..." She waved him off dismissively. "I'm not going to keep talking about this. It's a waste of time." She turned toward Chyron and said impatiently, "Why did you bring them here? Of what use are they?"

"We are going to ransom them, of course," said Chyron.

The Phey looked at each other with mixtures of incredulity. "Ransom us?" said Graves. "To whom?"

"To the others of your kind. The ones in the Spires."

"Are you out of your mind?" said Gant. "First of all, I can assure you that they aren't going to give a damn about us. And second, what could you possibly ransom us for? What do the Phey have that you desire?"

A female Whoresman strode forward and came up next to Chyron. "Weapons, of course."

Chyron nodded toward her but addressed the Phey. "This is my mate, Nessa."

"I don't care," said Graves. "Weapons? What makes you think we have weapons?"

"Everyone knows that the Phey are the most formidable fighters in the Damned World," said Nessa, smiling confidently. "The weapons you wield are legendary."

"Really. Certainly 'legendary' is the right word, because they are simply legends," said Gant. "The Phey have never been interested in conquest, and we've certainly never developed weapons to aid us in that which we do not choose to pursue."

"I have heard differently," said Nessa.

"Then you heard wrong," Graves said. "We have only ever fought when someone was foolish enough to attack us, and in those instances, we have utilized magiks."

Chyron and Nessa exchanged looks and then Chyron said, "Fine. Then you can teach us your magiks."

"You aren't Phey," said Graves. "Our magiks would be useless to you."

"You can find a way to make it work."

"No. We really cannot."

"Then," Chyron said to Graves, "you had best hope that you are wrong about the low esteem in which your kind holds you. Because if they do not meet our demands, you will surely die."

"All things surely die," said Graves with a shrug. "It's just a matter of when."

"Then settle in," Chyron instructed them. "We will send a messenger, while you will definitely be here a while."

"Shorter than you think," said Graves.

"I assume you have no further need of my services," said Tania in a formal manner to Chyron. "Am I free to return to my quarters?"

Chyron nodded to her and she turned to head back to the structure.

But then Nessa said, "Take that one with you," and she pointed at Gant.

"Absolutely not," Tania said immediately. "I have nothing to say to him."

"That is when the most important things are often said," Nessa replied. "Do as you are instructed."

Tania growled low in her throat but then bowed slightly. "As you wish," she said. She walked to the door of her home, opened it wide, and gestured for Gant to enter. He hesitated briefly but then strode forward and through the door. Tania followed him in and closed it behind her.

It was sparsely decorated. There was a couch, some sort of food preparation area, and a small curtained off room in the back that Gant assumed to be a sleeping chamber. Tania did not ease herself onto the couch, but instead turned and faced him in the middle of the room, her arms folded, looking annoyed. "Stay here for ten minutes and then let yourself out. They will certainly be distracted by other matters at that point."

"No, I'm not just going to stand here. How in the world did you wind up with these people?" he demanded. "They captured you, I assume."

She looked as if she were about to argue the point, but then rolled her eyes in exasperation. "Yes, okay, fine, they captured me. Satisfied?"

"How?"

"I was sleeping in the woods. I didn't know that they were around and they surprised me."

"And you did nothing to escape?"

"The Serpenteens made it impossible. They kept me a prisoner here and every time I would begin to regain any sense of feeling in my body, they would spit on me again." There was an edge to her voice that barely contained the anger she was obviously feeling at the recollection. "They grabbed me for the same reason they captured you: blackmail for weapons. Fortunately I managed to convince them that I would be of more use to them as a Visionary. That is how I have served them for…" She shrugged. "I've no idea how many turns. More than I like to think about."

"And you never tried to escape—?"

"*I can't go through it again!*"

The vehemence, the anger in her voice caught Gant off guard. It took Tania by surprise as well; she seemed startled at her reaction. She closed her eyes, reaching into herself to calm her nerves.

Gant approached her and tried to reach out, to put a hand on her shoulder. Somehow she sensed his approach and pulled away, turning her back to him. He withdrew his hand but spoke in a low, gentle voice. "I understand."

"You understand nothing."

"Of course I understand. Tania, you are the proudest individual I have ever met. What they did to you—spitting on you, immobilizing you—that must have been incredibly humiliating for you. A huge blow to your pride and sense of superiority. And don't scowl at me. I know you're scowling. You always have thought of yourself as superior, don't try to deny it. Yet these…these beings…brought you down low. How devastating to your ego that must have been."

He spoke the words simply, plainly. He sounded utterly sympathetic to her cause, not condemning her in the slightest. Gant wasn't sure if Tania was wiping away tears, but she was bringing her arm across her face for some reason. Finally she turned to face him and he was pleased to see that there was no hostility in her eyes. He couldn't remember the last time she had regarded him with anything other than revulsion.

Then she shook her head as if she were a large animal that had gotten wet and was trying to dispatch all the water from its body.

It seemed she was attempting to dispel the thoughts in her brain through physical action. "We aren't going to discuss this," she finally said.

"Fine. We won't." He regarded her thoughtfully. "Why were you out on your own, Tania? Why did you leave the Spires? Why did you leave your friends and family behind?"

She stared at him with astonishment. " You have to ask that? You, of all people?"

"What do you mean me, of all people?"

"They turned on me, Gant. Because of what I did to you. No one understood that you provoked me."

"I did *not* provoke you!" He gestured wildly. "Did you think that I wanted you to transform me into a green mass? That I had any desire to try and live my so-called life in that form? As I said earlier, I thought you didn't want to be with me anymore!"

"And so you took up with my sister?!"

"She reminded me of you!"

Tania was about to tear into him once more but then, to his surprise, she actually laughed. It was an amazingly lilting noise and reminded him of the beautiful Phey woman that he had loved before she had changed him. "Of me."

"Of course of you. She's your sister, for gods' sake."

"And did you ever tell her that?"

"Certainly not. No woman would want to think that you started a relationship with her out of a sense of nostalgia."

"Yes, I suppose that's true." She shook her head. "I have no idea what to say right now. Plus I find it hard to look at you while you're in that…that thing."

"Fine. Change me back."

"It isn't that simple."

"Why isn't it that simple?"

"I would need ingredients that I don't have, including things that don't even exist in this dimension."

"Wonderful," grumbled Gant.

At that moment, the door was yanked open and Trott was standing there. As typical for the usually silent Phey, he didn't speak but instead simply gestured that they should follow him. Tania and Gant exchanged uncomprehending shrugs and then followed Trott out into the main camp area. Graves was standing there waiting for them. "We're leaving," he said.

There were Whoresmen and Serpenteens sitting or standing around in various forms of leisure, but Graves' words immediately stirred them to action. They started to converge on Graves, but Graves did not seem especially perturbed at their aggressive nature. Trott was a short distance away, stroking the head of his draquon, keeping the creature calm. Gant caught Graves' eye and Graves simply nodded as if everything was under control.

When Graves spoke, it was to the entirety of the camp. "You wish to know about Phey magiks. Is that correct, Chyron?"

Chyron was standing off to the side, and he nodded. "Yes. It is. Do you intend to teach us some magiks now?"

"I intend to provide something of an education," said Graves. "The thing that you need to understand about so-called Phey magiks is that there are things in the world which we understand and you do not. As a result, we are able to use these things to our advantage. In that way, we are able to overcome our foes. I will give you an example, if you are interested."

"Very much so," said Nessa. Chyron and the others nodded in agreement.

"I want you to consider the draquons, our faithful beasts. They are more than just our mounts. They are our protectors."

"They didn't do much of a job of protecting you from us," one of the Serpenteens said smugly.

Graves studied the Serpenteen. "Do me a favor," he said. "Take a few steps forward."

The Serpenteen clearly didn't understand why Graves was asking him to do so, but he did indeed move forward several paces to accommodate him.

"The reason they were unable to protect us from you," Graves said to the Serpenteen as if he were answering a question, "was because of that paralysis venom of yours. The draquons were never exposed to it before. Here's the thing about draquons, though: once something has been used against them in that manner, they generate a resistance to it. And not just one of them: all of them."

A darkness moved from the shadows and Gant's draquon slowly slithered into sight. If it was possible to discern intent in the eyes of such a beast, then it was evident to anyone who was looking at it that it was incredibly pissed off and seeking some degree of vengeance against the creature that had paralyzed it.

"Go ahead," said Graves. "Try and stop it."

A sudden look of concern crossed the Serpenteen's face as the draquon very deliberately advanced on it. Quickly one of the snakes atop his head spat a wad of his toxin. It sailed through the air and struck the draquon squarely on the forehead.

The great beast snarled.

"Kill him," said Graves calmly.

With a roar of fury, the draquon unleashed a blast of flame that enveloped the Serpenteen. He let out an alarmed shriek as he erupted, and despite the scales on his skin, it did nothing to prevent the fire from searing him alive. He threw himself to the ground, rolling around frantically to try and snuff out the flames, but it didn't work. It was as if the fire had taken on a life of its own as it consumed him eagerly, like a creature devouring its prey.

The draquon didn't even slow. It roared once more and a huge jet of flame ripped from its maw as it swept the entirety of the encampment. The Whoresmen and the Serpenteens scattered in the face of the assault.

The other two draquons immediately joined in and now there was fire everywhere. The trees caught and started burning furiously. The air was thick with black smoke that curled lazily into the night sky.

"*Mount up!*" shouted Graves, and immediately the Phey clambered onto the backs of their mounts. Gant charged forward, hauling Tania along, and he leaped onto the back of the beast, yanking her on behind him. He hoped that her additional weight would not prove daunting to the beast, but the draquon didn't even seem to notice the presence of the additional rider.

And suddenly Chyron was directly in their path, and he had a long bow in his hand and an arrow nocked and drawn. He didn't even bother to issue a warning but instead fired an arrow directly at Graves.

Graves caught it.

It happened so quickly that Gant could scarcely follow it. One instant the arrow was in the bow, the next it was flying, and then Graves was holding it calmly in his hand, the feathered end still quivering slightly. Without a hint of hesitation, Graves reversed it and flung it at Chyron even as the Whoresman endeavored to prepare another arrow for flight. It thudded into Chyron's left shoulder. The Whoresman let out a strangled scream of pain and the arrow that he had been attempting to nock into his bow fell from his fingers, clattering to the ground.

"*Yaaah!*" Graves shouted and his draquon charged forward, the other two following suit. The Whoresmen and Serpenteens were so busy running around in confusion, trying to find something, anything that would stem the flames, that no one else tried to intercept their path. They galloped away, leaving the flaming camp alive with commotion.

Long minutes they galloped through the forest and then they burst out of it onto the paved road. Once they were on the smoother surface, the draquons were able to increase their speed, alternating between galloping and gliding. For a time they did nothing but continue on their expedited path down the road until finally Graves slowed his draquon and raised a fist to indicate they should follow suit. They did so and then Graves turned to Trott. "Check," he said.

Trott had been crouched low on the back of his draquon, but now he pulled himself fully upright. He closed his eyes and scented the air. The others simply sat and watched until finally Trott opened his eyes and said, "Nothing. We're not being pursued."

"You're sure?" asked Graves.

Trott nodded. "I'm not sensing any vibrations."

"Could they follow us without vibrations?" asked Tania.

"If they are pursuing us very slowly, yes," Graves told her. "But it is very unlikely that they would do that. No, the chances are that they are busy trying to stop their forest from burning down, so they have matters of far greater priority than trying to continue after us."

"Good," said Gant. "Then let's go."

"Where are we going?" said Tania. "The Spires are that way," and she pointed behind them.

"That is true. But Dizz is that way," said Graves, pointing down the road.

"Dizz?" Tania raised her eyebrows quizzically. "Why would you—?" But then her voice tapered off as she understood. "Because the Overseer is dead but the world is still here, and you want to ask Obertan for guidance."

"Exactly right," said Graves. "So you have a choice. You can come with us, or you can depart us here and go off on your business."

She made a face of impatient annoyance. "Right, absolutely. I would love to set off on my own so I can be recaptured by Whoresmen or Serpenteens."

"So you're coming with us, then?" said Gant.

"Yes, I'm coming with you."

"Do you wish to switch mounts?" said Graves. "Ride with Trott or myself, in order to distance yourself from Gant?"

Tania stared at Gant for a long moment and then said, with a shrug of forced indifference, "It does not matter to me. I can stay here. If that is acceptable to Gant."

Gant's voice caught for half a heartbeat in his throat and then he loudly cleared it. "I have no objection to that," he said.

II.

"YOU ARE AN IDIOT!" NESSA said angrily, and to underscore just how irritated she was with her mate, she punched him in his injured shoulder.

Chyron tried not to let out a yell in order to underscore that he was not remotely pained by the blow. Unfortunately he failed spectacularly and instead cried out from the impact, and then snarled, "*Bitch!*"

The Whoresmen and Serpenteens were frantically trying to halt the burning before it destroyed the entirety of the woods. Their storage of potable water was rapidly being depleted as they threw it upon the larger burning areas to try and bring it under control. The Whoresmen were also kicking up large chunks of dirt from the ground and were hurling it in clouds against the swells of flame, serving to smother it. Chyron, meantime, had been endeavoring to bandage the wound on his shoulder, but it wasn't being helped by Nessa's having struck it in anger.

"How could you have let him wound you like this?" she said furiously.

"It wasn't my idea! How was I supposed to know he would catch the damned missile and throw it back at me? How could anyone know that? Who does such a thing?"

"The Phey do. You should have known that!" Her body was almost trembling in ire. "Letting them escape was an idiotic move!"

"It was the perfect move! They were heading away from the Spires when we captured them. So it is obvious that they are not returning home. Therefore we want to see where they are going. It is entirely possible there is another enclave of Phey out there to which they can bring us. Stethno!"

The name he shouted brought one of the Serpenteens forward. He was covered in black ash and looked extremely unhappy with the way that matters were progressing at the moment. "What would you?" he said impatiently.

"Stethno," Chyron said to Nessa, "is the best tracker we have.

He will be able to track the Phey no matter how far they go. We will let them get what they will no doubt consider a sufficiently safe distance so that they can be confident that they have escaped, and then Stethno will lead us in pursuit of them."

"To where? Another Phey stronghold? And what will we do once we are there?"

"We will attack them," said Chyron confidently. "We will see just how well they defend themselves when we strike from hiding. So the Phey caught one arrow. Let them try to catch a thousand arrows raining down from on high. We will destroy them, Nessa," and he placed his hands on her shoulders and spoke with quiet intensity. "We will destroy them and take their weaponry for ourselves. That will be the fate of the Phey, at the hooves of the Whoresmen."

Nessa's eyes narrowed suspiciously. There was clear worry in her voice. "I don't trust the Phey. They are perfectly capable of coming up with some sort of means of avoiding a plan…"

"Not if they do not know it's coming. And this will be something that even the damnable Phey cannot anticipate." He kissed her lovingly on the forehead. "The Phey will never know that the attack will come until it is far too late to do anything about it. Trust me, my sweet. "

She forced a smile, reached up and stroked the underside of his chin. "I do."

"Then ready the attack party," she said. "Let us go and pursue the Phey."

THE CITY/STATE OF VENETS

{"GORKON IS BACK!" "GORKON IS back!" "Have you heard? Gorkon has returned!" "Is it really him?" "Gorkon has come back to us!"}

{Gorkon is impressed by the reactions of the Markene. The truth is that he had not been certain that they would even remember him. The memories of his people had always been, in the best of cases, fuzzy. That was because of their addiction to the mind-altering substance they called Klaa. Now, however, Klaa no longer exists, and Gorkon was not certain how his people would be able to function with its permanent loss. The answer to his concern appears to be: just fine. Obviously the Klaa did no permanent damage to their brains. That is just the thing that Gorkon had been hoping for.}

{Slowly they approach him from all directions, their flippered feet guiding them with certainty. Gorkon waits for them, politely greeting them as they approach. All of them respect him greatly, for they see him as the great Markene who led them against the oppressive Merk. The Merk, who had been planning to use the Markene as bait to wage war against the Travelers, a war that they neither wanted nor could they have likely won. Gorkon saved them from that endeavor, and the Markene have clearly not forgotten that.}

{It takes long minutes for word to filter through the loosely structured Markene community, but eventually most of them have gathered. They sense that he is there with a purpose; that he has something to say to them. They are eager to hear his words. He finds that very heartening.}

{"My friends," he says, his burbling voice carrying through the depths of the waters, "I have a job for many of you. A job that will challenge your trust in me, for the facts of the matter are this: I do not know what the job entails."}

{This causes a hum of confusion among the Markene. They clearly do not know what to make of this pronouncement. How are they supposed to commit to Gorkon if he is not telling them what he requires of them?}

{Gorkon senses their uncertainty. Indeed, he had expected it. He knows his next words are going to be vital. "The Liwyathan needs our help."}

{Immediately the name of the vast being echoes through the assemblage. The Markene are second to none for their worship of the mighty Liwyathan, oldest of all creatures that walked or swam or flew in the Damned World. It was the Liwyathan who had flooded Venets in their final strike against the city of the Merk. Their respect for him knows no bounds.}

{"The Liwyathan has had a vision. I do not know whence it has come, but when the Liwyathan says something is going to occur, I feel it is my duty to believe him. Furthermore, he says that the Markene will need to help with whatever is going to happen."}

{"Is it a war?" asks one of them. "Will we be required to fight?"]

{"I do not know," Gorkon admits. "The Liwyathan simply says that we are needed. I trust him. The question is: Do you trust him as well?"}

{"Except that is not the question. The question is: Do we trust you?"}

{It is the same Markene who had inquired as to whether fighting would be required. It is a young female Markene, and she clearly regards him with suspicion. "Who are you?" asks Gorkon.}

{"I am Miira." There is an arrogance and challenge in her tone. "And I object to you asking us to follow you without telling us where or what will be expected of us."}

{"I already told you. I do not know."}

{"Yes, you have made that abundantly clear. And yes, we followed you against the Merk. But I do not believe that—"}

{"*Quiet*," rings out a new voice.}

{Gorkon is visibly startled at the voice of the speaker. He recognizes her immediately. It is his mother.}

{"Pendara," he says. The Markene do not typically utilize the terms of "mother" and "father." A name is a name, to be used by any who address each other.}

{"Gorkon," she replies. For ages she had barely acknowledged his presence. Honestly, part of him is surprised that she remembers him at all. She stares at him placidly and then continues in a voice so low that even he has to strain to hear her. "It was you, wasn't it." It is not a question but a statement. But he doesn't understand it, which he makes clear with a quizzical look. When she continues, however, then he comprehends. "You made the Klaa go away."}

{He has no idea what to say. Even worse, he senses what the next question is going to be even before she asks it. But ask it she does.}

{"You are responsible for the death of your father."}

{He desperately wants to lie. It would be so easy to do so. There is nothing that directly connects him to the url that was spread upon the Klaa, obliterating it forever from the Markene. Nor did he force his father to throw himself onto the url in a desperate and ultimately failed attempt to access the Klaa, inadvertently covering himself in it and causing him to smother to death. All he has to do is lie to Pendara. That should be a fairly simple thing for him to do.}

{Indeed, the lie comes to his lips and he is about to speak it, but almost as if it is choosing to do so on its own, the truth emerges instead. "Yes," he says simply. "It was I. I did not foresee my father's death, but other than that, I was responsible for the url. I am very sorry. But I do not regret destroying the Klaa, for it was slowly killing our race. If you wish to turn away from me, I would not blame you."}

{She stares at him as if truly seeing him for the first time. Then, to his astonishment, she shrugs. "We are better off without it. And I am better off without him." Her acceptance of their situation, her matter-of-fact dismissal of her mate, are astounding to Gorkon, but he is hardly in any position to reject it.}

{Without hesitation she turns to the Markene and speaks in a loud, stentorian voice that reverberates through the water. "I believe in my son. He is the greatest of the Markene. The Liwyathan chose him for a reason, and Gorkon chose us for a reason. I say we follow him to the gate of the underworld, if need be, for he is Gorkon."}

{"Gorkon!" calls another, and "Gorkon" a third cries out, until his name is ringing loudly through the area, booming in all directions.}

{Gorkon smiles and nods to his mother in acknowledgment of what she has done. She returns the gesture and reaches out with one of her flippers. He wraps his around hers and they float there, basking in the adulation of the Markene.}

{He wonders if they will all survive whatever is to come.}

PERRIZ

JEPP WAS STUNNED BY THE architecture of the underground tunnels. It was her understanding that they had been designed to transport Mort sewage long ago. She would have thought that, as such, they would mostly just be designed for pure functionality. But the design, the brickwork, the layout of miles upon miles of tunnels that seemed to go on forever…it was staggering. For all the time that she had lived amongst the Twelve races, she had never seen anything designed in such a monumentally amazing way. It made her wonder, not for the first time, how in the world the races had managed to destroy her people so easily. There must have been so many of them, once upon a time. Thousands, maybe hundreds of thousands. Now they were down to a handful. Maybe less. Maybe she, Jepp, was the last of humanity. What a cheerful speculation *that* was. The notion that when she passed away, her kind would be extinct.

Then she forced her mind back to her surroundings. It was wasteful and even self-obsessed to be worrying about her own situation. They were delving deep into Piri territory, and her mind had to be focused.

Norda was leading the attack party, and at that moment she was barely recognizable in her own form. She was on all fours, crawling along on the ground like an animal, her nostril holes flaring as she scented the area, maintaining her trail of Clarinda's scent. Arren was directly behind her, his sword out and in his hand.

Karsen was in front of Jepp, his battle hammer likewise out and ready for potential use. The amusing thing, of course, was that Jepp was actually more formidable in combat situations than was Karsen. It was just that her battle instincts would not trigger unless Karsen himself was in mortal danger. Jepp was actually perfectly fine with that notion. Although she appreciated her usefulness as an object of war, especially in light of where she currently was and what she was expecting to happen, she disliked the notion of being a weapon. She far preferred to make people feel good about themselves to the idea of beating them to bloody pulps. None of that mattered, though. If someone threatened Karsen, she was perfectly sanguine about the idea of tearing them apart. They had it coming. They all had it coming.

"Into the breach of battle we descend," Rafe Kestor was muttering, his tail whipping back and forth. "To rescue the fair Clarinda, we travel deep into the enemy's lair, braving the—"

"Oh gods, shut up, Rafe," Zerena snapped at him. She was looking none too happy to be part of this expedition. In a way, it prompted Jepp to admire her for her determination to remain with Karsen and try to keep him safe.

"I am endeavoring," Rafe said archly, "to compose a ballad to this day."

"Save it. Focus on living through the day," said Zerena. She carried no weapon, but the way her fists were clenching and unclenching, she seemed to be spoiling for a fight. Jepp felt sorry for anyone who dared to cross her path.

The Ocular seemed to be the only ones who were having difficulties with their surroundings. They had to bend over nearly double to deal with the contained area, and several times one of them happened to stand up a bit too tall and bang their heads on the ceilings. They would grunt in pain as pieces of brickwork would fall to dust from the impacts. "I hate this place," growled Turkin.

"Deal with it," snapped back Kerda, clearly having no patience for his complaints, no matter how understandable they might be under the circumstances.

"All of you be quiet," said Arren. "If you have nothing of use to say, then keep it to yourselves. Norda, any idea how far we are?"

"I have no way of knowing," said Norda. "Her scent is growing stronger the further we go, but that gives me no clue as to how much more we must travel to reach her." She paused and blinked thoughtfully. "Should I be concerned about anything else right now?"

"No," Arren said. "Just the scent you're tracing."

"All right," she said with a cheerful tone. turning down a seemingly infinite number of corridors.

The one who was clearly the most concerned was Eutok. He had his battle axe at the ready in the same manner that Karsen and Arren seemed prepared for a fight. But Jepp noticed that he was also mumbling to himself. She could not discern every word he said, but as near as she could determine, he was providing encouragement for himself. Telling himself that he was going to save Clarinda, that she shouldn't be concerned, that he was coming for her. It was as if he were speaking to an invisible version of Clarinda, assuring her that there was nothing to worry about. Help was on the way. Jepp considered that to be somewhat sweet.

They kept moving, following Norda's lead, and then slowly started to become aware of something. Jepp wasn't entirely certain what it was, but she could sense that something was watching them. "Karsen," she said in a low voice, "we are not as alone as we think we are."

"What?" he said.

"We're not alone," she repeated.

"Arren, stop a second!" he called immediately.

Arren immediately did so, whispering to Norda that she should cease moving forward. "What is it?" he said.

"Jepp says we're not as alone as we think we are."

The shadows were thick around them. The only illumination that was being provided was from torches that were situated at long intervals on the walls around them. Jepp couldn't help but think that was fortunate, because without them…

Without them…

"Where did these torches come from?" she asked abruptly. "Why are they here?"

Karsen was about to toss off an easy answer but then seemed to realize that he didn't have one. The others exchanged confused glances as well. They had just accepted the presence of the lighting as a given without thinking to wonder whence it had originated.

It was as if Jepp's senses were expanding moment by moment. The imminent threat of danger, especially danger to Karsen, was rendering her hyper aware of everything that was happening. "We're being watched," she said, "I'm positive of it. I can feel their eyes on us, as if they were crawling on my skin. They're hiding in the shadows. So many shadows…"

"They can't be," said Arren. "Norda would know if there were other scents around us."

"Oh, there are," Norda said immediately. "They're everywhere."

"*What?!* Why didn't you say something?!" cried out Arren.

"You said I shouldn't be concerned about anything except tracking Clarinda," she said, sounding slightly annoyed that she had to point this out.

And with a screech, a Piri dropped down from overhead and landed squarely on Zerena's back.

She let out an alarmed cry and instantly Turkin was there, his huge hand wrapping around the Piri and yanking it clear of her back. He spun and threw it against the wall and it struck with a crunching of bones.

But he was hardly the last of them. Piri were suddenly coming at them from all directions. They were screeching like uncaged animals, their eyes burning with deathly fire, their howls echoing through the bricked sewers stretching in front and behind them.

Eutok's response was to unleash a shout of pure joy, as if thrilled finally to have an enemy in front of him that he could assail. He swung his axe around in a circle, assuming that the Piri would be throwing themselves at him in an attempt to overwhelm him. In that regard, he was absolutely correct. It didn't matter which way he swung his axe, he still came in contact with a Piri. They were not warrior creatures by nature. They had no battle plan, no strategy.

They counted on purely their numbers to overwhelm their prey, and typically this was more than sufficient to serve their needs.

That wasn't getting the job done this time. This time their prey was fighting back, and it seemed that no matter how many Piri assailed them, the Clarinda rescue squad was up to the task of combating them.

Jepp hid behind Karsen, waiting for her battle mechanism to kick in, but it didn't happen. Karsen was more than up to the challenge that was being presented to him. Any Piri who came close was unable to pierce the defensive shield of his war hammer as he swung it viciously back and forth.

Suddenly a Piri leaped in low from the side, striking Karsen in the legs. His knees buckled and Karsen went down. He tried to bring the hammer up and around, but another Piri darted in and knocked it out of his reach.

And Jepp went insane.

With a high-pitched screech, she leaped forward and landed on the back of the Piri that had knocked Karsen down. She slammed her open palms on the Piri's ears, causing a ringing within the creature's head that compelled him to cry out in pain. She threw one arm around his neck, the other around his head, and twisted fiercely. The sharp crack of the Piri's neck reverberated in the enclosed area and she tossed it aside, lunging for the other that was just starting to reach for Karsen's fallen hammer.

The Piri saw her coming, saw what she had done to his fellow, and he required no urging to release his grip on the hammer and back up, never taking his eyes off Jepp. Clearly she intimidated him. Jepp didn't even realize it. Instead she was focused entirely on the Piri who were all around them. Since Karsen had been attacked, she was now in full battle mode.

That was when another Piri burst out of the shadows at a dead run. Mingo saw him coming and endeavored to intercept him, but astoundingly, he was unsuccessful. The Piri was larger than any of the other creatures, much larger, and heavily muscled. He crashed into Mingo, who managed to maintain his footing for only a moment before being knocked backwards off his feet. Mingo slammed into the floor with such force that the tip of his right horn snapped off from the impact. The massive Piri grabbed up Mingo, hissed into his face, and then sank his fangs into Mingo's throat.

"*Mingo!*" shouted Zerena, and then Berola and Kerda were on either side of him, grabbing his arms and yanking him clear of Mingo, who sank to the ground with a moan, clutching at the bleeding punctures in his throat.

"I remember you!" said Berola angrily. "We attacked you in the woods! You barely escaped!"

"I could say the same about you," the Piri snapped back at her, and suddenly he had pulled free of the two of them. The abrupt shift in weight caused them to stumble and they almost fell as their limbs became tangled in each other.

He spun to face them and then let out a startled, infuriated yell that was utterly overwhelmed by a bellowing roar. It was so deafening that it snapped a startled Jepp out of her defensive fugue state as she stared in shock at the roar's origin.

It was Mingo. He was directly behind the Piri and he had driven both of his horns into either side of the Piri's back. Mingo threw back his head and lifted the Piri right off his feet. The other Piri froze, seemingly in shock at this display of strength, as Mingo snapped his horns around and sent the huge Piri flying off to the right. The Piri crashed to the ground with a sickening thud.

Yet clearly the battle wasn't done as the Piri clambered to his feet, ready to charge once more into battle. A thick, black ooze was streaking down his back, but he ignored it. Mingo faced him, stomping his feet repeatedly, gearing up to charge at him.

Before he could move, however, a loud female voice shouted, "*Stop! Everyone just stop!*"

Every individual who had been locked in combat ceased doing so immediately. The Piri withdrew, not so far into the shadows that they became invisible once more, but far enough to indicate that they were going to attend to the order that had been hurled at them.

A tall, female Piri emerged from the far end of the tunnel. She was, to Jepp's utter astonishment, one of the most beautiful creatures that Jepp had ever seen. Her only clothing was some sort of lengthy breechcloth that covered her nether regions. Her long black hair fell over her chest area, but Jepp could see from the way that her hair lay flat against it that she had no breasts. Instead Jepp saw the hints of scars beneath the strands of hair. Jepp couldn't fathom why her breasts had been severed from her chest. Disease, perhaps?

She came to within a short distance from them and swept them slowly with a level, even slightly amused gaze. Then her attention locked in on Eutok and the smile that had teased the edges of her mouth briefly disappeared before being quickly restored, as if she were reminding herself to appear pleased to see them. "You would be the Trull, I assume. Her Trull."

Eutok was cradling his axe in his hand. "And you are her mother."

She bowed slightly. "Sunara Redeye. You have created quite a disturbance in my family. A Trull taking a Piri as a lover. Quite the breaking of rules."

"Love doesn't give a damn about rules," said Eutok. "Let Clarinda go. I will take her far away from here and you will never have to see her again."

"I haven't made up my mind about her yet," Sunara said lazily. "I had been planning to kill her after the birth of her child, but I've been wavering on that. She is my daughter, after all, so perhaps—"

"Wait, wait," said Eutok, confusion on his face. "The birth of what child?" His eyes widened and his temper rose as his rage built. "What did you bastards do to her? Did one of you rape her? Did you hypnotize her into—?!"

Now it was Sunara's turn to look surprised. "You don't know? You don't—?" Then, to Jepp's surprise, Sunara dissolved into laughter. Jepp couldn't imagine what it was that Sunara found so funny that caused her to allow such hilarity to sweep over her. But something had clearly set her off.

"What's so funny?" demanded Eutok. "What is so damned funny?!" His fists were twisting on the handle of his axe. He looked as if he were ready to attack her. Indeed, the overly large Piri who was standing nearby discerned the fury that was building in Eutok's heart and stepped defensively in front of Sunara to anticipate any assault.

Sunara waved the Piri off dismissively even as she managed to regain her control. "You Trulls. You are always so wonderful in providing us amusement."

"Rape is not an amus—"

"It's your child, you idiot."

Several of the group gasped in astonishment. Jepp wasn't sure how to react. She knew that the Twelve races aggressively frowned on interracial relationships. Then again, since she, a Mort, was involved with Karsen, a Laocoon, she didn't feel that she was exactly in a position to render judgment on anyone for committing the same "crime" that she had done. But an interracial relationship creating an offspring? As far as Jepp knew, that was simply unprecedented. She wouldn't even have thought it was possible.

Eutok's mouth moved for several seconds with no words coming out of it. Finally he managed to find his voice. "*My* child? That... that cannot be..."

"Once upon a time, I would have wholly agreed with you," said Sunara. "But it would seem biology had other thoughts on the matter. Your timing is actually rather fortuitous. She is in labor even as we speak."

"*In labor?* How...how is that—?"

"Possible?" Sunara smiled. "The Piri gestation period is quite short. It is how we have managed to remain the most populous race on the Damned World. Actually, in this case, it was a bit longer than usual. I would have to assume that that is due to the Trull influence. Come. Stand aside," and she spoke just a bit louder to prompt the other Piri to move out of the way. Then she extended a hand to Eutok. "Come. No doubt you want to see her."

"This is a trick," growled Eutok. "All of this. It's…"

"A trick? What sort of trick?" Sunara sounded genuinely confused. "Did she trick you into making love to her? Fool you into impregnating her? I suppose it should not surprise me that you would be reluctant to assume your fair share of involvement in this situation. The Trulls hardly excel in taking responsibility for—"

Eutok bellowed out a roar and charged her. Two things stopped him: The oversized Piri who was standing in front of him, and Karsen who was behind him. Karsen was the main actor in the drama, grabbing him by the arms and preventing him from advancing. It was not an easy endeavor because the stout but heavily muscled Eutok was clearly stronger than Karsen. Karsen was nearly yanked off his feet, and indeed would have been had not Mingo stepped in and added his weight to Karsen's. Between the two of them they managed to halt Eutok in his tracks.

"This is helping nothing!" Karsen snarled in his ear. "Not Clarinda, not you, nothing is going to be served if you assault their queen."

"I am not their queen," Sunara promptly corrected him. "Their leader, yes, but the Piri have always disdained titles. 'Mistress' Sunara is more than satisfactory. Now: are you going to accompany us to see your lover, or are you going to remain here?"

"It's a trap," Eutok said suspiciously.

"What sort of trap?" said Arren. "You were prepared to fight your way to her. Here they are offering to bring us there. Pick and choose your battles, Trull. If they do lead us into a snare, we can fight our way out as easily as in. Let us go where they lead us and perhaps we can actually conclude this insanity on a positive note."

Eutok just stood there for a moment and then he nodded curtly.

"Very well. Off we go," said Sunara as cheerfully as if she were taking a group of younglings on an outing. "Bartolemayne, lead the way."

The huge Piri simply grunted. He was clearly not thrilled about the endeavor, but was willing to do as his leader commanded. "This way," he growled and gestured for them to follow him as he headed down a side tunnel. The rest of the crew fell into step behind them.

Rafe Kestor approached Eutok from behind and said in his booming voice, "Why the downturned face, Trull? You are going to see your lady love. That is the purpose of this quest, yes?"

Eutok didn't respond.

Rafe appeared not to notice his silence. Instead, carrying on as if Eutok had replied, he continued, "Smile, Trull! The end of a quest is always to be devoutly wished! The smile of gratitude from your lady as her eyes fall upon your visage, and she congratulates you and even embraces you for accomplishing your—!"

"*Shut up!*" bellowed Eutok. He turned and swung his meaty fist. It slammed into the side of Rafe's head, knocking him backwards, and only his curled tail cushioned him and prevented him from falling over completely.

Once again it was Karsen who interceded, grabbing Eutok's arm by the wrist. "Stop it! You aren't helping!"

Rafe was rubbing his chin. "Do not worry yourself, Karsen. Fortunately, he hits like a Trull. I barely felt the assault."

Karsen released his grip and Eutok pulled away without further comment. The trek continued after that in silence.

Bartolemayne approached a large metal door and gripped the handle on it. He pulled it open and it creaked loudly as he did so. It echoed through the sewers and the sound chilled Jepp deeply. She felt as if they were willingly striding toward their deaths. But it was too late for her to quit this endeavor now. Karsen was going, so she was going, and that was all there was to it. Besides, as much as she hated to admit it to herself, she was curious to meet this Clarinda. What sort of creature must she be to be able to attract a Trull, who were a notoriously hostile and discriminating race?

The door opened onto a narrow metal stairway that led down into darkness. Jepp was worried that perhaps the Piri had staked out the stairway and were going to leap out at them, cloaked in shadow, and drain them all. Yet no assault was forthcoming and one by one they made their way down.

"Through here," Sunara's voice echoed from ahead. There was a tunnel off to the right and they passed into it. As they moved down it, there was a slow, steady moaning ahead of them. It sounded more like chanting, though, than anyone in pain. The closer they got, the louder it was.

"What is that?" asked Evanna.

"The birthing ritual," replied Sunara. "Granted, this child is unnatural. A freak. But it is nevertheless at least partially Piri and so there are certain customs to be followed."

Then they started passing groups of Piri. None of them were so much as glancing at the strangers who had entered their midst. Instead they were, as one, focusing on something in front of them. Jepp was quickly able to make out what it was: a Piri woman, her belly swollen, lying on straw matting upon the ground. She was moaning softly as the other Piri continued to chant. They were saying words but Jepp couldn't understand them. They were not in any language she had ever heard. If they weren't all saying the same thing in unison, she would have thought they were just stringing together nonsense syllables. The area was dimly illuminated by torches that a number of Piri were holding in their hands, swaying back and forth slowly, causing light and shadow to shift continuously.

"Clarinda!" Berola cried out. She started to go forward, but Turkin put a hand on her shoulder and prevented her from doing so. Instead he nodded toward Eutok to indicate that the Trull should be the first one allowed to approach.

Clarinda, gasped and groaned for a prolonged moment and then her head thumped back onto the straw. Then she blinked in the dimness and her eyes fell on Eutok. She cried out his name, stretched out a hand.

He approached her very slowly, moving as if he were some undead being who had just been brought back to life and was taking the first, hesitant steps of his supernatural rebirth. "Clarinda…?" he whispered.

She nodded and, despite her pain, actually forced a smile. "You returned to me…"

"What," and he pointed a trembling finger. "What *is* that? What have you done?"

"We." She continued to stretch out her hand. "We did this. You and I."

"No. No, it's not possible. A Piri and a Trull can't…we can't…"

"We can and we did," she said. "We…" Then her voice cut off as another wave of pain swept through her. She cried out, her hand still outstretched, yet Eutok did nothing to move forward and take it. The wave of pain reached its crest and finally subsided and once more her head slumped back onto the straw. "Eutok…come to me…come…"

Eutok remained exactly where he was, staring at Clarinda as if he had never seen her before.

Clarinda switched her attention to her mother, and she snarled, "What did you do to him? Say to him?!"

It was Karsen who spoke up. "She said nothing. She's…actually been rather polite. I think he is just having problems grasping what he is seeing here."

"We all are," said Mingo.

"I think I have a reasonable grasp of it," Rafe said.

"You cheated on me," Eutok insisted. "That must be it. You had another lover…"

"No, she did not," Sunara said with quiet conviction. "I can smell the baby's scent; I was able to from the beginning. He is a half-breed and one half is Trull. I very much doubt that she copulated with another Trull, so you are most definitely the father. The only question that remains is: what are you going to do about it?"

"Do?"

"The child cannot remain with her. That much is a given. She is to stay with the Piri, and the Piri would never abide such a monstrosity residing with them. But if you are interested, I might be persuaded to allow you to take it with you. I would even provide you with several containers of mother's blood to take with you until it is old enough to feed itself…"

And Eutok let out a horrified howl. *"This is not happening!"*

"Oh, it definitely is," said Sunara. She sounded almost cheerful about it.

"Eutok, get me out of here," said Clarinda. Blood-red tears were streaming down her face. "I don't want to stay here. I want to be with you. Our baby and me. We can be a family. We can—"

For the first time, Eutok actually drew closer to her, his fists shaking. "A family? You, me and that…that obscenity? Are you insane? Are you completely mad? That thing should not exist! *We* cannot exist! I—" He reined himself in for a second and then turned away. "I'm leaving. We're all leaving."

"*No!*" screamed Clarinda. "Help me! Don't go! Don't abandon me! Please—!"

"Karsen," and Jepp pulled on his arm. "Maybe we should…"

"This is Eutok's undertaking,' replied Karsen. "We do as he says."

Eutok pushed past Karsen without even slowing down.

"I am sure you can find your way out," Sunara said, "but nevertheless I will have a squad of Piri escort you to make certain that you do not get lost."

"Come back! Come back!" Clarinda called. "Berola! Help me!"

Berola clearly wanted to do so, but Turkin and Kerda stood on either side of her and Turkin shook his head. "This is wrong," he said in a low voice. "It's against the most fundamental rules of the Twelve. If we help her, we are forever damned." Berola reluctantly nodded and turned away.

Clarinda continued to shriek, and the last person out was Jepp. She stood there and stared at the poor Piri woman, her heart going out to her for her unanswered pleas for help. Ultimately, though, even Jepp walked away, leaving Clarinda to keep screaming for aid until they were far enough away that they could no longer hear her. And even then, her cries continued to echo in Jepp's brain for a long, long time.

THE ARGO

I.

IT HAD TAKEN JASON NEARLY forever to find what he was looking for in storage. Hours of searching through a seemingly endless number of crates, hoping against hope that he would find what he was seeking. The thing that made it so problematic was there had never been any inventory made of personal possessions. Since there were none of what he was looking for as part of the ship's equipment, he had to hope that someone had brought one along on their own initiative. Which didn't seem terribly likely since the ship's computers were able to provide any information that anyone could reasonably require.

Eventually, though, he finally managed to locate one.

It was in the crate of one Bill Tucker, a geneticist from Ames, Iowa, and Jason let out a deep sigh of relief when he finally located it. It was a personal computer. In terms of years since it had been manufactured, it was positively ancient. But considering that manufacturing of them had halted decades earlier, he supposed it would be considered state of the art.

It took him no time at all the locate the power cord and within minutes he had jacked the computer into an outlet. He waited anxiously for it to gain enough power so that he could switch it on. "Be patient, be patient," he muttered to himself until an hour had passed, and then he pressed the "on" button.

Instantly the computer fired up with a soft hum of a few bars of music. He had no idea what the tune was and didn't especially care. All he needed was for the thing to be functional.

The screen flared to life and then asked him for the password.

"*Dammit!*" he snarled, ready to take the thing and smash it against the nearest bulkhead. How the hell was he supposed to know what the damned password was? Should he awaken Taylor and ask him? That was certainly an option, but he wasn't going to enjoy being asked the inevitable questions that would arise from him doing that.

He took a shot at entering some obvious possible passwords. Taylor's name and as many variations as he could come up with. All received negative responses. Then he wracked his brains for the names of famous geneticists but continued to strike out.

Quickly, desperately searching for answers, he started looking through Taylor's belongings, hoping to get some clue as to what the password could possibly be. It certainly appeared that Taylor was something of a hoarder. Granted, there were copious handwritten notes of his research into genetics, but there was also an abundance of personal items. He found an old passport and tried entering Taylor's birthday into it. That also came up empty.

Then he found two pictures. One was Taylor with a pair of children, grinning into camera. A little boy and a little girl. They were in a garden somewhere. The little girl appeared to be around eight or nine years old, and she was wearing a necklace with the name "Isadora" in a delicate scrawl. The boy was a year or two younger and wearing a baseball cap and a demented grin on his face. What was odd was that there were spots on the picture, the nature of which Jason could not determine at first. But then he realized what they were. They were tears.

Then he found another picture and it all became clear. There was the little boy, now several years older, again posing next to his father. This time they were on a beach and the boy already had the beginnings of a sunburn. Of the girl there was no sign.

"She died," Jason whispered, and then he put the computer back on his lap and typed in "Isadora" into the password slot.

The computer immediately flipped to the welcome screen.

Bingo thought Jason and he set to work.

The plan was simple: Use the personal computer to gain access to the ship's mainframe and utilize it to restart the ship's engines.

He worked on it for three hours, coming up with every angle he could think of to tie into the ship's onboard computers. Exactly three hours, as it so happened. And at three hours and one minute, he let out a frustrated roar of fury, lifted the personal computer over his head and smashed it repeatedly against the floor. The first couple of times he just managed to dent it, but eventually the casing busted apart and the computer's works flew everywhere. Not for a moment did he consider what would happen if and when Taylor ever came out of his hibernation and demanded to know who in hell had destroyed his belongings. The notion that Taylor, that any of them, were going to survive this insanity never factored into his considerations.

He lost track of how long he sat on the floor, his head between his hands, grieving over his situation. He wracked his brains, trying to come up with some alternative, and realized that he was never going to discover it down in the tech bay. No, the place to go was the observation deck. It was there that Jason typically took refuge to clear his head and ponder his next move. Granted, he had never been faced with a situation quite like this one. A situation that the entirety of the crew, deep in its slumber, was depending upon him to solve. Nevertheless, the observation deck called to him and so he heeded its summons and headed down to it.

The observation deck was three levels below and on the ship's starboard side. There were comfortable chairs strewn about, bolted to the deck as were all the ship's furniture should there be some sort of turbulence that could cause it to hurtle about and present a danger. They all faced a large bay window that provided observers an excellent view of the depths of space. The view was naturally always shifting as the ship continued in its steady orbit around the Earth.

Of course, with the engines dead, the *Argo* was not going to be able to maintain its circuitous route. It would deteriorate steadily and eventually plummet into the Earth's atmosphere. Its uncontrolled reentry would transform it into a mass of blazing metal that would spiral from the heavens and either break apart or just slam into the ground or, more likely, water, and be crushed upon impact. Unless, of course, Jason could discern another way for this to end.

He walked into the observation deck, wondering if he was doing so for the last time. He dropped into one of the chairs that provided the best view and gazed outward. Jason knew the names of many of the stars that peered steadily at him. There was no twinkling of the stars out in space since there was no atmosphere to cause that effect. He stared at them and thought about the fact that the beams of light he was seeing were many thousands of years old. It was entirely possible that some of the stars did not even exist anymore. Hell, what if none of them existed? What if there had been some great cosmic catastrophe and Earth was in fact the last inhabited planet in the whole of the universe?

"Yeah, that's the way to think," he grumbled.

The more he thought about it, the more he came to a grim but inevitable conclusion: the only individual who could be of any help in this damnable situation was his father. No one knew the ins and outs of the ship the way that Isaac did, and if anyone could possibly figure out some means of accessing the shattered remains of the database, Isaac was definitely the one to accomplish it. The truth was that Jason didn't have the faintest idea if the computer was even functional anymore. It was possible that its inner core was irreparable. After all, the safety mechanisms and back-ups for the system had never been designed to handle a full on assault with an axe. But if anyone could determine if it was still salvageable, and the engines capable of being ordered to reignite, it was Isaac.

Jason detested the idea of seeking him out and asking for his help. After all, Isaac was responsible for this catastrophe in the first place, no matter how much he attempted to blame it on Jason's deceased mother. But with that being the case, was it really reasonable to condemn the man for doing what his disordered brain had commanded him to do? Isaac was clearly not in his right mind. Could Jason really hold him to ask for—?

"Damned right I can," said Jason, but it was as much to convince himself of his right to blame his father as anything else. Considering that the man was around the bend, was it not a far more effective use of Jason's time if he consulted with Isaac on a way to fix what he had done, rather than just focus on the fact that he had done it in the first place?

His mind wandered and he found his thoughts going back to his youth, and the way that Isaac had treated him as a small boy. Whereas Debbie had oftentimes seemed to have little time to pay him any attention, Isaac delighted in bringing the boy on his rounds and teaching him about the intricacies of the ship's systems. Even from a young age, Isaac had taken very seriously the notion that some day the vessel would be Jason's to manage and determined that he would be ready for it when that day came. Plus Isaac always made certain to keep time for leisure activities, running movies featuring stars that were long dead, or playing classical music by ancient composers that nevertheless found ways to speak to him. Many was the time that Jason would sit in the observation deck while musical movements from Gustav Holst's "The Planets" or Wolfgang Amadeus Mozart's Symphony No. 41, "The Jupiter Symphony," would be piped over the public address system. If Mozart or Holst could have had the view that he had, he wondered what masterpieces they might have been inspired to compose.

The hell with it. Maybe Isaac could be of help at that. Jason would have to apologize, of course. You couldn't just belt your father in the jaw and expect to simply walk away from that. He would have to tell his father he was sorry and maybe even cop to the possibility that his mother was still alive. He needed his dad to forgive him his assault so that they could move onto subjects that would be mutually beneficial, such as finding a way to stop the ship from crashing to the Earth.

And then Jason saw something horrific that brought all such speculation to an end.

II.

ISAAC STOOD NEAR THE PORTAL, hesitating for what seemed forever. Most of him had made up his mind, but nevertheless the finality of the decision was causing him to pause in his actions.

Debbie rested her hand on his shoulder from behind. "What's the problem, Isaac?" she said softly.

"It's nothing."

"Oh, it's something. It's most definitely something. Come on, Isaac," she remonstrated him, "we've known each other for so long. You think I can't tell when there's something on your mind? Me, of all people?"

"It's just…I hate abandoning Jason this way."

"Abandoning? Honey, he doesn't love you. He's made that abundantly clear, hasn't he. He hit you, for God's sake."

"He thought I destroyed the engineering computer."

"And nothing you're going to be able to say will possibly convince him otherwise," she said. "You know that as well as I do. He is never going to forgive you. Ultimately, it doesn't matter. Once the ship crashes, he will be with us and we will live on forever as a family."

"So he's going to hate me for eternity."

"No," she said vehemently. "It doesn't work that way. Once you cross over, you come to terms with everything in your life that upset you. You can't help it. Your mind just sort of gets skewed that way. So once he is with us, he will have forgiven you for whatever it is he thinks he's mad at you about."

"Are you sure?" he said uncertainly.

She laughed at the idea. "Of course I'm sure! I'm always sure. So what are you waiting for?"

Once more he hesitated, and when he spoke again, his voice was so soft that Debbie had to strain to hear it. "Will it hurt?" he asked.

"Not at all."

"I won't explode?"

She laughed yet again. "Of course not. Don't you remember anything that they taught you? Your skin will expand, yes, due to ebullism. Gas bubbles will form in you because the boiling point of your body decreases below your normal body temperature. But your skin is much too tough to explode. And yes, that would hurt, but within ten to fifteen seconds you'll be unconscious due to the lack of oxygen, so you won't even feel it. You'll die in your sleep."

"That doesn't sound so bad."

"It's not. Furthermore, it's far more predictable than if you take an overdose of sleeping pills. After all, Jason could find you and pump your stomach, and who needs that aggravation?"

"You're right. You're so right. You're always right." He grinned broadly. "I'm ready."

"Good."

In Isaac's mind's eye, it was Debbie who reached over and punched in the code that caused the inner airlock door to swing open. It was, in fact, his own hand attending to the job, but he didn't see it that way. A light lit up blinking above it to indicate that it was ready to be opened, and Debbie helped him step through, taking care that he didn't trip on the entryway's upright base. Seconds later the door swung shut behind him.

There were all manner of warning signs within the airlock itself, most of them cautioning anyone who had entered to make damned sure that their suit was secure and alerting them of the catastrophic consequences if they failed to heed the admonitions.

Debbie was still behind him, rubbing his shoulders. She always gave the best messages and he relaxed into it.

"Are you ready, dear?" she whispered in his ear.

He nodded and reached up to the keypad, tapping in the same code that he had used to enter the airlock. And just as he tapped the final number, something in his vision shifted and he saw, not Debbie's finger pushing the last digit, but his own. That final sight tripped some sort of switch in his mind, and suddenly the pure insanity of what he was doing flooded through his mind, illuminating it as if it were a bulb that had long been dim but was suddenly filled with blinding light.

He reached for the override button, but it was too late, because the airlock cycled open. The air within rushed out, carrying Isaac with it. He tried instinctively to scream, which as it turned out was the correct move because doing so caused all the oxygen to escape from his lungs. Had he been holding his breath when he was blown out into space, it would have caused his lungs to rupture and set off all manner of unpleasant consequences. As it was, he hurtled out into the depths of space with no air in his lungs. Consequently it meant that he could last up to two minutes in the vacuum, which would have been extremely useful if Jason had been aware of what was happening, throwing on an extravehicular suit to pursue him and had leapt out after him seconds after Isaac had been blown out into space. None of that was going to happen, though, because Jason was in the observation deck, completely unaware of what his father had undertaken.

Isaac hurtled through space, skimming along the outside of the ship, trying to grab at it for no reason that he could readily discern. Whether he was gyrating through the void or clinging onto the *Argo*, neither made the slightest difference in terms of what was going to happen to him. He thrashed his arms, numb to the cold air, and he drifted past the observation deck. Jason was at the window, staring out, and his eyes widened when he saw his father's flailing body. He screamed something but Isaac couldn't hear anything, and Jason slammed his fists on the window as if somehow he could shatter the impregnable barrier between them and come riding to his father's rescue.

I'll be damned, he does love me, thought Isaac, and then the blackness of unconsciousness overwhelmed him and he thought and felt nothing more.

NOWHERE IN PARTICULAR

A NIGHT AND A DAY had passed since the Phey had broken free of their captors and they had continued to ride steadily on their way to Dizz. Conversation between Tania and Gant had been sporadic at best, and when Graves had finally signaled for them to stop and establish an encampment, Gant honestly hadn't been sure how he had felt about the proposition.

Tania was, after all, the one who had gotten him into this ludicrous position in the first place. She had mercilessly transformed him into a shapeless green blob, and the fact that her doing so had effectively alienated her from friends and family only provided him with a small bit of pleasure over contemplating it. So often had he mulled over what he would do to Tania if their paths should ever cross again. Yet now that it had, despite all his desire to perhaps savage her in her slumber courtesy of his Piri fangs, instead he found himself just feeling sorry for her. That was, to put it mildly, a most disconcerting state of affairs.

As the sun crawled below the horizon line, the Phey found an abandoned building off to the side of the road where they believed they could take refuge. The words "Holiday Inn Express" decorated the outside of it, but none of the Phey could have read it, nor would they have understood what it referred to even if they did. There were couches in the main entrance way and that was more than satisfactory for the Phey as they flopped down onto them. The Pheys' endurance was greater than most creatures, but nevertheless they had worn themselves down somewhat in the endless riding and were now eagerly looking forward to getting some rest.

There was no power being generated to the building and so

the main area slowly descended into darkness. Trott, as it turned out, had some glow sticks on him, and he placed the green gems at several points in the large room to provide illumination. Gant was lying down on one couch and he saw that Tania had set herself up on a chair. She seemed quite comfortable in it, sitting upright with her eyes closed and her chest rising and falling slowly. It seemed to Gant as if she were working on shutting her brain down in order to fall asleep.

Yet with her eyes closed, she was able to startle him as she said, "Stop staring at me."

"I wasn't staring," he said immediately as he looked away.

She didn't sound angry. Instead she came across as amused. "I suppose I couldn't blame you if you were. I am quite attractive."

"I guess you are."

"You 'guess?'"

He shrugged. "Well, it has been quite some time since I looked at any female with an eye toward that. Then again, I haven't exactly been in shape to do so."

"I suppose," she said.

"*You* suppose? You're the one who put me into that position in the first place."

"Yes, I am very aware of that. I…"

She stopped, her voice trailing off. He waited for her to continue on her own, but she failed to do so. Instead she sat there, saying nothing, until he could bear the prolonged silence no longer. "You what?" he prompted her impatiently.

"I am…" She seemed to be choking on the words. "I am… sorry…that I did it."

From nearby, Graves—who was overhearing the entire discussion—muttered, "I never thought I would hear her speak *those* words."

"Shut up, Graves," Gant said with a growl.

"Don't silence him," said Tania. "He can say anything he wants. In point of fact, what I did to you…if nothing else, it was beneath me. I allowed my emotions to govern my magiks, and that was wrong of me. No magiks user should allow her heart to guide her. Magiks is far too dangerous a discipline to indulge in if one is not doing so with thoughtfulness and logic. I didn't just betray you. I betrayed the discipline in which I have spent my entire adult life. I—"

Suddenly her breath caught in her throat. Her eyes went wide and her body started to tremble.

Gant was immediately up off the couch, as was Graves. They moved to either side of her, instantly knowing what was wrong with her.

"A vision," Gant said. "They never get easier for her, apparently."

But even as she was reacting as violently as she was, Tania was not the only individual in the large chamber that was clearly upset over something. The three draquons were also clearly stirred up. Graves' draquon was the first to react, but moments later both Gant's and Trott's draquons were likewise clearly stirred up. They had been resting comfortably, enjoying the carpeted floor, but now they were moving around, pacing with great agitation. They were looking at each other nervously and then toward the glass doorway that led into the large room. To Gant's imagination, it seemed as if the shadows outside were now starting to move, as if they were concealing something.

"I do not like this," said Graves. He shook Tania's shoulder. She was staring at nothing, her eyes wide with fear. "Tania! What is it? What's coming?"

Her lips were trembling as she whispered, "It's a queen."

"Queen? What queen?" demanded Graves. "Which queen from...?" Then his voice trailed off as he suddenly understood. "It's a draquon queen."

"A what?" Tania's mind was slowly clearing. She shook her head as if doing so could dispel random, unwanted thoughts from her brain. "What's a draquon queen?"

Graves gaped at her. "You're a Phey. How can you not know?"

"I've never ridden a draquon before I ran into you idiots," she said. "How am I supposed to be familiar with something that I have no personal experience of?"

Graves was clearly about to scold her again, but Gant had no patience for it. He pulled her aside and spoke to her with quick urgency. "We acquire our draquons by invading the nests of the queens. They live out in the wild and we find them and steal their eggs. The draquons are hatched into captivity and raised that way."

"Nice. Very nice," she said sarcastically.

"Don't judge us. It's just the way it's always been done. The problem is that the babes remain connected to queens, even in adulthood. And the queens don't tend to like us very much."

"Of course they don't," Tania said. "You steal their eggs."

"But they remain connected to all their draquons. And when they encounter them, especially when they are in the company of the Phey, they get angry."

"At the draquons?"

"At the Phey."

Graves spoke up, even as he faced the doorway and reached beneath his cloak. "They blame us for enslaving their youth."

"Well, technically they're correct."

"Yes, that's helpful," said Graves. He whipped the blade back and forth and it hissed through the air.

"You have a sword and you didn't use it against the Whoresmen?" Tania said in surprise.

"I wasn't interested in having a huge battle."

"How very restrained of you."

There was a series of loud, angry roars from outside that were drawing nearer. The draquons, in response, huddled together at the far side of the room and audibly whimpered to each other. Tania glanced toward them in annoyance. "They're not going to fight on your behalf?"

"Not if they can help it," said Gant. "Typically when a queen attacks, the draquons try to stay out of her way."

"Wonderful."

"Don't criticize my draquon," Trott warned her. He was standing several feet away from them and he had likewise drawn a sword. Gant wondered how in the world Graves and Trott had managed to carry the things without giving the slightest indication that they were armed. He decided not to ask.

The glass doors shook. Gant had taken up a position in front of Tania, instinctively blocking her from the direct path of the queen.

Suddenly there was a blast of fire that, astoundingly, was deep blue. The door melted and a large, dark form appeared in the doorway. It was definitely a draquon, but it was much larger than any of the others. Its eyes were a gleaming red and it slowly surveyed the room, growling deep in its massive throat.

"Get ready," Graves said in a low voice.

"For what?" said Gant.

"To move."

"Which way?"

"Either way."

Gant didn't have the opportunity to inquire any further as to exactly what Graves meant, because it immediately became clear. The queen opened her mouth wide and another huge blast of flame erupted from it.

Gant felt no heat from it. Instead it was very cold. Its power came from the force with which it was being emitted. If it had struck him, it wouldn't have burned him, but it would very likely have shattered every bone in his body. As it happened, though, he had attended to Graves' instructions, and so it was that even as the flame ripped through the air, Gant lunged to the right, shoving Tania along with him so that they both hit the floor, clear of the blast. Graves, by contrast, leaped to the left, and so both of them were able to avoid the flame's destruction.

"She needs to recharge!" shouted Graves the instant the flame dissipated. *"Attack now!"*

Even as he spoke, he came at her with his sword. Trott shoved Gant out of the way and moved in from the other direction. The queen backed up, snarling, and the blade of Graves' sword glanced off the creature's right flank. It inflicted no visible damage whatsoever, although the creature let out an angry roar. It might well have been that its dignity was injured by the Phey attempting to assault it. Trott leaped forward, disdaining to slash at it but instead stabbing forward, driving the point right at it.

The sword snapped. The blade simply broke in half, leaving Trott with an impotent half of the weapon in his hand. Trott actually gasped aloud in shock, evincing emotion for the first time that Gant could recall since he had met him.

The queen roared once more and leaped right at Trott. Trott barely managed to vault out of the way, but the queen whipped her tail around and it slammed into Trott broadside. The Phey was sent flying, banging into a couch and knocking it over.

Graves once more leaped forward, quickly shifting his attack. Instead of settling for aiming at the creature's overly large body, he chose to assail the queen's face. His plan was clear: try to blind the beast and thus gain an advantage. If the beast couldn't see, the Phey would clearly have the upper hand.

The queen instantly realized what he was trying to do. It whipped its head back and forth, keeping its face out of his way, and it kept roaring in protest at his attack.

Gant, for his part, did nothing except keep Tania back. If he'd had some manner of weapon…

Then he realized that he did. He wasn't a Phey. He was a Piri, and within him he could sense the personality of the creature that he had taken over desperate to leap to the attack. The Piri saw a massive meal and was eager to chow down.

Gant released his control on the Piri's personality enough to tap into its bloodlust, and even as the queen backed up, Gant took two steps and then leaped onto the queen's back.

The queen let out an alarmed shriek, and Gant brought his fangs down onto the creature's neck. He did so with all the violence and strength at his command.

It didn't work. Instead the tips of his fangs snapped off as he brought his teeth down against the queen's hide. It was only at that point that he remembered its skin had effortlessly thwarted a sword being thrust into it, and he suddenly realized he was in deep trouble.

The queen threw itself onto its back, its full weight slamming down onto Gant. He grunted from the impact and then the queen kept rolling, scrambling back to its feet. It opened its mouth and before Gant could get out of its way, it unleashed another blast of flame.

It struck Gant directly and the only thing that saved him was the fact that he was lying on the ground. So all the flame did was send him skidding across the floor at a high velocity, putting distance between him and the queen. He slammed into a wall on the far side and his head spun dizzily. It occurred to him that maybe he'd have been smarter to emerge from the Piri and take the creature on in his green gelatinous form, but just as quickly he discarded the idea. If he did that, the Piri would doubtless escape during the battle and it was doubtful that they would be able to retrieve him.

Graves and Trott were circling the queen, trying to find an opening that they could use to assail her, and then to his shock, Gant spotted Tania moving toward the queen. "Tania!" he shouted. "*Get back!*"

She ignored him. Instead, as if she were casually striding through a garden and studying the foliage, she walked toward the queen, her face calm. She was whispering something in what sounded like a comforting tone, and she was swaying slightly back and forth. Her hands remained relaxed at her side. She was displaying no aggression at all, and that alone seemed to capture the queen's attention.

"Get back!" Gant repeated, this time dropping his voice to a harsh whisper. Tania continued to pay him no mind. Instead she drew to within several feet of the queen and then stopped. She had a soft smile on her face.

"It's all right," she said, still moving from side to side. The queen was noticing it and, to Gant's surprise, began to match it. It was as if she was hypnotizing it. "Everything is going to be okay. You can calm down. There is no need to attack or fight here."

The three draquons who had been cowering over in the corner tilted their heads in curiosity, sensing that something in the dynamic of the room was changing.

Very slowly and delicately, Tania stretched out her hand and cupped the underside of the queen's chin. To Gant's astonishment, the queen had ceased its roaring and even its growling. Instead now it emitted a soft trilling noise, as if endeavoring to communicate directly with Tania. For her part, Tania continued to speak to her. "I know you are angry," she said. "I know that you feel your offspring are being ill-used. And perhaps there is some validity to your anger. But the facts are these: this is the only life that these draquons know. They are accustomed to it and they fear you. Meanwhile their riders treat them with love and respect. You are doing nothing here except terrifying the very beings that you want to aid. Please: leave here. Leave knowing that your offspring are in safe hands and that there is nothing for you to accomplish."

The queen inhaled deeply and let out a final, low sigh. Then it grunted once as if acknowledging the truth and reasonableness of all that Tania had said. With an indifferent twist of its head, the queen rose to its feet, turned away from all of them, and walked out of the large room. Its tail swept side-to-side as if it were cleaning up after itself, and seconds later it was gone.

For long moments the Phey continued to stare at the door, as if suspecting that this was all some trick and the queen was suddenly going to charge back in and attempt to assail them once more. Such, however, was obviously not the case, which was especially discernible because the three draquons promptly settled down and began to drift to sleep.

"You did it," said Gant.

She shrugged. "Of course I did."

"How?" asked Graves. "Do you speak the draquon language?"

"Did I *sound* like I was speaking a different language?"

Trott walked forward and stared at her as if trying to gaze into her soul. "You empathized with it."

"Stop calling her 'it.' She is a she. And yes, I was able to empathize with her." She smiled. "Empathy can be the greatest weapon in the world if you use it properly. Yet it has become something of a lost art to the Phey ever since we landed on the Damned World. But to those of us who remember it, it can be quite potent."

"Obviously," said Graves. He glanced over at the slumbering draquons. "I suggest we follow the leads of our mounts and get some sleep."

The others nodded and moments later they had righted the couches and were stretched out on them. Gant watched as Tania headed over to her chair and he rested a hand on her shoulder. She looked at him quizzically. "You can stretch out on the couch if you prefer."

"No, the chair will suffice." She started to move toward it but his hand on her shoulder held her in place. She turned back to him and stared in confusion. "What?"

"With your empathy, you can sense what someone or something else feels?"

"If I am inclined to do so, yes."

He paused, licked his lips briefly, and then asked, "When you transformed me…did you feel what I felt?"

Tania hesitated and then said, "Yes. And it was the most devastating sensation I had ever experienced. The moment I performed the act, the moment I made you into what you were, I knew I had done the wrong thing. That no matter how much you might have betrayed me, no one deserved to suffer the way that you did. The change was unworthy of me."

He released his grip on his shoulder and they stared at each other for a time.

Then she said, "You know what? I'm going to take you up on your offer. Good night, Gant."

"Good night, Tania."

She moved past him and draped herself on the couch. Amazingly, within seconds she was asleep. He was still standing there staring at her and she was already deep in slumber.

"Women," he muttered and headed toward the chair in hopes that he would be able to follow suit and sleep as well. He wasn't counting on it. Yet astoundingly he was soon asleep.

The rest of the night passed uneventfully, as they slept unaware that the Whoresmen and Serpenteens were closing in.

PERRIZ

I.

CLARINDA LAY UPON HER STRAW mat and stared at the rocky ceiling above her. The terrible pain of the birthing had passed and was already receding into her memory. For a long moment after the child's birth there had been silence and she had thought that perhaps, mercifully, it was stillborn. But then there was a long, pronounced wail that indicated the damned thing was still alive. She never even had a chance to see it before it had been whisked away.

She assumed that it was dead.

She wondered why she felt nothing.

Was it because she did not love it? How was one supposed to love such a thing, anyway? She had never seen it. Instead it had simply bounced around inside her gut, occasionally ricocheting off her internal organs. Truthfully, it had really been nothing more than a very lively tumor. Loving it seemed an impossibility.

And worse, it had cost her Eutok.

She had wanted to be angry, so angry with him. It was clear that he had intended to mount some manner of rescue mission, but once he had been confronted with her—once he had seen for himself her distended belly and learned there was a creature growing inside her—then he had fled the scene. He had wanted nothing to do with her. Indeed, he was repulsed by her.

Her first reaction had been to feel overwhelmed by the unfairness of it all. She knew for a fact that he had been the one who placed the seed in her belly. There had been no one else for her. So unless the gods had decided to impregnate her, she was certain that Eutok was the father. How dare he reject her for something that he himself had done to her. Perhaps it should indeed not have been possible.

Nevertheless he had done it and it was up to him to answer for it.

Wasn't it?

But as time had passed and her heated emotions had cooled, and as she had become distracted by other demands her body was placing on her, she had come to realize that he had every right to be repulsed by her. The creature in her belly had been an abomination. Eutok was within his rights to want to have nothing to do with it, or her. That was what her calm, considered conscience told her.

And now she knew that she was never going to see him again. Certainly he would never want to have sex with her any more, knowing that their copulation could result in yet another monstrosity. Clarinda had no idea how to feel about that. Against all odds, she had fallen in love with a Trull, and now she had no idea what to do with her emotions. Should she hate him now? How could she hate him when she didn't blame him for abandoning her…?

Yes, you do. You blame him. You hate him, despise him. How could he have done that? How could he have returned to you, given you hope for an escape from your mother, and then turned around and left you behind? Accuse you of being unfaithful? How could that bastard have treated you so?

She closed her eyes as if she could shut them against the emotions that rampaged through her own mind. She knew she should not feel this way against him, and yet she did. He knew how much she detested her mother, and yet he had left her to the bitch. If he had loved her, he could never have done that. Obviously he did not know what love was.

Clarinda heard a movement at the entrance to the area of the sewers where her mother had left her. She didn't know who or what it was, nor did she care.

"Good day, my dear."

Clarinda rolled her eyes. It figured. She said nothing in response to her mother. What was there *to* say?

Actually, there was one thing.

"Are you going to kill me now?" There was no tone or inflection in her voice. It was just a simple question and the truth was that she had little to no interest in the answer.

When no response immediately came to her, she turned her gaze to her mother and gasped when she saw her.

Sunara was standing in the entranceway, holding a small bundle wrapped in a blanket. There was peace on her face. For a heartbeat, Clarinda wondered if her mother was bringing her her child's corpse just to further torment her, and then she heard a soft, gentle coo from the infant. Sunara slowly walked toward her, cradling the infant and even bouncing it gently. "He just fell asleep," said Clarinda. "He had his first meal."

"His first...?"

"He has fangs. The fangs of a Piri, but the skin tone and the hair of a Trull. Whether he would grow to become as tall as one of us or be a runt like his father, I couldn't begin to guess. But I thought you might want to see him."

"What did he feed on?"

"Me," said Sunara. She pointed at two tiny pinpricks at the base of her throat. "No doubt he gorged himself, but I was scarcely aware of how much he drank." She paused and then said, "Would you like to hold him?"

The question "Why?" immediately leaped into her mind, plus a dozen other questions besides. But she uttered none of them. Instead all she did was nod and stretch out her arms. She sat up as Sunara approached her. She had been nude when she delivered the child, but now she had donned a simple white shift that covered her down to her knees. Sunara crouched to the level of her daughter and extended the small bundle, and Clarinda took him into her arms. Until the moment she touched him, part of her was convinced that this was all some horrific joke on Sunara's part. That she had already killed the child, had made the small sounds herself so that Clarinda would think the infant was still alive, and was handing her a corpse. But no. The child's body was warm and he was gently breathing, his chest slowly rising and falling in a steady motion.

Sunara had been correct in her description. Two remarkably tiny fangs protruded from its otherwise toothless gums. They peeked over the baby's lower lip. He had no talons or claws, and his skin was indeed darker than that of a Piri, although still paler than someone who lived above ground. Piri children were typically born bald, but this baby had a thick head of brown hair adorning his head.

"What are you going to name him?" asked Sunara.

Clarinda could scarcely believe the question. Could it be possible? Had Sunara changed her mind? Was she going to allow Clarinda's baby and Clarinda herself to live?

She realized she didn't have the faintest idea what to call him. She had become so disconnected from the child growing in her body that she had not thought of him as a person at all. "Why are you asking?" she said.

"Because as you well know, names have power. In this case, it has the power to connect a mother to her infant. That will be important when you kill him."

The words seemed to freeze in the air. The baby gasped softly in his sleep because Clarinda's arms tightened around him. "I...what?"

Sunara strolled in leisurely fashion around the room, as if she were engaged in a casual discussion about the weather. "I have been thinking it over. A good deal has been said and done since the Trull entered your life and you, in some fit of dementia, allowed him to engage in sexual conduct with you. I believe that it is my obligation to be as magnanimous as possible when it comes to dealing with your lapses in judgment. So having given the matter much thought, I have come to this resolution. If you drain your child's blood, then I will spare your life and restore you to your rank among the Piri. You will once again be my heir, entitled to all the power and privilege that that entails. Does that not sound fair to you?"

In point of fact, it sounded eminently fair. Yet Clarinda's insides were repulsed by the notion. "But...he's helpless..."

"As are the various animals that we devour to survive. I've never seen you balk at sucking them dry when you were hungry.

Furthermore, I can assure you that you've never eaten anything quite like this. He is a virgin, after all."

"He's a baby!"

"Doesn't matter. Drinking virgin blood…there is nothing like it." She sighed, reliving the sensations of consuming something so rare and intoxicating. "It is an aphrodisiac. After consuming it, you can just lie back and stare at nothing and find the beauty in it all. I am providing you a rare honor, Clarinda. The chance to get back into my good graces while simultaneously drinking the best blood you will ever have. But you are going to have to decide what you want to do. Drink or don't; it's up to you. If you do, then all is forgiven. If you do not, then I will drink the child dry and have you killed afterward. When you get right down to it, it isn't that hard a decision to make."

It really wasn't. Sunara had lain out the options quite plainly. One was homicide, the other was suicide. One choice was no choice. And really, what was this infant to her, anyway? Was he worth her life? Gods knew that she didn't get along with her mother, but was death truly preferable to living with that anger?

She held the baby close, staring down at his tiny throat. She wondered if it was really true about virgin blood having that kind of affect on the drinker. She'd heard tales of it, but had never truly had the opportunity to find out for herself. As she drew his neck toward her fangs, she wondered what it would be like. She wondered…

Without knowing that she was going to do it, she lay the baby down on the straw matting and turned away. "I can't," she whispered. "I can't, I…"

"As you wish," said Sunara. She leaned over, picked up the child, and started to bring him up to her mouth.

"*Wait!*" Clarinda cried out.

Sunara froze with her mouth open, her fangs glistening in the dim lighting around them. "For what?"

"I'll do it." Clarinda tossed aside the sheet that had been covering her and got to her feet. She wavered slightly but then managed to recover rather than fall over. "Give him to me. I'll do it."

Sunara did not hand him back immediately. "His name?" she prompted.

"Eutok," said Clarinda. "I'll name him after his father. No use in wasting a new name on someone who will be dead in a minute anyway."

"That's good thinking, my daughter." Sunara smiled and handed the baby back to Clarinda. Clarinda took the infant into her arms and then looked up at her mother. "I'm sorry," she said quietly. "I am so sorry."

"Your sins are forgiven," said Sunara magnanimously.

"Not for those. For this."

Her right hand flew so fast that Sunara never saw it coming. The claws of her fingernails ripped across Sunara's face, shredding the skin and leaving trails of blood welling up on the left side of her face. Sunara let out an ear-piercing scream and Clarinda lashed out with one foot, striking Sunara right in the gut. Sunara doubled over and Clarinda kicked upward, catching Sunara's chin. Her head snapped back and Sunara went down. She was not, however, unconscious, and she screamed out Clarinda's name in a white-hot fury.

Clarinda vaulted over Sunara's body. Sunara grabbed at her ankle but she just missed and Clarinda sprinted past her and out the entranceway. Little Eutok continued to sleep blissfully in her arms.

She ran down the sewer tunnels, having no idea where she was going or the slightest clue how she was going to get there. She knew there were Piri everywhere who would not hesitate to throw themselves upon her and bring her down. But that didn't matter to her. Even if she died within the next few moments, she would do so knowing that she had fought until her last breath. Because despite her earlier disconnection from the child, she now felt completely bonded with him, as insane as that sounded. She was unsure how one could go from indifference to love in a matter of seconds, but she supposed that was one of the mysteries of motherhood.

A couple of Piri wandered directly into her path and looked at the running female in confusion. She didn't slow but instead ran right through them, shoving them aside and plowing past. They let out startled yelps which were then transformed into angry roars, and over their shouts came the bellowed order of Sunara: "Stop her! *Stop her!*"

She kept running, her bare feet splashing along some water that was trickling on the ground.

The baby was starting to stir in her arms, his voice crying out in confusion. He had been napping quite soundly and clearly wasn't thrilled with this business of being jostled around by a running mother. She was already holding him as tightly as she could and had no means of calming him down, short of coming to a halt, taking a seat, and rocking back and forth while singing him a song. That was not really an option at that moment.

She turned a corner and banged head on into a huge obstruction. She stumbled backwards and fell to the ground, taking care even as she did so to cushion the child and protect him from harm. She looked up in confusion and then saw what it was that had blocked her path.

It was Bartolemayne. He stood over her, glowering at her. There were several Piri surrounding him, giggling and cavorting over the sight of Clarinda's direct impact into the unmoving behemoth.

"Where do you think you're going?" he rumbled.

She scrambled to her feet, still clutching the baby close to her, and she started to back up. Then she heard more Piri closing in behind her. There was nowhere to run.

"I told Sunara you wouldn't have the nerve to do it," Bartolemayne said. "A sneaky little bitch like you couldn't possibly take direct responsibility for her sins."

"Drop dead, Bartolemayne," she snarled, her mouth twisted into a sneer.

"I'm ending this now," said Bartolemayne, and he took two steps toward her as the Piri squealed with glee. He didn't manage the third step, however, because suddenly an explosive roar filled the sewers, causing everything else to plunge into silence. Of even greater significance was the fact that a large, dark splotch had appeared on Bartolemayne's right shoulder. He let out a shocked roar and looked down, not understanding what in the world had just happened. Then his legs buckled and he fell to the floor. Where once the other Piri had been laughing in amusement, now all was silent save for the echoing of the explosion.

Norda Kinklash was standing there, and smoke was wafting from some object that she was holding in her hand. "Well, that worked," she said cheerfully. "I wonder if it will work again." She swung the weapon at one of the Piri and an instant later it made the same deafening noise. It was hard to understand how something that small could be that loud. The Piri's head exploded and it collapsed. She fired again and again and each time another Piri went down, either dead or in far worse shape than it had been.

"*Stop!*" It was Sunara, pushing past the retreating Piri and striding forward to face the young Mandraque. "Stop that this instant!"

"No," replied Norda and she pointed the weapon directly at Sunara and pulled what was obviously the trigger. Rather than another explosion, however, there was instead an impotent click. Norda pulled the trigger several more times but kept being rewarded with absolutely nothing. "Well, *that's* annoying," she said.

Sunara indicated with a gesture that the other Piri should fall back, and naturally they obeyed their mistress. She advanced, her face twisted in a snarl, blood still streaming from the slashes on her left cheek. "You," she said. "I thought you had the intelligence to depart with your friends."

Norda didn't seem to be paying the slightest attention to what she was saying. Instead the Mandraque was staring in confusion at her, as if she couldn't comprehend the words she was speaking. "Something's wrong," she said.

"What's wrong," said Sunara, "is that you're going to—"

"*Shh! Quiet!*" Norda told her. "I've almost got it. Almost got... yes! I see the problem! One half of your face is injured."

Sunara blinked in surprise, clearly not understanding the way

Norda's mind was working. Then she forced a ragged smile. "Yes, that's correct. My daughter did this to me. Do you," she added sarcastically, "have a problem with it?"

"I do," said Norda. "The problem is that it makes your face uneven."

Before Sunara could register her words, Norda spat out a glob of green liquid that sailed through the air and splattered against the right half of Sunara's face. Sunara let out a shriek of agony as it began to eat away at her skin.

Clarinda couldn't believe it as Norda grabbed her by the side of her arm. "That's better. We should go now."

"*Stop those bitches!*" howled Sunara as she grabbed at her face, staggering and almost following.

A swarm of Piri moved around her, coming at them with incredible speed. Worse, there were several Piri ahead of them, cutting off their escape route. Clarinda's heart fell. Norda was formidable, but there was no way they were going to be able to fight their way through this many opponents.

And then, surprisingly, astoundingly, the Piri that were blocking their departure were tumbling forward, bereft of their heads. Directly behind them stood Rafe Kestor, his sword covered in Piri blood. "Go," he said tersely. "I will hold them off."

"What are you doing here?!" said Clarinda.

"Some may believe that allowing a damsel in distress to remain unrescued is a proper way to behave, but we do not," said Kestor. "Get out. Now." He held his sword up defensively as the Piri who were behind them advanced. "*Now!*"

Clarinda needed no further urging as Norda yanked her away. They sprinted down the sewer corridor as Rafe Kestor remained behind to face the oncoming Piri.

II.

THEY SWARMED TOWARD HIM, TRYING to move past him, but he didn't permit it. Instead he bounded from one side to the other, greeting all comers with sweeps of his sword. None managed to get beyond him. Instead he cut them all down, one after the other. Their wounded or dead bodies were piling up on the floor, themselves creating a barrier. The entire time that he battled them, Rafe Kestor cried out in delirious joy, thrilled to be swept up in what he perceived as the greatest battle of his life.

"Come, all of you!" he shouted. "Come meet your deaths, you sewer vermin! Come and be cut down by the greatest warrior in the history of the Mandraques! You thought that you could imprison a woman and get away with it! Never! *Not while Rafe Kestor lives!*"

That was when Sunara moved toward him. The best aspect of the right side of her face was that it made the left side look lovely by comparison. It was covered with massive burns; if it had gone any deeper, parts of her skull would have been peeping through. She was lucky that Norda's aim had been slightly off and it had only been a glancing blow. Had she hit her full on, Sunara would be lying on the floor with half her face completely eaten away.

"Really," she managed to say. It was the only word she could get out because she was in such massive amounts of pain. It was all she could do just to move forward. She stopped, the world swimming around her as she steadied herself, and then her fangs flashed out and she came at him.

Rafe swung his sword and if she had been so much as a second slower, he would have beheaded her. But instead she ducked under the sweep, and before Kestor could swing the sword back, she leaped upon him and sank her fangs into his throat.

There was nothing delicate in the way that she drained him. She had neither the time nor the patience for it. Instead she ripped his throat out with her fangs, caring not for drinking his blood but rather simply desiring to stop his battle against the Piri. In that respect, she was completely effective. Rafe's eyes widened in surprise and he went down. She did not even bother to taste his blood, but simply stepped back from him and gazed down at his dying moments.

Yet when he focused his waning gaze upon her, she saw to her astonishment that there was triumph in his eyes. "You will never win...I have seen it..." he somehow managed to whisper even as his lungs filled with blood. "You...cannot...deny love..."

Then his head slumped to one side and he was gone.

"Watch me deny it," she snarled at him. Then she abruptly became lightheaded, the pain from her wounds slamming through her head as if someone had taken a 2 x 4 and struck her in the back of the skull. She staggered and almost fell. It was Bartolemayne who caught her, saving her from stumbling and helping her right herself. She tried to take a step forward but was unable to do so without nearly collapsing. Only Bartolemayne's strength prevented her from falling once again, and he grunted slightly as he did so thanks to the pain in his shoulder.

"Get them," she said to the other Piri. "Get them and bring them back to me. I will kill them both myself for this."

The Piri almost fell over each other as they sprinted past her to track down her daughter.

Sunara gritted her teeth and whispered to Bartolemayne, "Get me back to my quarters before I faint."

III.

CLARINDA KNEW THAT THE PIRI were gaining. The damned things weighed almost nothing and so could move far faster than she could, considering she was burdened with running as carefully as she could so as not to injure the baby. For a moment she actually considered the notion of dumping it so she could move faster, but as quickly as the idea occurred to her, she dismissed it. This tiny being was hers, and if he was going to die, it was going to be in her arms.

Norda led her unerringly through the sewers. Her sense of direction was apparently infallible. "This way! Hurry!" she said with brisk determination, and Clarinda followed as best she could. The torches flickered, aiding them in their escape.

Then Clarinda's feet went out from under her. A brick was missing in the ground directly in front of her and she never had a chance of seeing it. Her foot went into the hole and she fell, feeling her ankle twist as she went. She lost her grip on the baby and he flew from her arms. Clarinda cried out but Norda was quick. She caught the hurtling infant and held him in her arms, staring down at him in amazement. "He weighs nothing," she breathed in surprise. Their fleeing from the Piri went straight out of her head. Instead she was entranced with the tiny being in her arms.

That was when the sewer behind them filled up with Piri. They had overtaken them and they skidded to a halt, clearly suspecting some sort of trap. They saw Clarinda on the ground, trying to haul herself to her feet, and Norda standing about a yard behind her, holding the baby.

Norda looked up at the Piri and completely forgot that they were being pursued by killers. "Do any of you want to hold him?" she offered. "He smells amazing. Like violets and piss. Which you'd think wouldn't go together, but it really does."

The Piri glanced at each other collectively, and then as one they charged forward.

Clarinda let out a scream of despair, and that was when a massive jet of fire ripped through the air. It blew right over her head and she felt the heat searing her scalp, and then it enveloped the closest Piri. They ignited and shrieked, and then did the exact thing they shouldn't have done: They ran right at their fellows, flailing their arms and only succeeding in igniting others of the Piri.

Clarinda's head snapped around and she saw Evanna, the Firedraque, her mouth still open as she continued to hurl a jet of flame at their pursuers. The Piri who weren't aflame were screaming as loudly as the ones who were, and they stumbled back into the recesses of the sewer tunnels.

Evanna closed her mouth, moved forward quickly and hauled Clarinda to her feet. Clarinda limped instinctively, concerned over having twisted her ankle. "Let's get out of here," said Evanna.

"That other Mandraque—" Clarinda began.

"He's dead," Norda said softly. "He died fighting."

"How do you know…?"

"I wouldn't question her," said Evanna. "Let's get you out of here."

"Where am I supposed to go?" asked Clarinda. "Eutok doesn't want me…"

"That's the next thing we're going to settle. Now hurry up, unless you think you'd fare better with your own people."

Clarinda was quite positive that she most definitely would not fare better with them. Without another word, leaning on Evanna for support, she limped after Norda, who was cradling the child, bouncing it lightly, and mentally wondering if she should eat the infant just to see what it tasted like.

IV.

THE PIRI WERE NOT EXACTLY exceptional when it came to matters of medical care. If one of them was dying, they tended to stay out of his or her way until they passed, and then drank the blood while it was still warm. If one of them was injured, they would steer clear while the hurt member of their tribe either managed to recover on his or her own, or otherwise succumb and once again be drained. It was a fairly simple system and all of them knew where they stood when it came to matters of survival.

Sunara, however, was a different case altogether.

She sat in her quarters and screeched to high heaven as Bartolemayne gently applied salve to the burned side of her face. He had already bathed the part that Clarinda had scratched up and applied bandages to it, but the scorched half was of a far more serious nature. She gripped the arms of her chair to prevent herself from lashing out at Bartolemayne as he tended to her wounds. Every time he touched her it sent more pain through her, and it was all she could do not to lash out at him. She managed to control herself through the long minutes until finally he stepped back, wiping the remaining salve on his chest. "How's that?" he asked.

"It's fine," she said through gritted teeth. It was in fact anything but fine. She had not known agony like this since the day she had mutilated her genitalia and severed her breasts to become the creature she was. But she would be damned if she admitted that to anyone. "Where are they? They should have caught up by now…"

That was the moment that a Piri came stumbling into her chambers. He was, to her shock, sobbing. Then she immediately figured out why. "They got away, didn't they," she said without preamble.

He managed a nod. "There was this Firedraque, and she—"

"I don't care. Be thankful I don't have you killed. Get out." She was about to repeat the order in a louder, angrier voice, but he didn't give her the opportunity because he was already gone. She heard the sounds of his feet scampering away. Scowling, she turned her attention to Bartolemayne. "When night falls, we go after her."

Bartolemayne rubbed the part of his shoulder where that bizarre weapon that the Mandraque female had wounded him. There was a hole both in his front and his back. Whatever it was that she had fired at him had gone clean through him. He was much too tough to admit that he was in pain, and he was doing everything he could to ignore it. "Perhaps we should wait," he suggested. "Give you time to heal…"

"You mean give her time to escape." She had been lying down on her bed, but now she pulled herself to sitting. "Is that what you're suggesting, Bartolemayne. Are you in love with her now?"

"No!"

"Supporting her? Trying to let her get away?"

"*No!*"

"Then don't fight me on this," she said, barely quelling her anger. "We move on her when the sun goes down. And we find her even if we have to kill every creature in Perriz to accomplish it. This ends tonight."

THE VASTLY WATERS

{GORKON HAS NEVER THOUGHT THAT he would become sick of the Markene again. Yet it is starting to become that way again as they continue their long trek through the Vastly Waters.}

{When they were under the influence of the Klaa, their minds were so disconnected from their bodies that he was never able even to engage them in conversation. They would stare at him and through him, off in their own little worlds, enveloped in the drug-induced haze of Klaa. It infuriated him that they so willingly handed control of their minds over to the narcotic, and he had been thrilled when the url had spread its poison on the Klaa and disposed of it. It was possible that it might manage to regrow somehow, but such an event was hundreds of turns into the future and so not of the slightest concern to Gorkon. Of far greater concern now is that his people are dutifully following him on this quest, but they are not especially happy about it. The one who is the least happy is Miira, and hardly any time passes where she does not hesitate to make her lack of enthusiasm known. Furthermore, she is making certain to swim within range of him while she has incessant discussions with other Markene as if she is unaware that he can hear every word she says. Her attitude is seriously annoying him, but he is uncertain what he can do to shut her up. Yell at her? Threaten her? Kill her? All of these strike him as over-the-top responses to someone who is just saying things to annoy him. But what *should* he do, then? That is the question to which he continues to have no answer.}

{"We have been swimming endlessly," Miira says to someone near her. It's not even anyone that Gorkon recognizes, which may well be part of the point. She may be enjoying selecting random

Markene to address because she is fully aware that he can hear her. "I respect the Liwyathan as much as anyone, but why are we following Gorkon? He claims it is the Liwyathan's desire, but none of us have seen him. And considering his size, that is quite an accomplishment. Is it possible that Gorkon has been lying to us all this time?"}

{For some reason, that is the final straw. Gorkon pivots and faces Miira, who comes to a halt in her swimming and looks at him with confusion that he is reasonably sure is feigned. She knows exactly why he has turned to confront her. She arches a brow. "Problem?" she asks.}

{"I am tired of your endless carping," he tells her. "How dare you call me a liar? For what purpose would I be lying to you?"}

{"Is it not obvious?"}

{"No. Explain it to me."}

{"You," she says, her voice laced with contempt, "wish to be our leader. You desire to be needed. So you concoct this elaborate 'quest' to send us on for no reason other than that you get to be the head."}

{The other Markene have slowly come to a halt. They are floating nearby, watching the heated discussion. Gorkon mentally punches himself in the head, because all he has done now is draw closer attention to all the nonsense that Miira is spouting. Why did he confront her? He should have anticipated that any such battle would serve Miira. But why? Why is she doing this? Is it simply because she is that genuinely suspicious? Or does she have another motivation? Ultimately it doesn't matter what her reasons are. He is now in the middle of this battle and he must see it through.}

{"You do not know me. You cannot begin to fathom what goes through my mind. The fact is that I have no interest in leading the Markene. Truthfully, if I never saw any of you again, I would not care. I am indifferent to your fates. The only reason that I returned—"}

{"Was because the Liwyathan told you to, yes, you have made that abundantly clear. And I do not know what the rest of them think," and she gestures widely toward others nearby, "but if you ask me, I think it is insulting."}

{"Insulting? How is it insulting?"}

{"Because," she says with rising anger, "it is abundantly clear that you have your own motivations on bringing us on this waste of time, and you are using the sacred Liwyathan as an excuse in order to do it. It is insulting that you are doing so."}

{He is stunned that she is saying these things. *Insulting? To whom?* None of this was making the slightest bit of sense. "Who am I insulting?"}

{She replies as if the answer should be obvious. "The great Liwyathan, of course. You try to meet your own ends by...by..."}

{Her voice trails off and her eyes widen in shock. The other Markene are reacting in the same manner. Gorkon turns to see what it is that they are staring at and when he does, he actually smiles for the first time in a long while that he can recall.}

{The massive shadow that is approaching them is immediately recognizable. It is the Liwyathan. The vast creature is taking its sweet time in approaching, and its looming presence is able to sink into the minds of the onlookers.}

{As he and Miira had been arguing, he had been watching the Markene assessing what she was saying and clearly trying to decide if there was some validity to her observations. But the arrival of the Liwyathan has quieted all of them. Miira's reaction is the most delightful, although it is hardly unique. As much contempt as she might have and display for Gorkon, her reverence for the Liwyathan is undeniable. She drifts backward and her mouth is moving, but she is producing no words. That's good. A moment where Miira is unable to speak is inherently a good moment.}

{The Liwyathan draws closer and closer. Gorkon maintains his position while the other Markene back up. None of them are looking directly at the Liwyathan now. Instead they have all bowed their heads in respect. Gorkon momentarily wonders if he should do so as well and then immediately dismisses the idea. He is not a worshipper of the Liwyathan. He is an aide, a helper. He is not about to bow down to it.}

{The water bobs fiercely, creating sub-aquatic waves through water displacement. The Markene try to stay in place but they can't help it; they are being pushed backwards by the Liwyathan's approach. As if it senses what he's doing to them, the Liwyathan stops a distance away. His voice echoes in Gorkon's mind: *"Come to me."*}

{"He summons me," Gorkon informs his followers with a hint of imperiousness. "Wait here for me."}

{"Yes, Gorkon," they say as one.}

{He turns his back to them, pausing only long enough to cast a triumphant, sneering glance in Miira's direction. She does not see him because her face is still downcast. He takes pleasure in that.}

{He swims a distance, swims until his people have dwindled to small shapes who are drifting far away. They are so small to him, they look like motes of dust. It is not difficult for him to swim so quickly, because he is being hauled along in the Liwyathan's backwash. He ceases endeavoring to swim and just allows the Liwyathan's movement to continue hauling him along.}

{Eventually the Liwyathan stops his forward motion, and it takes long moments for Gorkon to slow to a halt. Once he does so, he floats in place and waits for the vast beast to address him.}

{*"I do not like your mate. She is abusive."*}

{Gorkon has no idea what he is referring to. "My mate? What mate?"}

{*"The female challenging you. Her opinions irritated me."*}

{"She isn't my mate."}

{*"She will be."*}

{Gorkon has absolutely no idea how to respond to that assertion. The notion that he can put together some sort of relationship with Miira is unthinkable. He does not dare tell the Liwyathan that he is wrong, because, well, he's the Liwyathan. Gorkon has no business challenging anything that he says. So instead he chooses to simply bow his head and reply, "I will endeavor to restrain her in the future."}

{*"That is wise."*}

{For a long moment the Liwyathan says nothing more. Gorkon wonders if he is thinking about something. Contemplating the vastness of Gorkon's thoughts is almost overwhelming to him.}

{Finally he speaks. *"You have brought them."*}

{"Yes. What should I have them do now?"}

{*"Have them wait."*}

{"For what?"}

{*"For when they are needed."*}

{This is not exactly the answer that Gorkon had desired. The vagueness of the Liwyathan's needs, the lack of specifics that he is being presented with, is beginning to frustrate him. He intensely dislikes the notion of having to return to his people with no further knowledge of what is required of him and what he has to ask his people to do. He is extremely reluctant to challenge the Liwyathan on the subject, but having to go back and present no updates as to what is needed...}

{"I require more," he says. He is surprised to hear the words coming out of his mouth. Is he actually going to challenge the oldest creature in the Damned World? Indeed, in the entirety of everything that is known? "My people require more."}

{He wonders if the Liwyathan will be angry. Instead he sounds amused. *"You issue terms?"* he says.}

{"I have obeyed you consistently. Blindly. I have served you well. But that was when I was acting on my own. Now my people have been pulled into it. You asked me to bring them in, and I did. But I need to know what is expected of us. If I am going to be exposing them to any danger. If I am to be their..." His voice trails off for a moment as he seeks the word, and finally musters the courage to say it. "If I am to be their leader, then I have to know what I am leading them into." Then he falls silent and waits for an answer. For all he knows, the answer will be terminal. The Liwyathan may turn around and depart without saying a word to him. For that matter, the Liwyathan may lash out in fury at being questioned. There is no doubt in Gorkon's mind that the creature could dispose of him with a single slam of his gargantuan tail.}

{He seems to wait for an eternity, and then the Liwyathan says something very surprising: *"Open your mind."*}

{Gorkon wants to know why, but he does not inquire. He has no idea how to go about "opening" his mind, but he does his best to obey the instruction. He closes his eyes and lets the wave of the tides cause him to drift. He tries to think about absolutely nothing, but in that respect he utterly fails. All he can think about is his duty to his people, and his determination to live up to their expectations. His thoughts continue to drift, and then he feels, senses something brushing up against his mind. It is as if fingers are reaching in and gently kneading his thoughts.}

{He begins to relax.}

{And then the world explodes within his head.}

{Visions erupt through him and the future, far from being a closed book, is instead open and overwhelming him. Events tumble one over the other, and all the answers that he might seek present themselves to him. He sees what is going to happen, or at least what the Liwyathan believes will happen. He sees what his people are going to be required for. He sees the future, every future, and every possibility that presents itself as something that could occur.}

{*"Do you understand? Are you satisfied?"*}

{Gorkon manages to nod and then says, "Yes. I am satisfied."}

{*"Convince your people of their necessity."*}

{"I will."}

{His audience with the Liwyathan is over. He has seen more than enough. Gorkon quickly swims away from the great beast and hurries over to his people, who are waiting eagerly for him to return so that they learn what they are supposed to do next. He makes his way over to them and at first, once he arrives, he says nothing. Instead Gorkon makes them wait for him to make a pronouncement.}

{Finally it comes. "We are to wait here for the event that the Liwyathan has foreseen. We will wait and we will provide aid."}

{No one says anything at first. Then, naturally—naturally—it is Miira who speaks. "What are we waiting for?"}

{He does not reply. Instead he drifts over toward her until he is mere inches from her face. He gazes squarely into her eyes and is pleased when she drops her gaze, suddenly seeming quite interested in gazing down toward her flippers. "Did you say something?" he asks.}

{Her mouth moves and at first nothing emerges. Then she manages to say, with what seems great effort, "I said...nothing of importance."}

{"Good," he says. "That is wise." Then he raises his voice, addressing the entirety of the Markene. "Does anyone else have nothing of importance that they wish to say to me?" No answers are forthcoming. They are all of them staring downward, none of them wanting to make eye contact. Only one member of the Markene is looking right at him, and that is his mother. A broad grin is across her face. Clearly she approves, and because of that, Gorkon's heart soars with pride. It was not all that long ago that she seemed to have no awareness of his existence at all. Now she is proud of him. He remembers, though, that her pride in him stems entirely from his association with the Liwyathan. But there is no shame in that. The Liwyathan chose him to represent the beast's interest, and he has every right to take pride in that. He is satisfied with his status, and Gorkon nods to her in acknowledgment of how positive she feels toward him.}

{"So we wait," he says, and the words, "So we wait" are echoed by the Markene. It is universal endorsement of his status and their task.}

{Life is good.}

THE ARGO

JASON HAD NO IDEA HOW long he stood there as he watched his father's body spin away into the depths of space. At some point he realized he was no longer standing. Instead his knees had given way and he had sunk to the floor, his gaze still riveted to the outside. His father grew smaller and smaller and eventually his body was indistinguishable from the sea of stars that spread out across the void.

He was alone. Jason was now alone in the *Argo*. The ship's orbit was in the process of disintegrating, he had no way of restarting the engines, and he had just watched his father commit suicide.

"I should have stopped him," Jason muttered to himself. Of course to himself. There was no one else on the ship for him to speak to. There was no reasonable means by which he could have prevented his father from hurling himself into space, but that did not deter him from blaming himself for it.

Had he driven Isaac to destroy himself? He'd struck him, after all. Jason had punched his father in the jaw, knocked him to the ground. What if Isaac had taken that as an indicator that he had lost his son's love and respect once and for all? If he had decided that that was all the proof he needed to hurl himself into the vacuum?

Would he really do that? Was his mental acuity, or lack of such, sufficient to cause him to take such a final, fatal step? Maybe he'd actually been trying to get back at Jason. To effectively say to him, "See what happens when you raise your hand against me? You drive me to end my life, you stupid bastard. Well done."

Or maybe...

Maybe Isaac had hallucinated his wife, Jason's mom, and she had encouraged him to come outside and join him. *Come be with me and we can walk among the stars together.* Could Isaac have been so far gone that he would have attended to the words of a ghost that only he could perceive?

Yes, that made a hell of a lot of sense.

But that left him right where he'd been before. He had no means of accessing the computer. He had no way of restarting the engines. There was no way to keep the *Argo* in space.

So what the hell was he going to do now?

Slowly he got to his feet and he began to walk. He had no clue where he was going to head to or wind up. He just started wandering aimlessly, and as he did so, he began to wonder if perhaps his father had had the right idea. The simple fact was that there was nothing more for him to live for. He was helpless to save the *Argo* from its deteriorating orbit. All that was left for him to do was to remain on the ship and effectively go down with it, as all good captains were supposed to do with their vessels when they met their end. Of course, the logic was that the rest of the crew was supposed to vacate the ship in an endeavor to save their own lives. The captain, the sole symbol of the crew that had once populated it, was supposed to sink along with it. Why? Probably to symbolize his failure to keep it afloat.

So now what? The captain was going down with his ship as was his duty, but so was the rest of the crew. Not that they were aware of it. They were all slumbering, trapped in their somnambulant state, assuming that they would be awakened once the ship landed and the creatures who had taken control of their world had wiped each other out.

Right. Just like all the criminals who were deported to Australia did, he thought grimly. Yes, that plan had certainly worked out perfectly, hadn't it.

What should I do? What the hell should I do? The words kept slamming through his mind as he wandered and wandered until he lost track of how long he had been making his way through the ship. Finally he looked around as if he was waking from a protracted dream, and saw where he had wound up. Despite the upcoming fatality of the situation, he nevertheless smiled and even chuckled slightly.

He was standing in a row of dreamers, directly in front of Medea Nussman's pod.

"Why am I not surprised?" he muttered. Of course he had wound up in front of Medea. Who else but?

The emptiness of his life, as abortive as it was going to be, was arrayed in front of him. For the first time in ages, he actually found himself jealous of his father. Say what one would about him—and considering he had effectively doomed humanity to oblivion, Jason could certainly say quite a lot—at least he had been in love. At least he had had a woman by his side whose life had transformed his own. He had been a loving husband, and that love had in turn produced a son. He had tried to be the best father that he could, and even if he had effectively become insane, wasn't that also as a result of love? He had loved her unto death, and when she had passed, his mind went on the trip with her.

If it hadn't resulted in the end of humankind, it would be kind of sweet.

So despite the madness of his father's passing, Jason still wound up envying him. How screwed up was that? Because his father had had a soul mate, and Jason was going to wind up with nothing except for his endless fantasies about Medea.

Jason dropped to the floor and stared up at the container in which Medea slumbered for pretty much ever. He would never hear her voice, never have the chance to talk with her. Never have the chance to speak words of love to her, and perhaps even have sex with her. He was going to die a goddamned virgin.

And the longer he stared at her, the more he began to wonder just why exactly that was.

He could wake her up.

He was so stunned by the notion that he actually physically reeled from it and had to steady himself lest he fall over. It was, of course, the most obvious answer in the world, and yet it had only just now occurred to him.

Immediately he balked at the idea. These people, these crewmen, were intended to be humanity's last hope. That was what they had signed on for. None of them had expected to be woken up for the purpose of being informed that their lives were going to be ending imminently. It just didn't seem fair somehow. How could he do that to them?

But...then again, didn't they deserve to know what was going to happen to them? Rather than simply dying in their dreamlike state, shouldn't they be able to be aware that they were entering their final moments? Hold hands, kiss, pray to the unhearing God for their salvation? Didn't they deserve to know what was going to happen to them—?

"That's all bullshit," he said, blinking in mild surprise at the harsh language coming from his mouth. Why not, though? He no longer had a father around to scold him for using inappropriate words. He could say whatever he wanted to say, do whatever he wanted to do. He could strip off all his clothing and meet his final moments stark naked if he so chose. No one was around to tell him no.

Because yes, the truth of the matter was that it was indeed all bullshit. He didn't really give much of a damn about the rest of the passengers, beyond his duty to try and care for them and see them through to the successful conclusion of their mission. The only one he cared about was Medea. What he was really trying to do was rationalize reviving her, returning her to life. Telling her how he felt about her, knowing that she wouldn't possibly feel that way in return considering he didn't even exist when she was first placed into suspended animation. That was all that was important to him.

So he could safely put aside all the other considerations and focus on her. Should he awaken her and tell her the fate that awaited her? Or let her die peacefully?

Like this father.

And Jason's heart hardened then. The loneliness of his situation, the fact that his father had effectively abandoned him, all descended upon him. Compassion and concern were replaced with deep, burning rage, and the longer he gazed upon the sleeping Medea, the angrier he became.

Why should she get off? Why should I have to face it all alone? Why should she end her life in peace and happiness and I have to be here to experience it all by my lonesome? His thoughts grew darker. *Stupid bitch. She's probably dreaming about her whole wonderful life with her perfect man while I'm here by myself watching humanity come plunging down from the skies. Screw it. Screw her.*

The irrationality coursed through his brain and he did nothing to stop it. Instead he went to the control devices on her crystal and, with several quick steps, disengaged the sleep status that was keeping her in suspended animation. He stepped back and grinned as he watched the pod start to reverse itself, and as he did so, the rage that had so thoroughly consumed him began to dissipate. The reality of what he had done, the selfishness of the act, overwhelmed him. Quickly he attempted to restart the sleep crystal, but he was unable to do so. It was powering down and did not have the capability of recharging so quickly. He realized it would take at least three hours to get it charged up once more, and that would be of no use to him at all. She would be awake and there was very little likelihood that she would be willing to return to her slumber quite so readily.

Nevertheless, he couldn't help himself. His attention was entirely caught up in watching this woman whom he had been dreaming about for years, slowly returning to consciousness. His hands fell away from the sleep pod's controls and his gaze remained fixed upon her. Despite the fact that he had taken this action purely out of misplaced spite, and should have felt ashamed of himself, instead he was completely into the prospect of finally, *finally,* interacting with the female of his dreams.

Mist swirled around within the sleep pod, moisturizing her skin, while her heartbeat was slowly sped up to the standard resting pulse rate. Very slowly her eyes opened, but at first they were not focused on anything. Instead it was as if she was gazing inward, not yet processing that she was being restored to the land of the living. Her lips parted slightly and mist drifted from between them. She said something, but he couldn't discern what it could have been. *You missed her first words. Nice going. Don't get too worked up about it, though. They were probably something along the lines of, "What the fuck?"*

He remembered belatedly that she was in her underwear. Quickly he went to a nearby supply closet and withdrew a folded up bathrobe, one of the generic ones that had been created for crewmembers. He unfolded it and absently tried to smooth it out. Then he just stood there, unsure of how to proceed. He knew what he was supposed to do technically when awakening one of the passengers, but now all of that information departed his brain and he just stood there and waited.

Endless minutes passed, and then he heard a series of clicks as Medea reached for the unlocking mechanism inside the pod. He realized that he had forgotten to keep breathing and forced himself to inhale deeply. Moments later the door swung open and Medea was standing there, looking around in confusion. Her gaze seemed to drift everywhere before she finally noticed Jason standing there, holding the robe. She was wearing blue panties and a loose fitting undershirt. She didn't seem the least bit perturbed by her relative lack of clothing. She tried to speak but at first nothing emerged from her throat except for a croak. She reached up to rub her eyes but only had the strength to raise her arm partway before it dropped back to her waist as if all muscle strength had left it. The pod was upright and she tried to take a step forward out of it, but she had no more muscle power in her legs than she did her arm. She sagged forward, her legs giving way, and it was only Jason's quick movement that prevented her from falling to the ground. She stumbled into his arms and he supported her, draping the bathrobe over her to cover her semi-nudity. She looked around blankly, clearly trying to wrap herself around what was happening. When she finally managed to speak, her voice was thick with confusion. "Are...are they gone?"

"Are who gone?"

"The monsters. The invaders."

"Oh, right," said Jason, remembering. Naturally she would assume that was the case. For what other reason could she possibly be revived save to be informed that it was safe to return to Earth? "No. Not to my knowledge."

Medea's eyes seemed to focus on him for the first time. She tried once more to stand on her own and failed as her legs wobbled again, but this time there was a bit more strength to them. She still required Jason to support her, but there was some more of her own strength in them this time. "Who are you?" she asked. "I don't know you, do I?"

Only if I somehow managed to invade your dreams in all the years that I was staring at you longingly. That, though, did not seem to be the thing to say, and so he kept that line to himself. "No, you don't. My name is Jason Tanner. I'm..." He paused, trying to figure out the best way to describe himself, and then shrugged. "I'm in charge of the *Argo.*"

"In charge? You mean you're the captain?"

That hardly seemed to be the most appropriate title, but he had to suppose that it was as accurate a description as any. Giving thought to appointing an actual commander had seemed a waste of time considering how hurriedly the entire endeavor had been thrown together, and the fact that with nearly everyone on the ship in suspended animation, there would certainly be no one around to command. Jason's family was simply the maintenance staff. That was all that had been deemed necessary.

But that didn't seem to be the answer to give.

"I would say so, yes," he said, although that didn't exactly sound authoritative. However she was still working on getting her brain to function normally, so she was hardly in a position to take note of the vague indecision in his tone. He straightened her up a bit and said, "Let's get you walking."

"I'm fine, I'm fine," she said hurriedly, and indeed she did seem to be recovering with a good deal of speed. She began to walk forward slowly, and although Jason provided her with some support, she was walking on her own with greater confidence as each moment passed. "How long have I been out, anyway?"

"A long while. Decades," he said. "Take it easy. You have plenty of time to get your legs back."

"I said I'm fine." She was speaking with greater insistence and was now removing her arm from around his shoulders. It was astounding how quickly she had recovered control of her limbs. He envisioned her wrapping those legs around him and then quickly dismissed the notion from his mind. She was hardly going to be in the mood for copulation. Meanwhile she glanced around and saw that everyone else was still in suspended animation. She frowned, running a hand through her askew hair. "Why is everyone else still asleep? Why was I the only one woken up?"

It was a reasonable question and it was one to which he did not have a reasonable answer. What was he supposed to say? *I've fallen in love with you and since we are going to be dying shortly, I thought it would be nice to say good-bye and perhaps have someone to share the ride down.*

His lack of response began to be reflected by the growing concern in her face. "What's wrong?" she said and then her tone of voice sharpened. "Are we being invaded? Do you need me to fight?"

"What? No! God, no. Nothing like that."

"All right," she said, working on keeping her voice flat and even. "There is obviously something going on that you're having trouble discussing. I'd like to say that I'm patient enough to draw it out of you slowly, but I'm really not. Patience has never been my strong suit. So how about I give you five seconds to tell me what's going on, or I beat it out of you. How's that work for you?"

He started to laugh, but then saw the silent expression in her eyes and realized that she was one hundred percent serious. Her hands were already curling into fists and he suddenly knew that she was unquestionably going to start pounding on him. Considering that she was half an inch taller than he was and that her bare forearms seemed quite well muscled, there was no doubt in his mind that she could probably wail the tar out of him. He'd never been in a fight in his life, and he certainly wasn't going to get into a slugging match with the woman that he had secretly worshipped for as far back as he could remember.

"My father went insane," he said quickly. "So insane that he shut down the engines and destroyed all the computer links so that I can't access it, and then he threw himself into space. Not too long from now, the ship's decaying orbit is going to send us plummeting to Earth and we're all going to die, so I arbitrarily brought you back to life so that I would have company for the ride down."

She stared at him, blinking several times. She had actually cocked her fist in preparation for delivering a beat down, but his hurried explanation froze her and instead she just kept looking at him as if she expected him to sprout a third eye or perform some similar physical marvel. "Are you serious?" she finally asked.

"Well, I hardly think I'd make something like that up."

"No, no, of course you wouldn't." She absently drew the robe tighter around herself, considering the hurried explanation that he'd provided. "That was a pretty selfish thing of you to do, you know. I mean, you could've just let me die in peace."

"Yeah, it was pretty selfish." *Now ask me why I picked you,* he mentally urged her. Because he knew that once she asked, he would provide the real explanation. He would divulge his feelings to her, and the chances were huge that she would stare at him with incredulity, or dismiss him out of hand, or perhaps even yell at him in a white fury because he had reduced her to some sort of object of adoration. But he felt as if he couldn't say anything until she asked. He couldn't volunteer the information, only provide it as a response to a question.

A question that she didn't ask. Instead she stood there and stroked her chin thoughtfully, as if they were on Earth discussing the weather and she was speculating as to whether a storm was going to come rolling in. (He had heard that storms could be quite formidable; since he had spent the entirety of his life within the confines of a satellite, naturally he had no idea what it was like to experience one first hand.)

"Where are the lifeboats?" she asked.

He stared at her. "The what?"

"The lifeboats. The escape pods. Whatever was built into this thing for us to climb into and escape from the ship in the event that it started to fall out of the sky, which is—let's face it—exactly what it's doing."

"There aren't any," he said.

Her eyes widened in obvious incredulity. "There aren't *any*? Who the hell designed this ship and thought that including escape ships wasn't a good idea! Did they totally forget about the *Titanic*?"

"The titanic what?" he asked, having no clue what she was talking about.

She clearly couldn't believe that he had to ask that. "The *Titanic*. It was a big, unsinkable cruiser except it hit an iceberg and sank. And thousands of people died because apparently the ancestors of this vessel must have been the ones who decided that not having enough lifeboats on it to accommodate everyone was a good idea."

"You're joking now, aren't you," he said uncertainly. He realized belatedly that he was having genuine issues talking to her, if for no other reason than that she was the first person he had ever had a conversation with that he wasn't related to.

She rolled her eyes, clearly annoyed with the question, but her mind was already racing on to other concerns. "We need Ada," she said briskly, seemingly having come to some manner of conclusion.

It was not, however, a conclusion that Jason immediately understood. "We need what?"

"Not what. Who. Ada Miller. She's a brilliant engineer. If anyone could figure how to get the engines restarted, it would be her. And she's probably going to need some people to assist her. You know what?" her mind was racing. "We might as well wake up everyone. This is a state of emergency. You never know who's going to be the one who's going to come up with a life-saving idea."

If Medea had started speaking in alien tongues, the things she had been saying could not have sounded more otherworldly to Jason. This was all a waste of time. He had already tried every possible remedy in order to fix the damage that his father had inflicted. The kind of solution that Medea was attempting to implement simply didn't exist. The ship could not possibly be saved, no matter how brilliant Medea's engineering pal was. All she was going to do was fritter away the last hours, or days at most, that were left to her. "So you're saying we should awaken all one hundred and seventy five people so they can go down with the ship? Die conscious of what's happening to them."

"No!" she replied in clear irritation. "I'm saying we should save the damned ship!" She clapped her hands briskly. "So let's get to it!"

Jason hadn't really had any idea how his first meeting with Medea was going to go, but this certainly hadn't been it. Wake everyone up so they could all die together? It seemed the height of cruelty. But he suspected that pointing that fact out to Medea wasn't going to make the slightest bit of difference. If he refused to aid her, she would just bring everyone else back to life herself. And God knew what would happen then.

He checked the ship's directory and located where Ada Miller was sleeping. He lead Medea over to her and quickly turned the switches that would bring her out of her slumber. Once more the door hissed open and once more mist filled the corridor, but this time Jason felt no sense of excitement or anticipation. Instead all he felt was guilty. He was, by restoring Ada to consciousness and cooperating with Medea, simply perpetuating the cruelty of Medea's false hope that people working together could forestall the inevitable. It made his mind go back to the days when his father was sane and warned him against the futility of getting into arguments with women because it was impossible for a man to ever win such an endeavor. "Just always say, 'Fine,' and give up fighting. Because otherwise you're just wasting your time," Isaac said wearily on more than one occasion.

"This is going to work," Medea said with total conviction.

"Fine," said Jason, watching the dials to make sure that the resuscitation proceeded properly.

Long seconds passed and then, just as Medea had, Ada slumped forward. She was clad in similar fashion to the way Medea had been, and her legs seemed no stronger initially. Jason started to reach forward toward her, but Medea intervened, stepping between them and catching Ada as she slumped forward. Ada's eyes wandered for a moment, drifting separately from each other as if she were a chameleon before she suddenly focused on Medea's face.

"*Maddy!*" Ada cried out, and to Jason's utter shock, she kissed Medea firmly on the lips. To Jason's even greater shock, Medea was passionately returning it.

"Oh, you've *got* to be kidding," he muttered so softly that neither of the women could have heard him, provided that they had been the slightest bit interested in listening to him. It certainly appeared that that was not the case.

Finally their lips parted and Ada gasped out, "Is it over? Are the creatures all dead?"

"No," replied Medea. "The ship's broken and we need you to save it."

Ada was stepping out of the pod and Medea was supporting her as Jason had done. Ada kissed Medea once more and then looked in puzzlement at Jason. "Who's that?" she asked.

"That's…" Medea's face went blank.

"Jason," he reminded her tonelessly.

"Yes, right! Jason! That's Jason. He's the captain. He woke us up to save the ship."

"Yeah, you said it was…broken?" Ada clearly didn't understand what Medea meant by that. "Broken how?"

"The engines are shut down and I can't access the computers to restart them."

Ada considered that for half a moment and said, "Then we jumpstart them. No big deal."

"I tried that."

"Are you an engineer?"

"I'm everything," said Jason.

"Well, I'm just an engineer, so since it's my specialty, how about if I take a look at it and see if we can get this thing up and running."

"Fine," said Jason with a shrug. He studied the two of them. "I take it you two know each other."

"She's my fiancée," said Medea.

Jason nodded. "Of course she is. Well, let's go save the ship because, y'know, we all have so much to live for."

DIZZ

I.

GANT COULD SCARCELY BELIEVE IT. They had been riding for what seemed endless days. The draquons were exhausted from the lengthy trip. They had certainly done their best to attend to their beasts' needs, but food and water had not always been plentiful during their excursion.

Yet now it seemed that their journey was nearing its end. The inner guidance system that drew all Phey, with unerring accuracy, to large gatherings of their kind was drawing them with one hundred percent certainty to the land that was known was Dizz.

No one knew whence had come the name "Dizz." As was the case with all places on the Damned World, the moniker was left over from the days when the Morts had populated the region. They were the ones who had dubbed it "Dizz" or at least something along those lines. Gant didn't especially care about the whys and wherefores of how the Morts had come up with the names for things: they just were what they were.

Nevertheless, the signs that were posted had the name "Dizz" with such frequency the closer they drew to it, it was almost impossible to miss. At least that was what Gant assumed that the words in the signs were saying. But he saw the word "Disney" printed on any number of large signs along the road that they were speeding down and simply assumed that that was the word that indicated the advent of Dizz.

Tania continued to sit behind him as the draquon sped down the large highway. Her arms were draped leisurely around him. He had gotten quite used to the sensation, and although he never would have admitted it aloud, had even come to like it. He tried to tell himself that there was no way that he was falling back in love with the little twit. He could not ever trust her again. After all, she had transformed him into a green gelatinous mass. He would have to be totally insane to trust her never to do such a thing again. He couldn't expect to go through the rest of his life being worried that he would say or do something that would set her off. That was no way for anyone to live, and Gant had absolutely no intention of existing that way.

But still…it was so nice.

He was reasonably sure that she was actually sleeping against his back. It was astounding that she had become so accustomed to the slow, steady rhythms of the draquon that she was capable of falling asleep while riding it. Indeed, the very thought of it nearly caused Gant to start to drift off, and he forced his mind to snap back to reality and focus on the world around him. Gant's draquon was currently in the middle of the array, with Graves in the lead and Trott bringing up the rear. The blazing sun was hanging high above them, and the only thing that was preventing Gant's skin from being severely burned was the protective hood and cloak that was streaming behind him.

"Not much further," Graves called back, but it wasn't necessary. Gant had an inner sense that they were drawing closer and closer to his people. He sensed his heartbeat speeding up, and he was even breathing faster. To his annoyance, he also felt his inner persona of the Piri whose body he had taken over roiling around within his mind, trying to shove his way out. He was hyper aware of how exposed Tania had left herself. If he allowed the Piri to seize control for even a moment, he would turn around and sink his teeth into her throat, draining her life's blood in a matter of moments. And the sad fact was that, once upon a time, Gant would have been perfectly happy to let him do that. Forgiving Tania was not something that he lightly thought about doing, considering what she had done to him.

But perhaps she could find a way to change him back. It was a faint hope, granted, but anything was possible.

It took no effort at all for Gant to shove the protesting Piri back into the inner recesses of his mind.

The closer they drew to Dizz, the more puzzling the landscaping became. Once upon a time, decades ago, there might well have been an array of decorated bushes, carved into random shapes. Now, though, thanks to the lack of attention and the inevitability of nature, the bushes had become overgrown and held only dim throwbacks to the manner in which they had once been carved. The road was still relatively smooth, so that was something.

They passed large signs that were decorated with some sort of bizarre, smiling creatures. They appeared to be anthropomorphized versions of animals: mice, dogs—one on two legs and wearing pants, one of them on all fours—ducks and other beasts. Perhaps they were intended to provide entertainment value. What that entertainment might actually be, Gant could not begin to guess, and so he mentally shrugged it off as unimportant.

Graves suddenly brought his draquon to a halt and raised a fist, indicating that the others should stop their forward motion. They immediately did so, drawing up their draquons and gazing ahead into the emptiness. There was no noise of any kind; all was silent. Not even random animals were squawking around them.

After a long moment, Graves called out, "I know you're here. Come out where I can see you."

Gant didn't know what Graves was talking about, but he had enough confidence in him that he was sure Graves had a reason to be speaking to empty air.

They had stopped moving directly in front of what seemed to be a major archway. It was obviously just for decoration since it wasn't supporting anything. It must have served to welcome Morts who were coming to Dizz for whatever reason. An acknowledgment that they had arrived at their destination, perhaps. Gant still had no idea what purpose Dizz had served, but it was certainly large enough to accommodate hundreds of thousands, perhaps even millions of Morts at any one time.

For a long moment, nothing happened, and suddenly a Phey

was standing directly in their path. He was holding a bow and an arrow was nocked, ready to be released. His eyes were narrowed in suspicion, and then they cleared. "Graves?" he said slowly. "Is that you after all this time?"

"Sebore, as I suspected."

Sebore had been wearing a hood. He flipped it back to reveal that his own skin had indeed been changing color in the same way that the other Phey's skin had been doing. His face was much thinner and gaunter than Pheys' faces typically were, and his eyes were more sunken. He stared down at Graves and there was obvious suspicion in his gaze. "You are somewhat far away from your general residence. That's Trott with you, is it not?" Trott nodded curtly and his attention shifted to the others. "The female?"

"Tania," she said.

"Tania. The one who cursed Gant?"

She did not even bother to ask how he had heard of her. Instead she simply nodded.

"And who in the world is that?" and he stared at the hooded figure on draquonback seated in front of her. "That looks like a Piri?"

"Actually it's Gant," Gant informed him.

"I'll be," said Sebore. "I knew she had transformed you, but I'd no idea she had changed you into a Piri."

"She didn't. I possessed a Piri."

"Then what are you when you're not possessing something else?"

"Introduce enough alcohol into my system and perhaps I will show you."

Sebore nodded as if he took Gant's offhand comment for a promise of future revelation. "So can I safely assume that you are here because you wish to seek a meeting with Obertan."

"That is correct," said Graves. "Out of curiosity, do you know why?"

"Because the Overseer is dead. Killed by a female Mandraque."

"You have a Visionary," Tania said immediately.

"We prefer the term 'Farseer,' but the purpose and skill set are very much the same," said Sebore. "He tells us the things that he sees, and we take that information and make use of it, or ignore it, as we see fit."

"Has he seen the skies open up and unleash pitch blackness upon it?" said Graves. "Have our exilers sent retribution for the slaying of their agent?"

"He has seen nothing of that nature at all. There is no hint of punishment being inflicted upon us in response for the Mandraque's actions."

"Incredible," said Graves softly. Gant, for his part, just let out a sigh of relief, while Trott slowly shook his head as if he could not believe what he was being told. "But why not?" continued Graves. "The Banishers made it clear that if something happened to the Overseer, that our world would effectively end."

"Yes, they did," said Sebore. "And since we are all still here, then what conclusion can we draw from that threat?"

"That it was a bluff," said Graves. "Something to keep us in place. To enable the Overseer to control us."

"Which he did, quite well," Sebore agreed. "At least, that is one theory."

"What other theory is there?"

Gant was able to provide the answer. "That something bad is coming. That it wasn't immediate, but with the Overseer now dead, his passing has put something into motion that none of us is going to be especially thrilled about."

"Very good," said Sebore. "You certainly possess something of your Phey heritage, even if you wear the shape of a Piri. How long do you plan to remain that way?"

"That's up to her," said Gant, inclining his head toward Tania.

"Hunh," said Sebore. "Considering your proximity to her, you seem to be getting on quite well with someone who has cursed you. Were it me, I would kill her as soon as look at her."

"I thought about that," said Gant, "but then I would have no chance of her transforming me back."

"That much is true," said Sebore.

It was at that moment that the Phey heard the galloping of feet approaching from the distance. It was three more Phey, their cloaks fluttering behind him, astride draquons. Most startlingly, instead of the black or grey of the Spires draquons, these beasts were pale white. Gant was astounded. He had never seen draquons of such light color before. He reasoned that it must have had something to do with the area in which they were currently residing, but he wasn't entirely sure how it was possible. Nevertheless, there they were, and they seemed most suspicious of their brethrens' dark shadings.

They reined up a short distance from the new arrivals, and the leader bellowed, "State your business!"

"They're Phey from the Spires," Sebore spoke up. "There is no reason to treat them as anything other than allies. They were present at the death of the Overseer."

"Ah," said the leader. His hand had been hovering near the hilt of a sword that was hanging from his left hip, but upon hearing that information from Sebore, he appeared to relax. Then he grunted. "Was never much of a fan of the Overseer."

"None of us were," said Graves.

Anticipating their needs, the leader said, "And now you wish to confer with Obertan, yes?"

"That is exactly right," Graves told him.

The leader shrugged in a manner that seemed indifferent. "I am not sure what he will tell you that he hasn't told us."

"What did he tell you?" asked Graves.

The leader snorted. "He laughed. He thought it was funny."

The Phey from the Spires exchanged confused looks and then Graves said, "Perhaps he will be more forthcoming for us."

"Perhaps he will. It is not for us to second guess the mind of Obertan," said Sebore.

The leader's response to that was to pivot his draquon and snap the reins. The beast leaped forward, and the two others accompanied it, heading back the way they came. Graves glanced at his companions and then prompted his own mount forward, and Gant and Trott followed him. Seconds later the newcomers were in full pursuit toward the land of Dizz.

Tania angrily elbowed Gant in the ribs and he gasped. "What was that for?" he demanded.

"You thought of killing me as soon as you looked at me?!"

"Can you blame me?" he demanded.

She was about to snap back a response, but then her face softened and she shrugged. "I suppose not."

Progress, he thought grimly.

II.

GANT HAD BEEN UNSURE OF what to expect from the famed Dizz. Supposedly it was unlike anywhere else on the Damned World, and he had to admit that—as they made their way down the main street of the land—it certainly lived up to that reputation.

There was no consistency to it at all. Unlike other Mort cities that were built upon a common theme, Dizz was a bizarre agglomeration of different styles. The main thoroughfare of the land seemed quite antiquated, even by Mort standards. The street dead-ended into a large circle, and from there it transformed depending upon which way you looked. One direction seemed even older in its construction, while the other appeared to be some attempt to divine the future. All of that, however, paled in comparison to the small castle that stretched toward the heavens. It reminded Gant a bit of the chief residence of the Ocular. The closer he drew to it, though, the more that he perceived the trickery in its design. From a distance it seemed quite big, but the nearer he got, the more he saw that it was designed in such a way to force one's perceptions to see it far larger than it was. Somehow the Morts had actually managed to create some manner of trick in perspective to deceive the common eye. It was certainly not the first time that Gant had been impressed by the collective cleverness of the departed Mort society, but it was the first time he had actually perceived an ability for true deceit. In a way it frustrated him that he would never be able to converse with the individual who had come up with the castle design and had so flawlessly executed it. Once again he wished that he were able to read Mort language because perhaps the name of the person who had developed it was somewhere on display.

The other Phey who had been wandering in the land of Dizz had halted whatever they were doing to stare at the new arrivals. Gant felt as if most eyes were upon him. His companion were Phey, after all, and so would garner at most mild curiosity. But a cloaked Piri riding through the main street of Dizz on a draquon? That would certainly prompt major interest.

He wanted to shout at them, "Are you through looking? Find something else interesting to stare at for a while?" But he sensed that his sarcasm would likely go past them, so he kept his mouth shut.

To his surprise, he felt Tania's hand on his back, as if she was being supportive. "Steady," she murmured as if she sensed his discomfort. He felt oddly gratified by her touch.

The leader of the Phey guard was leading the expedition, and he brought them straight to the castle. Once they were inside the main entrance area, he dismounted and turned to face the others. "Come with me," he ordered.

They followed suit and moments later were following the leader up a flight of stairs. There was a door at the top and the leader knocked on it tentatively. "Obertan?" he called in a soft voice.

"You may enter...while there is time," came a deep, aged sounding reply from the other side.

Gant and Graves looked at each other briefly and then shrugged. Who were they to try and decipher the warnings of the elderly? They were hard enough to understand under even the best of conditions.

The leader pushed the door open and the four of them entered a quite nice set of rooms. Everything had an odd red emblem on it: the velvet red bedspread, the blue window drapes, and a large circular carpet in the middle of the room. None of them had the slightest idea what it represented. They just took mental note of it.

Seated at a desk with papers spread everywhere was Obertan. He was easily the oldest Phey that Gant had ever seen. Surprisingly, he had very long, white hair, which was something of a rarity among Phey. Even more startling was the color of his skin.

It was dead white.

Gant actually gasped in surprise. He knew that Obertan was of advanced age, but he had no idea that the passing years could inflict that sort of damage upon Phey skin tone. Or maybe it was damage caused by the Damned World itself. Or maybe—

"It's not damage," said Obertan without even glancing at them, still focused upon the pages upon his desk. "This is simply what happens when a Phey lives long enough. Most of us have the good sense not to."

"We don't?" said a surprised Graves. Apparently his thoughts had been running in the same direction as Gant's.

Slowly Obertan turned his chair to face them. Gant gasped once more and this time he had company because Graves had the same reaction.

Obertan had no eyes. Instead two blackened pits resided in his face.

Tania could not restrain herself. "What happened to your eyes?" she gasped. An annoyed Gant slugged her in the shoulder to remonstrate her, but the truth was that he was just as curious as she. He simply would not have had the nerve to inquire.

He did not seem the least bit perturbed by the question. "I sacrificed them for a spell. We still do spells on occasion, as I'm sure you're aware."

"What kind of spell means that you have to sacrifice your eyes?"

"One that enables me to see."

"See what?" asked Gant.

He smiled. "Better." The he tilted his head as if he was gazing directly at them. "But my eyes, or lack thereof, are not the only thing that disturb you, yes? You have never seen any of the Phey die of old age, have you?" He chuckled. "When your parents age sufficiently, they simply go on the Final Quest. But you have never actually watched one of your fellows pass of natural cause, have you."

They shook their heads. So did Tania. Trott made no motion, as was his custom.

"Typically," said Obertan, "a Phey simply tires of existence. Once that happens, we just…" He shrugged. "Fade away. No pain. No fuss. The air just takes us and we dissipate. It's truthfully a very considerate way to dispose of oneself. Then again, the Phey were once a very considerate race until we eventually developed into…" He frowned. "What was the Mort word? Oh. Right. 'Dicks.' The Mort considered us to be 'Dicks,' whatever those are."

"How do you know what the Morts called us?" asked Gant.

"I had a servant many years ago. He was quite the tormented soul. He was a youngster when he fell into my hands. Eventually I managed to domesticate him and he became rather useful. Taught me many things. That," and he pointed to the icon on the bedspread, "is the letter 'D.' It stands for Disney. This land was built by him. A man called Disney."

"Was it?" said Gant.

"It was indeed. It was called Disney World. Morts came here for entertainment and diversion."

"All this for entertainment and diversion?" Gant said incredulously.

"Oh, this is only a very small portion of it. You could spend an entire day walking from one end to the other and still never reach it. Apparently Morts were quite serious about their amusements. But you do not care about any of that, do you?"

"No," said Trott.

"No, you are concerned about the death of the Overseer."

"I would like to meet with your Farseer," Graves said, walking up to Obertan. "See if he has any other visions that he might share with us."

"You are speaking with him."

Graves did not attempt to keep the surprise from his face. "You?" Then he nodded in understanding. "You sacrificed your eyes so that you could be a Farseer. Why did your men not tell us that?"

"They are not especially inclined to share our secrets with newcomers and strangers. Come, sit. Sit. Take your leisure time while you can still avail yourself of it."

"Why do you keep saying that?" said Tania.

"The explanation will come when it is time." He gestured for them to take seats, which they readily did. "So you wish to know why the world is still here with the passing of the Overseer."

They nodded. "It does seem strange," said Graves.

"Not really. What did you think was going to happen? The Magisters were going to rain down death upon us? That the skies would run red with blood and they would annihilate us from existence? Don't you think that if they were capable of doing such a thing, they would have done so in the first place?"

"Then why did they not?" said Gant.

Obertan did not answer immediately. Instead, surprisingly, he was "staring" at Gant even though he had no eyes with which to see him. His nostrils flared and then he said, "You are a Piri. With a Phey within you."

"I am."

"How came you to this situation?"

Gant had become fed up enough with having to keep explaining his situation that this time he just pointed at Tania and said, "She did it," without considering that Obertan could not actually see who he was pointing at.

Obertan, for his part, simply nodded. He turned his non-existent eyes straight toward Tania and asked a curious question: "Has she apologized?"

"Yes, she did."

"Was she sincere?"

"I would like to think that she was."

"Well then," said Obertan. "That is all that matters."

"Except she cannot transform me back. She requires special ingredients…"

"Really." Obertan gave that a moment's thought. "It is entirely possible I may be able to aid you in that regard. Over my years I have accrued more ingredients than is probably good for me to have. If I can use them to help her restore you to your true form, I would be perfectly happy to share them with you."

Gant couldn't believe it. It was the best news that he had ever received for as…well, for as long as he could recall, really. Impulsively, he turned to Tania and embraced her, and she let out a startled gasp. "I haven't done it yet," she reminded him as he lifted her off her feet.

Regaining control of himself, he set her back down and then said, "Well, here is hoping for the best."

"Hope quickly," said Obertan. "Hope can vanish as quickly as it comes."

Graves was beginning to lose patience and he was making no effort to restrain his growing lack of enthusiasm. "There you go again," he said angrily. "Why do you keep saying depressing things like that? What is going on?"

"I suppose Sebore could tell you," said Obertan.

"Well, then fine. Bring him here."

"That isn't possible," said Obertan.

A slow dread was beginning to build in Gant's heart. "Why," he said slowly, concerned that he already knew the answer, "isn't it possible for Sebore to be brought here."

"Because he's dead," said Obertan. "Right about now."

III.

SEBORE FELT THE RUMBLING BEFORE he heard it, and heard it before he knew what the source was. However as it turned out, it didn't matter at what point he saw it, because the moment he became aware of it, it was already too late.

From his hiding place in the trees, he became aware of the sudden and steady vibrations of something massive, a herd of some sort, stampeding in his direction. He didn't have the slightest idea what it was, because wandering herds simply didn't tend to live in this particular part of the country. He understood that they did tend to wander about in various parts of the Midwest, but definitely not hereabouts, and he couldn't fathom what might be heading his way. Whatever it was, however, it warranted investigation.

He descended from the tree branches and dropped to the ground below. He called out in sounds that to any stranger would have seemed like animal noises, but the Phey who were within earshot were easily able to discern it as Sebore urging caution while he investigated the creatures approaching.

He peered around a tree trunk, giving himself a full view of the oncoming approach while providing little target for anyone who was coming.

Sebore squinted, trying to discern exactly what was approaching. It was remarkably hot and humid out, and waves of heat were radiating from the pavement, making it difficult at first to make it out. The thundering of what sounded like hooves were getting progressively louder as whatever it was got closer. Then he was finally able to make out forms speeding toward them. He gasped, barely able to believe what he was seeing.

It was a herd of Whoresmen, and Serpenteens were riding on their backs.

He wasn't sure which was more astounding: that the Whoresmen were apparently mounting a full on attack on the Phey, or that the Serpenteens had formed an alliance with them, since alliances were virtually unknown among the tribes.

He began to cry out a warning to the other guards, and suddenly an arrow buried itself in his forehead. He pitched backwards and fell into view of his fellows.

One of the Phey, stationed toward the back, was a telepath. He immediately sent word into the heart of Dizz of what had just happened, and then seconds later a volley of arrows hurtled through the air, slamming home and bringing a wave of death and destruction down upon the Phey. It was the first time in memory that any had ever dared launch an attack upon them, and it would live forever in their memories. That was assuming that any of them survived it.

IV.

THEY WERE STUNNED BY WHAT Obertan had just told them. "Why?" demanded Graves. "What happened?"

"He was shot by a Serpenteen," said Obertan calmly. "It's impressive. The first of our kind to fall to violent ends in quite some time. Unless the Overseer killed someone. I'm getting old and it is occasionally hard for me to remember."

"A Serpenteen?" Graves looked around in confusion. "Where did—?"

"They followed us," said Trott grimly.

Gant was about to deny the possibility out of hand, but the presentation of the facts before them gave him an unavoidable conclusion. "How?" he whispered.

"It doesn't really matter, does it," said Obertan in his calm, almost detached voice. "They are here and their means of achieving it are beside the point."

Tania was on her feet and she said urgently, "A ward. We need to create a ward."

"It's already under way." He gestured toward a window. Tania crossed to it and stared down at the main entranceway to the home of the Phey. A group of them had formed a straight line and were gesturing into the air. Green sparks were dancing between their fingertips.

"What's happening?" said Gant. He was standing right next to her, but it was readily apparent that he wasn't seeing the same thing that she was.

"They're creating a barrier. One that will prevent anyone with the intention of hurting us from entering."

"How long will it last?"

Tania wasn't sure and she automatically glanced toward Obertan, confident that—despite his lack of eyes—he would be aware that she was staring right at him, waiting for him to reply.

Her faith was seemingly well placed, because Obertan looked right at her and said, "It will last indefinitely. Unlike, as you've seen yourselves, the spells crafted to render the human weapons helpless. That wore off once the humans were destroyed since there was no need for any to maintain it. But the ward is different. It is governed by the will power of those creating it, and as long as they wish to keep it in place, they should be able to sustain it." He sighed. "It's a shame that it won't matter."

"Why?" said Gant. "Why won't it matter?"

Graves' reaction was angrier. His voice rising, he strode forward and stopped only a foot short of Obertan. "Why do you keep doing that? Why do you keep speaking so fatalistically? What in the Damned World is the matter with you?"

Obertan actually seemed surprised at Graves' attitude. "Nothing is the matter with me. Something is the matter with the world. Haven't you figured that out yet? It is going to end."

"What do you mean, end?"

His voice dropped to a whisper and for the first time the age so prevalent in his body seemed to be overwhelming him. He steadied himself, placing a hand against the nearest wall. "I can't see," he said. "Beyond the next turn. The world is closed to me."

Tania walked toward him, pushing Graves aside, and she rested a hand on his arm. "Do you...do you think you are foreseeing your own death?"

"It is beyond that. If I was seeing my own end, I am certain that I would be able to discern it. I am perceiving something far greater than that. The Whoresmen, the Serpenteen...they will be able to invade us. There are tunnels beneath the streets that they will be able to access. They will descend upon us, but that is irrelevant. Something else will come. Something massive. Something that will end life as we know it. Perhaps it is indeed the work of the Magisters. Perhaps they are angry over the death of the Overseer and this will be their final vengeance upon us. Or perhaps none of it matters. Maybe fate has simply decided that it is our time to end. Everything ends, sooner or later."

"Well, I refuse to accept that!" said Graves.

Obertan actually seemed amused by the declaration. "It is not up to you to accept it or reject it, Graves. What will happen, will happen, whether you are able to deal with that or not. I suggest," and he gestured toward the windows, "you watch outside and see how the battle goes. The chances are that you will be in the thick of it. And then we will see who, if anyone, survives." He rubbed his hands together. "I'm sure it will be very exciting."

PERRIZ

I.

EUTOK HAD CHOSEN THE BUILDING he was residing in at random, mostly because he liked the exterior. There was some sort of odd structure on top of it that was bright red with what seemed to be four paddles extending from its center. He had seen similar structures out in random fields in his travels, and in those instances the arms had spun when a strong enough wind would happen upon them. He didn't know what their function was, and had no idea what it represented here in Perriz, but it was certainly unique in the city. So when he had required somewhere to rest his head, this was the place that he had selected.

He had thoroughly barricaded the front door of the place, blocking it with an assortment of chairs and tables and finally a large counter that he had dragged from its place in the entranceway. Eutok did not wish to see anyone, to speak with anyone. He just wanted to be left alone and deal with the thoughts that were slamming through his head.

He was in a room that appeared to be designed for gatherings. There were tables and chairs strewn around in no particular order, and there was some manner of stage at the front of the room. Eutok was lying upon it, his stone axe to his right as he stared at the ceiling.

He was still trying to process what he had learned when there was a loud banging coming from the door. Immediately he scrambled to his feet, grabbing his axe and clambering into a defensive squat. He briefly considered hiding somewhere so that he could get the drop on whoever was attacking, but then decided to maintain his ground. A Trull did not hide from an opponent. A Trull met him head on and let the best of them win.

Whoever was attempting to enter continued to pound away at

the outer doors and for a moment Eutok thought that his barrier was going to hold. Suddenly a loud smashing reached his ears and he heard the doors shatter from the impact as his assailant crashed through them. Eutok braced himself, not knowing what he was going to be fighting but pretty much ready for anything.

The inner door, which Eutok had not bothered to secure, burst open and Karsen Foux was standing there with his war hammer cradled in his hands.

"Oh, for gods sake!" said an annoyed Eutok. "Karsen, what are you playing at? If I'd had a bow or a spear, I would have punctured you before I realized it was you."

It was as if Karsen hadn't heard a word. "*How could you*?!" he bellowed. He took several steps forward, so filled with rage that his legs were shaking. "How could you have done that to Clarinda? How could you have abandoned her that way?"

"You think her mother was going to just let her go?" said Eutok, his voice thick with contempt. "Then you're an even bigger fool that you would believe me to be. Her mother would just have attacked both of us, and you as well. I saved your damned life by getting us out of there."

"We would have fought for her," said Karsen tightly. He drew nearer toward Eutok and the Trull's defensive systems went alert. Karsen was getting close enough to take a swing with his war hammer. "That's what we went down there to do. And you stopped us. You made us withdraw. Because of the child."

"That child should not exist."

"*You* put it there!"

"How was I supposed to know that was possible?" Eutok demanded. "I didn't want children! I had no idea we could possibly conceive a child!"

That seemed to surprise Karsen for a moment. He lowered his war hammer and said, "Why didn't you want children?"

"Aside from the fact that it's taboo, you mean?"

"Your entire relationship is taboo," Karsen pointed out. "Not sure why you should stop now."

"Look at the world!" said Eutok. He gestured vaguely in a way that indicated he was including the entirety of the Damned World. "Filled with nothing but races that want to kill each other! My own brother and mother wanted me dead! How are we truly supposed to bring any offspring into this…this cesspool of insanity? What kind of place is this to bring a child into?"

"It's the only one we've got, Eutok." He still appeared angry, but at least he no longer seemed interested in attacking. "And who knows? Maybe children who are combinations of races can wind up improving it. Did you ever consider that?"

"No," said Eutok, "I didn't."

Karsen's face hardened. "And what of Clarinda? You're perfectly happy to leave her to the tender mercies of her mother?"

"Sunara won't do anything to her," Eutok said dismissively. "Kill the child perhaps, yes, but not—"

Karsen moved so fast that Eutok never even saw him coming. One moment he was on the far side of the room, and the next he was across it and grabbing Eutok by the leathers he was wearing strapped across his chest. His action was so quick that Eutok didn't have time to react, and Karsen reached behind the Trull and knocked the battle axe out of his hand. Eutok's eyes widened in shock and for the first time he actually thought his life might be in danger.

"She was going to kill her! The only thing that prevented her from dying was that some of our people went back in and rescued her! Rafe Kestor died helping her to escape, you idiot!"

Eutok's already pale face went even whiter. "Wh-what?"

"You heard me," said Karsen. Angrily he shoved the Trull back, causing him to stagger. "Clarinda is fine. She is back with the Ocular. They love her and are protecting her. The only question now is, What the hell are you going to do about it?"

Eutok said nothing. He turned his back to Karsen and just stood there with his arms folded across his chest.

"That's what I thought…coward." He wadded up a mouthful of

spittle and sent it flying at Eutok. It landed on his back and dribbled down it. Eutok did not make a move to wipe it off, and he remained there with his back to Karsen as Karsen stamped out.

II.

"THE PIRI ARE GOING TO attack."

Arren stood at the far end of the long table around which the heads of the Five Clans were grouped. They were leaning forward, listening intently to his words, and he considered that a good sign. Typically when the Clan heads were engaged with incessant discussion with each other, that was when it was difficult to accomplish anything. Such meetings were usually filled with an overabundance of crosstalk, arguments, challenges, and borderline battles that were oftentimes, but not always, shouted down in favor of more threats and counter threats. In this case, though, the four of them seemed to be listening to him.

Evanna was seated off to the side, in the chair that had typically been occupied by her late father. She barely seemed to be paying attention to the meeting. That was not unusual for her. Since she had learned of her father's horrific fate, she had oftentimes withdrawn into herself, allowing the matters of the world to pass on without contributing anything of herself to them. Arren supposed that he could not blame her. She was likely running her father's last moments through her head, imagining those bleak seconds as his body plummeted toward its death on the streets far below. She was likely blaming herself for not being there and maybe saving him from his horrific fate. That was hardly realistic, though. If the Overseer was determined to kill her father, he would have not hesitated to dispose of her as well, and that would have been the end of the two most important Firedraques in Perriz.

Arren jolted his wandering mind back to the situation at hand. He knew he had drifted off topic for only a couple of seconds, but he was well aware that it was necessary to remain focused. He gestured toward the colored window that shone down upon them. "At the moment," he said, "the glowing orb hovers above us, providing us with its radiance and protection. But soon the turn will be complete and the Piri will rise from their haven below our feet."

"We are certain that they are there," Gorshen said cautiously, glancing around at his peers as if seeking an echo of his uncertainty. "This is not some manner of fantasy dreamt up by one of the Ocular."

"I have seen them. Fought them," Arren said with conviction. "Their leader, a female called Sunara, dwells with them. She is the mother of Clarinda."

"The Piri who arrived with the Ocular."

"Yes, Gorshen, that is correct. Clarinda, however, escaped from her. She was brought up with the aid of Evanna," and he gestured toward her, "and several others."

"With her child."

It had been Jormund who had spoken, his deep voice rumbling and making no effort to keep the disgust from his tone. "Her child…a mixed breed."

"Mixed?" Gorshen sounded astounded. The surprised looks on the faces of Thorda Odomo and Bazilikus registered that they were likewise previously uninformed of the half-breed's existence.

Thorda remained the unknown element to Arren. She was the daughter of the late Thulsa Odomo, who had been slain during his unwise attempt to take over Perriz for himself. Thorda, by reputation, was the exact opposite of her father, tending to give great thought to every action before doing anything. Some considered that rendered her indecisive, but Arren figured that made her quite the opposite: once she made a decision, she stuck to it and typically carried it off flawlessly. There were rumors that she was her father's battle strategist, and that she had not been involved in his ill-advised endeavor to conquer Perriz. Were that true, it might well have explained why it failed.

"Yes," said Arren. "Mixed. Her and a Trull."

"Gods," whispered Bazilikus.

"I doubt the deities are involved or have any particular feelings about it," said Arren, trying to keep the sarcasm out of his tone. "However, if it is of any use to you, I am sure you will be happy to know that the Piri's mother has the exact same attitude as you do. To be specific, she wants the child killed. Quite possibly the child's mother as well; I am still a bit unclear on that. In any event, the point is that she is going to launch an assault on us, very likely this very evening."

"How many Piri are we talking about?" asked Thorda.

"I am uncertain. Very likely hundreds. But we outnumber them, and if we fight together, we can most certainly defeat them."

"Why?" said Jormund.

The question stunned Arren. He couldn't quite believe that Jormund was asking it. "What do you mean, why?"

"I mean why should we battle the Piri?"

Arren slowly came around the table until he was standing directly in front of Jormund. The Mandraque's towering form enabled him to glower down at Arren, but Arren did not display any air of intimidation. "From my understanding," he said carefully, "you approached the Ocular with the notion of sending them in to battle the Piri. You were concerned about exactly this. Yet now you would refrain from battling them even though they represent a direct threat to you?"

"Sending the Ocular in to battle them is a far cry from engaging them ourselves."

"Since when is a Mandraque afraid of battle?" Arren demanded.

"For my own needs, wants, desires, I will battle to the death," Jormund said. "But on behalf of some Piri bitch and her half-breed spawn? Of what use to me is that? How would you suggest I rationalize it to my people when they demand to know the reasons for this battle?"

"You tell them that we are fighting for our safety! That Piri are residing in the sewers below us and they are moving to attack!"

"But wait," said Bazilikus. "You said they are attacking because of the female and her child. If we turn them back over to her, they would refrain from the assault, yes? I mean, I don't claim to have your level of intelligence, but that is what you are basically implying?"

"I am not implying anything. I am telling you outright, the Piri are going to attack. Besides," he continued, "I am telling you there are Piri residing below us, something that Jormund is already well aware of. If they are going to present themselves to us for battle, why in the world should we not take this opportunity to dispose of them?"

"There should always be a purpose for battle," said Jormund. "There is no purpose in battling an onslaught of Piri in order to defend a female we've no interest in defending."

"If she spawned an offspring with a Trull," Thorda spoke up, "let the Trull handle this. Let him call in his people to attend to the Piri."

"That's a good point," said Bazilikus. "They both dwell underground. Certainly the Trull would be fully equipped to—"

To Arren's surprise and also his dismay, Evanna suddenly lent her voice to the discussion. "The father will not battle on her behalf. Once he learned of the child's existence, he did not even desire to be near it. He considers it as much of an abomination as you do."

Arren closed his eyes in pain and a silence fell upon the other Clan leaders.

"The *father* wants no part of it?" said Thorda.

Evanna shook her head heavily, as if a great weight was resting upon it. "We attempted to bring her to him after we rescued him. He refused to see her, to speak to her. Karsen endeavored to convince him otherwise, but he would not be moved."

"All right, then!" said Jormund as if his point had been established beyond all question. "That would seem to be that! If even the father does not wish to be involved in this discussion, then that would settle it."

"No, it does not settle it," said Arren, making no attempt to hide his irritation. Although he was speaking to the others, he was glaring squarely at Evanna, but she didn't appear to be paying the slightest attention. Slowly he realized he couldn't truly blame her. After all, she had learned only recently that her father had died at the hands of the Overseer. She should have been deep in mourning, but matters had progressed far too quickly for her to take the time to actually allow the tragedy to consume her. He was seeing it happen now, and he felt sorry for her, having to cope with the loss under these circumstances.

Still, he couldn't help but wish that if she didn't have anything useful to contribute, she would just keep her maw shut.

"How does it not settle it?" demanded Thorda. "If the father himself does not care whether the female and child live or die, why in the world should we risk our own against the Piri?"

"Because Mandraques do nothing in half measures. We rescued the girl. A heroic Rafe Kestor, died in the assault. To back away from her now, to surrender to the Piri…that is not our way."

"The rescue," said Gorshen, "was not a decision that was collectively arrived at. You and yours unilaterally decided to undertake the excursion, and now you are asking us to step in and clean up your mess. I have no more love for the Piri than anybody else, and if they were assaulting us simply because they wanted to hunt us, that would be a different issue. But if they are coming up here because they demand back one of their own, then yes. We should give her to them."

"These are *Piri*," said Arren with open incredulity.

"Yes, and so is she!" Gorshen said. "Let Piri take Piri and her freak offspring and they can all be damned!"

Arren could not take it anymore. "*Coward*!" he snarled, and spat at Gorshen's feet. The green liquid sizzled on the floor.

Gorshen was immediately on his feet, his mouth twisted into an angry snarl. His hand went to the hilt of his sword and Arren matched the gesture with his own weapon.

Jormund was on his feet as well, and his arms were spread wide. "Now, now," he said in a voice that was surprisingly soothing. "There is no need for this."

"He spat at me!" said Gorshen, pointing at the smoking area of the floor.

"Did he strike your body?"

"Well…no…"

"Then don't complain. He is frustrated. Allow him his frustration. Arren," and he gestured toward him, "come. Walk with me. Let us speak in private."

Arren had no idea why Jormund was abruptly acting in a conciliatory fashion, but he saw no reason not to indulge him. Gorshen was still glaring at him as he came around the table to Jormund who indicated that he should follow him out of the meeting hall.

The two Mandraques exited. Arren didn't trust Jormund in the slightest, but he was well aware that Jormund's words carried weight with the others. He was the oldest of the Mandraques, and he was quite capable of helping to direct opinions in whatever direction he wanted them to go.

They found another, smaller room. The wall was cluttered with what Arren assumed was some manner of religious iconography, left over from when Morts resided in the place. Crosses with an obviously dead man dangling from it were strewn around, so Arren assumed that this was the office of the lord high executioner. He would have liked to meet him; he was sure they would have had a good deal to discuss.

There was a desk on the far side of the room and Jormund leaned against it. His attitude and demeanor were entirely different from the way that he had been conducting himself earlier. "The fact is, Arren, that I agree with you," he said.

This pronouncement startled Arren and he made no attempt to hide it. "You were one of the ones who was the loudest in saying we shouldn't oppose the Piri!"

He shrugged indifferently. "You may be our leader, Arren, but you are still young, and there is much that you do not understand. When you are negotiating with others, it is not advisable to be wholly honest with them or, worse, to come across as needy. Neediness is not attractive and generates no sympathies from those you wish to ally with. In point of fact, you are correct. I already approached the Ocular about mounting an invasion upon the Piri in order to wipe them from existence. And they said no, obviously," said Jormund, who was clearly still irritated over the fact that that his attempted alliance did not go the way he had planned. "They did not have the stomach to risk themselves in battle. For all their size, all their power, they are still children who have seen far too much, especially the deaths of their parents and families. They lacked the resolve such an undertaking would have required."

"But the Mandraques do not lack that resolve."

"That is true, provided that it can be seen to be in their interest." Jormund drummed his clawed fingers upon the desk surface. "Let us speak candidly, Arren. Although you are our leader, the fact is that the Five Clans are not truly united. Everyone is involved with their own concerns, and there is still much in-fighting and cross-interests. That is *really* the problem that you are dealing with. Battling the Piri will force the Mandraques to be united, and thus far they aren't. And I am not sure that you alone can bring them together."

It was all beginning to make sense to Arren as he smiled grimly. "You are asking me to step aside so that you can take charge," he said.

To his surprise, Jormund immediately shook his head. "No. Absolutely not. If I try to shove you aside, that will simply result in more division. The Clans will split along lines of loyalty, some allying with you, others with me. And while we are all plotting and fighting against each other, the Piri will attack with impunity and have no one to stand against them."

"Then what do you suggest?" asked Arren, who was genuinely curious as to the response.

"An alliance, beyond the notion that you are the leader of the Clans."

"What sort of alliance?" Arren's eyes narrowed, his suspicions welling up once more.

"I propose the traditional way: marriage."

"I'm…I'm sorry?"

"Marriage."

Arren had no idea how to respond to that. "Jormund, I have… great respect for you, but I am not attracted to you in that man—"

Jormund actually laughed at that. "Not you, Arren. Your sister."

"Norda?"

"Unless you have another."

"You…" He was having trouble processing it. "You want to marry Norda. You know that some consider her insane, yes?"

"She strikes me as a rather singular individual, to be sure. But she is nothing I cannot handle."

"I have been handling her for quite a few turns, and I can assure you that you are vastly underestimating her. To say nothing of the fact that I can hardly speak for my sister when it comes to a choice of mates."

Jormund eased himself off the desk and placed a friendly hand on Arren's shoulder. "You are the leader of the Clans. Your word is effectively law. If you command your sister to wed me, she will adhere to your words."

Arren stepped back, allowing Jormund's hand to slip off his shoulder. He turned away, his mind racing with uncertainty. As he thought about what Jormund had proposed, Jormund continued speaking in low, convincing tones. "You know I'm right, Arren. This alliance will show all of the Clans that we are united. Together we can bring the rest of the Mandraques into line. Together we can form an army to battle the Piri so that your precious Piri mother can remain here. Together—"

"Together we can do all sorts of things."

"Yes," said Jormund eagerly.

"As long as I surrender you my sister."

"Well," Jormund said hesitantly, "I do not think that 'surrender' is the right word…"

"Yes, it exactly is." Arren's voice was becoming more forceful, his entire deportment changing. He took several more steps back from

Jormund, not in fear, but in decision. "You are asking me to give her hand to you without consulting her, but simply by ordering her."

"You are her brother and her lord," Jormund reminded him. "She is bound to do as you command."

"The only thing she is 'bound' to do is trust me, and I will not betray her."

"Are you saying," Jormund said, and his voice was beginning to rise, "that there is something wrong with me? That I am, in some way, not worthy of her?"

That was when Arren decided to toss away any hope of civility. Instinctively he knew it was the wrong thing to do. The fact was that he needed Jormund's support. But he was not willing to sacrifice Norda's freedom in order to achieve it. And besides, the mental image of Norda writhing under him sexually made him want to vomit. There was every likelihood that she would wind up killing him. Arren decided that there was no way he was going to give her that opportunity.

"It has nothing to do with worthiness and everything to do with the fact that Norda has the right to decide what to do with her life and with whom she should share it. At this point she has expressed not the slightest interest in sharing it with anyone. I am not going to command her to share it with you, and if that causes the Five Clans to fall apart, so be it."

Jormund's face soured, and Arren watched carefully, but Jormund's hand did not drift to the hilt of his sword. "You are making a most unwise decision, Arren," he said warningly.

"Perhaps," Arren admitted, "but it is the only one with which I am comfortable. And if you find it difficult to live with, well, that is your problem, not mine."

"Oh, but it is most definitely going to be your problem," said Jormund. He strode past Arren, bumping him roughly in the shoulder and ignoring that the impact caused the thinner Mandraque to stagger. "I am going to call an assemblage of the Five Clans in the great square of the monument. I will tell them of your decision to face down the Piri in order to protect the rights of a female Piri and her bastard freak offspring. And we will see just how much they welcome your attitudes. Once they know what their leader prioritizes, it is quite likely that they will desire a new leader. You may find yourself wanting to revisit my offer, Arren, but guess what? That is no longer an option for you. You have made your decision, and now let us see how well you live with it!"

He stormed out of the room and Arren took a few moments to compose himself. Then he strode back out into the main room and saw the puzzled looks of the remaining Clan members. "This meeting is adjourned," he said without breaking stride and moments later had left Firedraque Hall behind.

III.

ARREN STRODE TOWARD THE PLACE where he knew Eutok was hiding out. Karsen had relayed the results of his frustrating meeting with the Trull and now Arren was fit for a repeat performance. He saw the evidence of Karsen's earlier visit: the outer door shattered and the objects that had been used to block it scattered in pieces all over the floor. He moved quickly past all of them and into the main room of the facility.

Eutok was sitting on what appeared to be some sort of stage. The Trull barely glanced up when Arren came in. Arren stopped several feet away and simply stood there, waiting for Eutok to speak up, to demand what Arren was doing there, perhaps even challenge him to battle. In short, Arren was ready for anything.

"Do you think I'm a coward?" Eutok asked.

Arren wasn't ready for that.

He cocked his head and said, "Excuse me?"

"I said," and Eutok swung his legs around and hopped off the stage. "Do you think I am a coward." He paused and then added, "A coward is someone who is afraid—"

"I know what a coward is," said Arren testily. "I'm not an idiot."

"Fine. So do you think I am one?"

The truth was that Arren hadn't the faintest idea. He thought about Eutok's fearless leading of the strike team into the heart of Piri country, and he had done so without the slightest hesitation. "Not that I have observed," he said judiciously.

"Then why does the accusation sting? I don't believe I am a coward either, but…" His voice trailed off.

Arren didn't know what Eutok was talking about, and admitted to that. "I've been talking to someone," Arren said, "and now I want to talk to you."

Eutok frowned. "What do you want?" he finally asked.

Arren answered him.

IV.

IT WAS ALL WORKING OUT exactly as Jormund had wanted it to.

He stood at the base of the gargantuan arch that towered over him. Briefly he wondered what occasion had prompted the Morts to create such an amazing structure. After considering it for a few moments, he decided that it was likely due to a triumph in some war. That was really the only reason to build such massive things. Say what one would about the Morts, they certainly had a knack for construction. The entire city of Perriz was evidence of that.

Now Jormund stalked around the base of the arch as Mandraques moved toward him from all directions. He was pleased to see that they had heeded his summons. It had been so easy to gain their obedience. He had simply demanded that they all show up and they had done so. Now was the time to make his move. Arren had given him the grounds to muster alliances to his house. All he had to do was rally the Mandraques to his cause, and soon he would be in charge.

Would Arren fight back, he wondered? Arren had never been much for face-to-face confrontations. His method of operation was to outthink his opponent and typically find someone else to do his dirty work. That was the way his mind worked. On some level, Jormund could respect that. However that strategy would do him no good this time. This time Arren had underestimated just how much power his opponent had.

The crowd of Mandraques surrounding him had grown to sufficient size that he decided it was time to begin speaking. "My friends, my family," said Jormund. His family consisted of only his son, Jordund, who was standing off to the side. Jordund had always been something of a disappointment. Thinner and less muscled than Mandraques typically were, Jordund was also a terrible fighter. If he had been son of a lesser Mandraque than Jormund, the chances were that he would not have lasted beyond his teen years. He was smart, there was no denying that. His intellect was far beyond that of other Mandraques. But he was never going to be of much use in full battle situations.

He was useful for crowd control, however. He certainly had an impressive enough speaking voice. "*One side*," Jordund called repeatedly. "Leave a path!" That seemed to be a good idea. There was a straight path of visibility right up the middle of the crowd so even those in the back had a clear view of him. Jordund may have been scrawny but Jormund liked the way he thought.

"Thank you for coming here," Jormund continued. "Thank you for coming to attend my words." The arch was helping his words carry as they echoed and rebounded off the smooth interior. "I am here to deliver a warning to you. This evening we are likely going to be attacked by the Piri."

This caused a vast rush of whispers and words of concern among the Mandraques. They were certainly not afraid of the Piri, but they were well aware of the damage the creatures could cause in a full-blown assault.

"However," he continued, "the Piri do not especially want to assail us. To the best of my knowledge, they are content to dwell in the sewers below us, finding sustenance where they can: random animals, and admittedly the occasional Mandraque who has grown too weak to be able to sustain himself and fight on behalf of his or her people. Mandraques, in short, who are of no use to us."

"But why are they going to assail us?" called one voice.

It was exactly the question he was waiting for. "Because we have someone they want. One of their own. The daughter of their queen...and her offspring." His face twisted in disgust. "And the father isn't even a Piri."

"*What?*" There was incredulity, shouts of horror over the mere concept of a infant born of a mixed assignation. "What is the father?"

"A Trull," said Jormund. "A disgusting Trull. He spawned this freak, this monstrosity, and now he wants no part of it. And Arren, our fearless leader, is expecting us to fight on behalf of this thing. *But why?*" and his voice rose as his tone thundered through the area. "Why should we risk our lives to fight on behalf of a Piri? They want her back? Give her back! Our lives should not be at stake while a Piri and her half-breed freak of a child—!"

There was a sudden rush of air and something sped right up through the divide in the crowd, the one that Jordund had carefully maintained. It spun around like a wheel and then it thudded squarely into Jormund's chest. He looked down in astonishment and saw, to his shock, that a stone axe was lodged in his sternum. The wooden handle was still shaking from the impact. He staggered, tried to remove it, but discovered that he was unable to raise his arms. He did, however, manage to lift his eyes just enough so that he was staring directly at the person who had thrown the axe with expert precision.

It was a Trull. He was stalking toward Jormund and his lips were twisted in a snarl of hatred.

"No one," rumbled the Trull, "has the right to call my son a freak. Least of all a gods damned Mandraque." He paused, glanced at the stunned Mandraques surrounding him, and muttered, "No offense."

He kept walking, grabbed the handle of the axe and yanked it out of Jormund's chest. "I don't give a damn," he continued, "what you think of me or the child's mother, but he's not a freak. He is *not a freak!*" With that howled declaration, he swung the axe around and slammed the blade into Jormund's skull. It crushed in the side and green liquid oozed out of the newly appeared cracks in his head.

"Not a freak! Not a freak!" He kept shouting it and continued to slam the axe into Jormund's head until there was nothing left of it except a bloodied mass. Jormund's effectively decapitated body slumped over to the ground, and then the Trull turned and shouted at the crowd, *"Does anyone else have something to say?"*

"I do," came a familiar voice. It was Arren and he was striding forward. He rested a hand on the Trull's shoulder. "Thank you, Eutok. That should be enough to drive home your point."

Eutok was breathing heavily over the strain of having pounded Jormund to death.

Jordund was standing next to Arren, but he did not seem the least bit put off that his father had just died, or that his murderer was standing there with apparently no fear of being held to account for his actions. One would almost have thought that he was entirely sanguine about his father's death.

Arren took in the entirety of the assemblage with a single glance and when he spoke, his voice was thick with disdain. "You are soft," he said contemptuously. "When you lived upon the vast plains of this world, you did not have to be talked into defending yourselves. If someone looked at you sidelong, that was all the inspiration you required to grab up your weapons and launch yourselves into battle. Yet now you learn that the Piri are going to be attacking this very night, and you have to be *convinced* to go into battle? This city, this Mort construct," and he gestured at the whole of Perriz, "has weakened your resolve. Made life and food and sanctuary far too simple an endeavor. It has dampened and nearly extinguished the fire of war that should be burning within your bellies.

"Yes, the fact is that the Piri are coming here for one of their own. They are coming here for his female," and he pointed at Eutok. "But the whys of their advance are irrelevant. Their motives are immaterial. What matters is one thing and one thing only: Perriz is ours. Not the Morts' and not the Piris'. *Ours.* Anyone who trespasses on it, for any reason, is subject to full retaliation by the Mandraques."

His gaze now took in the other members of the ruling council.

Gorshen, Thorda and Bazilikus were all grouped nearby. "Your leaders have forgotten what we are supposed to be. They have forsaken what the Mandraques stand for, and they offer excuses or compromises that promise self-gratification." He was pleased to see that they dropped their gazes, unable to continue staring into his eyes.

Arren turned back to the rest of the assemblage. "But I have not forgotten. I do not give a damn about those who would hold us back. I care about the Mandraques' thirst for battle. I care about the havoc that we can and should wreak upon those who would challenge us. I care about the might of the Mandraques being inflicted upon anyone who would attack us for any reason. And I now call upon the Five Clans to unite behind me to destroy the Piri!"

He waited for a roar, a cheer of unity to erupt from the throats of the Mandraques.

Nothing. Dead silence.

They stood there staring at each other, clearly waiting for somebody to step forward and take charge of the situation.

Suddenly Arren noticed that the ground was beginning to tremble beneath his feet. He realized that it had been occurring for the recent minutes but now it was becoming more violent, more pronounced. Was it the beginnings of some sort of quake? No, it didn't feel like it. It was steady and rhythmic. Like something very large that was walking toward them extremely quickly.

Then there were startled gasps from the other Mandraques as two very large and apparently very angry Ocular—a male and a female—were heading straight toward them. They were wearing those large covers over their eyes that enabled them to see the world in daylight and they appeared, by all accounts, to be quite irritated.

The Mandraques hastened to get out of their way as the Ocular stormed straight up to the area beneath the arch. They glanced briefly at Arren, then turned to the assembled Mandraques.

"You will aid us in battling the Piri," the female announced, "or else all the Ocular in this land will come out and stomp you into the ground. Do we understand each other?"

One more moment of silence, and then Thorda called out loudly, *"Death to the Piri!"*

Her cry was immediately taken up by others, and *"Death to the Piri! Death to the Piri!"* became the repeated chant as every Mandraque took up the call.

Arren looked in astonishment at Eutok and the Trull simply shrugged. "I called in some friends," said Eutok.

V.

JEPP IS SOUND ASLEEP, HER mind wandering as it typically does when she is in the throes of a dream. It used to be that she was terrified of her dreams; that her visions brought her great concern over what she would see. Now, though, she has come to accept them for what they are: her mind giving her insight into the land around her. She sees everything, even if she does not always understand it. She wishes she knew how it was that she has fully acquired this ability.

You did not.

The words slam through her mind. She had been in the midst of a glorious dream in which she was love-making with Karsen. She had been very much enjoying it, unsure of whether it presaged something for her future or was simply a nice indulgence from her mind. But now something new has intruded, and she cannot even begin to grasp its origins. "Who is that?" she asks as her love making scenario vanishes into the ether. She is now floating in darkness, and she senses that there is someone or something gazing at her.

We have met, *the voice informs her.* You have ridden on me.

It takes Jepp a moment to understand the sentence, but then she gets it. "The Liwyathan. The creature that befriended Gorkon."

I befriend no one. I simply use them to varying degrees.

"How are you communicating with me? I was dreaming…"

You still are. I know your dreams. I know the dreams of humanity, for I was there at the beginning and will be there when it ends. I have had all your history to bond. And I am tired. Very. Very. Tired.

"You're showing me something, yes? You're showing me that...I don't know. Something."

I am showing you that your time is arriving. That the future of your kind depends on you.

"How? I'm just me. I'm no one for anyone to depend on. I am no one of significance."

You have absolutely no idea who you are, or what your significance is. I, who have lived far beyond your understanding, am still learning my place in the vast scheme of things. How can you, who have lived less than an eye blink, have the faintest idea of your place in the world?

"I...guess I can't," she admits. Then, very tentatively, she says, "Can you...show me?"

Yes.

The world around her suddenly wavers and she is now standing somewhere that is incomprehensible. It is some manner of structure. The walls around her are glistening metal and silver. There are devices set into them that she cannot begin to understand. They are flat and seem to be made out of glass, but there are images dancing across them. Numbers, it appears, and letters, but she cannot understand any of them or discern what they could possibly stand for.

And there are Morts. Humans. Dozens of them, and they seem most focused on their environment. It is all most alien to Jepp, but they seem utterly comfortable in it and involved in doing...whatever it is they're doing. "Where is this?" she whispers, but the Liwyathan does not respond to her.

Having no idea what else to do, she starts walking. She continues to look around in bewilderment, moving through different areas of this vast building, still without understanding.

And then she stops.

And stares.

And gapes.

She is standing in front of a large window, and she is gazing down at something she cannot begin to comprehend. It is a vast ball of blue *and green, turning beneath her, and it is surrounded by the blackness of night skies. In the far distance is the glowing ball that climbs into the air every morning and provides them light and visibility. And there are far more glowing balls scattered throughout the night sky, hundreds, even thousands of them. Stars. They are called stars, she recalls. But they are not twinkling the way they do when she gazes up at them at night. Instead they glow steadily, and they are far more beautiful than she ever would have thought possible.*

"Gods," she whispers again. "What is this place?"

Then a face is being reflected back at her in the glass. She spins to see the face's owner. It is a young man, and he looks confused. She realizes that he is not looking directly at her, but where her reflection would be in the glass if she were casting one. But that makes no sense at all. How can he possibly be seeing her?

All things are possible, *the voice of the Liwyathan echoes within her once more.*

"Who are all these people?" she asks. "Is this a dream? Am I imagining it?"

These people will die unless we help.

"How am I supposed to help?"

The Liwayathan does not answer, but suddenly she feels her body being yanked through space. She is standing in a new, vast area, filled with machinery she does not understand. Most of the Morts have congregated here, and they seem to be very focused on the large devices that occupy the area. Everything around her is silent save for the babbling of the Morts, who are speaking with obvious concern. They are worried because something called "engines" are not working. Apparently if they continue not to function, this "ship" is going to crash…

A ship. She is on a ship. She has been on ships before, when the Travelers—the Phey—were bringing her to the Spires. But that traversed only water. This ship…

Gods, it traverses air. That has to be it. That vast green and blue image that she had been staring down at without the faintest idea of what it was…that had to be the Damned World. She is above it, in the land of the stars. And this ship is going to descend to it because these "engines" are not functioning properly.

It will plummet and, judging by the worried voices she is hearing, it is not going to survive. She is surrounded by walking dead people.

She cannot allow that to happen.

So she focuses on restarting the engines.

She has no idea how it works. She has no clue as to its operation. All she knows is that this ship requires it to be operational so that the vessel will not be destroyed, and so she focuses all her energy upon it. "Live," she orders it. "Live. LIVE!" She shouts with all the energy of her desire to see others of her kind, to change her world from what it is to something that is evocative of what it once was. She screams with a passion that is partly supplemented by the Liwyathan, but stems also from what can only be described as the depths of her soul. "LIIIIIIVE!" she bellows into the silence.

The engine roars to life.

THE ARGO

I.

IT WAS THE STRANGEST THING that Jason had ever seen.

He had been gazing out the window, staring at the Earth as the *Argo* steadily approached it. Despite all the people whom he had awakened, he was certain that they were not going to be able to revitalize the engines. It was hopeless; the ship's orbit had already deteriorated to the point where re-entrance into the Earth's atmosphere was simply inevitable. The only question was whether they were going to be able to withstand reentry and burn up in the atmosphere, or survive but end up crashing to the ground. Yes, granted, the Earth was three quarters water, so they would likely land on some wet area, but the ship would then sink like a rock and they could all live out their lives at the bottom of the sea. That sounded exciting.

But all those depressing notions fled his mind when he stared into the window and saw someone else looking back at him. At first he had tried to tell himself that he was imagining it, yet he knew that he wasn't. Someone had been staring straight back at him. It had definitely been a female. He hadn't been able to determine much beyond that; he couldn't even discern her hair color. He was certain he hadn't imagined it. She had seemed as surprised to see him as he was to see her. No, it was more than that. He realized that she had been surprised that he had been able to see her. He wasn't entirely sure how he had come to understand that, but he was certain that he was right.

That meant that she was another individual who had been spying on him from…from some other realm. But that made no sense at all. Jason was many things, but being superstitious was not among his attributes. He was not inclined to accept the idea that there was some ghost from a dimension over who was watching them. That, though, left him with the question of who was she? Then he realized that it was a question to which he would never be able to find an answer, because the *Argo* was going to be plummeting out of the sky before much longer.

Then he was startled by a sharp whistling noise from his left, and he realized that it was the ship's intercom. The device hadn't been used much, but it was obviously functioning. It wasn't the most efficient thing on the ship: The summoning whistle sounded all over the ship, followed by the caller's request of who they wanted to talk to. Once you tapped the "receive" button it was routed directly to you and you had privacy, but it was still annoying as hell.

"Jason Tanner," Medea's voice barked over the intercom. *"Pick up please."*

Jason stepped over to the unit and punched the receive button. "Jason here. Go ahead, Medea."

"You need to get down to the engine room, right now."

The urgency in her voice sounded combined with genuine excitement, as if she had good news for him. So that, at least, was positive.

"On my way," he shot back, and then turned and sped down the corridor as fast as possible.

He ran past a number of the newly thawed survivors of the *Argo*. Upon seeing him many of them tossed off a salute that he hurriedly returned without even bothering to make eye contact. The ship's imminent crash was hanging over him like a sword of Damocles, and if Medea had any sort of good news to impart to him, he was extremely anxious to hear it.

Jason descended into the engineering section and even as he did so, he heard a sound that made his heart jump. There was noise coming from the engines. They had been brought back on line. He hadn't the slightest idea how they had managed it, but somehow they had bypassed the main controls and gotten them up and running. It was a miracle in a world that didn't generally seem to believe in miracles anymore.

But even as he jumped down to the main entranceway, he realized that something was wrong. The engines were generating noise, yes, but they were still not firing at full power. He wasn't at all sure whether there was enough power to push the ship back into orbit, or if they were even firing on all cylinders.

Medea and Ada, along with several other engineers, approached him as he came down the main catwalk. "What have we got?" said Jason.

"The reverse thrusters came back on," said Ada, moving past Medea and stepping in close to Jason. "We don't have sufficient power to get us back into orbit, but we can at least do something to control our landing."

"Control it how much? Can we guide our course?"

"Not at the speeds we're moving. The thrusters can't guide us; just slow down our descent."

"So we could still come down pretty much anywhere."

"That's correct."

"How long?"

"Hours," said Medea. "We're descending pretty fast."

"Okay, then," said Jason with authority. "Let's haul ass to the command post. I'm going to try and steer this thing to a safe landing."

Medea, to his surprise, rested a hand on his arm. "Can you really pilot the ship?"

"I've lived my whole life here," he said with a touch of grim amusement. "I know the ins and outs of how to handle this thing. Maybe I'm not quite the engineering genius that you and your fiancée are, but…"

Suddenly Medea's eyes flashed. "You're the captain of this vessel, right?"

"Yes."

She reached out and her right hand curled around the fingers of Ada's left hand. "Can you marry us?"

Oh my God...

Ada looked completely stunned. "What? This...Maddy, this is so sudden..."

"Honey," Medea said, working to keep her voice even. "I don't know if you've noticed, but we're likely not going to survive. We've got the thrusters on line to slow us down, but no engines to guide us. Jason, what are the odds of us making a safe landing under those circumstances?"

Jason cleared his throat. "About fifty-fifty."

"You're being overly optimistic, I think."

"Even if we manage to survive a fall into the ocean, the ship has no means of flotation. So we'll sink to the bottom of the ocean with no means of attaining the surface. If we're able to land in a body of water that's shallow enough for us to land, the chances are the impact of the landing will crush the ship despite the thrusters. So our chances of prolonged longevity are not good." He paused and then lay a hand on her shoulder. "But I'll do my best."

"I'm sure you will," she replied, patting his hand, and for an instant his soul soared. He imagined her touching him all over, imagined the two of them making love as the ark sped toward Earth and its likely doom. But then she reached over and took one of Ada's hands in both of hers. "In case we don't make it, though, this may well be our last chance to getting around to marriage. Ada, please..."

"Fine, fine!" Ada said and she laughed, pulled Medea's head to her and kissed her soundly.

For an instant Jason considered asking both of them to kneel, then getting a baseball bat and smashing their heads in. Just as quickly, though, he sighed and said heavily, "Join hands."

They did so.

"Do you, Medea, take Ada, and do you Ada, take Medea."

"Couldn't do anything more fancy?" asked Ada.

He glared at her. "We don't have a ton of time. This is the best you're going to get. Do you or don't you?"

"We do." "Yes." "Of course." Their voices overlapped each other.

"Fine. I now pronounce you wife and wife. If you're going to go off on a honeymoon, I would say you have," and he glanced at his watch, "about an hour and a quarter. So go off and hurry."

"No, sir," Medea said, sounding formal. "Our allegiance right now is to the ship and whatever we can do to help."

"Good. Then haul your asses back to the engineering room and see what you can do about getting us full engine power."

"Yes, sir," said Ada, and she tossed off a salute.

Jason realized that he liked it. He appreciated the idea of people in the ship treating him as if he were in charge. In point of fact, he was. Nobody else knew the vessel as well as he did, and his father's suicide rendered him in charge by default. He was truly okay with that.

Now if only they could survive.

II.

THE COMPOST.

That was what Jason realized the abbreviation for "command post" should be.

Seriously? The compost? He wasn't entirely sure what compost was, exactly, but he was reasonably sure it had something to do with excrement, and really anything that had to do with excrement couldn't be especially positive.

He figured that he would continue to call it by its full name, the command post, in order to avoid smirks of those around him.

And there were certainly people around him. Several of the people that he had defrosted had offered to help him try and land the vast ship, and he didn't have any real reason to refuse their offers. He wasn't entirely sure what sort of orders to give them because there was nothing they could do that he couldn't do faster and more easily himself.

The only one who really inspired any confidence in him was Matt Ciccone. More formally, he was lieutenant Matt Ciccone, one of the four-dozen soldiers who were part of the crew. Their main job was defense, but they also had various specialties that made them useful. Ciccone was in his late thirties, early forties, with a buzz cut and what seemed to be permanent five o'clock shadow. In addition to being a straight up soldier, Ciccone was a skilled navigator, and he was guiding the descending vessel as best he could.

The surface of the Earth seemed to be reaching up toward them, the great hand of unseen gravity pulling them down. Aside from Ciccone, he hadn't bothered to remember the names of his "officers" because he reasoned that he would wait until he was in a situation where he had to learn them. If the ship impacted with any great deal of force, or in the wrong place, the crash would kill everyone immediately, so what would be the point of getting all their names down?

The ship's exterior was superheating as it slammed through the atmosphere, but fortunately enough the heat shields combined with the ship's hull seemed to be doing the job. "Reverse thrust in three… two…one…trigger," said Jason.

His words were instantly relayed down to engineering where the tech crew was able to jump the reverse thrusters back to life again. The ship thundered and shuddered as the thrusters did their job, slowing down the ship's descent yet again. Fuel consumption was a concern, which was why they could not simply keep the thrusters on line the entire time.

Jason timed off ten seconds and then ordered the thrusters shut down. They immediately went off and the ship continued to fall. He continued to follow procedures over the next hour as the *Argo* kept plummeting to its inevitable termination point.

"Where are we coming in?" he asked.

Ciccone at the navigation console studied it. "The North Atlantic. About two hundred miles East of the United States."

"Little far to swim," Jason muttered.

"What was that, sir?"

"Nothing useful," Jason said.

Three more times Jason cycled the thrusters through, and finally one of the people informed him that they were thirty seconds from impact.

"Ignite thrusters and keep them going until we land," he ordered.

Seconds later the thrusters once more came to life and Jason…

Jason prayed.

He had never prayed. He had never believed in God, because he simply could not accept the notion that there was some divine being who was willing to stand aside and let creatures from legend annihilate his creations. If such a being did exist, then Jason did not have the slightest interest in praying to him. Why should he worship such a thorough bastard?

Yet now, with the potential end of humanity hanging before him, he could not help himself.

If you're there, if you're listening…this is your chance to help us after abandoning us to those creatures. You can make up for it by allowing us to survive somehow. Enable the ship to float. Bring the main engines on line so we can control our landing. Something, anything. Don't let this be the last moments of your greatest creation. Save us. Please. I'll even start praying to you. There are one hundred and seventy five people on this ship and every single one of them deserve to live. I know, I know: Mark Twain said that if you existed, then the odds were that you were a malign thug. I always bought into that. You have a chance to prove him wrong. Come through for us. Come through.

He honestly didn't know what to expect. Lightning crashing across the sky accompanied by a loud burst of thunder. A gigantic hand reaching down and catching the ship. Something, anything. But there was nothing, not the slightest indication that some vast invisible, unknowable sky deity was listening and remotely interested in doing anything to save them. "Figures," he said softly, and then seconds later the ship slammed into the water.

"What do we do now, sir?" one of the men asked.

"Keep the thrusters firing," he said. "Order all crew to the life pods…wait. Damn. We don't have lifepods. Medea was right. Idiots."

"Sir!"

"Quiet! I'm thinking!"

"But sir—!" Ciccone now spoke up.

Jason was on his feet and he said loudly, "Did you not hear me?"

"Perfectly, sir, but I think you should know we're not sinking! We're moving!"

That announcement immediately got Jason's attention. "That's… that's not possible. We can't be moving."

"We are, sir! Our underside is on some sort of raised land, like an island, and the island is moving us!"

That made absolutely no sense to Jason, but he decided there was only one way to test it. "Kill the thrusters," he said.

They promptly did so, and to Jason's complete astonishment, the ship was indeed moving forward. It wasn't propelling itself at all. It was just somehow sailing along on the surface of the water.

"How is this happening?" said Jason. He received nothing but confused looks from those surrounding him. "Okay, fine: I'll find out myself."

He descended from his command chair and headed quickly to the airlock. Certainly there was no issue with space's vacuum considering they were on Earth, but it was the nearest exit out of the ship. To his surprise, Medea and Ada were arriving at the same place, along with a number of other crew members. They were staring at Jason in confusion and curiosity, clearly interested to see what he was going to do.

"Let's go see what the hell is going on," he said, and started the airlock's opening process. The door hissed loudly and then swung open. Were they in space, this would have been the point where he would close the inner door and then open the outer exit. Instead he began the exit process while keeping the inner door open.

"Warning," the computer shouted and red lights began to flash.

Jason ignored them, tapping a six-digit code into a nearby keypad, which promptly overrode the safety mechanisms. The red flashing lights shut down and the outer door cycled open.

He stepped forward and was immediately sprayed in the face by a fine mist of water.

He gasped in astonishment as the water continued to spray at him. But that paled in comparison to the sensation of sunlight that burnished him. He couldn't believe. He was feeling overwhelmed by what he was experiencing. It was beyond anything that he had ever encountered before. It was overwhelming, these feelings that he knew anyone born on Earth underwent so routinely that they didn't even think about it. Sun, air, and spray…these were all normal things that didn't strike any human being as remotely unusual. But for Jason, it was just unbelievable.

He heard the hushed voices of other humans behind him. They likely wanted to push him out of the way so that they could likewise feel what he was feeling, but collectively they held back out of respect. Jason's legs began to shake wildly and he suddenly sank to his knees, feeling as if his entire body had become heavy. He realized immediately the reason for it: the Earth's gravity. Thanks to the rotation of its inner core, the *Argo* likewise had gravity, but it was doubtless lighter than the pull of Earth's gravity. He needed time to adjust as likely did everyone else on the ship. "Sit down!" he shouted to everyone behind him. "Grab some ground before you collapse! Send word throughout the ship!" His words were immediately relayed to everyone within earshot as Jason sat there on the edge of the airlock, starring out raptly at the vast vista of oceanic nothingness that was laid out before him.

"This is Earth. This is Earth," he kept whispering, not quite able to wrap his consciousness around it. The planet where his ancestors had been born, the world that he had been certain he would never be able to experience on his own.

But how the hell were they moving?

That was the immediate question that he needed to answer. A close second was, Where were they going?

He edged his way further out of the airlock and then very carefully slid out of it completely and settled onto the land that the ship was resting on. He lay his hand flat on it. It was like nothing he had ever touched before. He knew what dirt was but had no clue what it should feel like. But he had a feeling that this wasn't it. Instead it felt as if it was some sort of smooth rock, yet there was a deep warmth to it. If he hadn't known better, he would have thought that the moving island was alive. That didn't make any sense, though, but…

"Hello."

His head snapped around and his jaw dropped.

There was something in the water looking up at him. It looked like a cross between a human being and a walrus. Its skin was grayish/brown and it was studying them with intense curiosity.

And it spoke English.

It spoke English?!

"You speak English?" said an astounded Jason.

"I do?" it said. Then it shrugged. "All right."

"Get down!"

The voice came from behind Jason and his head snapped around just in time to see a crewman holding a gun. He was swinging it up and aiming it straight at the creature. The creature, clearly having not a clue what the gun was, stared at it with curiosity.

"No!" shouted Jason, and he grabbed at the gun just as it went off. It ricocheted off the ground directly in front of the creature, and it jumped back in clear surprise at the projectile. An extended Jason snagged the gun and for half a second found himself staring straight down the barrel. If it went off, that would be the instant end of him. His instinct was to release it, but instead he held on and once again shouted, "No! Let go of it!"

The surprised crewman did so and Jason yanked the gun from his hand. "It's one of them!" whispered the crewman.

"You think I don't know that? Is it attacking?"

"Well, it—"

"Is it attacking?"

The crewman paused and then shook his head. "No, sir. But I thought it might."

"Well, how about you keep your damned thoughts to yourself. Anyone else?" He raised his voice. "Anyone else have a gun?"

There were a few hesitant nods. Apparently some of them had taken the time to swing by the armory before the ship had landed. Perhaps they had believed they were going to be trapped in a gunfight the moment they hit the planet's surface, having forgotten that the creatures had somehow managed to render all shooting weapons useless when they'd first arrived.

"Holster them," Jason ordered. "All of them. I swear to God, if I see even a hint of steel, I'm going to put a bullet in them myself. Is that clear?"

There were reluctant nods from all around.

"Good," he said and turned back to the floating creature. "Do you have a name?"

"Gorkon," replied the creature.

"What are you?"

"I am a Markene. My kind lives in the water, as does the Liwyathan."

"The who?"

"The Liwyathan." Gorkon tapped the surface that was supporting the vessel. "This."

The truth of what Gorkon was saying to him slowly fed through to Jason. He stared down, truly stared at the surface under the ship and realized that it wasn't remotely dirt. It was alive. They were riding on a living creature.

"This thing is a beast?"

"It is *the* beast. It is almost as old as the damned world. At least so it says. It..." Surprisingly, Gorkon shrugged. "It is the Liwyathan." That seemed to be all the explanation that was required.

"What is it doing here?"

"He brought you here. He brought all of us here." Gorkon nodded his head behind himself and Jason saw, to his amazement, an entire herd of the creatures. They were swimming in the near distance, and there had to be hundreds of them. Some of them were watching him guardedly with obvious suspicion. They seemed to be worried that…well, hell, that he might pull out a gun and shoot them.

"Why did he do that? And is he bringing us somewhere?"

"Yes," said Gorkon. He had been swimming alongside the moving beast, but now he had splashed forward and had pulled himself up onto the surface of the Liwyathan. He was utterly hairless and Jason couldn't even begin to guess what his skin felt like.

He. Jason realized that he was now thinking of this Markene, this "Gorkon," as having a personal pronoun rather than being an "it."

"Where is he bringing us?"

"To Dizz," Gorkon said, which was not exactly the degree of help that Gorkon might have considered it would be. "Once we get close enough, my people are going to transport you off the vessel individually and bring you to dry land. There you will help battle on behalf of the Phey. They are under attack. Or will be under attack." He frowned. "It is not always easy to understand the world in the way that the Liwyathan understands it. As long as he does, though, I suppose it makes sense."

"I have no idea what you're talking about," said Jason. "We aren't soldiers. Well, some of us are. But mostly we aren't."

"If you have sufficient arms and sufficient gratitude, then I believe you can fight."

"What do you mean sufficient gratitude?"

"Well," Gorkon said patiently, "the Liwyathan desires your efforts in this matter. And he is currently keeping your vessel afloat. If you decide you do not want to aid him, I am unsure as to how he will react. He might continue to transport you. Or he might simply submerge and leave you to go on your own. If you wish to take your chance, I will convey your desires to him."

"No, don't," Jason said immediately, his mind racing. "Let me bring the situation to my people."

"As you wish," said Gorkon. "However, may I suggest that you do not attempt to lie. The Liwyathan is quite skilled at perceiving lies and I do not think he would appreciate any falsehoods." He slid beneath the ocean's surface and was gone.

Jason sagged back, stunned over what he had just witnessed. And he had absolutely no idea what he was going to tell his people.

But he had a feeling there was one thing he was going to have to confirm right now.

He crawled back into the interior. Standing near the front of the corridor was Ciccone. He was leaned up against the wall, and it seemed as if he wasn't being as drastically affected by the heavier gravity as Jason was. He stretched his hand down to Jason and Jason gripped it firmly and allowed himself to be hauled up. His legs wavered but he balanced himself against the wall.

"Lieutenant," he said in a low voice, "who's in charge here?"

Ciccone did not even hesitate in his reply. "You are, sir."

"Good. Get me to the assembly hall and then get everyone else there as fast as you can. People who can walk should walk. If they need rides, find wheelchairs or even just have the sturdier people help them. We need to discuss some stuff and we need to do it fast."

"Yes, sir," said Ciccone.

Jason had never been quite so pleased to hear those two words said in conjunction with each other.

III.

THE ASSEMBLY HALL HAD BEEN designed specifically to be used for what it was now being employed for: somewhere for as many people on the crew as possible to gather to hear announcements or have meetings.

Jason was seated at the front of the room. He kept flexing his feet, endeavoring to make certain that he had full strength and would be capable of standing when next he endeavored to. Every time he pumped his legs he felt stronger, so he considered that a hopeful indication. He felt as if he could not allow himself to display any manner of weakness.

The people in the room were staring at him with obvious astonishment, because he had just got done informing them of the specifics of their situation, and they were clearly processing it.

Characteristically—indeed, typically—it was Medea who stood first and said with slow incredulity, "They want us to fight…on their behalf?"

"That is the case," said Jason.

"But they invaded us. Assaulted us. Tried to destroy us."

"And now, as near as I can tell, they are turning against each other. If that's the case," said Jason, trying to sound reasonable, "then it would certainly be to our advantage to develop alliances. Wouldn't you say?"

"I…"

"He's right," said Ada, and suddenly Jason was as in love with her as he had ever been with her wife.

Medea looked at her in surprise and there were murmurs from throughout the room.

"He is?" said Medea.

"Of course he is," said Ada and she rose, pushing back her chair. "Look, I know that it would be great to pretend that what happened didn't happen. But it did, and we don't have a time machine to scroll it back. We need to live in the world we're currently in, and if one group is fighting another, we have to come down on somebody's side. Otherwise, for all we know, they may just turn around and unite against us."

"I think she's absolutely correct," Jason said immediately as relief began to surge within him. It seemed as if he was actually going to be able to pull this off. "We need allies and these 'Phey,' whatever they are…"

"Phey are fairies," called out one voice. "At least according to old stories."

"See there? Fairies. Fairies are being assaulted. Certainly we'd want to help fairies, right?"

"You're out of your mind."

It was Bill Tucker, the guy whose computer Jason had destroyed. He didn't think that Tucker was petty enough to want to screw this up for Jason simply because Jason had smashed up his computer.

Honestly, though, at that point Jason wasn't beyond putting anything past anybody.

Tucker rose to his feet and there was clear anger on his face. "I mean it, Jason. You are completely out of your mind."

"I would appreciate it if you could convey your thoughts minus the insults, Tucker," Jason said carefully, keeping his voice flat and neutral. He realized he was gripping tightly onto the arm of his chair and endeavored to prevent it from trembling.

"My thought is this: it is insane to demand that we fight alongside any of these creatures, whether they're fairies, elves or leprechauns. They killed billions of humans, Jason, and doubtlessly enslaved any who managed to survive. And now they're asking for our help, and you think we should go along with it?"

"The one who is asking for our help is currently preventing us from sinking to the bottom of the ocean."

"Then fine!" said Tucker in clear frustration. "Say that you'll help them, and then once it gets us to land, we bolt as fast as we can."

"So you're saying we should lie."

"Yes! *Obviously!*"

"It's my belief that that would be a bad idea. That the creature would be able to tell that I was being less than honest, and that could rebound to our disadvantage. Besides," he continued before Tucker could speak over him, "you're right! These creatures did kill billions of us. And if we can join together and inflict some payback against them, where's the harm in that?"

"The harm is that they could then turn around and slaughter us, too!"

"I get the impression that wouldn't happen."

"You get the *impression*?" He made no effort to hide his astonishment. "We are supposed to fight and die on your impression?"

Slowly Jason got to his feet. His legs were shaking, but only slightly, and he was reasonably sure that no one in the room could see it happening. "That, Mr. Tucker, is exactly what you are supposed to do. I have maintained this vessel and kept you alive for the entirety of my life. Responsibility for the future of the human race is what I was born for, trained for, lived for. When you signed onto this vessel, you signed documentation that deferred power over your lives to whoever was in charge of this ship. That would be me. My thoughts on the matter are simple: the creature that has rescued us from living out the rest of our lives in the bottom of the ocean is now seeking our help. We need to help him."

"If we sank to the bottom of the ocean, that would give us time to repair our engines!"

"We do not have sufficient fuel to lift off again, even if we could fix the engines. This is our only shot."

"I disagree," said Tucker, "and if we can't do anything because you're in charge, then I say we have elections and see if we can put someone else in charge!"

There was now a rapid series of murmurs spreading through the room. It was obvious that a number of people in there were agreeing with him. This entire thing was rapidly skidding off the rails, and Jason had no idea how to deal with it.

Then the means to do so instantly leaped into his head. He wasn't sure he was thrilled with it, but it seemed literally the only answer.

"Lieutenant Ciccone," his voice suddenly thundered over the people who seemed determined to discuss whether he should be remaining in charge.

Ciccone was toward the back of the room. He immediately drew himself up and strode across the room, clearly immune to any affects from Earth's gravity. Ciccone was at least a head taller than just about anyone else in the place and everyone looked up at him as he walked across the space between him and Jason and stood at attention before him.

"Lieutenant Ciccone, who is in charge here?" he asked.

"You are, sir."

"Good. Three things: you are now Captain Ciccone."

"Thank you, sir," said Ciccone, and he snapped off a salute that Jason immediately returned.

"Play your cards right, you could be General before the day is out. Second: I want you to secure the armory."

"Already done, sir."

Jason blinked in surprise at that. "Really?"

"First thing I did when we landed, sir. Four guards outside. I had no idea what sort of situation we were descending into and decided it best to secure our weaponry."

"Good lad. Last thing: that fellow over there, Mr. Tucker? He's being insubordinate. Would you be so kind as to put a bullet in his brain?"

Ciccone blinked in surprise at that, but then without hesitation he nodded, withdrew his service revolver, and swung it around, pointing it straight at Tucker's head.

All the blood went out of Tucker's face. Jason couldn't be quite sure, but...yes, he was right. A large spot of discoloration had appeared on the front of Tucker's trousers. Poor bastard had peed himself. *"Wait! Wait!"*

"Hold up, Captain," said Jason. Ciccone immediately lowered his gun. "Have any final words, Mr. Tucker?"

"You'd really do this? Have this guy shoot me?"

"If you wish, I can do it myself."

Jason calmly withdrew the gun that he had taken off the guy earlier, the one who had tried to shoot Gorkon. He aimed it at Tucker, trying not to allow the trembling in his arm to reveal the horror he was facing in what he was doing. "Do you find this preferable?"

"No! I..." Tucker swallowed deeply, his gulp sounding throughout the entire silent room. For a moment Jason was worried that others might put themselves in between Jason and his gun. That they might seize this moment to take a stand and insist that if he was going to shoot one of them, then he'd have to shoot all of them. If that happened, he'd have to fold. "I just...I don't want to die. Not here and not fighting beside those things."

"Those things," Jason said slowly, "have been part of Earth's history for millennia before anyone on this ship was born. The creature that's

supporting this vessel may well have been here before the dinosaurs."
He sighed deeply although he was careful to keep his gun leveled.
"I've been reading up on those things during my time here. Studying
every last broadcast, every report, every bit of information I could
garner about them. And I am telling you all that they have their own
enemies, their own problems, and their own situations. We have
drones surveying the Earth's surface, are you aware of that? I don't
pretend to understand everything that I've seen, but some of it has
been horrific. There was a city of giants down there, and they're all
dead now from some sort of nuclear mishap. There was an attack on
Paris. They are constantly trying to kill each other. I think that maybe
our involvement may actually turn things around. May convince them
to live together, and to live with us. Right now the ones who have
saved us say our help is needed. I tend to believe them. And if you
don't want to believe them, and you're going to fight against me, then
I'm going to kill you. Right now." He notched back the hammer on
the gun.

Tucker immediately said, "I'll fight with you. I mean, alongside
you."

"Really." Jason did not sound as if he believed him.

"Yes, really. I swear. You've convinced me. I'll follow you into
battle."

"Okay. Because if you say you will and then turn against me,
Captain Ciccone will be sure to kill you." His glance swayed to
Ciccone. "Gut shot. He'd died slow from that, yes?"

"Yes, sir. Two, three days."

"Good." He put the hammer back into its original position. "Do
we have skipjacks, Captain?"

"Yes, sir. Plenty."

"Excellent. Make sure they're tuned up. Everybody else: rest up.
We have a war to fight, and a chance to get some payback on some
of the bastards who destroyed the human race."

A ragged cheer went up. Jason figured he'd settle for ragged,
under the circumstances.

DIZZ

"I'M NOT STAYING HERE." GANT said, staring out the window at the Phey who were just completing the ward. "Somehow, we're responsible for those monsters showing up here. I'm not going to hide up here while those bastards come crashing into Dizz, killing whatever they see."

"They'll kill you if they see you," Tania warned him.

"If that is to happen, then so be it," said Gant. He glanced around. "Graves. Trott. Are you with me?"

For a moment they stared at him silently, and then Graves shrugged. "I suppose. It's not as if I have anything else planned. Trott?"

Trott just nodded indifferently, as if he were being asked to take a stroll in the woods.

"All right, let's get out there, then." Gant pulled up the hood of his cloak and then turned to Tania. "You stay here."

"But—"

"You're not a warrior, Tania."

"Neither are you!" she protested. To his surprise, she stroked his cheek in what seemed to be definite affection. "I don't want you to go out there and get killed."

"It's not my top vote either," Gant said reasonably. "But I'm not going to hide up here. Obertan, make damned sure she stays here."

Obertan shrugged. "I will make my best efforts to keep her here, but that is certainly not up to me."

He had no idea how to respond to that, so he simply repeated, "Stay," to Tania and then turned and headed for the door. Before he exited, though, Obertan spoke up. "I perceive you have swords. You may wish to grab some shields. Might be useful." He waved a hand languidly towards some shields that were mounted on the walls, and the three Phey immediately took them down. Then Gant exited. Graves followed close behind him and Trott took up the rear.

They emerged onto the main street and Gant could sense the energy humming in the air. He felt as if it were charging the hairs in his nostrils. It was early evening, and lights were illuminating the main street. They were very pale, however, flickering on and off. It reminded him of the unpredictable hotstars that had powered the van of the Bottom Feeders, and how they had been running out of power more and more frequently.

Gant slid back his hood, grateful for the non-existent sunlight so that the Piri body he was inhabiting was not going to present any problems.

"You all right?" said Graves, one eyelid cocked in curiosity.

"Yes, yes. I'm fine."

The three of them strode forward into the center of the street, where the mystics were just finishing placing up the wards that were to serve as their protection. Gant stepped in close to one of them, who seemed older and the likely leader of the spells. "Obertan claims these are going to be useless," he said in a low voice. "That the enemy has discovered some manner of tunnels?"

The older Phey turned and stared at him with a confused look. "When did he say that?"

"Just a few minutes ago."

"No. No, he would have said something earlier."

Lowering his voice as much as he could, Gant murmured, "He claims that he has seen the end of everything. Perhaps he simply does not care anymore."

"That can't be," the older Phey shook his head with determination. "Obertan would never give up on us."

"Either that or he would never tell you what he knew in order not to dash your hopes," said Graves, stepping forward and looking impatient. "Did you ever consider the possibility that he was trying to shield you?"

"Magister!" said one of the Phey, approaching with a confident stride. "It's finished. We are protected."

The one addressed as Magister nodded his head and smiled as he turned toward Gant. "You see? Nothing to worry about at all."

That was when all hell broke loose.

There was a collection of noises that sounded like whinnies combined with the roars of full-grown men and suddenly walls from all around them were being smashed apart. Pieces of wood flew everywhere, but it wasn't as if those shards were any real problem. No, it was rather the collective causation from the stampeding creatures who were blasting it apart and slamming forward into the main street. Whoresmen came piling out onto the street, swinging swords, wielding bows and arrows and howling challenges to all surrounding them. On their backs were Serpenteens, each of them wielding what appeared to be short spears with sharp, curved heads that bore a strong resemblance to fangs. That somehow made sense to Gant. Naturally their armament be modeled upon their natural weapons.

"Fall back!" bellowed the Magister, and Gant and his friends, as well as a contingent of armed Phey, immediately did so. The Magister and several other spell casters charged forward, their hands moving quickly, blue glows emanating from their palms. A blast of the energy erupted from their hands, slamming forward and hurling the charging Whoresmen backwards. The Serpenteens fell from their backs, crashing to the ground, momentarily helpless. But only momentarily, for they scrambled to their feet and charged forward, their weapons out.

"Don't kill them unless you have to!" shouted one of the Whoresmen, who Gant immediately recognized as Chyron. "We want their magic!"

"You want it? Here's more if it!" the Magister shouted, and he waved his hands. Instantly the ground beneath their hooves began to crack, and thick vines extended from the dirt beneath them.

The Whoresmen tried to kick their way through the rapidly

gathering vines, but the plants were extremely insistent, gathering thicker and thicker as they endeavored to tangle their hooves and impede their approach.

But then the Serpenteens slid toward them, practically slithering on their scaled arms and legs, and they spit thick green venom at the vines. The vines struggled against the poison, actually seeming to writhe in agony as the venom seeped in through them. Immediately the venom became brown instead of green, twisting away and into themselves as if they were sentient beings in pain. The Magister looked stunned as he watched their plant defenders moving away from the oncoming Serpenteens as if they were afraid of them.

More were now coming at them from all directions. The Magister hesitated, clearly unsure of what spell to throw or where to cast it. The Whoresmen were giving out shouts of triumph, and that was when Gant lunged forward with his sword out, leaping over the dying vines and swinging his blade at the nearest Serpenteen. The creature spotted him at the last minute and drew back, but Gant struck him on the upper shoulder and blood welled from the slash. The Serpenteen let out a horrified gasp of pain, and now the other blade wielders charged forward, coming in fast and aggressive. The Serpenteens aligned and began spitting their green venom once again. They were clearly going for the kill, rather than the paralysis their heads of snakes could cause. Gant and the other swung their shields up, intercepting the globs, and they sizzled against the surfaces of the shields but didn't penetrate.

Now the Whoresmen took the charge. Their hooves were vicious weapons, and they had both swords and massive clubs in their hands that they were swinging around in wide circles. And the Phey fell back, driven backwards by the strength of their charges.

Chyron battled forward and Gant intercepted him just before he could club down the Magister. Chyron actually grinned when he saw him. "I owe you a great deal," he snarled. He was wielding a broadsword and he brought it down again and again on Gant's shield. The shield was made of metal and every time Chyron struck it, it actually dented it severely. Gant struggled, his knees buckling from the impact, and then he fell. Chyron's hooves slammed down toward him and he barely managed to roll out of the way in time.

There was now a full-on battle raging through the main street of Dizz. It seemed as if Whoresmen and Serpenteens were coming from everywhere, and it was far too many attackers for the Phey to have to deal with. The Phey were accustomed to being the wandering servers of the Overseers, the formidable Travelers who everyone lived in fear of. And when they had gone up against the Morts, their magic had defused the Morts' weapons so that they were helpless before the charges of the others of their kind. It had been ages since the Phey had been forced into pitched battle and they were sorely out of practice.

Then Gant heard a Phey scream and his head snapped around. It was one of the swordsmen, clutching at his face as venom from a Serpenteen poured down his eyes and his cheeks, blinding him and searing away the skin. He stumbled backwards and a Whoresmen finished the job, galloping in and swinging his sword, sending the poor Phey's head flying.

"They can be killed!" shouted one of the Whoresmen, and from that moment it seemed as if it was going to be an all out slaughter.

The Phey fell back, but there was nowhere for them to go. Serpenteens and Whoresmen were on all sides, driving in a circle maneuver that gave the Phey nowhere to run. Gant had gotten to his feet and was backing up, trying to keep his shield between him and his attackers, but it was no good. There were too many attackers, too many ways to die.

Chyron was looming over him, and he pointed with his sword at Gant and shouted, *"This one first!"*

It was the last thing Chyron ever said, because his head exploded. Everything stopped.

The explosion was accompanied by a roar that sounded through the suddenly still air, a noise that no one there had ever heard.

Then another bang rang out, and another. Another Whoresmen's head exploded, and then the chest of a Serpenteen erupted in blood and he pitched forward, dead before he even struck the ground.

And from the far end of main street, a Mort came forward. He was holding something under his arm that was, at best guess, some manner of weapon. Smoke was wafting from the front of it.

He had company. A lot of company.

They were not walking. They were standing on some manner of small, hovering platforms with handlebars mounted on poles on the front of them. Gant couldn't quite discern what was enabling them to hover above the ground. Upon looking closer, he was sure he was able to see gusts of air that were emanating from the underside.

There were dozens of Morts, and they were clearly armed with some manner of weaponry that had easily disposed of Whoresmen and Serpenteens and could quite possibly attend to the others.

The Serpenteens spun and a number of them let fly with their venom. But the Morts quickly backed up and the venom fell to the ground, sizzling the pavement. It did not deter their weapons at all, and they spat out what appeared to be some sort of pellets that were flying far too fast for anyone to discern. They ripped into the Serpenteens and they shrieked as they went down, their heads and chests torn apart by the impact of the pellets. They went down, their blood flowing everywhere, and the leader of the Morts shouted, "All of them except for the caped ones! Every centaur, every one of those scaled things…take them all!"

The Whoresmen and Serpenteens tried to mount a response, but there was nothing for them to do, no way for them to attack. The pellets spat out with lethal rapidity and there was just no defense against them. Their bodies were rapidly piling up; they were tripping over themselves, trying to get away and not being able to make any progress.

Finally they bolted, heading for the only exit they could reach: the hidden doors that they had used to get in in the first place. The Morts endeavored to prevent them, their small flying platforms swiftly angling around to try and cut them off. They were able to open fire on a considerable number of them, but a handful of Serpenteens and Whoresmen were able to make it through the doors and escape into the tunnels that they had used to make their entrance.

"Blue squad, following them!" shouted the Mort who had managed to dispose of Chyron so easily that he had made it seem like nothing. A number of the Morts accompanying him headed after the Whoresmen and Serpenteens, while others gathered closer toward the leader and eyed the Phey suspiciously.

The lead Mort swung his weapon down, the muzzle pointing toward the ground, which filled Gant with some relief. He didn't think the Phey would fare particularly well against it, and began to appreciate seriously for the first time just how fortunate the Phey had been to be able to disarm the Morts' weapons during the invasion. There was no impediment of these arms, though, and it was only because of that that the Phey had not been overrun by their invaders.

The Mort guided himself over toward the Phey and hovered a few feet away from them. The others were backing him up and were making no attempt to hide their obvious distrust. For all Gant knew, they would open fire on the Phey and he was quite sure that they would not be able to withstand the pellets that these weapons had spat out with such lethal effects.

"My name is Jason," he said. "And these," and he nodded toward the others, "are the Argonauts. Who is your leader?"

The Magister stepped forward and rumbled, "Obertan."

"Bring me to him," said Jason. "Because we have a lot to talk about.

PERRIZ

I.

SUNARA REDEYE WAS SUSPICIOUS. WHICH made sense, because she was always suspicious.

It was all she could do to ignore the pain that was still radiating through her face from the burns. She kept resisting the temptation to reach up and touch it, stroke it. It wouldn't do any good and would make her seem weak. And when one was leading an invading force consisting of all one's followers into an assault on the Mandraques, that was not the time to display even the slightest hint of weakness.

I'll kill them. I'll kill them all, she kept whispering to herself.

It was very late at night, a new moon hanging in the sky and thus providing them no light in their endeavors. The Piri naturally had superb night vision, but Sunara still would not have minded having at least some light provided by nature. Sunara and the Piri had emerged from their hideaway below the streets of Perriz, and they were eagerly looking forward to devouring any Mandraques they encountered. It had been ages since Sunara was in a genuine battle, throwing herself against enemies and draining them dry. No one knew just how much power she had coursing through her veins, but she was more than happy to show any doubters exactly what she was capable of.

Except…

There weren't any.

The Mandraques were certainly not as nocturnal beings as were the Piri. Nevertheless she had lost count of the many times when she would be wandering the sewers, passing under the grates, and she would hear Mandraques at all times of night, chattering and snarling and fighting and guffawing with each other. That was what she had anticipated they would run into this night, but so far there had been nothing. Had they all just gone to sleep quite early for them? Were they all hiding within their homes?

Had they fled?

That last option came to her and at first she was having trouble believing it. Was it possible that the Mandraques knew that the Piri would be attacking them and had somehow decided that now was the ideal time to leave Perriz altogether? On the surface, the notion was unthinkable. Mandraques running from a battle en masse? Was it possible? She supposed that on some level it was. After all, why should the Mandraques throw themselves into battle with the Piri considering that they would be fighting on behalf of a Piri female and her half-breed offspring? That was certainly not the sort of thing that the Mandraques would necessarily oblige themselves to protect with any spirit. So perhaps they were indeed gone, having abandoned Clarinda and her whelp to the will of the Piri.

But she didn't think so. Somehow she just couldn't buy it.

Which still left her wondering where they were.

She gestured for Bartolemayne to come over to her, which he briskly did. He leaned down toward her and she said in a low voice, "Spread out. Stay in shadows, but survey the area. See if you can find any Mandraques."

"Do we kill them if we do?"

"No. Just watch and observe and report back to me."

"You suspect a trap?"

"Always," she said.

Her orders were quickly carried out as Bartolemayne selected six scouts to make their way in different directions through Perriz, trying to find somewhere, anywhere that the Mandraques might be hiding.

Even as the Piri did their sweeps, Sunara wasn't thinking about them at all. Instead she was focused on sniffing the air, trying to catch a whiff of the scent that she knew better than her own. Somewhere in this damnable city, Clarinda was hiding from her. Clarinda and her insufferable half-breed brat, Eutok. All Sunara needed to find her was one moment of sloppiness on Clarinda's part. If she stepped too near to a window, for instance. That was all she would need for her scent to be carried to her, provided the wind was working for her. Sunara's nostrils flared and she cursed to herself. The wind was preternaturally still this evening, making it nearly impossible for her to catch even the slightest hint of her daughter's whereabouts.

"We have something."

The pronouncement was from Bartolemayne and so soft in her ear that it caused her to jump slightly. Her head whipped around and she stared at him with impatience. "What? *What*?" she whispered, having no idea why she was speaking so softly considering there were only Piri within range.

"We found a Firedraque, standing by herself in the great plaza within range of that huge tower the Morts constructed."

Sunara's suspicions flared even more. "Just standing there? By herself? Is it that same Firedraque who came into our lair earlier?"

"Not sure, but I think so."

"Are there any others around?"

He shook his head.

"What's she doing out there?" Sunara wondered. "Out in the middle of nowhere in the dark of night? Does that make any sense to you?"

"You think it could be a trap."

"Are there any other Mandraques there?"

"None that we can see. We've scattered around all the grounds and have yet to spot anything. As near as we can determine, she's alone."

It didn't seem right to her. Why would she be there so vulnerable with no one around should she be attacked?

Could it be self-confidence? Did she seriously think that she could take on any challenges herself? Or perhaps she genuinely wanted to die. Perhaps she wanted to undergo death by Piri. Anything was possible when dealing with surface creatures.

"Launch an attack," she said finally.

"I think you should remain back," Bartolemayne warned her. "In case it is a trap of some sort."

"Yes, I agree. I will remain right here and will be fine on my own."

"Without any guards…?"

She scowled at him. "Do you think there is truly any jeopardy that I cannot deal with on my own?"

He automatically bowed. "No, Mistress. There is nothing that you cannot dispose of yourself."

She patted the side of his head. "Well said."

Bartolemayne turned from her and then, in a low voice, growled, "Everyone, with me. We have a Firedraque to kill."

"You don't necessarily have to kill her," Sunara reminded him. "If she is indeed the one who attacked us, she might well be useful for some sort of ransom."

"Very well, Mistress. If it is possible."

The Piri then turned away from her and headed out in the direction that the scouts were leading them.

And then, at that moment, the wind shifted slightly.

Sunara's nostrils flared.

She had her. She had Clarinda.

Sunara headed away from the spot where she had said she would remain, in search of her daughter.

A final reckoning was coming.

II.

THE CLOSER HE DREW, THE more convinced Bartolemayne was that it was not a trap. There were no Mandraques, none, hiding near the buildings. The site of the tower was fairly desolate, surrounded by looming statues. There were no buildings that they could be hiding in. It was entirely possible that the Firedraque had indeed simply come out into the middle of nowhere for some manner of ritual, or who knew what else?

Slowly they approached the vast tower that was cloaked in darkness. The statues were likewise hard to discern, although they were certainly impressive even in the shadow. Bartolemayne studied the shadows carefully to make sure that no Mandraques were lurking within, but there was a total lack of movement. He was positive that nothing was hiding in the shadows of the statues as the Piri drew ever closer.

The Firedraque was standing with her back to them. It was hard to discern whether she was even aware that she was being approached. Bartolemayne gestured widely for the others to fall back and he crept forward, taking the lead. If she had any tricks, any stunts, they would be utilized upon him first and he had no doubt that he would be able to withstand anything that she inflicted upon them.

His nostrils flared. A scent was wafting to him that he did not know. It smelled strong, and it was nearby, but he hadn't the faintest idea what it might be. It probably wasn't dangerous, though, and so he ignored it.

He gestured for his troops to gather in closely behind them as he got closer and closer to the Firedraque. Something prompted him to stop several feet away from her, and he glanced behind himself. All of his followers were pushing in behind him, shoving each other for position. Piri were not the best when it came to a measured offense. Their preferred method of combat was simply endeavoring to overwhelm whatever they wanted to assault through sheer numbers.

"I know you're there," said the Firedraque abruptly.

Her comment caused all the Piri to stop their movement, but Bartolemayne's eyes narrowed in suspicion. Was she unaware of just how outnumbered she was?

She turned to face them and incredibly she actually smiled. "Hello. I remember you from when we assaulted your lair. You were quite the combatant. Norda wounded you in your shoulder."

"It is nothing," he said, which wasn't quite true. Actually it hurt like hell, and the shoulder was becoming stiffer. But he'd be damned if he admitted that to her. "Thank you for providing me her name, however. I look forward to tracking her down and exacting revenge upon her."

"Oh, you won't be tracking down anyone," she said. "That will not be an option for you."

"Really. And why would that be?"

"Because you're going to die here."

Bartolemayne laughed at that, triggering mirth from the other Piri as well. It seemed a ludicrous claim, far more reckless bravado than anything actually attached to the real world. "Is that a fact," he said with no question in his voice.

"Yes, it is."

"Let me tell you what is going to happen," he said with a snarl. "You are going to tell me where Clarinda is. Then you will lead us there. And then you will die."

"Really," said the Firedraque. She seemed to give it a moment's thought, and then said, "I'm afraid that I have completely different plans for the evening."

"Yes, you've made that clear. You intend to kill us. Would you care to tell me how?"

"Well, I think it's always better to show rather than tell."

She turned and spat a short jab of flame to her right.

It hit the ground and immediately fire roared to life all around them.

The Piri stepped back, startled, and their first impulse was to run. But the flames were moving too fast and too quickly, and a huge roaring inferno surrounded them within seconds. Bartolemayne and the others shielded their eyes since they were wholly unprepared for the sudden shift in illumination from darkness into light.

"It's a flammable Mort liquid," she said. "Not sure what they called it, but it can be quite formidable. Has a rather strong scent to it that helps prevent you from noticing other smells that might have warned you off."

She strode backwards then and although there was a wall of fire there, she simply walked right through it. The flame licked at her scaled skin but didn't bother her at all. Then, over the roar of the conflagration, she raised her voice and shouted, "Get them!"

That was when two of the statues moved.

Bartolemayne gaped with astonishment as the statues leaped off their pedestals and thudded to the ground mere yards away from them. Their single eyes snapped open, covered by clear shells that apparently enabled them to see. They were Ocular and they were ready to kill any of the Piri around them.

The Ocular charged forward and there was no grace in their assault. They simply just started stomping on the Piri. Normally the Piri would have rallied, would have endeavored to overwhelm the Ocular. But they were so startled by the turn that matters had taken and clearly so blinded by the flames that they were thoroughly disconcerted. They had no idea where to look or what to do.

"Assemble yourselves!" shouted Bartolemayne. "It's only two Ocular!"

Except it wasn't, because Mandraques were hurtling over the flame walls. No, not hurtling: they were being thrown over them by their fellows.

Bartolemayne saw where they were coming from: the great tower. In the darkness, they had spanned the entire height of the structure, hiding along the vast crossbeams. Now that they were attacking, however, they were not attempting to be stealthy at all.

They descended from the tower like a massive living wave and more and more were being thrown over the tops of the flames, landing squarely amidst the Piri and cutting them down. The Piri were largely unarmed since they typically depended upon their fangs and their usual superior numbers to carry the day. But that wasn't working for them this time. The Mandraques were heavily armed and much too savage for the Piri to withstand.

Which did not stop Bartolemayne from battling back fiercely. Despite the fact that they had been lured into a horrific trap, that was not going to deter him in the slightest from fighting back against the forces that were rapidly cutting down his fellows. Because Bartolemayne did not require weapons; he had his own muscles and ferocity to carry the day as he tore into anyone who got near him. He literally ripped Mandraques apart, either yanking their heads or arms off or even, at one point, tearing one of them in half. He roared defiance at those who were trying to bring him down.

"Come on, you bastards!" he shouted furiously. "Come on! I'll kill you all!"

"Hi there," said a voice from right nearby.

He turned and looked down just in time to see Arren Kinklash with a can of something, although he didn't know what it was. Before Bartolemayne could do anything, Arren hacked the top of the can off with a sword and hurled the entire contents of the can onto Bartolemayne. It was some sort of liquid with a noxious smell that spattered all over him, and belatedly he realized that it carried the same stench of whatever the substance was that had been laid out in a circle on the ground and lit up to imprison the Piri.

"Evanna!" shouted Arren. "Care to do the honors?"

Even as he spoke, he backpedaled as the Firedraque strode forward. A couple of fleeing Piri got in her way and she shoved them aside as if she was barely noticing them. She drew within range of Bartolemayne and simply waved good-bye to him. Then her jaws snapped open and she unleashed a flame blast right at him.

Bartolemayne went up.

He screamed, beating furiously at himself to try and extinguish the fire, but it did no good. Whatever the hell Arren had tossed on him, it was igniting with far greater ferocity than he could ever have expected.

The charging Mandraques, to add insult to injury, were grabbing up Piris and throwing them directly at the burning Bartolemayne. They quickly went up as well and within seconds there was a massive bonfire of Piri blazing, illuminating the area with the light of their own flaming carcasses. Bartolemayne's arms dropped and his body collapsed as his brain liquefied.

"Where's the queen?" shouted Arren. "Did we get the queen?"

Evanna shook her head. "She's gone. And we've got to find her, fast, if we have any hope of ending this."

III.

"OF COURSE." WHISPERED SUNARA. "I should have known."

The scent could not be mistaken. Clarinda was hiding within Firedraque Hall, the immense structure that must have been one of the centerpieces of Perriz when the Morts had resided there. It towered high in the sky, although she couldn't help but notice that the upper tower had apparently been shattered. She wasn't sure what could have smashed it apart so thoroughly; perhaps there had been some sort of an attack that had included an assault on it. Whatever it was, the Firedraques would doubtless have to rebuild it at some point. But that was not going to be happening anytime soon.

Slowly, cautiously, Sunara approached the vast building. She had no idea where within Clarinda was hiding, but there was no doubt in her mind that she was going to be able to locate her. But once she did, what then?

Kill her, of course. Simple, straightforward. Sunara was no longer interested in taunting her daughter or playing with her or providing her hope that she might spare her and her unnatural son. No, she was focused on one thing and one thing only: ending her damned life.

And she wouldn't hesitate. She wouldn't even talk to her. She would just charge forward and savage her, drain the blood from her... no. Not drain. She would rip open Clarinda's throat and then throw her to the floor and allow her to bleed to death. And as Clarinda did so, her warm life spilling out all around her, the last thing she would see would be her mother drinking out the life of her hell spawn infant. Yes, that would be perfect. Sunara wondered what the blood of a half breed would taste like? Some sort of odd mixture of Piri and Trull? It was impossible to say, but Sunara knew that she would be the first to drink the blood of a half breed.

She approached the great wooden doors, wondering if they were barred against her. Then, as her feet touched the great steps that led upward, she heard something that sounded like water rushing.

She looked up.

Water was pouring down out of the mouths of statues above her. And steam was rising from the water.

Sunara judged the distance and quickly sprinted forward. She flattened against the door just as the water cascaded down where she'd been standing and even from several feet away, she could perceive the massive heat radiating off the fallen water.

Someone had attempted to dump boiling water on her.

Her lip twisted in a sneer. So that was how they were going to play it. Try to ambush her. Whoever had dumped the water must have alerted whoever was waiting inside for her, which meant she was going to be in for a fight.

Fine. Let them.

Sunara stood there for a long moment, bringing the palms of her hands together and breathing slowly in and out. She was summoning the strength that typically lay dormant within her, and then she slammed her fists forward. The doors had been locked, but whatever was keeping them closed shattered as Sunara smashed them open.

She strode into the entry area, looking left and right warily, knowing that an attack was going to be forthcoming. The only question was, from where?

Suddenly the ground began to shudder under her. Her head snapped around just in time to see a huge Minosaur bearing down on her, his head lowered, his sharpened horns glistening at the points.

Sunara twisted so that the horns wouldn't gore her, and instead he banged into her with only his head. She gripped the horns, allowing him to push her bare feet across the floor, and then she leaped forward and bounded over his head. She landed behind him and he tried to skid to a halt, but she lashed out with her leg and her foot slammed into the small of his back. The impact sent him skidding forward and crashing into the door.

Immediately she turned and now two Laocoon, the mother and son who had attacked her earlier, were charging at her. And off to the side…

Perfect. The Trull. The little bastard who had convinced her daughter to get herself impregnated. He would definitely be the last.

The male Laocoon was coming at her with a large hammer, and the female was bearing a sword. The Trull had a stone axe. How charming.

Sunara wiggled her fingers, encouraging them to charge. Her lack of concern was certain to only aggravate them further, which was Sunara's intention. Angered foes became sloppy, and she could use their sloppiness.

The female Laocoon reached her first and she swung the sword furiously with little attempt at actual technique. As powerfully muscled as she was, she didn't seem someone who embraced the art of war with any frequency. It was entirely likely that she did not have tons of experience since Laocoon were not particularly warlike, one of the few of the races that could make that contention. Clearly, though, she was willing to fight on behalf of her son, and Sunara figured that she deserved praise for that, at least.

The attacking female slashed back and forth with her sword. Sunara gauged the angle of the thrusts and effortlessly dodged right, left, right, backing up steadily. But she slowed each dodge, causing the Laocoon to come closer and closer. Sunara watched as the creature's bare breasts, naked out of the clothing habit of her kind, swayed back and forth. Then Sunara snapped her fists forward and struck the Laocoon squarely in her tits. The Laocoon cried out and it was at just that moment that Sunara sensed pounding feet coming up behind her. Apparently the Minosaur was making another run at her. Sunara timed it perfectly and leaped straight up, allowing the Minosaur to run right past her and slam into the already injured female Laocoon. His right horn skewered her upper chest, just below her clavicle, and the two of them went down in a tangle of arms and legs, her sword clattering away.

"Mother!" shouted the male Laocoon, and Sunara took his distraction as the perfect opportunity. She leaped forward and he only spotted her at the last second. He swung his battle hammer but she dodged it easily and she collided with him, driving him to the floor. She clambered atop him and drove her fangs into his throat.

"*No!*" shouted the Trull and he swung in fast and efficiently with his axe. Sunara rolled off the Laocoon, smiling with red-stained lips as she saw his blood flowing from the wound. He grabbed at it, trying to cease it before he bled out.

Eutok the Trull was not as easily distracted as the Laocoon had been. He brought his axe up and around and suddenly changed course, with the result that Sunara actually dodged the wrong way. The axe struck her in the right shoulder and she both heard and felt a sharp crack in the bone. She cried out and the Trull, becoming overconfident, charged at her at full speed. Sunara hit the ground and swung her legs around in an arc, knocking his feet out from under him. The Trull hit the ground and she leaped at him, but he countered by bringing his own feet up and catching her squarely in the solar plexus. She gasped, the air knocked out of her, and he slammed the butt end of his axe into her face. Her head snapped back and she tumbled to the floor.

And to her immediate right was the fallen sword of the Laocoon female.

The Trull charged her once more, swinging back his axe, and Sunara grabbed the sword from the floor and whipped it around with preternatural speed. It sliced directly into the Trull's left wrist and his hand went flying.

He screamed and it was a glorious sound as he lost his grip on his axe. It tumbled away and he stumbled, grabbing at his handless left wrist with his right hand. His pale skin went dead white as he stared at the blood gushing from it.

This was glorious. It could not have gone better. The Laocoon female and Minotaur were on the ground, both moaning, the Laocoon male was clutching his throat as he endeavored to halt the blood flow, and the damnable Eutok was crippled and on the ground before her.

Sunara strode forward and jammed the sword in Eutok's leg. He cried out and went down and she brought the point of the sword to his throat. "I could have just killed you immediately," she whispered to him. "But I think I will leave you here long enough for you to hear Clarinda's scream as I kill her. Yes, I believe I will do you that fa—"

"*Karsen!*"

The alarmed shriek caused Sunara's head to snap around.

It was that Mort female, the one called Jepp. She was crouched next to the fallen Laocoon, her hands moving in vague helplessness. Quickly she ripped off the small bit of clothing that covered her breasts, wadded it up, and placed it onto the wound.

"Very clever," said Sunara. "It may even sa—"

She was unable to complete the sentence, because Jepp let out a roar that sounded as if it had been ripped from the throat of a wild beast. It was only at that moment that Sunara remembered that her warriors had told her that the Mort girl had gone berserk when the male Laocoon, Karsen, had been injured. She had dispatched several Piri with absolutely no effort whatsoever.

And her full attention was on Sunara.

Jepp's eyes seemed to glaze over and she bolted straight at Sunara.

Sunara was waiting for her and just as Jepp got to her, Sunara slammed the sword forward.

Jepp caught it.

Sunara couldn't believe it. Jepp had brought her hands together and caught the blade just as Sunara had jabbed it toward her. It was mere inches from her chest but it might as well have been yards. Sunara focused her strength and tried to drive it forward, but she was no match for Jepp in her demented, attacking phase.

Once more Jepp screamed incoherently and twisted, and she snapped the blade. Sunara gasped and backpedaled. Jepp came after her…

…and slid on the puddle of blood that had poured from either Karsen's throat or Eutok's wrist, or both.

With Jepp fallen, Sunara could have attacked her. For the first time, though, her confidence was wavering in the face of Jepp's ferocious assault. So instead she opted for the more obvious and useful tactic:

She ran.

Piri may have had many weaknesses, but one of their greatest strengths was their speed. Sunara sprinted up the stairs, taking two at a time, moving so quickly that the walls were practically blurring around her. Her nostrils flared as she sought out where Clarinda was hiding from her.

Up she went, faster and faster, leaving Jepp far behind her. That was all she needed to do. She had to get away from her. Nothing was going to be gained by battling Jepp, even though she was still sure that she could defeat her. Her goal was her daughter, and enjoying the pleasure of tearing her apart.

She was three quarters of the way up the stairs when suddenly a door to her right caught her attention. Calinda's scent was strongest there.

Instantly excitement welled up in Sunara's heart. This was it. This was going to be her opportunity to get her revenge. She knew that Clarinda was behind the door, doubtlessly cowering in a corner, clutching her mewling infant. Sunara would throw open the door, go in fast, and be upon Clarinda before she even knew what was happening.

She yanked open the door and Clarinda was standing right there, and she raked her hands out before Sunara had a chance to properly react. She ducked her head back and if she had been even a microsecond slower, Clarinda would have gouged out her eyes. As it was her fingernails slashed across Sunara's forehead and blood immediately started pouring down from the gash.

Sunara stumbled back, desperately trying to wipe the blood from her eyes, and suddenly to her alarm she heard Jepp hurtling up the stairs, still continuing to snarl without forming any words. The Mort's speed was absolutely alarming.

For a heartbeat she considered remaining where she was, attacking Clarinda, trying to dispose of the bitch before Jepp got there. But Jepp was moving too fast, and the fury in her face was simply too intimidating. Cursing herself for her weakness while believing she truly didn't have any other choice, Sunara sprinted up the steps.

With every step she took, Jepp grew closer. Hoping she could get the drop on her, and aware that Jepp was only seconds behind her, Sunara grabbed a torch off the wall and swung it around, shoving the flame directly toward Jepp's chest. She struck home, and she fully expected Jepp to fall back in pain.

Jepp didn't even appear to notice it. She did not back away from Sunara at all, even as the flame pressed into her flesh. Instead she remained frozen in place, howling not in pain but fury. Sunara's eyes widened in shock as Jepp's arm swept up and knocked the torch away, sending it rolling down the steps.

Sunara lashed out with her right foot and got lucky, catching Jepp on the chin. Jepp stumbled back, fell a few steps, but that was all. She scrambled to her feet and launched herself at Sunara.

The Piri Mistress darted back, just barely ahead of her, and suddenly realized that she was at the top of the stairs. There was a door to her left and she slammed through it. Darkness and cold air hit her face and she realized that she was standing at the top of the shattered tower, bricks and broken wood all around. There was nowhere for her to retreat to.

Jepp burst through the door and charged at her. Sunara moved to the right, attempting to dodge her, to send her running past her and ideally off the edge. Jepp was too quick. She pivoted and came at Sunara.

Sunara's lips pulled back to expose her fangs and she charged forward, crashing into Jepp. She slammed her fangs down into Jepp's throat.

She had never tasted the blood of a human being before and it was like nothing else she had ever sampled. An insane giddiness swept through her and for half a moment she thought she was flying.

And then she was, because Jepp had never stopped driving herself forward when she had barreled into Sunara. The thrust of her legs carried the two of them over the edge of the tower.

Sunara let out a horrified shriek and she released her hold on Jepp, reaching for the edge of the huge building, trying to grab onto something, anything to halt her fall. That was when Jepp drove her foot forward and into Sunara's face, sending her hurtling away from the building. Now nothing was reaching up toward her except the blackness of a very, very long fall.

As she plummeted, the one thing she saw that gave her a shred of pleasure was that Jepp was falling as well.

Then, suddenly, Jepp wasn't.

She had been tumbling past an outstretched gargoyle and something that was holding onto that statue had caught her. The shadowed creature moved slightly forward and Sunara's perfect night vision saw that Norda Kinklash was perched atop it, having snagged Jepp before her plunge could really gain speed.

"*Enjoy your fall!*" Norda shouted at the Piri.

Sunara screamed all the way down.

IV.

SLOWLY THE CLOUDS CLEARED AROUND Jepp's head. Then she gasped as he realized she was hanging hundreds of feet in the air, a great pool of blackness beneath her that looked ready to swallow her whole.

"Don't worry, I've got you."

Norda was dangling from the head of a gargoyle outstretched from the wall. It seemed to Jepp that it was sneering at her derisively.

"Did I…did I do it again?" asked Jepp in an unsteady voice.

"You mean turn into an unstoppable killing creature because Karsen was threatened? Yes, I am pretty sure you did."

Jepp heard a thud from far, far below, which halted the scream that had been accompanying it. "Who was that?"

"No one important," said Norda. She started to pull Jepp up toward her. "Here we go. Come on up."

That was when the gargoyle gave way.

Norda had clearly not been expecting it, which Jepp briefly had the time to be surprised at since it seemed that nothing ever startled Norda. At most she tended to react with mild bemusement. But this was not one of those instances because Norda actually cried out as her hold on the wall gave way.

Yet even as she started to fall, she grabbed Jepp with both arms and swung her around onto her back. *"Hold on!"* she shouted as gravity overtook her and began to drag her down.

She flung herself forward with every ounce of strength in her muscles and managed to bang against the wall. She lashed out with her claws and they scraped against the brick face as she continued to skid. Norda was already moving too quickly, however, and all her claw-grabbing managed to do was slow them down a bit before the brick crumbled under her grip.

If it had been merely a matter of her own weight, she might well have been able to stop her descent. But Jepp, clutching onto her back, added drag onto her that prevented her from getting the job done. Yet interestingly it never occurred to Norda to shrug Jepp off, to send her plummeting to her doom in order to save herself. To her mind, either both of them were going to survive or neither of them were.

And so it went, down the entire side of Firedraque Hall. She would clutch at the wall, lose her grip, drop another few hundred feet, try to stop her fall once more and again be reclaimed by gravity. She did, however, manage to keep slowing their descent, and if she had had another few hundred yards of building, she might well have managed the feat.

Unfortunately she ran out of building, and she hit the ground with a horrifying thud. Once Norda hit, Jepp lost her grip on her back and bounded away from her. She hit the street, rolled a distance, and came to a halt nearby a pile of bloodied mass that had once been Sunara, Mistress of the Piri. Jepp lay there for a moment, her eyes focusing on the fallen corpse, and then—for no particular reason— stuck out her tongue at her. Then Jepp rolled onto her back and slipped away into unconsciousness.

All was still.

DIZZ

I.

JASON WAS HAVING TROUBLE BELIEVING where he was.

He had read about Disney World on any number of occasions. It had been one of the most extraordinary amusement parks in the history of the planet, which was hard for Jason to understand since he knew nothing about the origins of amusement parks. It was all a very startling concept for him to wrap himself around.

Now here he was in a strange bedroom apartment that was situated in a castle, of all things, that was related to the fairy tale character Cinderella in some way. It looked quite lovely and if he were a simple tourist, he would have been delighted to spend a night or two in there. But that was certainly not the situation now. No, instead he was sitting there, backed up by Ciccone, Medea and Ada who were seated in scattered seats. Also present were several of what were referred to as Phey. He had managed to pick up their names: Graves, Trott and Tania. There was also another who didn't look remotely like the others. He claimed that he was a Phey as well, but his skin was remarkably sallow and he really looked like someone in truly awful vampire makeup. But he said he didn't know what a vampire was and Jason wasn't in the mood to push it. His name was Gant.

And there was a senior member of the Phey to whom they all appeared to defer. His name was Obertan, and he had just gotten done telling them the most unbelievable story that he had ever heard.

"So...let me see if I'm understanding this," Jason said slowly. "You're telling me that humanity as a whole is responsible for these..." He gestured toward a dimly growing crystalline rock that was situated in the center of the table. "...these...hotstars, is what you called them…and the power that goes to them?"

"That is a very simplistic version of what I've told you, but that is essentially correct."

"And you know this…how?"

"I saw it."

"What did you see again?" asked Medea. She cast a sidelong glance at Jason that clearly conveyed to him that she was as puzzled by what she was hearing as he was.

"I saw a conversation between a Firedraque and the Overseer."

"Right," said Jason. "A Firedraque is kind of a fire breathing dragon on two legs, and the Overseer was in charge."

"That is correct."

"And the Firedraque put forward this idea? How did the Overseer react to it?"

"He threw him off the top of a building."

Jason again exchanged looks with his partner. "He threw him off a building?"

"Yes. I assume he had reasons for doing so, although I cannot speculate that they were particularly good ones."

"It's crazy," said Medea. "The notion that humanity is responsible for providing energy for these hotstars…"

"As I said, that is a simplistic summary. It is not merely the presence of humans. It is your capacity for thought, for imagination, for speculation. Through your actions, you shape the world."

"Through *building* stuff."

"That is part of it, yes. But there is far more to it than that. Your contribution to the whole of the universe occurs on a level that you would refer to as…" He hesitated, trying to summon the word. "Metaphysical. It stems from your imagination, your desires, your sheer want to change things. I have no idea if it was the intention of the gods in the designing of the universes, nor do I know if that is a similar set up in other, further away realms. But that is apparently the way things have turned out in this one, and it impacts the Elserealms as well. Can't be helped, you see."

"Well, that's great," said Jason, "but whoever this Firedraque was, he was out of his mind. He's putting forward a situation that simply cannot possibly exist, in this realm or any other."

Obertan studied him for a long moment, which was odd considering he had no eyes, and then he gestured toward the hotstar. "Pick it up, if you don't mind."

Jason sighed and rolled his eyes, but obediently picked up the faintly glowing rock.

"Hotstars are connected, one to the other," said Obertan. "I am not quite sure how that could be, because they are certainly not alive. At least I don't think they are. But that connection remains, nevertheless. Here is what I want you to do, human. I want you to focus on the hotstar being filled with light and energy. Go ahead."

Jason stared at the rock, unsure of what to do. He also knew that he felt uncomfortable as his friends stared at him. Gamely, he closed his eyes and tried to focus on what Obertan was telling him, but he was having trouble taking it seriously. It all seemed some tortured game that he couldn't even begin to comprehend.

"You're not trying," said Obertan.

How the hell would he know? He's blind, for God's sake.

Still, Jason resolved to at least cooperate with the old man... Phey...whatever he was. He truly began to imagine the hotstar becoming suffused with life and power.

Suddenly the rock became blindingly illuminated, so much so that even though Jason's eyes were closed, it seared right through his eyelids so that he was aware how bright it was. He gasped and dropped it to the table, but that did nothing to diminish the intensity of the brightness. The others pulled back from it and even the other Phey raised their arms to shield their eyes. Only Obertan gazed at it, naturally.

That was when Disney's Main Street lit up, along with the rest of the park.

Music slowly came to life and Jason stared out the window at the merry-go-round, the source of the tune that was floating through the air. Other things likewise sprang into action. Flying elephants with huge ears started moving, as did what appeared to be an array of giant cups. Lights lit up everywhere, and the music continued to speed up until it was playing at its full tempo.

"It's amazing," Jason whispered, his breath taken away by the sights he was seeing.

"I am sure that it is," said Obertan. "Your entire world can be like this. All you have to do is imagine it. You can rebuild the...what is the name of this planet again?"

"Earth."

"Hunh. What an odd name." Then he shrugged, giving it no more thought. "The point is, you can restore life to this world. We, the Phey, will provide protection for you all. You can reside here, in Dizz, or in one of the many buildings that surround the area. There is plenty of food to be obtained from nearby buildings. At least we think they are good." He reached over to a bookshelf and withdrew a can. "This is food, yes? What does it say?"

"Spaghetti-Os," said Jason.

'That is a type of food, yes?"

"Yes. And canned food pretty much lasts forever."

"Well, there is plenty of that around. And with your continued presence, you will help provide energy to both the entirety of the Earth, and even into the Elserealms. And the Elserealms will realize just how important humanity is to our world, so that eventually you will become protected and cherished..."

Ciccone pulled out his gun, aimed it at the hotstar and fired. The hotstar exploded, shattering into a hundred pieces.

The explosive blast startled Obertan into silence. Ciccone was standing now, and for a moment Jason was sure that Ciccone was going to put the next bullet directly into Obertan's head. Instead he held his gun out for a long moment, and then slowly he slid it into his holster.

"Your people," Ciccone rumbled, "killed my brother. My father. My mother. I was ordered onto the *Argo* by my superiors who absolutely did not give a crap that my family—all in the army—died battling you and your kind. I've no idea whether it was one of the Phey who did it or another of your accursed races. And I don't care. What you're proposing is that we cooperate with you and your kind for the betterment of all you creatures, and for the home world that banished you. Is that supposed to be a selling point? Is that supposed to convince me that I should care about you?"

"I was trying to give you the best of a bad situation," said Obertan.

"It is not a bad situation. It's an unlivable situation. You're telling me that the only way humanity can survive is if we serve as a means for you to survive as well."

"That's a negative way to look at it…"

"What if we don't?" said Medea.

The question astounded Jason. It also seemed to surprise Ada as well.

"If you do not survive, you mean?" said Obertan. He shrugged. "Then eventually the hotstars will die. We will have no means of energy. And if we believe the words of the Firedraque, the entirety of the world and the Elserealm will begin to deteriorate. It could take many thousands of turns but eventually all life on this world will end, and very probably it will be likewise in the Elserealm since it will not be able to maintain its integrity. But I very much doubt that you will be interested in…"

"Killing ourselves?" Medea whispered the question.

"That is what it would require, yes. But what purpose would that serve?"

"It would end you," said Ciccone. "That's better than living our lives as enforced slaves of the Phey, and passing that fate onto our children."

"Wait, wait," Jason said. He had been sitting but now he rose and stood in front of his crew. "Are you…are you serious about this? You're talking about the entirety of humanity just…extinguishing itself? Just…what? Everyone drinks poison or something and we all die?"

"Do you want to perpetuate their world?" said Ciccone.

"No, of course not, but—"

"There's no 'but' here, Jason," Ciccone told him. "We know that's what they're going to do, no matter what Obertan here promises us," and he gestured toward the elderly Piri. "He can make all the promises he wants as to what they're going to do for us, but eventually they're going to turn on us. Probably limit our population. Keep us at a nice controlled number so they don't have to worry that we'll rise up and overthrow them. But these bastards killed my family, and I'll be damned if I do anything to make their lives easier for them. And if we can end their lives, then that's fantastic."

"Killing ourselves is not fantastic!"

Ada leaned forward and when she spoke it was as if she was talking from very far away. "Maybe we should vote. Go to our people, explain the situation, and have them vote on it."

"This isn't a democracy," said Jason. "I'm in charge. Ciccone, you said so yourself…"

"Not of this," said Ciccone. "Not of this."

"Yes, of this!" He flailed his hands in frustration. "The rest of humanity can't simply decide it's time to pack up shop, to end it all. I don't understand how you could—"

"*Because you weren't there!*" Medea shouted, and the volume of her voice startled Jason into silence. "Because all of us lost family! Parents, siblings, nephews and nieces, aunts and uncles. No one was spared. Before the broadcast system was destroyed, they put it out there on television. All other channels were canned except for news, and we witnessed it both on TV and in person! We saw these races slaughtering humanity, and you know what they did? They laughed! They laughed at the helpless humans that they were killing because none of our weapons worked!"

"That was our doing," said Obertan.

Slowly she turned and gaped at him. "*Your* doing?"

He nodded. "We cast spells to render your weaponry ineffective. Had your weapons been functioning, you would very likely have defeated us. So we had to make sure that didn't happen."

Medea let out a scream and lunged for him, her fingers outstretched, determined to wrap them around his throat. The only thing that prevented her from doing so was the Phey named Graves, who intercepted her before she could reach Obertan. She struggled in his grasp as he carefully but firmly pushed her back until she was seated in a chair. "Enough of that," he said.

Slowly Medea took in a deep breath and then let it out. She shifted her attention back to Jason. "You don't know what it was like because you weren't here. You weren't even born yet. And me, I've been dreaming about it, for decades. Did you know that? We dream in suspended animation and I've had these creatures destroying us in my mind for all that time. Now we're being presented with an opportunity to either destroy them or enable them, and if it means putting an end to these bastards, then I will do it whole heartedly."

"I agree," said Ada. She reached over and squeezed Medea's hand, and tears were rolling down her cheeks. "If it will end them, I'm all for it. The whole purpose of the ship was to keep us in orbit while these monsters killed each other in their endless wars. We weren't supposed to live on it with them, and I've no interest in doing so."

"Fine," said Jason. "Fine. We'll have a vote. Will that make you happy?"

They all nodded.

"Okay. Let's go to them. But I can guarantee you that by the time I'm done talking to them, they'll never go for it."

II.

HUMANITY WAS HAVING A BALL in the streets of Disney World.

They were running hither and yon, riding all the rides with naturally a complete absence of lines. It took them no time at all to figure out how to run them, to lower or stop the elephant rides or halt the merry-go-round so that people could get off and on. Screeches of joy erupted from what Jason learned was called "Space

Mountain" and people strolled the streets, grabbing t-shirts and hats and whatever else they felt like stealing from them.

Jason was seated on a bench near the entrance area, staring up at the new moon. He heard a noise near him and glanced over, and saw that the odd looking Phey named Gant was standing there. "May I join you?" asked Gant.

"Go ahead," said Jason, gesturing to the empty part of the bench beside him.

Gant did so, drawing his cloak more tightly around him even though it didn't seem especially cold to Jason. "So I understand that the conversation with the others of your kind did not go as well as you had hoped."

Jason found it hard to speak, his voice choking in his throat. "It was unanimous," he finally said. "None of them wanted to live in the world with you and your kind. Parents who lost their children in the battles said they couldn't wait to be with their kids. The soldiers followed Ciccone's lead. And frankly, most of them are afraid of me or outright hate me. The bottom line is that they would rather be dead than remain alive."

"They seem to be having a good time for people who are suicidal," and he gestured in the general direction of the festivities.

"It was decided that we should have one last, big party. A farewell bash. So that's what we're doing. They're all running around having fun and then tomorrow at twelve noon exactly we're all going to walk into the water down there," and he gestured toward the water that came up to the docks. "And we will collectively drown."

"That doesn't sound especially pleasant."

"Well, we could have all shot each other, but all those guns going off...it just seemed too violent. Plus gunshots aren't always fatal. People have been known to shoot themselves in the head and not die. Drowning is final."

"I suppose it is." Gant hesitated, and then he said, "I did not always look like this. I used to be a normal Phey."

"What happened?"

"My lover transformed me into a mound of green goo. I lived like that for quite a long time before I ended up taking over his creature, this Piri. And do not think that for a moment, in all that time, I didn't consider ending my life."

"Why didn't you?"

"Because I always had hope that things would improve somehow. Always." He shrugged. "That and I had no idea how to do it."

Jason laughed at that. The noise sounded odd coming from his throat. "Thanks for sharing that."

"Not a problem."

"You know," said Jason, "for a creature that's part of a massive race of beings that wound up wiping out all humans on Earth, you're not so bad."

"That's very kind of you to say."

Jason leaned back on the bench and yawned widely. "Man, it's getting late."

"Perhaps you should find a bed somewhere to get slumber."

"No, no way," said Jason. "If this is my last night on Earth," and he yawned again, "I want to be awake for every minute of it."

Within five minutes, he was asleep.

PERRIZ

JEPP IS UNDERWATER. SHE IS not certain how she wound up there, but she knows that it is where she is.

Since she has no idea which way to go, she picks one arbitrarily and begins walking. Then she begins to see structures of some sort, the supports of piers, and she knows she is heading in the right direction. She moves faster, not out of fear that she will drown, because she knows that at this moment she is invulnerable to harm.

She has been in this state before. It was not long ago that she was walking about on that vessel in the sky. She also remembers walking through the streets of the Spires and encountering Norda for the first time, so she knows this is far more than a mere dream. She cannot recall how she managed to tumble into this state; she just knows that it has veracity.

Jepp continues to walk forward and suddenly she is no longer underwater but is instead standing on a shore. She has seen many villages, many cities, but she has never seen anything quite like this. There is a large wall that lines the exterior of it, and what she can glimpse beyond it seems utterly charming and also somehow unreal.

That, however, is not what concerns her. What she is stunned to see is humans, so many humans. They are standing in a long line on the shore, staring out at the water, and their hands are linked. They are looking at each other apprehensively, speaking softly to one another, seemingly preparing themselves to do something. Jepp cannot imagine what that will be.

And then they start to move.

In a flash, Jepp suddenly understands what is about to happen. The humans are going to stride into the water and drown themselves.

They are committing mass suicide.

She stands there, frozen, and then she screams, "Stop!"

The word causes them to freeze. They are all looking around as if trying to determine from where the cry had come, and then someone is looking right at her. She recognizes him instantly. She had seen him the last time she had a dream like this, out on that vessel that was in the depths of space.

"You!" he cries out. "I know you! I remember you!" Now all eyes are following his gaze and they all see her. They are clearly stunned. They have no idea what they are looking at.

"What are you doing?" she asks.

"We're...we're going to kill ourselves," he says.

"Are you insane? Why would you do that?"

"Because the Phey want to use us to improve the world for them. To power their hotstars and also help the dimension that shoved them over here in the first place."

"I don't understand. What would you have to do?"

"Well...nothing, really. Just live. Who are you—?"

She doesn't respond to his question because she is still having difficulty processing what he has said. "You...don't have to do anything? Just live?"

"We would be their slaves."

"Are they making you do work for them? Live with no means of leaving them if you want?"

"Not really, no..."

"And you would rather die than simply live?"

Another man steps forward. "Why should we cooperate with the bastards who helped destroy our world?"

"They didn't destroy the world! Look around," and she gestures widely all about them. "There it is! It's all here! And it's yours to live in! Are they going to protect you from any who would attack you?"

"Well, yes," says the man who had just spoken. "But that's not the point..."

"That is the point!" Jepp is shouting at them. "Life is for living,

not for abandoning! As long as you live, there is hope for a better tomorrow! How can you terminate your lives? Kill yourselves and end the lives of any children you might have had before they even begin? How can humanity be so cruel! Do you have any idea..." Her voice catches for a moment and she has to fight past sobs. "Do you have any idea how long I have lived in hope of encountering other humans? I have lived here by myself for so many turns! My parents long dead! Me endlessly dreaming of eventually somehow meeting other humans, and now that you're here, you're going to deprive me of that?"

"It isn't a matter of you," the man she first met in space says. "It's wanting to put an end to the Elserealms and to these creatures who took the world from us..."

"Then you're a fool," she tells them heatedly. She raises her voice to speak to all the humans who are staring at her. "You're all fools. Yes, there were evil beings amongst those who took this world. But there are good ones, as well. Many good ones who just want to survive. Do you think they wanted to come here? They were exiled *here. Cast off by the rulers of their home, consigned here to try and live as best they could. None of them wanted to be here. They are all victims of what the rulers of the Elserealms wanted. I would think that humanity would be sympathetic to those who were wronged by others. If anyone should be able to understand, it's you!"*

The humans look at each other, confused, uncertain.

"The Phey wish to make peace with you. The reason doesn't matter. They will work to protect you from any who wish to do you harm, and they will reach out to all other races to endeavor to end this hostility. Humanity can work together to repopulate this world, to live as one beside..."

"Those who tried to destroy us?"

"Those who want to make up for their vast mistakes! I know what you want. You want vengeance for all those loved ones who died. But tell me...do you think your loved ones would want this? Would they want you to end your lives? I don't believe that for a moment! I

think they would want you to live! Live for their sakes and the sake of humanity. You owe them that. You owe it to all your loved ones to survive! To build strength from weakness and order from chaos. You need to make the right choice, and I swear to you, mass suicide is not the correct one. Please. Please do not do this thing. Please put aside your hatred. Live. Live and give humanity a future. I'm begging you. I'm begging y—"

"Jepp?"

Jepp snapped awake and looked around in confusion. Sunlight was filtering in through the high windows in the room that she had no idea how she had gotten to. She sat up and immediately her head felt like it was splitting open. She moaned and flopped back into it, and then she looked and saw that Karsen was staring down at her in concern. His throat had been bandaged up, and although he seemed a bit more pale than usual, he was clearly all right

"Karsen!" she cried out and she sat up again. The world spun around her but she didn't care as she embraced him as tightly as she could. She felt as if she were going to pitch off the bed, but Karsen held her securely until the world stopped tilting around her.

"You're all right," he whispered. "Thank the gods, you're all right." Then she withdrew from him slightly so that she could look him in the eyes. "The others. They were all injured."

"They're all fine. They're on the mend," said Karsen. "My mother's wound was bandaged and Eutok, well…he's not thrilled. Left hand's gone and there's nothing to be done for that, although knowing him he'll fashion a weapon and attach it. But he'll be okay."

The door in the small bedroom creaked open and Clarinda was standing in the doorway, cradling her infant. "I see my savior is awake."

"Are you all right?" asked Jepp.

"Of course I am. Thought I'd bring Eutok by. Junior. Senior is sleeping after having drunk enough alcohol to fell seven of his kind." She came over to Jepp and knelt down beside her.

Then, before Jepp could even ask about her, Norda entered. She was not moving with her typical bouncy style, but rather slowly and stiffly. She was not alone; she was hanging onto Arren's shoulder.

"You're alive!" said Jepp in relief. "Oh, thank the gods!"

"Thank the building," said Arren. "She was able to sink her claws into enough places to slow down both your falls. She's somewhat banged up, but she'll recover."

"Which is more than can be said of the Piri lady. I am very glad she's dead. No offense," she added to Clarinda, and then she glanced at Arren. "That's what one says, right? No offense? When one has said something that one really means but could upset someone else whose feelings you really don't care about but do not wish to upset?"

"Yes," said Arren after a moment, deciding to provide the simplest answer to the question.

Jepp was staring with fascination at the baby. "Can I hold him?" she whispered.

"Of course," said Clarinda and she lay the child down in Jepp's arms.

Jepp stared down at him, amazed. She had never seen anything quite so tiny and helpless. She stroked under his chin and his eyes opened narrowly for a moment as he gazed up at her before drifting back to sleep. "He's beautiful," Jepp said softly. Then she turned her attention to Karsen. "We should absolutely make one of these."

"That's not happening anytime soon," Karsen assured her.

"Can we think about it?"

"Absolutely not," he said.

"All right…"

Then her thoughts came swimming back to her and she shook so violently that the baby almost tumbled from her arms. Karsen steadied her but there was concern on his face. "What is it? What's wrong?"

"Humans," she said. "I saw humans. Many of them. Standing on a far off shore."

"What were they doing?"

"They…" Her voice choked a moment and she embraced the

child even more tightly. "They were going to kill themselves. All of them. Just walk into water and drown."

"Why in gods' name would they do that?"

She looked up at Karsen. "Because they hate all of you that much."

"Then they're idiots and don't deserve to live," Karsen told her.

"That's more or less what I told them."

"Did they listen?" He had learned not to question Jepp's dreams.

She sighed. "I have no idea. And we'll probably never know."

DIZZ

JASON AWOKE WHEN SOMEONE PUSHED at his shoulder. He turned and saw that it was Medea. Ada was right behind her. "It's time," said Medea.

He glanced around and saw no sign of Gant. The bright sun seemed far too high in the sky, though. He glanced at his wristwatch and blinked. "It's 2:30. I thought we were doing it at noon."

"Yeah, well, everybody fell asleep," said Medea. "We were out partying pretty hard. There were benches, and there's first aid areas with beds. And actually the grass is pretty soft, too."

"I used to love Disney World," Ada said with a sigh. "If I'm going to spend my last day on Earth anywhere, I'm glad it was here."

"Me, too," said Medea. She squeezed Ada's hand. "Happy honeymoon." She leaned over and kissed her.

"I was in love with you," said Jason.

Medea's head snapped around and she stared at him in confusion. "What?"

"For years." The words were tumbling over each other. "Since I was a kid. Because of your name, that's what first attracted me. Because in myth Jason was joined with Medea. And as I got older I dreamt up us spending our lives together. I lost track of the number of times I imagined making love to you. That's why you were the first person I woke up when we lost power. Because I didn't see any way to fix it and frankly I was picturing making love to you while the ship spiraled to its death. But no. You're gay and I married you to her," and he gestured toward Ada, "and now my life is going to end before I've done anything with it, because you're all insane and I don't have the strength to be the only man left on Earth. So let's go. Let's do this."

Medea didn't move. She just stared at him.

"*Let's go!*" he shouted, and it startled both Medea and Ada forward. Jason turned his back on them and strode through the main entrance to the park, out to the docks.

The rest of the crew was already out there, massed. Many of them were rubbing their eyes, clearly still fighting against the sun. They were mumbling to each other and then all fell silent as Jason approached them. He gazed at them for a long moment. His people, whom he had fought beside. Whom he had planned to grow up, grow old with. His people, who he was about to walk into oblivion with. The more Jason thought about it, the more it had the ring of a Greek tragedy after all. Apparently his parents had named him well.

Slowly he walked forward and the crowd separated around him. He walked to dead center and then stretched his arms out right and left. Medea took his left hand, Ada his right, and now others began to join as well as they slowly formed a long line that stretched in either direction. Everyone was looking at him, as if waiting for him to say something.

So he was startled when a voice spoke to him from behind. "Are you sure about this?"

He turned and saw Obertan was standing behind him, along with other members of the Phey. "There is no coming back from this," he said solemnly.

"Well, we weren't planning to come back, so that works out," he said. He took a deep breath and then let it out slowly. He stared at the welcoming waters, which seemed to be begging him to just end this useless life of his.

Then he laughed.

"What's so funny?" said Ciccone. He was standing a few feet away.

Jason shrugged. "I was just hoping a beautiful girl would show up out of nowhere and talk us out of it."

"Wait, what?" said Medea. She had released her grip on his hand and was looking right at him. "Why would you say that?"

"It's stupid."

"*Why* did you say that?"

"I had this dream," he sighed. "This beautiful girl. Long black hair. Scantily clad. She tried to—"

"To talk us out of doing this?" said Ada.

"Yeah, why?"

"I had that dream," said Medea. She was looking past Jason to Ada. Ada was nodding and tapped her own chest. "So did I."

"The dream girl?" said Ciccone. He had released his grip on the hands of others and had walked over, looking bewildered. "The one who said we shouldn't do it? That we were idiots?"

And now Bill Tucker came over from the other side. "And that our dead family members wouldn't want us to do it?"

Jason's eyes widened. "Yes!"

Now the entire crew of the *Argo* was babbling to each other, all of them comparing notes. None of them could quite believe what they were all saying to each other. Their voices rose as they shared their recollections, and they were matching up exactly with each other.

"*You!*" Ciccone was shouting at Obertan, pointing at him angrily, apparently not caring that Obertan couldn't see the gesture. "You did this!"

"What did I do?" Obertan was clearly confused.

"You put a dream into our heads!"

Obertan shook his head, and his sincere confusion didn't seem as if it could be faked. "That is beyond the power of any Phey I know of. It is certainly beyond mine. Can some of us scan thoughts? Yes. Some. But none can project thoughts into a mind, and certainly not so many as this. I have no explanation for your shared vision."

"Then how did it happen?" demanded Ciccone.

Obertan shrugged. "Perhaps it is a vision from your gods. Is that possible? You have gods, I assume."

"God. One God," said Jason. He was standing there, trying not to tremble. "My God. Maybe it's…"

"No! It had to be him!" said Ciccone, indicating Obertan. "It had to—"

"*Shut up! It wasn't him!*" Jason had shouted so loudly that it stopped all other conversation. "Don't you get it? We shared something! Whatever it was, it was miraculous! Are you so far gone that you can't believe in miracles anymore? You don't believe in God, is that what you're telling me, Ciccone?"

"I do," Ciccone said, and he was actually sounding defensive. "But that doesn't mean that—"

"That what? That He abandoned us to these invaders but now He's giving us a second chance? That He might've sent an angel for us to see? For us *all* to see?" He pointed broadly at everyone within hearing distance. "You all heard the things she said! If you want to be like Ciccone and pretend that the Phey did this, go right ahead! That doesn't change the fact that every damned thing she said was true! You know it! You all know it! And I have had it with this…this bullshit!" He gestured toward the waters. "I'm out! If you want to spit into the eye of an angel from God, you go right ahead! But I am goddamn staying here! If the human race dies when I do, then so be it, but I'll croak knowing that I never gave up until my dying breath. And the rest of you can go screw yourselves!"

Then he turned away from them and strode up to Obertan. "Six months," he said to Obertan. "I'll give this thing with you and me working together six months. If at the end of that I'm not happy, I'm just gonna go off on my own."

There was a pause and suddenly Medea was at his side. "I can see holding off for six months," she said. "We really aren't losing anything. If we kill ourselves now or six months from now, what's the difference?"

He lowered his voice to a whisper and said, "That stuff I said…I thought we were going to die and I didn't figure that—"

She pulled his cheek to her face and kissed it. She whispered back to him, "If I were straight, I'd totally be all over you."

"That's nice to know."

Ada was by her side now, and then others walked toward them, slowly massing around them. Within moments only Ciccone and a number of other soldiers hadn't joined them. Jason regarded them with a raised eyebrow.

Finally, Ciccone shrugged. "The hell with it. What's six months?"

"I completely agree," said Obertan. "What's six months?"

"That's my attitude," said Jason.

"No," said Obertan, "I was asking. What's six months? I have no idea. What is even one month?"

Jason studied him and then laughed. "We'll teach you."

THE VASTLY WATERS

{"HUMANITY HAS DECIDED NOT TO kill itself," Gorkon informs the Liwyathan. "I and all my people were beneath the waters, just as you instructed, to haul them back to land if they attempted to do so. But they did not." He pauses. "And you knew they were thinking of doing so ."}

{"*Yes, they were. But their actions have been averted.*"}

{"How did that happen?"}

{"*The same way all miracles occur...with help from me. I suppose that makes me their God. I have not been worshipped...in quite some time.*"}

{"So..." Gorkon hesitates, unsure of what to say. "So what do we do now?"}

{"*You? You go off and mate with that female.*"}

{"Miira, you mean? No. No, you're wrong. She's not at all interested in me, nor I in..."}

{"*Do as I say.*"}

{"Yes, great one. I shall." Then he pauses before asking, "What will happen to the humans?"}

{"*We shall see, Gorkon. We shall see.*"}

FIVE YEARS LATER

PERRIZ

KARLINDA AND HER LITTLE PLAYMATE sprinted into Firedraque hall, startling Arren and Evanna. Their mouths parted and they jumped back from each other, looking extremely embarrassed. "Karlinda! Eutok! You should knock before entering!" Arren scolded them.

Karlinda ignored the remonstration. "Where's mommy! I need to see mommy!" She stamped her little hooved foot. "Where is she?"

"Here, darling."

Jepp hurried down the stairs and threw her arms open, expecting her child to run into her arms and embrace her. But Karlinda did not seem remotely interested in hugging her mother. "Someone's coming!" she declared, pointing behind her.

"Someone? What someone?"

"I dunno. He said he knew you. He came in a boat. He's a trav…" She stumbled over the word. "Travler?"

"Traveler," Jepp corrected her, but now there was concern in her face. Despite all that she had learned about the Phey, and that the Overseer had been dead for years, she was still concerned. She crouched and drew Karlinda and Eutok to her. "Run upstairs and stay there until I tell you to come down…"

"That won't be necessary."

The voice was loud but calm and she looked up to see that it was too late, that two Travelers had entered the great hall. They did not seem especially aggressive, however. The one in the lead flipped his hood back. It was someone that she had never seen before. His companion slid their hood back as well, and Jepp saw that it was a female. The male was smiling, which was as odd an expression on a Phey as Jepp had ever seen. "Hello, Jepp," he said softly. "It's been quite a while."

"Do I know you?" she said, her head cocked slightly.

"My name is Gant."

Her jaw dropped and slowly she stood, releasing her hold on the children. She heard the clop of hooves behind her. It was Karsen coming down the stairs, clearly having awoken from his nap, and he had heard enough of the exchange to gasp in disbelief. "Gant?" said Karsen.

"Hello, Karsen," said Gant.

"Oh my gods," and Karsen sprinted past Jepp and the children, his arms thrown wide open. Gant stepped forward and the two embraced, Karsen slapping him on the back repeatedly. "I can't believe it!" said Karsen as the two separated. "Who did this? Who changed you back?"

"She did," said Gant and he chucked a thumb at the female next to him. "This is Tania. Tania, this is my old friend, Karsen."

"Tania? Isn't that the name of the female who first cursed you?"

"Yes, that's right," said Tania as she stepped forward, extending her hand. "That was me."

Karsen froze and didn't take the extended hand. Instead he stared at her in confusion before turning his attention back to Gant. "Seriously?"

"Seriously," said Gant. "We…worked things out."

"And what about the Piri you inhabited?"

"I let him go. If he can find more of his own kind, that's fine, although I doubt he will."

"But how did you get here?" asked Jepp.

Gant didn't immediately answer. He was staring at the children. The little girl had the legs of a Laocoon, but her hips and the rest of her looked entirely like those of a Mort. She was wearing a small loin cloth but was otherwise unclothed. Her companion looked like a Trull, but his mouth was pulled back in a ready smile that exposed a small pair of fangs. "Are they…hybrids?" he asked. "Mixtures?"

"They are children," said Jepp, resting her hands on their shoulders. "That is all that is needed to be known about them. And I'd still like to know how you got here."

"We sailed," he said. "We've been doing quite a bit of sailing about lately. To all parts of America, and other countries in Europe."

She looked confused. "Where...are those?"

"You've been there. I'm just using the original names, in deference to our companion." He glanced over his shoulder and was mildly surprised to see that no one was there. He raised his voice and called, "Jason!"

A human walked in. A human.

Jepp gasped. His hair was long and he had a full brown beard. He was saying, "Sorry, I was just looking around. This building is amazing, it's..." Then his voice trailed off as he stared at Jepp. "Oh my God. Oh my God, it's you. You're her. You're the angel."

Then she recognized him. It was the first time she had seen him with her mind clear, but once she realized, it should have been obvious. "You're the human I saw out in the skies. And at the waters. You were going to kill yourselves."

"And you stopped us." He crossed the room to her and stood in front of her. "I feel like I should kneel or something. Do you...do you have a name?"

"Jepp. My name is Jepp."

"I'm Jason. Jason Tanner."

"It is a pleasure to meet you."

They shook hands firmly, and then she gave into temptation and embraced him. For the first time in her life, she felt a sense of belonging. "What about the other humans? Are they all right?"

"Thriving," he said. "We've built farms, growing food. Domesticated some cows we found, so we have milk. And we're building alliances."

"We are," said Gant. "We are slowly overcoming the impulses all our races have to wage war with each other."

"That's wonderful!"

"The world is changing, Jepp," said Jason. "Much of it is because of you. Would you...would you be interested in going back with us? Meeting your brethren?"

"Oh, I couldn't," said Jepp. Then she paused and turned to Karsen. "Could I?"

"Jepp," said Karsen, putting an arm around her, "you don't have to ask me. You're an independent woman. If you want to go, we go."

"We?"

"Always we," he said, kissing her.

Karlinda scampered over to her and said, "Are we going on a trip, Mommy?"

"Yes, honey. Yes, we are."

"What are we going to see?"

Jepp smiled.

"The world," she said. "The whole damned world."

# # #

ABOUT THE AUTHOR

PETER DAVID is a prolific author whose career, and continued popularity, spans nearly two decades. He has worked in every conceivable media: Television, film, books (fiction, non-fiction and audio), short stories, and comic books, and acquired followings in all of them.

In the literary field, Peter has had over one hundred novels published, including numerous appearances on the *New York Times* Bestsellers List. His novels include *Tigerheart, Darkness of the Light, Sir Apropos of Nothing* and the sequel *The Woad to Wuin, Knight Life, Howling Mad,* and the Psi-Man adventure series. He is the co-creator and author of the bestselling *Star Trek: New Frontier* series for Pocket Books, and has also written such Trek novels as *Q-Squared, The Siege, Q-in-Law, Vendetta, I, Q* (with John deLancie), *A Rock and a Hard Place* and *Imzadi.* He produced the three *Babylon 5* Centauri Prime novels, and has also had his short fiction published in such collections as *Shock Rock, Shock Rock II,* and *Otherwere,* as well as *Isaac Asimov's Science Fiction Magazine* and *The Magazine of Fantasy and Science Fiction.*

Peter's comic book resume includes an award-winning twelve-year run on *The Incredible Hulk,* and he has also worked on such varied and popular titles as *Supergirl, Young Justice, Soulsearchers and Company, Aquaman, Spider-Man, Spider-Man 2099, X-Factor, Star Trek, Wolverine, The Phantom, Sachs & Violens, The Dark Tower,* and many others. He has also written comic book related novels, such as *The Incredible Hulk: What Savage Beast,* and co-edited *The Ultimate Hulk* short story collection.

Peter is also the writer for two popular video games: *Shadow Complex* and *Spider-Man: Edge of Time.*

Peter is the co-creator, with popular science fiction icon Bill

Mumy (of *Lost in Space* and *Babylon 5* fame) of the Cable Ace Award-nominated science fiction series *Space Cases*, which ran for two seasons on Nickelodeon. He has written several scripts for the Hugo Award winning TV series *Babylon 5*, and the sequel series, *Crusade*. He has also written several films for Full Moon Entertainment and co-produced two of them, including two installments in the popular *Trancers* series, as well as the science fiction western spoof *Oblivion*, which won the Gold Award at the 1994 Houston International Film Festival for best Theatrical Feature Film, Fantasy/Horror category.

Peter's awards and citations include: the Haxtur Award 1996 (Spain), Best Comic script; OZCon 1995 award (Australia), Favorite International Writer; Comic Buyers Guide 1995 Fan Awards, Favorite writer; Wizard Fan Award Winner 1993; Golden Duck Award for Young Adult Series (*Starfleet Academy*), 1994; UK Comic Art Award, 1993; Will Eisner Comic Industry Award, 1993. He lives in New York with his wife, Kathleen, and his four children, Shana, Gwen, Ariel, and Caroline.

THE HIDDEN EARTH CHRONICLES

On the Damned World, it's every man for himself. Only it's not just mankind who inhabits this crumbling, desolate world. Twelve very different species, creatures out of Earth's mythology that live on the land, in the sea, and underground, vie for survival in a hostile land. Humanity is nearly extinct. But now the Twelve Races have discovered that their own fortunes are inextricably linked with the remnants of the human race.

As a result, a young slave girl named Jepp may hold the key to the future of the world. But can she and her new companions survive long enough to save everyone . . . or will they damn the world instead?

CRAZY 8 PRESS
www.crazy8press.com

THERE'S A LOT AT STAKE HERE!

Meet Vince Hammond. He has a secret that, if his mother finds out, she will absolutely kill him.

No, he's not dating a girl she'd hate. No, he's not gay.

He's a vampire. And Mom is a vampire hunter. And all of his friends are vampire hunters. And his fiancee is a vampire hunter, and so are his future in-laws.

Need an antidote to every other vampire novel out there? Then you're going to want to be *Pulling Up Stakes*. After putting a silver bullet in werewolves in his classic *Howling Mad*, *New York Times* Bestseller Peter David now sinks his teeth into vampire lore, with bloody good results.

CRAZY 8 PRESS

www.crazy8press.com

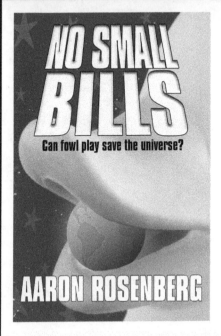

GREAT BOOKS BY GREAT AUTHORS
DIRECT TO READERS

WHY?
BECAUSE WE'RE CRAZY!!!

CPSIA information can be obtained
at www.ICGtesting.com
Printed in the USA
FSHW02n0618251018
53286FS